NEW YORK TIMES
BESTSELLING AUTHOR
JUDE DEVERAUX
IS "ONE OF THE ALL-TIME GREATS"
(*MIDWEST BOOK REVIEW*).

Acclaim for her bestselling novels
of marvelous romance . . .

"Deveraux's touch is gold."

—Publishers Weekly

"Jude Deveraux's writing is enchanting and exquisite."

—BookPage

"Packed full of warmth, humor, sensual tension, and exciting adventure. What more could you ask . . . ?"

—Romantic Times

"Filled with excitement, action, and insight."

—Harriet Klausner

"Satisfying."

—Booklist

"Incredible, wonderful, fantastic, superb. . . . An unforgettable read."

—Romance Reviews Today

Books by Jude Deveraux

Jude Deveraux

Velvet Song
Velvet Angel

Pocket Books
New York London Toronto Sydney

POCKET BOOKS, a division of Simon & Schuster, Inc.
1230 Avenue of the Americas, New York, NY 10020

ISBN-13: 978-1-4165-1716-0
ISBN-10:   1-4165-1716-2

This Pocket Books paperback edition January 2006

10 9 8 7 6 5 4 3 2 1

POCKET and colophon are registered trademarks of Simon & Schuster, Inc.

Cover art by Shasti O'Leary Soudant

Manufactured in the United States of America

For information regarding special discounts for bulk purchases, please contact Simon & Schuster Special Sales at 1-800-456-6798 or business@simonandschuster.com

Velvet Song and *Velvet Angel* were previously published individually by Pocket Books.

Velvet Song

PART I

❧

The South of England

❧

January 1502

Chapter One

THE LITTLE VILLAGE of Moreton was surrounded by a high stone wall, the gray of the stones casting a long, early-morning shadow over the many houses packed inside. Well-worn pathways connected the buildings, radiating out from the central position of the towering church and the tall white town hall. Now, in the dim light of the morning, a few dogs began to stretch, sleepy-eyed women lazily walked toward the town well and four men waited, with axes over their shoulders, while the gatekeepers opened the heavy oak gates in the stone wall.

Inside one house, a plain, narrow, two-story, white-washed house, Alyxandria Blackett listened with every pore of her body for the creak of the gates. When she heard it, she grabbed her soft leather shoes and began tiptoeing toward the stairs, which were, unfortunately, on the other side of her father's bedroom. She'd been dressed for hours, waking long before the sun rose, slipping a plain, rather coarse woolen dress over her slight figure. And today, for once, she didn't look down in disgust at her body. It seemed that all her life she'd been waiting to grow up, to gain some height and, most of all, to gain some curves. But at twenty she knew she was always going to be flat-chested and hipless. At least, she thought with a sigh, she had no need for corsets. In her father's room, she tossed him a quick glance to make sure that he was sleeping, flipped the wool of her skirt over her arm and started down, skipping the fourth step, as she knew it creaked badly.

Once downstairs she didn't dare open a window shutter. The sound might wake her father, and he very much needed his rest now. Skirting a table covered with papers and ink and a half-finished will her father was drafting, she went to the far wall, gazing up with love at the two musical instruments hanging there. All thoughts of self-pity for what God had forgotten in her physically disappeared when she thought of her music. Already a new tune was beginning to form in her head, a gentle, rolling melody. It was obviously a love song.

"Can't make up your mind?" came her father's voice from the foot of the stairs.

Instantly, she ran to him, put her arm around his waist and helped him sit at the table. Even in the dark room she could see the bluish circles under his eyes. "You should have stayed in bed. There's time enough to do a day's work without starting before daylight."

Catching her hand for a moment, he smiled up into her pretty eyes. He well knew what his daughter thought of her little elfin face with its tip-tilted violet eyes, tiny nose and curvy little mouth—he'd certainly heard her wail about it enough—but to him everything about her was dear. "Go on," he said, pushing her gently. "Go and see if you can choose which instrument to take and leave before someone comes and complains they must have a song for their latest love."

"Perhaps this morning I should stay with you," she whispered, her face showing her concern for him. Three times in the last year he'd had horrible pains in his heart.

"Alyx!" he warned. "Don't disobey me. Now gather your things and leave!"

"Yes, my lord," she laughed, giving what, to him, was a heart-melting smile, her eyes turning up at the corners, her mouth forming a perfect cupid's bow. With a swift, practiced gesture she pulled the long, steel-stringed cittern from the wall, leaving the psaltery where it was. Turning, she looked back at her father. "Are you sure you'll be all right? I don't have to leave this morning."

Ignoring her, he handed her her scholar's box, a lap desk containing pen, ink and paper. "I'd rather have you creating music than staying home with a sick old man. Alyx," he cautioned. "Come here." With a familiar gesture he began to plait her long hair into a fat braid down her back. Her hair was heavy and thick, perfectly straight without a hint of curl and the color was, even to her father, very odd. It was almost as if a child had thrown together every hair color possible on one very small young woman's head. There were streaks of gold, bright yellow, deep red, a golden red, mouse brown and, Alyx swore, even some gray.

When her hair was braided, he pulled her cloak from the wall, put it about her shoulders and tied the hood over her head. "Don't get so engrossed you forget to stay warm," he said with mock fierceness, turning her about. "Now go, and when you return I want to hear something beautiful."

"I'll do my best," she said, laughing as she left the house, closing the door behind her.

From their house at the very back of the town wall, directly across from the big gates, Alyx could see nearly all of the town as the people were beginning to stir and get ready to greet the day. There was a matter of inches between the houses and in the tiny alleyway that ran along the wall. Half-timbered and stone, brick and stucco houses sat side by side, ranging in size from the mayor's house down to the tiny houses of the craftsmen and, like her father's, the lawyers'. A bit of breeze stirred the air and the shop signs rattled.

"Good morning," a woman sweeping the gravel before her house called to Alyx. "Are you working on something for the church today?"

Slinging the cittern by its strap onto her back, she waved back at her neighbor. "Yes . . . and no. Everything!" She laughed, waving and hurrying toward the gate.

Abruptly, she stopped as she nearly ran into a cart horse. One look up showed her that John Thorpe had purposefully tried to trip her.

"Hoa, now, little Alyx, not a kind word for me?" He grinned as she sidestepped the old horse.

"Alyx!" called a voice from the back of the wagon. Mistress Burbage was emptying chamber pots into the honey wagon John drove. "Could you come inside for a moment? My youngest daughter is heartbroken, and

I thought perhaps a new love song might make her well."

"Aye, and for me," John laughed from atop the wagon. "I have need of a love song, too," he said, ostentatiously rubbing his side where two nights before Alyx had given him a fierce pinch when he'd tried to kiss her.

"For you, John," she said very sweetly, "I'll write a song as sweet as the honey in your wagon." The sound of his laughter almost hid her answer to Mistress Burbage that she'd see her after evening mass.

With a gasp, Alyx began to run toward the gate. In another few moments she'd get caught and would never get her time alone, outside the walls, to work on her music.

"Ye're late, Alyx," the gatekeeper said, "and don't forget the sweet music for my sick babe," he called after her as she ran toward the orchards outside the walls.

Finally, she reached her favorite apple tree and, with a laugh of sheer happiness, opened the little desk and set about preparing to make a record of the music she heard in her head. Sitting down, leaning back against the tree, she pulled her cittern across her lap and began to strum the tune she'd heard this morning. Totally absorbed, working with melody and lyrics, recording on paper the notes, she was unaware of the hours passing. When she came up for air, her shoulders stiff, fingers sore, she had written two songs and started on a new psalm for the church.

With a long, exuberant stretch, she set aside her cittern, rose and, one hand on a low, bare branch of the apple tree, gazed out across the fields of crops, past them to the earl's enclosed sheep pastures.

No! she would not let herself think of the earl, who'd pushed so many farmers from the land by raising their rents and then fencing it and filling the space with his profitable sheep. Think of something pleasant, she commanded herself, turning to look the other way. And, of course, what else was there really beautiful in life besides music?

As a child she'd always heard music in her head. While the priest droned on in Latin at Mass, she'd occupied her mind with creating a song for the boys' choir. At the Harvest Festival she wandered away, preoccupied with songs only she could hear. Her father, a widower for years, had been nearly insane trying to find his lost child.

One day when she was ten, she'd gone to the well to draw water. A troubadour visiting the town had been sitting with a young woman on a bench, and beside the well, unattended, was his lute. Alyx had never touched any musical instrument before, but she'd heard enough and seen enough to know basically how to make a lute play. Within minutes, she'd plucked out one of the hundreds of tunes chorusing through her head. She was on her fourth song before she realized the troubadour was beside her, his courting forgotten. Silently, without a word between them, needing only the language of music, he had shown her how to place her fingers for the chords. The pain of the sharp strings cutting into her small, tender finger-tips was nothing compared to her joy at being able to hear her music outside her mind.

Three hours later, when her father, with a resigned air, went to look for his daughter, he found her surrounded by half the townspeople, all of them whispering that they were seeing a miracle. The priest, seeing a wonderful possibility, took her to the church and set her before the virginals. After a few minutes of experimenting, Alyx began to play, badly at first, a magnificat, a song of praise to the church, softly speaking the words as she played.

Alyx's father was thoroughly relieved that his only child wasn't light in the head after all, that it was just so filled with music that sometimes she didn't respond to everything said to her. After that momentous day, the priest took over Alyx's training, saying her gift was from God and as God's spokesman, he would take charge of her. He didn't need to add that as a lawyer, her father was far away from God's holiness and the less she associated with such as him, the better.

There followed four years of rigorous training in which the priest managed the loan of every instrument created for Alyx to learn to play. She played the keyboard instruments, horns, strings with and without a bow, drums, bells and the huge pipe organ the priest shamed the town into buying for the Lord (and for him and Alyx, some said).

When the priest was sure she could play, he sent for a Franciscan monk who taught her how to write music, to record the songs, ballads, masses, litanies, whatever she could set to music.

Because she was so busy playing instruments and writing down notes, it wasn't until she was fifteen that anyone realized she could sing. The monk, who was nearly ready to return to his abbey, since Alyx had learned all he could teach her, walked into the church very early one morning and was surrounded by a voice so powerful he could feel the buttons on his cloak trembling. When he was able to convince himself that this magnificent sound came from his very small pupil, he fell to his knees and began to give thanks to God for letting him have contact with such a blessed child.

Alyx, when she saw the old monk on his knees at the back of the church, holding his cross tightly, tears running down his face, stopped singing immediately and ran to him, hoping he wasn't ill, or, as she suspected, offended at her singing, which she knew was dreadfully loud.

After that, as much attention was paid to her voice as to her playing and she began to arrange choral groups, using every voice in the little walled-off town.

Suddenly, she was twenty years old, expecting any day to grow up and, she desperately hoped, out. But she stayed little, and flat, while the other girls her age married and had babies, and Alyx had to be content to sing the lullabies she'd written to teething infants.

What right did she have to be discontent, she thought now, hanging onto the apple tree? Just because the young men all treated her with great respect —except, of course, John Thorpe, who too often smelled like what he hauled—was no reason to be discontent. When she was sixteen and of marriageable age and not so old as now, four men had offered her marriage, but the priest said her music was a sign that she was meant for God's work and not some man's lust and therefore refused to allow any marriage. Alyx, at the time, was relieved, but the older she got, the more she was aware of her loneliness. She loved her music and especially loved what she did for the church, but sometimes . . . like two summers ago when she'd had four glasses of very strong wine at the mayor's daughter's wedding, she grabbed her cittern, stood on a table and sang a very, very bawdy song, which she made up as she went along. Of course, the priest would have stopped her, but since he'd had more wine than anyone else and was rolling in the grass, holding his stomach with laughter at Alyx's song, he certainly wasn't capable of stopping anyone. That had been a wonderful evening, when she'd been a part of the people she'd known all her life, not something set aside by the priest's command, rather like a holy bit of St. Peter's skull in the church, awe inspiring but far from touchable.

Now as she always did, she began to turn her thoughts to song. Breathing deeply, spacing her breath as she'd been taught, she began a ballad of life's loneliness, of a young woman seeking her own true love.

"And here I am, little songbird," came a man's voice from behind her.

So intent on singing—and, indeed, her voice would have covered the sound—she had not heard the young men on horseback approaching. There were three of them, all big, strong, healthy, lusty as only the nobility could be, their faces flushed from what she guessed to be a night of revelry. Their clothes, the fine velvets and fur linings with a jewel winking here and there, were things she'd seen only on the church altar. Dazed, she looked up at them, didn't even move when the largest blond man dismounted.

"Come, serf," he said, and his breath was foul. "Don't you even know your own lord? Allow me to introduce myself. Pagnell, soon to be Earl of Waldenham."

The name brought Alyx alive. The great, greedy, ugly Waldenham family drained the village farmers of every cent they had. When they had no more, the farmers were thrown off the land, left to die wandering the country, begging for their bread.

Alyx was just about to open her mouth to tell this foul young man what she thought of him when he grabbed her, his hideous mouth descending on hers, his tongue thrusting, making her gag.

"Bitch!" he gasped when she clamped her teeth down on his tongue. "I'll teach you who is the master." With one grasp, he tore her cloak away and instantly his hand was at the collar of her dress, tearing easily, exposing one small, vulnerable shoulder and the top of her breast.

"Shall we throw such a small fish back?" he taunted over his shoulder to his friends, who were dismounting.

The reference to her lack of physical endowment above the waist was what changed Alyx's fear to anger. Although she may have been born this man's social inferior, her talent had caused her to be treated as no one's inferior. In a gesture none of the men expected, Alyx pulled up her skirt, raised her leg and viciously kicked Pagnell directly between the legs. The next instant pandemonium broke loose. Pagnell bent double in pain while his companions desperately tried to hear what he was saying as they were still much too drunk to fully comprehend what was going on.

Not sure where she was going or in which direction, Alyx began to run. Her lung power from her many years of breathing exercises held her in good stead. Across cold, barren fields she ran, stumbling twice, trying to hold her torn gown together, the skirt away from her feet.

At the second fence, the hated sheep enclosure, she stopped, slumped against the post, tears running down her face. But even through tears she could see the three horsemen as they combed the area looking for her.

"This way!" came a voice to her left. "This way!"

Looking up, she saw an older man on horseback, his clothes as rich and fine as Pagnell's. With the look of a trapped animal, she began to run again, away from this new man who pursued her.

Easily, he caught up with her, pacing beside her on his horse. "The boys mean no harm," he said. "They're just high-spirited and had a little too much to drink last night. If you'll come with me I'll get you away from them, hide you somewhere."

Alyx wasn't sure if she should trust him. What if he handed her over to those lecherous, drunken noblemen?

"Come on, girl," the man said. "I don't want to see you hurt."

Without another thought, she took the hand offered to her. He hauled her into the saddle before him and kicked the horse into a gallop, heading toward the faraway line of trees.

"The King's forest," Alyx gasped, holding onto the saddle for dear life. No commoner was allowed to enter the King's forest, and she'd seen several men hanged for taking rabbits from it.

"I doubt Henry will mind just this once," the man said.

As soon as they were inside the forest, he lowered her from his horse. "Now go and hide and do not leave this place until the sun is high. Wait until you see other serfs out about their business, then return to your walls."

Wincing once at his calling her, a freewoman, a serf, she nodded and ran deeper into the forest.

Noon took a very long time in coming, and while she waited in the dark, cold forest in a torn dress without her cloak, she became fully aware of her terror at what could have happened at the hands of the nobles. Perhaps it was her training by the priest and the monk that made her believe the nobles had no right to use her people as they wished. She had a right to peace and happiness, had a right to sit under a tree and play her music, and God gave no one the power to take such a thing away from another person.

After only an hour her anger kept her warm. Of course, she knew her anger came partly from a happening last summer. The priest had arranged for the boys' chorus and Alyx to sing in the earl's— Pagnell's father's—private chapel. For weeks they'd worked, Alyx always trying to perfect the music, driving herself to exhaustion rehearsing. When at last they had performed, the earl, a fat man ridden with gout, had said loudly he liked his women with more meat on them and for the priest to bring her back when she could entertain him somewhere besides church. He left before the service was finished.

When the sun was directly overhead, Alyx crept to the edge of the forest and spent a long time studying the countryside, seeing if she saw anyone who resembled a nobleman. Tentatively, she slowly made her way back to her apple tree—hers no longer, as now it would carry too many ugly memories.

There Alyx suffered her greatest shock, for broken

into shreds and splinters lay her cittern, obviously trampled and retrampled by horses' hoofs. Quick, hot tears of anger, hate, frustration, helplessness welled up through her body, spilling down her cheeks unheeded. How could they? she raged, kneeling, picking up a piece of wood. When her lap was full of splinters she saw the uselessness of what she was doing and with all her might began to fling the pieces against the tree.

Dry eyed, shoulders back, she started for the safety of her town, her anger capped for the moment but still very close to the surface.

Chapter Two

*T*HE BIG ROOM of the manor house was hung with brilliant tapestries, the empty spaces covered with weapons of every kind. The heavy, massive furniture was scarred, gouged from ax blades and sword cuts. At the big table sat three young men, their eyes heavily circled from a short life of little sleep and much wine.

"She bested you, Pagnell," laughed one of the men, filling his wine cup, sloshing it on his dirty sleeve. "She beat you, then disappeared like the witch she is. You heard her sing. That wasn't a human voice but one meant to entice you to her and when you went—" He stopped, slammed his fist into his palm and laughed loudly.

Pagnell put his foot on the man's chair and pushed, sending man and chair sprawling. "She's human," he growled, "and not worth my time."

"Pretty eyes," one of the other men said. "And that voice. You think when you stuck it in her, she'd cry out in some note that'd curl the hairs on your legs?"

The first man laughed, righting his chair. "Romantic! I'd make her sing me a song about what she'd like me to do to her."

"Quiet, both of you," Pagnell growled, draining his wine. "I tell you she was human, nothing more."

The other men said nothing and sat silently for a moment, but when a servant girl passed through the room, Pagnell grabbed her. "In the village, there's a girl who can sing. Who is she?"

The servant girl tried to twist away from his painful grip. "That's Alyx," she whispered.

"Stop twisting or I'll break it," Pagnell commanded. "Now tell me exactly where this Alyx lives inside your beastly little town."

An hour later, in the dark night, Pagnell and his three cohorts were outside the walled village of Moreton, tossing pronged, steel hooks to the top of the wall. After three tries, two hooks held, their attached ropes hanging down the wall to the ground. With much less expertise than if they'd been sober, the three men pulled themselves up the ropes to the top of the wall, pausing for a moment before retrieving the hooks and ropes and lowering themselves down to the ground in the narrow alleyway behind the closely packed houses.

Pagnell raised his arm, motioning for the men to follow him as he quietly went to the front of the houses, his eyes searching the street signs hanging over the silent houses. "A witch!" he muttered angrily. "I'll show them how mortal she is. The daughter of a lawyer, the scum of the earth."

At Alyx's house he paused, slipping quickly to the side of it and a latched shutter. One strong blow, one quick sound and the shutter was open and he was inside.

Upstairs, Alyx's father lay quietly, his hands clutching at his breast, at the pains starting there once again. At the sound of the shutter giving, he gasped, not at first believing what he heard. There had been no robberies in town for years.

Quickly striking flint and tinder, he lit a candle and started down the stairs. "What do you ruffians think you're doing?" he demanded loudly as Pagnell helped his friend through the window.

They were the last words he uttered for in a second, Pagnell was across the room, his hand on the old man's hair, a dagger digging deeply as he slashed the man's throat. Without even a second glance to the body as it thudded lifelessly to the floor, he went back to his friends at the window. When they were through, he started up the stairs.

Alyx had not been able to sleep after the day's ordeal. Every time she closed her eyes she saw Pagnell, smelled his horrible breath, felt his tongue in her mouth. She'd somehow been able to keep what had happened from her father, not wanting to worry him, but for the first time in her life something besides music occupied her thoughts.

So upset was she that at first she did not hear the sounds below stairs, only becoming aware of her surroundings when she heard her father's angry voice and the odd thud that followed.

"Robbers!" she gasped, flinging back the woolen covers to stand nude in the room. Quickly, she grabbed her dress, pulling it over her head. Why would anyone want to rob them? They were too poor to be worth robbing. The Lyon belt! she thought, perhaps they've heard of that. Opening a small wall cupboard, she expertly lifted the false bottom and removed the only thing of value she owned, a gold belt, and fastened it about her waist.

A noise in her father's room startled her as footsteps came toward her room. Grabbing a stool and a heavy iron candlestick, she positioned herself behind the door, waiting breathlessly.

The door on its leather hinges opened very slowly, and when Alyx had a good clear shot at the foreign head, she brought down the candlestick with all her might.

Crumpling at her feet was Pagnell, his eyes open for just an instant, seeing her before falling unconscious.

The sight of him, this nobleman, in her little house, renewed her terror of the afternoon. This was no ordinary robbery, and where was her father? More footsteps, heavy ones, pounding up the stairs, brought her to her senses. After one desperate glance, she knew the window was her only means of escape. Running to it, she didn't give a thought to how high she was when she lowered herself and jumped.

The fall slammed her into the ground, where she rolled back against the wall, stunned, breathless for a full terrifying minute. There was no time to lie in the dirt and try to collect herself. Limping, a pain in her side and left leg, she hobbled toward the side of her house where a shutter gaped open.

The moonlight was not a good source of light, but lying beside her father in a tilted candlestick holder was a glowing candle—all she needed to see clearly the great gaping hole in her father's throat, his head lying in a pool of his own blood.

Dazed, Alyx left the window and began to walk away from her house. She didn't notice the cold air on her arms, the chill piercing through her crudely woven wool gown. No longer did she care about Pagnell or what he intended to do to her, what he took from her house, because he had already taken all he could. Her father, the one person who had loved her not because she was a musician but just because he liked her, was dead. What more could the nobleman take than that?

Walking, not seeing where she was going, she finally half fell, half collapsed in front of the church, on her knees, her hands clasped, and began praying for her father's soul, that he be received in Heaven with all the welcome he deserved.

Perhaps it was the years of training Alyx had received that made her able to concentrate so single-mindedly, or perhaps it was her grief, but she heard nothing of the turmoil that went on about her, neither saw nor heard the crackling flames that consumed her house and cremated her father's lifeless body. The constant fear of fire within the walls brought most of the citizens from their houses, and in their terror they did not see Alyx's slight form huddled in the recessed door of the church.

At first light, the gates were opened, and waiting outside were six armored knights bearing the emblem of the Earl of Waldenham. The great stallions' hoofs cut into the narrow paths between the houses, the knights slashing with two-handed swords at any sign or roof projection that got in their way as they moved slowly, possessively, through the town. Women grabbed their children away from the dangerous horses, holding them, paralyzed, as they watched these massive, formidable, helmeted men make their way through the peaceful town.

The knights paused at the smoldering ruins of the Blackett house and the leader pulled a parchment from his saddle, nailing it to one standing, charred post. Without lifting his helmet, he looked down from atop his tall horse to the wide-eyed, frightened townspeople. With one swift gesture he took the lance he carried and deftly speared a dog, tossing the instantly killed body into the ashes.

"Read this and beware!" he said in a growl that reverberated off the stone walls of the town.

Without heed for the townspeople, the men kicked their horses forward and thundered out of the town, taking the opposite side, destroying yet another road before they vanished through the gates, leaving a stunned populace behind them.

It was some moments before anyone recovered enough to look toward the paper nailed to the post and the priest, who was able to read, stepped forward. He took his time in the reading of the parchment, and the townspeople were silent while they waited. When at last the priest turned, his face was white, drawn.

"Alyx," he began slowly. "Alyxandria Blackett has been accused of heresy, witchcraft and thievery. The Earl of Waldenham says the girl used her devil-given voice to entice his son, and when he tried to resist her, she profaned the church. At his further resistance, she smote him with her evil powers and robbed him."

For a moment, no one could even breathe. Alyx's voice given by the devil? Perhaps she was astonishingly gifted, but surely God had given her her ability. Didn't she use her voice in praise of the Lord? Of course, there were some songs she created that were far removed from church music, perhaps . . .

As one, they looked up as they saw Alyx walk across the ground that separated her house from the back of the church, saw her stumble slightly over a torn piece of earth cut by the knights' horses. With puzzled expressions, some with doubt on their faces, they parted to let her pass. She stood still and silent, gazing at what had been her house.

"Come, my child," the priest said quickly, his arm about her shoulders, as he half pulled her to the parish house. Once inside, he began to work quickly, tossing bread and cheese into a canvas bag. "Alyx, you must leave this place."

"My father," she said quietly.

"I know, we saw his body inside the flames. Hush, now, he was already dead, and I will say twenty-five Masses for his soul. We must worry about you now."

When he saw she wasn't really listening, he gave her a sharp shake, making her head snap back. "Alyx! You must listen to me." As a light began to come back into her eyes, he told her about the notice for her arrest. "There is a reward for you, either dead or alive."

"Reward?" she whispered. "Of what value am I?"

"Alyx, you are of great value, but you have angered an earl for some reason. I have not told anyone of the reward, but they will soon find out and they will not all protect you. Some greedy cur will be only too willing to give you away for the reward."

"Then let them! I am innocent and the king—"

The priest's laugh cut her off as he wrapped her in a heavy, too long cloak. "You would be found guilty and the best you could hope for is a hanging. I want you to go now and wait for me at the edge of the King's forest. Tonight I will come for you, and I hope I will have a plan that we can use. Go now, Alyx, and quickly. Let as few people see you as possible. I will come tonight and bring you an instrument and more food. Perhaps we can find a way for a young girl to earn her keep."

Before Alyx could reply to what was happening, she was pushed out the door, the bag of food about her shoulder, her hands holding the long cloak up. She hurried toward the gate, making no attempt to hide, but since nearly all the townspeople were still gathered at the ruins of Alyx's house, no one saw her.

Once in the forest, she sat down, exhausted, grief-ridden, her mind unable to comprehend or believe the events of the last few hours. An hour passed in which the image of her dead father stayed fixed before her eyes and she remembered their life together, the way he'd cared for her. At last, after a night of prayer and a hideous morning, she began to cry, and cry, and cry, and wrapping the cloak over her head, huddling down into a tight little ball, she gave vent to her grief. After a long while, her tired muscles began to relax and she fell asleep, still shaking, buried under the folds of the cloak.

It was close to sunset when she woke, her muscles aching, her left leg hurt from her jump from the window, her head throbbing. Carefully, she pushed back the wool from her face only to see a man sitting on a log not far from her. With a frightened gasp, she looked about for a way to escape.

"There's no need to run from me," the man said

gently, and his voice made her recognize him. He was the servant of Pagnell, the one who'd helped her escape the nobleman yesterday.

"Did you come for the reward?" she asked with a half sneer. "Perhaps I will tell how you helped me before. I don't think your master will like that."

To her surprise the man chuckled. "Have no fear of me, child," he said. "Your priest and I have had a good long talk while you slept and we have a plan for you. If you are willing to listen I think we can hide you well enough that no one will find you."

Nodding curtly, she looked at him, waiting for him to continue. As his plan unfolded, her eyes widened in a mixture of horror, fear and some feeling of anticipation at the prospect of adventure.

The servant had a brother who had once been a soldier for the king, but since the man had had the misfortune to live through all his battles to an old age, he'd been discharged from service with no means to support himself. For two years he had wandered alone, nearly starving until he happened on one of a band of outlaws, misfits and out-of-works who made their life in a vast forest just north of the town of Moreton.

For a moment, Alyx sat quietly. "Are you proposing I join this band?" she asked in disbelief. "As an . . . an outlaw?"

The servant understood her outrage. The priest had been full of praise for the girl's good qualities. "Yes and no," he answered. "A young girl such as yourself would not be safe with the band. For all they have a leader now and there is a measure of Christian goodness among them and some discipline, still a little thing like you would not last long."

With a sigh of relief, Alyx gave a little smile.

"And, too," he continued, "no one would hesitate to take you to the earl for the reward."

"I can sing. Perhaps someone would hire—"

Putting up his hand, he cut her off. "Only the nobles can afford their own musicians, or perhaps some rich merchant, but there again, a lone girl, unprotected . . ."

Dejected, Alyx's shoulders slumped. Was there anywhere safe for her?

When the servant saw that she was aware of the problem of hiding her, he went on with his plan quickly. "If you became a boy, you could hide with the outlaws. With your hair cut and boy's clothes, perhaps a binding about your chest, you might pass. The priest says you can change your voice at will, and your looks might well suit a boy as well as a girl."

Alyx wasn't sure she should laugh or cry at his last remark. It was true that she was no classic beauty with full lips and big blue eyes, but she liked to think . . .

"Come now," the servant chuckled, "there's no need to look like that. I'm sure when you reach an age, you'll fill out and look almost as lovely as a lady."

"I'm twenty years old," she said, eyes narrowed.

The servant cleared his throat in embarrassment. "Then you should be grateful for your looks. Now, come on, for it grows dark. I brought some boy's clothes, and when you're ready, we'll travel. I want to be back before I'm missed. The earl likes to know where his servants are."

This idea that she might be endangering him made her move quickly, taking the folded clothes he offered. At the touch of the cloth, she paused for just a moment before fleeing to the trees to change. It took only seconds to rid herself of the dress she wore, but the boy's garments were unfamiliar. Tightly woven cotton knit hose covered her legs up to her waist, where she tied them snugly. A cloth came next, and she tried not to give a sigh of disgust when she realized she needed very little binding to flatten her breasts. A cotton shirt, fine and soft, went on, a heavier wool shirt with wide sleeves over that and, on top, a long doublet of sturdy, closely woven wool. The doublet came to the bottom curve of her buttocks and was beautifully trimmed with gold scrollwork. Never had she had such rich clothing next to her skin, and she could feel the raw places, rubbed by her woolen dress, beginning to heal. And the freedom of the boy's clothes! she thought as she kicked high with first one leg and then the other.

Slipping on knee-high boots, lacing them at the sides of her ankles, she lifted her gold belt from the heap of her dress and hid the belt about her waist, under doublet and wool shirt. Ready at last, tying an embroidered sash about her waist, she went out to where the earl's servant waited for her.

"Good!" he said, turning her about, inspecting her, frowning at her legs, which were just a little too fine looking for a boy's. "Now for your hair." He took a pair of shears from a pouch at her side.

Alyx took a step backwards, her hand on her long, straight hair. It had never been cut in her life.

"Come on," the man urged. "It's getting late. It's only hair, girl. It will grow again. Better to cut your hair than have it burned, with your head, in a witch's fire."

With fortitude, Alyx turned her back to the man and let him have access to her hair. Surprisingly, as it fell away, her head felt strangely light and not at all unpleasant.

"Look at it curl," the man said, trying to please her, to make light of her horrible situation. When he'd finished, he turned her around, nodding in approval at the curls and waves that clouded about her puckish little face. He thought to himself that the short hair and the boy's clothes suited her better than the ugly dress she'd worn.

"Why?" she asked, looking at him. "You work for the man who killed my father, so why are you helping me?"

"I've been with the lad"—she knew he meant Pagnell—"since he was a babe. He's always had all he wanted, and his father's taught him to take what he should not have. I have tried at times to make amends for the boy's misdeeds. Are you ready?" He obviously didn't want to discuss the subject anymore.

Alyx rode behind the man on the gentle horse and they set off, staying at the edge of the forest, toward the north. All through the ride the servant lectured her on how she must act to keep her secret. She must walk as a boy, shoulders back, taking long strides. She mustn't cry or laugh in a silly way, must swear, mustn't bathe overmuch, must scratch and spit and not be afraid to work, to lift and tote, or turn up her nose at dirt and spiders. On and on he went until Alyx nearly fell asleep, which cost her another lecture on the softness of girls.

When they arrived at the edge of the forest where the outlaws hid, he gave her a dagger to wear at her side to protect herself and told her to practice the use of it.

Once they entered the dark, forbidding forest, he

stopped talking and Alyx could feel the tension run through his body. She found that her hands, gripping the edge of the saddle, were white knuckled.

The call of a night bird came softly to them and the servant answered it. Farther into the forest another call and answer were exchanged, and the servant stopped, setting Alyx down and dismounting. "We will wait here until morning," he said in a voice that was almost a whisper. "They will want to find out who we are before they let us enter their camp. Come, boy," he said louder. "Let's sleep."

Alyx found she could not sleep but instead lay still under the blanket the servant gave her and went over in her mind all that had happened, that because of some nobleman's whim she was here alone in this cold, frightful forest while her dear father's life had been cut short. As she thought, anger began to replace her fear as well as her grief. She would overcome this problem and someday, somehow, she'd revenge herself on Pagnell and all of his kind.

At first light, they were back on the horse and slowly made their way deeper and deeper into the maze of the forest.

Chapter Three

*A*FTER A VERY long time of tiptoeing through the tangle of trees and undergrowth, following no path that Alyx could see, she began to hear voices, quiet voices, mostly male. "I hear the men talking," she whispered.

The servant gave her a look of disbelief over his shoulder, for he heard nothing but the wind. It was quite some time before he, too, heard the voices.

Suddenly, surprisingly, a deep tangle of growth parted and before them was a small village of tents and crude shelters. A gray-haired man, a deep, old scar running from his temple, down his cheek, his neck and disappearing into his collar, caught the reins of the horse.

"You had no trouble, brother?" the scarred man asked, and when his brother nodded, he looked at Alyx. "This the lad?"

She held her breath under his scrutiny, fearing he'd see her for female, but he dismissed her as not of importance.

"Raine is waiting for you," the scarred man said to his brother. "Leave the boy with him and I'll ride out with you and you can give me the news."

With a nod, the servant reined his horse toward the direction in which his brother pointed.

"He didn't think I wasn't a boy," Alyx whispered, half pleased, half insulted. "And who is Raine?"

"He's the leader of this motley group. He's only been here a couple of weeks, but he's been able to whip some order into the men. If you plan to stay here you must obey him at all times or he'll have you out on your ear."

"The king of the outlaws," she said somewhat dreamily. "He must be very fierce. He isn't a . . . a murderer, is he?" she gasped.

The servant looked back at her, laughing at her girlish changes in mood, but when he saw her face, he stopped and followed her mesmerized gaze straight ahead of them.

Sitting on a low stool, his shirt off, sharpening his sword, was the man who was unmistakably the leader of any group of men in his presence. He was a big man, very large, with great bulging muscles, a deep thick chest, thighs straining against the black knit hose he wore. That he should be shirtless in January in the cold, sunless forest was astonishing, but even this far away Alyx could see that he was covered with a fine sheen of sweat.

His profile was handsome: a fine nose, black, black hair, sweat dampened into curls along his neck, deep set serious eyes under heavy black brows, a mouth set into a firm line as he concentrated on the whetstone before him and the sharpening of the sword.

Alyx's first impression was that her heart might stop beating. She'd never seen a man like this one, from whom power came as if it were the sweat glistening on his body. People often said she had power in her voice, and she wondered if it was like the power of this man, an aura surrounding all of his enormous, magnificent body.

"Close your mouth, girl," the servant chuckled, "or you'll give yourself away. His lordship won't take to a lad drooling on his knees."

"Lordship?" Alyx asked, coming up for air. "Lordship!" she gasped and reason came back to her. It wasn't power she saw coming from this man, it was his sense that all the world belonged to him. Generations of men like Pagnell had reproduced themselves to create men like the one before her—arrogant, prideful, sure that everyone was destined to be their personal servant, taking what they wanted, even an old, ailing lawyer who got in their way. Alyx was in this cold forest and not at home practicing her music where she belonged because of men like this one who sat on a stool and waited for others to come to him.

The man turned, looking up at them with blue eyes, serious eyes that missed little of what he saw. As if he were a king on a throne, Alyx thought, and indeed he made the rough stool look like a throne, waiting for his lowly subjects to approach. So this was why she had to dress as a boy! This man with his lordly, superior ways, demanding that everyone bow and scrape before him, bend down so he could place his jeweled shoes on their behinds. He was the leader of this group of outlaws and murderers, and how had he gotten that dubious honor? No doubt from all of them believing in the natural superiority of the nobility; that this man, because of his birth, had the *right* to command them and they, as stupid as criminals must be, did not question his authority, merely asked how low they should grovel before his lordship.

"That's Raine Montgomery," the servant said, not seeing the way Alyx's eyes hardened, a great change from her original softness. "The king has declared him a traitor."

"And no doubt he well deserves the title," she spat, still watching Raine as they drew nearer to the man, his strength seeming to pull them toward him.

The servant glanced at her in surprise. "He was once a favorite of King Henry's and was leading men to the king's own Wales when Lord Raine heard that his sister had been taken prisoner by Lord Roger Chatworth and—"

"A feud among themselves!" she snapped. "And no doubt many innocent men were killed to feed these nobles' taste for blood."

"No one was killed," the man said, bewildered by her attitude. "Lord Roger threatened to kill Lord Raine's sister, so Lord Raine retreated; but King Henry declared him a traitor for using the king's own men in a personal war."

"Lords!" Alyx snarled. "There is only one Lord and King Henry was right to declare the man a traitor, since he well deserved the title for using our good king's men for his own personal fight. So now he hides in the forest using the ruffians as his subjects. Tell me, does he kill them at will or is he content with having them serve his dinner to him on silver platters?"

At that the servant laughed, at last understanding her hostility toward Lord Raine. No doubt the only noblemen she'd met were Pagnell and his father. Using them as criteria, she had reason to despise Lord Raine.

"Come sit down," Raine said, taking the reins and looking up at the weary man on the horse.

Alyx's first thought was: He can sing! Any man with such a deep, rich voice had to be able to sing. But the next instant her kind thoughts were gone.

"Step down here, boy, and let's have a look at you," Raine said. "You look a bit thin to me. Can you do a day's work?"

Alyx had never ridden astride a horse before, and the new exercise had made the inside of her legs stiff and sore. When she tried to swing off the top of the horse with at least a bit of bravado, her hateful legs refused to obey, and the left one, still hurt from her fall, collapsed under her.

Raine placed a steadying hand on her upper arm, and to Alyx's chagrin her body reacted instantly to this man who represented everything she hated. "Get your hand off me!" she snarled at him, seeing the surprised look on his handsome face before she had to grab the saddle of the horse to keep from falling. The stupid horse shied away, causing Alyx to stumble again before she could right herself.

"Now, if you are quite finished," Raine said, his blue eyes alight, that delicious voice of his running across her like melted honey, "perhaps we can find out something about you."

"This is all you need to know about me, nobleman!" she hissed, drawing the knife at her side, pointing it at him, despising his easy assurance that she meant nothing while he was God's gift to the earth.

Completely startled by the boy's hostility, Raine was unprepared for the sharp little dagger lunging at him and barely had time to move away before it cut, not where it aimed, his heart, but the top of his arm.

Stunned at what she'd done, Alyx stood still, her eyes fastened to the slow trickle of blood coming from the man's bare arm. Never in her life had she hurt anyone before.

But she didn't have long to think on her rash act because before she could begin to apologize, or before she could even blink an eye, Raine Montgomery had grabbed the seat of her pants and her collar and sent her sliding, face down, across about half an acre of forest floor. She should have closed her gaping mouth because her lower teeth acted as a shovel and collected bushels of leaves, dirt and whatever other filth made the spongy floor.

"Now, you young devil!" Raine said from his place behind her.

Sitting up, using both hands and furiously gouging handfuls of Heaven-knows-what from her mouth, wincing at her sore leg, she looked up to see him standing at what seemed to be quite a distance from her. Between them was a deep, scoured path that had been made by Alyx's body. And what she saw renewed her anger. Raine Montgomery, that vile nobleman, was surrounded by a disreputable looking crew of men and women, all laughing, showing black, rotten teeth, choking on their tongues, generally enjoying her agony. Raine himself was laughing harder than anyone, and the sight of deep, long dimples in his cheeks emphasizing his mirth did nothing for her temperament.

"Come on," said a voice beside her, the man who'd brought her, as he helped her stand. "Hold your tongue or he may toss you out altogether."

Alyx started to speak but paused to remove a piece of stick from its hiding place between her gum and cheek and missed her chance.

The man used this opportunity to speak to Raine, his fingers biting warningly into Alyx's arm, fairly shouting to be heard over the raucous laughter. "My lord, please forgive the lad. Yesterday a nobleman killed his father and burned his house. He has reason to hate and I fear it extends to all men of your class."

Instantly, Raine sobered and looked at Alyx with sympathy, which made her stiffen and look away. She did not want his pity.

"What nobleman did this?" Raine asked, his voice full of concern.

"The Earl of Waldenham's son."

Spitting in pure disgust, Raine's face twisted for a moment, his fine lips curling into a snarl. "Pagnell," he said, his voice full of contempt. "The man doesn't deserve the title of man or nobleman. Come with me, boy, and I will teach you we're not all cut of the same cloth. I need a squire and you will do nicely."

In two steps he was beside her, his arm companionably about her shoulders.

"Do not touch me," she gasped, jumping away from him. "I do not need your pity or the soft job of serving your sweet cakes. I am . . . a man and I can hold my own. I will work and earn my keep."

"Sweet cakes, is it?" Raine asked as a dimple flashed in his left cheek. "I have a feeling, boy," he said, looking her up and down, "you have no idea what work is. You have legs and arms more suited for a girl."

"How dare you insult me so!" she gasped, scared that she was going to be revealed at any moment, grabbing for her dagger but finding only an empty sheath.

"Another of your mistakes," Raine said. "You dropped it to the ground." Slowly, with great show, he removed her little knife from the waist of his hose, those tight, tight hose that clung to his body, a triangular patch loosely tied over his maleness. "I'll teach you to keep your weapons about you and not discard them so lightly." Idly, he ran his thumb along the blade. "It needs sharpening."

"It was sharp enough to cut your thick hide," she said confidently, smiling back at him, glad she could repay him for some of his self-assurance.

As if just remembering the bloody cut, he glanced at it before looking back at her. "Come with me, squire, and tend to my wound," he said flatly, turning his back on her as if he expected her to follow him.

Alyx instantly decided that she did not want to stay in this camp at the mercy and whim of this man Raine, who attracted her so yet made her so angry. And she did not like these dirty, greedily staring people who surrounded her, watching as if she were part of a play put on for their entertainment.

She turned to the servant who'd brought her. "I don't wish to stay here. I will take my chances elsewhere," she said, turning toward the saddled horse.

"Neither do you know how to obey an order,"

came Raine's voice from behind her, an instant before his big hand clamped on her neck. "I'll not let a little thing like your terror of me keep me from acquiring a good squire."

"Get away from me!" she yelled as he pushed her ahead of him. "I don't want to stay here. I won't stay here."

"As I see it you owe me for spilling some of my blood. Now get in there!" he said as he pushed her inside a large canvas tent.

Trying not to cry at the pain in her leg, at the battering her already bruised body was taking, she clutched at a tent pole and tried to stay upright.

"Blanche!" Raine bellowed out of the tent flap. "Bring me some hot water and some linen and make sure it's clean!"

"Now, boy," he said, turning back to her and, for a moment, studying her. "You've hurt your leg. Take off those hose and let me look at it."

"No!" she gasped, backing away from him.

He looked truly puzzled. "Is it me you fear or"—he gave a bit of a smile—"that you're modest? Oh, well," he said, sitting down on the cot at the edge of the tent, "perhaps you should be shy. If I had legs like yours I'd be ashamed of them, too. But don't worry, lad, we'll put some muscle on your scrawny body. Ah, yes, Blanche, put it there and go."

"But don't you want me to dress your wound?"

Alyx looked from her scrutiny of her legs, thinking that they weren't so bad at all, to see the woman who spoke. Her sensitivity to sound and especially to voices made her look up sharply. The hint of a whine, the begging quality, somehow overridden by a touch of insolence, grated along her spine. She saw a plump woman with stringy, dirty blonde hair, looking at Raine as if she might devour him at any moment.

With pure disgust, Alyx looked away.

"The boy will dress the wound."

"I most certainly will not!" Alyx said vehemently. "Let the woman do it, 'tis woman's work and she looks as if she'd like the job." Smiling, Alyx thought perhaps she might like being a male and not having to do all the thankless drudgery tasks of a woman.

Raine, in one unseen, swift gesture, leaned forward, grabbed Alyx's thigh in one of his big hands and pulled. As her leg went flying out from under her she landed very hard on her already bruised rump.

"You need some manners as well as muscles. Go now, Blanche," he said pointedly to the staring woman. When they were alone he turned back to Alyx. "I'll be forgiving for a few days since you've not had a noble background, but if your manners don't soon improve, I'll take a switch to that puny body of yours and see if you can learn to behave. The water grows cold, so come and clean this wound and bind it."

Reluctantly, Alyx stood, rubbing her buttocks, limping a bit on her leg. When she reached Raine, he extended his arm, that large brown muscular arm, blood from shoulder to forearm, for her to clean. As she touched him with the warm cloth she realized how cold her hands were, how warm his skin—and how deep the cut. It did not set well with her that she had hurt anyone like this.

"The first time you've drawn blood?" Raine asked gently, his face near hers, his voice soft as he watched her.

She barely nodded, not wanting to meet his eyes as tears choked her throat and she remembered her life before two days ago.

"How did you hurt your leg?" he asked.

Blinking rapidly, refusing to cry, she glared at him. "By running from one of your kind," she spat at him.

"Good lad." He smiled and again those dimples appeared. "Don't let anyone scare you. Keep your head high no matter what happens."

She rinsed out the bloody cloth and started washing all of his arm.

"Should I tell you the duties of a squire?" he asked.

"Having never had your advantages of personal servants I am afraid I am at a loss as to what one should do for h—"—she had almost said "her"—"his master."

A snort from Raine was his reply to her answer. "You are to clean my armor, care for my horses, help me personally in any way you can, and"—his eyes twinkled—"serve me my sweet cakes. Do you think you can do all that?"

"There's no more?" she taunted.

"A true squire would learn the rudiments of training to be a knight, using a sword, a lance, that sort of thing, as well as write his lord's letters and at times deliver important messages. I do not expect so much from you though since—"

Alyx cut him off. "Since I am not of your class and you do not think I have the brain to learn? My father was a lawyer and I can read and write better than most of your nobles, I'll wager, and I can do it in Latin and French as well as English."

Raine tested his arm for a moment, curling his hand into a fist, making his bicep bulge, all the while smiling slightly, not at all offended by her accusations. Finally, he looked back at her. "You're still too small to do much heavy training," he said, "and it has little to do with your birth status. As for reading and writing, you must be better than I am, for I do not read more than the names of my family. Good!" he said as he stood. "You have a delicate hand with a wound. Perhaps Rosamund can use your help."

"Another of your women?" Alyx sneered, motioning her head toward the tent flap where Blanche had been.

"Are you jealous?" he asked, and before Alyx could sputter that she was jealous of no women, he added, "You'll have your share of women yet, when you get your first beard and we put a little meat on you." Cocking his head, looking at her, he said, "You're pretty enough if you don't get scarred on the battlefield. Women like pretty faces on their men."

"Such as yours?" she snapped and could have bitten out her tongue.

"I do well enough," he said, obviously highly amused. "Now I have some work for you to do. This armor needs cleaning and after that it must be polished to keep the rust off." Quickly, he piled pieces of steel armor together, back and front together forming a large shell which held arm and leg coverings. The helmet went on top.

Confidently, arrogantly, Alyx held out her arms and in the next moment she staggered backward and would have fallen had not Raine caught her at the small of her back.

"It's a mite heavy for a lad your size."

"My size!" she gasped, trying to steady herself. "If

you weren't as large as a pair of oxen the armor need not be so big."

"Your insolence is going to earn you some bruises, and I would advise you to show some proper respect for your leige lord." Before she could make a reply, he fairly pushed her from the tent. "There's a stream to the north," he said, piling several cloths on her burden of mud-encrusted armor. "Wash it well then bring it back. And if I find one new dent in it I will add five dents to your hide. Is that clear, boy?"

Alyx could barely nod, as she was more concerned with staying upright under her burden, wondering how in the world she was going to walk, than making any smart retorts to Raine. Slowly, one step at a time, she started forward, her arms already aching, her neck craned sideways to see around the high pile of steel she carried. When her body hurt so badly there were tears in her eyes, she finally saw the stream. At its side she started to drop the armor to her feet, but remembering Raine's threat, she braced her legs apart, squatted and carefully lowered all seventy pounds of it to the ground.

For a moment she sat there, her arms extended, wondering if they'd ever feel the same again. When feeling came back to them, and all the feeling was pain, she plunged her arms, shirt and all, into the cold clear water of the stream.

Several minutes later she glanced back at the pile of armor with a great sigh. So much for women's drudgery. What was the difference between washing dishes and washing armor? With another sigh she picked up the cloths and began removing the crust of mud, sweat, rust and whatever else held the filth together.

An hour later she'd succeeded in taking the dirt off the armor and placing it on herself. Never had she sweat so much in her life, and every drop made the dirt cling to her skin. Removing her tunic, she used a clean cloth to wash most of the dirt from it and left it to dry on a rock while she washed her face and arms.

As she came up from washing and reached for a dry cloth, someone handed it to her. Quickly drying her face, she opened her eyes to see an astonishingly handsome man. Dark wavy hair framed a perfectly formed, high-cheekboned face. Hot, dark eyes blazed under long thick lashes. Alyx blinked twice to make sure this dark angel was real and, in her stunned silence, she did not see the sword pointed at her belly.

Chapter Four

"WHO ARE YOU?" this man who was too perfect-looking to be real asked.

Alyx, unused to danger in her life, did not fully react to the sword, but what she did react to was the music in this man's voice. She'd felt that Raine, with his deep voice, could sing if he tried, but she was sure this man *did* sing. "I am Raine's new squire," she said quietly, using her voice and all her many years of training to bring the voice from deep within her chest.

For a moment he stared at her, puzzled, speechless, and very slowly he resheathed his sword, his eyes never leaving hers. "There's something about your voice. Have you ever done any singing?"

"A bit," she said, her eyes dancing, every ounce of her confidence making itself known in that simple statement.

Without another word he reached to his back and the quiver of arrows he carried there and pulled out a flute. He started to play a simple, common song that Alyx knew well. For a moment she closed her eyes, letting the music float about her. The last few days had been the longest she'd ever gone without music since that day ten years ago when she'd picked up the troubadour's lute. As the music filled her, her lungs filled with air and she opened her mouth to sing.

After only four notes, the young man stopped playing, his mouth dropping open in disbelief, his eyes wide. Alyx grinned, kept singing and motioned for him to continue.

With one quick glance of thankfulness raised toward Heaven and a laugh of pure joy, the man again put the flute to his lips.

Alyx followed the tune for quite some time, but her need to create was too strong to let it rest. Here was someone who could play, and she wondered what else he could do. Looking about for something to give her more sound, she saw a hollow log quite near. Still singing, never losing a beat, she grabbed the back, breastplate and thigh covering of Raine's armor and set them near the log. Sticks quickly made drumsticks and for a moment she stopped singing, tapping out sounds on the pieces of armor and the log. When she had the sounds down she began to hum some of the music in her head.

Fascinated, the young man watched her, and when she began to sing, a new song this time, he followed her on his flute, slowly at first until he caught the tune and rhythm. When he added a variation of his own she laughed, still singing, and followed him easily. It became a bit of competition after that, with Alyx going one way and the man another, yet both following each other, testing one another's skill.

And when the man tossed the flute to the ground and added his strong, clear voice to hers, it was Alyx's turn to be stunned for a moment, at least enough to make her miss a beat which, from the look on his face, gave the man great joy. Grabbing her hands, both on their knees, facing each other, they blended their voices together, sending them upward toward Heaven.

At last they stopped and all around them was utter and complete silence, as if the wind and birds had stopped to listen to their magnificent music. Hands still clasped, they were still, looking at each other with a mixture of love, awe, surprise, delight and kinship.

"Jocelin Laing," the beautiful young man finally said, breaking the silence.

"Alyx . . . ander Blackett," she answered, stumbling over the male name.

One of Jocelin's perfect brows lifted and he started to say something, but Raine's voice stopped him.

"Joss, I see you've met my new squire."

Almost with guilt, Alyx dropped Jocelin's hands and stood, only to find her sore leg going under her.

Roughly, Raine grabbed her arm. "If the two of you are through entertaining each other, you can bring my armor back and scrape the rust off of it. Joss, did you get any game?"

With what were surely spots of color on his cheeks, Jocelin faced Raine, his slim, broad-shouldered body appearing miniature next to Raine's massive form. "I have four rabbits by the stream."

"Rabbits!" Raine grunted. "I'll go and look for a deer or two later, but now, boy, come back to camp and let's have a look at that leg. You'll be no use to me if you're crippled."

With resignation, Alyx collected the pieces of armor and Jocelin loaded them into her arms, along with her damp tunic. She followed Raine back to the camp, wondering just how much of the singing he'd heard.

If he'd heard any of it, he didn't comment as he entered the tent and pointed for Alyx to set his armor down.

"Now pull off those hose and let's look at that leg."

"My leg is healing nicely," she said, standing firmly where she was.

Narrowing his eyes at her, he took a step closer. "You might as well understand now that everyone in this camp pulls his weight. We can't afford the time to deal with sick people. Get undressed while I get Rosamund," he said, slipping on a shirt and doublet over his hose before leaving the tent.

As soon as he was gone, Alyx quickly removed the tight hose, grabbed a cloth and tied it about her waist, bringing the end up and over the Lyon belt secreted beneath her clothes so that she formed a loincloth. A great deal of her thigh and hip were exposed, and as she looked down at them, thinking that they weren't bad-looking at all, she knew that now she'd be exposed as a female. Oh, well, she sighed, it was nice to think that some part of her, if not her face, was so pretty it could only belong to a woman.

A sound at the tent opening made her look up and there, in profile, was surely one of the most beautiful women ever made on earth. Lashes so long they looked unreal, curled over pretty green eyes, a perfect nose and mouth that curved back, its lips finely shaped, chiseled, a classic beauty, how every woman dreams of looking. And behind her was Raine. No wonder he never noticed his squire! she thought. With women like this one around, why would he look at something plain and ordinary like her?

"This is Rosamund, a healer," Raine said, and his voice held a sweet softness that made Alyx look at him in wonder. It would be nice to hear him use that voice when he spoke to her.

The next moment Rosamund turned and an involuntary gasp escaped Alyx, for the entire left side of Rosamund's face was covered with a deep pink strawberry mark—the sign of the devil. Instantly, her hand raised to cross herself in hopes of warding off the evil power, but her eyes were drawn to Raine's and those blue orbs were fastened on hers in warning and threat.

"If you'd rather I didn't touch you . . ." Rosamund began in a voice that showed she was perfectly used to being repulsed.

"No, of course not," Alyx said hesitantly, then gained strength. "There's nothing wrong with my leg, only what this great horse of a man thinks is wrong."

With surprised eyes, Rosamund looked up at Raine, but he only snorted. "The boy has no manners —yet," he added, his words carrying a threat. He seemed satisfied that Alyx was going to treat Rosamund with respect and turned away from them, never once glancing at Alyx's legs, she noticed with chagrin.

Gently, Rosamund took Alyx's leg, lifted it, turned it this way and that, seeing no external signs of injury.

"My name is Raine Montgomery," he said, his back to them. "I prefer my name to being referred to as . . . whatever animal you choose."

"And should I preface it with 'your majesty' or will 'your lordship' do?" She knew she was greatly daring and had no idea what his wrath would be like, but she was still angry over the way he'd forced her to stay in his camp.

"Raine will do fine," he said, looking back at her, smiling. "I find the rules of society are fairly useless in this place, and what may I call you?"

Alyx started to speak, but Rosamund pulled her leg in such a way that Alyx gave an involuntary squeal of pain and lifted straight off her seat. Trying to control the tears in her eyes, she clenched her teeth and said, "Alyxander Blackett."

"What's wrong with the lad?" Raine asked.

"He's pulled some of the muscles and there is nothing to be done except bind it and let it heal by itself. I can offer no medicine, perhaps a poultice tonight but nothing else."

Raine ignored Alyx's I-told-you-so look as he held the tent flap open for Rosamund and watched her leave.

In seconds, Alyx dressed again while Raine's back was turned, and she tried for a normal tone of voice. "She's a beautiful woman," she said, trying not to betray how interested she was in Raine's answer.

"She doesn't think she is," he said, "and it's been my experience with women that they must believe themselves to be beautiful before they are."

"And no doubt you are very experienced with women."

One of his dark eyebrows lifted as he smiled at her.

"Get up off that scrawny rear of yours and let's get to work."

Trying not to be hurt by his too personal comments on her body, Alyx followed him outside, his big legs eating up ground at a furious pace as she hurried along behind him. Without pausing, he grabbed a large loaf of black bread from a makeshift brick oven, tore it in half and gave a piece to Alyx, who looked at the loaf with some consternation, as the bread was more than she normally ate in a day.

Raine, eating his way through the heavy, solid bread, led her through the village of outlaws. All the shelters were shoddy things, not even hinting at permanence, and the smells emanating from them were horrible. Obviously, there were no sanitary ordinances here as there were in her pretty, walled town.

"Not much, is it?" Raine asked, watching her face. "What can you teach people who empty their chamber pots on their own front doorsteps?"

"Who are these people?" she asked, looking in disgust at the filthy, tired-looking women ambling about doing various housewifely chores while men sat and spit, now and then looking up at Raine and Alyx with insolent glares. Without realizing she was doing it, she stepped closer to Raine.

"There," he said, pointing, "that one killed four women." His voice held a great deal of disgust. "Stay away from him. He likes to terrorize anything smaller than he is. And that man with the patch over his eye is the Black Runner, the highwayman. He became so famous he had to retire at the peak of his career," he added sarcastically.

"And them? The men huddled by the fire?"

Raine frowned slightly. "They are suffering from melancholia. They are farmers, displaced by the enclosure acts. They know nothing except farming and, as far as I can tell, want to learn nothing new."

"Enclosures!" she gasped. "No wonder they hate you."

"Me?" he asked, truly astonished. "Why should they hate me?"

"You have taken their farms, put fences around what was their land and put your nasty sheep in the pens," she said smugly, letting him know that not everyone of the non-nobles was as uneducated as these louts.

"I have, have I?" he said, not smiling but a dimple giving away his amusement. "Do you always judge an entire group of people on the actions of one? Is there no villain in your little town? If this villain picked my pocket should I hang everyone in town for justice's sake?"

"No . . . no, I guess not," she reluctantly admitted.

"Here, eat this," he said, handing her a hard-boiled egg and taking away what was left of her loaf and eating it himself. "You'll never grow any bigger if you don't eat. Now we'll try to do something about your lack of muscle."

With that comment, he led her through the trees toward the sounds she'd been hearing since she'd arrived. When they reached a large, cleared area, she halted, eyes wide, staring at the scene before her. Men, many men, seemed to be trying to kill either each other, their horses or themselves. Men lunged at one another with swords, at stuffed dummies with lances or performed bodily contortions wearing stones strapped to their bodies.

"What is this?" she whispered, not knowing how to react.

"If the men are to survive, they must know how to fight," he said, his eyes on the men. "Here, you two," he bellowed so loudly Alyx jumped. With two furious strides, he reached two men who'd dropped their swords and gone after each other with their fists. Raine grabbed the back of the rags they wore, shook them like dogs and tossed them apart. "Men of honor do not fight with their fists," he growled. "As long as you are under my rule you will fight as if you were decent men and not the scum you are. If you break my training again, you will be punished. Now get back to work!"

Silent, somewhat awed by Raine's fierceness, Alyx stood stone-still until he turned back to her. The man's voice ranged from the sweetness he used with Rosamund to this terrifying bellow.

"Now," he said, in the cool voice he used for her, "let's see how strong you are. Lie down and push your body up using only your arms."

Alyx had absolutely no idea what he meant, and at her blank look he sighed as if greatly burdened, pulled off his shirt and doublet, dropped to the ground on his stomach and proceeded to lift his body repeatedly with his arms. It certainly didn't look difficult, so Alyx assumed the same position. On her first try only the front half of her body came up and on the second try, her arms raised her half way and then collapsed.

"Too much sitting!" Raine declared and grabbed the seat of her hose, pulling that heavier part of her up. "Now push! Do something with those puny arms!"

With that, Alyx rolled away from him and sat up.

"It's not as easy as it looks," she said, rubbing her shaking arms.

"Easy!" he snorted, dropping to his stomach again. "Climb on my back."

It took Alyx a few moments to believe what she heard. Climb atop that great, bare, sweaty expanse of sun-bronzed skin?

Impatiently, he pointed and Alyx straddled him. Using only one hand, he began to push up and down, her astride him, but the last thing Alyx was interested in was his show of strength. Never had she been this near a man before, and certainly she had never had one between her legs before. His sweat began to dampen the insides of her thighs, or perhaps it was her own sweat, but she certainly was becoming damp from someone. His muscles, popping out, straining as he lifted his own considerable body weight as well as hers with the one arm, rippled along the inside of her legs, sending waves of warmth through her body. Her hands, touching his hot skin, seemed very alive, very sensitive. His muscles and skin were making music, playing her body until it was singing a song she'd never heard before.

"Now!" Raine said, rolling to one side and dumping her in the dirt. "Someday when you're a man you'll be able to do that."

Sitting down, looking up at him and all that lovely skin of his, her body still humming, she thought that the very last thing she wanted was to be a man.

Behind Raine stepped Jocelin, his beautiful eyes alight, watching her, and it was almost as if he knew what she was thinking. Embarrassed, she looked away.

"I think you've shocked your squire into silence," Jocelin said to Raine. "You forget that people of our class aren't used to your physical vigor."

"You're too busy sitting around counting your money," Raine said in dead earnest. "And what's made you so happy today? Not enough work for you to do?"

Joss ignored the jibe. "Just curious, 'tis all. I was on my way to practice with my bow." With that, he left to go to the targets at the far end of the long field.

"Are you going to take root?" Raine asked, looking down at Alyx. When she stood, he took a long sword from a passing man and handed it to her. "Take the hilt in both hands and come for me."

"I don't want to hurt anyone," she said instantly. "I didn't even want to hurt Pagnell when—"

"What if I were Pagnell?" he said archly. "Come for me or I will go for you."

The pain, so recent, so deep, made her raise the heavy sword from where its tip dangled in the dust and she thrust at him. When the blade was a hairsbreadth from his belly, he sidestepped, evading her. Again she lunged and again, again, and still she couldn't touch him. She started for one side, changed in midthrust and made for his other side, but no matter what she did she could not hit him.

Panting from her exertions, she stopped, resting the sword tip in the dirt, her arms aching, quivering from the exertion, while Raine, smiling and confident, grinned at her until she longed to ram him with the steel she held.

"Now I will give you another chance. I will stand perfectly still while you swing at me."

"There's a trick," she said with such fatalism that he laughed aloud.

"No trick, but you must lift the sword above your head and come straight down. If you can do that you will strike me."

"I could not hurt someone. To draw blood—"

His face showed his belief in her swordsmanship. "Think of all my sheep, all the farmers I have caused to starve because of my greedy ways. Think of—"

Alyx happily lifted the sword straight up, planning to bring it down on his head, but at the moment she reached up the blasted, uncooperative sword started pulling her arms backward. Already tired and weakened, her arms could not hold it and for a few seconds it was a struggle—and the damned piece of steel won. The smirk on Raine's face as she stood there holding the long sword, its tip planted between her heels, made her furious.

"You're as weak a boy as I ever saw. What have you done with your life?"

She absolutely refused to answer that question as she twisted the sword around to the front of her.

"Lift it to the top of your head, lower it and do it again and again until I return. If I see you slacking, I'll double your practice time," he said as he left her.

Up and down, over and over she lifted the sword, her arms screaming with the exercise.

"You'll learn," said a voice behind her and she turned to see the scarred soldier, the brother of the man who'd brought her here.

"Has your brother left? I wanted to thank him, although right now I'm not sure this is any better than what could have happened to me."

"He needed no thanks," the man said gruffly, "and you'd better not stop because Lord Raine is looking this way."

With trembling arms, Alyx resumed her exercise, and it was several moments before Raine returned to show her how to hold the sword at arm's length, one arm at a time, lifting and lowering it repeatedly.

After what seemed like an eternity, he took the sword from her and started walking back toward the camp. Her arms and shoulders feeling as if they'd been put to the rack, Alyx followed him silently.

"Food, Blanche," he said over his shoulder on the way to his tent.

Gratefully, Alyx sat down on a stool while Raine took another and began to sharpen the point of a long lance. With her head leaning against a tent pole, she was almost asleep when Blanche came in bearing crockery bowls full of stew and curds and whey mixed with soft cooked lentils and more of the heavy black bread, with hot spiced wine in mugs.

As Alyx lifted her wooden spoon, her arms started to jerk spasmodically, protesting what she'd just done to them.

"You're too soft," Raine grunted, his mouth full. "It'll take months to harden you up."

Silently, Alyx knew she'd die if she had to take even a week of today's torture. She ate as best she could, too weary to pay much attention to the food, and she was falling asleep when Raine grabbed her upper arm and pulled her up.

"The day's young yet," he said, obviously laughing at her exhaustion. "The camp needs food and we must get it."

"Food?" she groaned. "Let them starve and let me sleep."

"Starve!" he snorted. "They'd kill each other for what food there is and only the strongest would survive. And you," he said, his fingers meeting as they encircled her upper arm, "you wouldn't last an hour. So we go to hunt to keep you alive as well as them."

With one jerk, she moved away from his touch. Stupid man, she thought, couldn't he see that she was female? Without another word, he was out of the tent and she ran after him, following him to the edge of camp where the horses were kept. All along the way she saw the people of the camp, resting, digesting their food, no one continuing to work except Raine.

"Could it be possible that you could ride?" he asked, his voice showing he had no hope.

"No," she whispered.

"What have you done with your life?" he demanded again. "I have never known a boy who couldn't ride."

"And I have never known a man who knew so little about the people outside his own world. Have you spent your life on a jeweled throne doing nothing but fighting with swords and riding great horses?"

Flinging a heavy wood-based saddle on his horse, he said, "You have a sharp tongue on you, and if it were not for us training to fight, who would protect you when there is war?"

"The King, of course," she answered smugly.

"Henry!" Raine gasped, one foot in the stirrup.

"And who do you think protects Henry? Who does he call when he is attacked if not his nobles? Give me your arm," he said and easily pulled her up to sit on the hard rump of the horse behind his saddle. Before she could say a word, they were off at a teeth-jarring pace.

Chapter Five

$\mathcal{A}$FTER WHAT SEEMED to be hours of banging up and down on the bony backside of the horse, her knuckles white from gripping the edge of the saddle, Raine abruptly halted the animal and Alyx came close to flying backward over the tail.

"Hold on," he growled as he grabbed the nearest part of her, which was her sore thigh, making her gasp in pain. "Quiet!" he commanded. "There, through the trees, see them?"

Dashing away tears of pain with her sleeve, she was finally able to see a family of wild pigs scrounging in the undergrowth. The pigs halted, looked up with their mean little eyes glaring out of their lean, tough bodies and snorted over the long sharp tusks protruding from their mouths.

"Hold onto me," Raine bellowed seconds before he spurred his horse forward and went after the largest pig, lance held point down. "Grip the horse with your knees," he said when Alyx, openmouthed, held her breath as the pig began to charge them. The animal was so big compared to the horse's thin legs.

Suddenly, Raine dipped sideways, his body parallel to the ground. Since Alyx was holding onto him, she went down with him. Unbalanced, falling, she held onto Raine with all her might as he thrust his lance into the backbone of the furious animal. The hideous scream was the voice of death, and Alyx buried her face in Raine's broad back.

"Let me go!" he growled, shaking the pig off his lance, then prying Alyx's fingers from his chest. "You nearly toppled us. Now hold the saddle with all your strength." With that command he was off again, tearing through the forest, dodging tree branches overhead, trees to both sides, as he ran after another pig. Two more were brought down as cleanly as the first before he stopped and again had to pry Alyx's fingers from his stomach. She had no idea when she'd grabbed him and was glad he made no further comment on her cowardice.

When he was free of her grip, he dismounted, took several leather thongs from his saddle and, after a cautious approach to the animals, trussed their feet. "Get down," he said and waited patiently for her to obey.

Her legs, unaccustomed to the exercise, buckled under her and she clutched at the saddle to keep from falling.

Ignoring her, Raine slung the dead pigs over the back of his horse, then went immediately to the horse's head to calm him as he pranced, not liking the smell of blood so close to him.

"Lead the horse and follow me," he said to her, turning his back to her and walking ahead.

After one fearful look at the stallion, its ears back, eyes wild, sweaty from its run, Alyx gave a deep swallow of sheer terror and reached for the reins. The stallion danced away once and Alyx jumped, glancing quickly toward Raine where she could just see him through the trees.

"Come on, horse," she whispered, approaching the animal slowly but again it moved away from her.

Frustrated, she stood still, eyes locked with the horse's and softly, she began to hum, trying different notes, different tempos until she sensed the horse rather liked a very old, simple round. As the horse seemed to calm, she reached for the reins and her voice gained strength as she gained confidence.

Several minutes later, swaggering with pride at her accomplishment, she reached the small clearing where Raine waited impatiently with the third pig.

"It's a good thing I have guards posted," he said, flinging the trussed pig on the stallion's back, "otherwise with all your noise anyone within a mile could have heard you."

Absolute shock nearly flattened Alyx. Since she was ten years old all she'd ever heard was the most profuse praise for her music and now it was being referred to as "noise." Without another word from her she allowed Raine to pull her into the saddle in front of him and together they rode back to camp, her back slamming into his chest.

Once back in the camp, Raine dismounted, ignoring Alyx, still in the saddle, as he untied the pigs and slung them in the general direction of a campfire. As

Jocelin came forward, Raine tossed him the reins. "Show the boy how to clean a horse," he said before striding toward his tent.

After a reassuring smile for Alyx, Joss led the horse toward the clearing where the other horses were kept.

"Boy!" Alyx muttered as she dismounted, holding onto the saddle for support. "Boy, do this; boy, do that. That's all he ever says." When Joss had unfastened the saddle cinch, Alyx stood on tiptoe, grabbed the saddle and pulled and promptly fell backward, landing in a heap with the heavy saddle on top of her.

Obviously trying not to laugh, Jocelin removed the saddle while Alyx rubbed her bruised chin where it had struck her. "Is Raine making your life miserable?"

"He's trying to," she said as she took the saddle from him and, after three tries, managed to set it atop a wooden construction. "Oh, Joss," she gasped. "I'm so very tired. This morning he had me scour his armor, then I spent hours with that heavy sword. Now it's hunting and looking after that great beast."

At that comment the stallion rolled its eyes and began to prance. Without a thought, Alyx sang six notes and the animal calmed.

Jocelin had to control his look of amazement at her unconscious use of her voice before he could speak. "Raine has a lot of people to care for."

"A lot of people to play the lord with, you mean," she snapped, following Joss's lead in wiping down the horse.

"Perhaps. Perhaps a man like Raine is so used to taking responsibility he takes it without thinking."

"For me, I'd like fewer orders," she said. "Why

does he command everyone? Why does he believe he rules everyone? Why doesn't he just let the people rest?"

"Rest!" Joss said from the other side of the horse. "You should have seen this place a few weeks before he arrived. It was like the worst sections of London, people slitting one another's throats for a few pennies, stealing so much you had to stay up all night to guard your possessions. Displaced farmers were at the mercy of murderers and—"

"And so this righteous Raine Montgomery set everything to rights, correct?"

"Yes, he did."

"Did anyone ever consider he did it because he felt it was his God-given right over his underlings?"

"You're awfully young to be so bitter, aren't you?" Joss asked.

Alyx stopped brushing the horse. "Why are you here?" she asked him. "How do you fit into this group? You're not a murderer and you don't look like someone too lazy to work. The only thing I can imagine is that some jealous husband is after you," she teased.

Instantly, Jocelin tossed the brush down. "I have to go back to work," he said in a hard, flat voice and walked away from her.

For a full, stunned minute Alyx could not continue. Never in her life would she have insulted Jocelin. He was the only one she could talk to, sing with and—

"When you finish that you can fetch me some water from the stream," came a whiny voice from behind her, cutting off Alyx's thoughts.

Slowly, with deliberation, she turned toward Blanche. For all Alyx's words on Raine's arrogance,

Alyx also had a great deal of class pride. This woman with her slovenly dress, her coarse voice, her uneducated accents, was certainly not of the same class as Alyx. Ignoring her, Alyx turned back to the horse.

"Boy!" Blanche demanded. "Did you hear what I said?"

"I heard you," Alyx said, dropping her voice to a low tremor. "And I'm sure half the camp did, too."

"You think you're too good for me, don't you, you in your pretty clothes with your fine manners. Just because you've spent today with him doesn't mean you'll spend every day with him."

With a sneer, Alyx kept working on the horse. "Go about your business, woman. I have none with you."

Blanche grabbed Alyx's arm, pulled her about. "Until this morning I waited on Raine, brought his food to him and now he orders me to prepare a bed in his tent for you. What kind of boy are you?"

It took Alyx a moment to understand Blanche's insinuations and when she did, her eyes blazed purple fire. "If you knew anything about the nobility you'd know that all the lords have squires. I merely perform the duties of any good squire."

Blanche, obviously attempting to appear as part of the nobility, tried to stand erect. "Of course," she snapped. "I know about squires. But just you remember," she said threateningly, "Raine Montgomery is mine. I care for him as his lady would—in every way." With that, she turned on her heel and left through the trees.

"Lady!" Alyx muttered, going after the horse with a vengeance. "What would a slut like that know of being a lady?" Angry, she was unaware of time passing until she heard Raine's voice close to her.

"Boy," he said, making her jump. "You've got to be faster than that with a horse. There's plenty more work to be done."

"More?" she whispered and looked so sad that Raine smiled, eyes twinkling, and Alyx straightened. She'd give him no reason to laugh at her again.

After setting aside the brush, whispering one last tune to the stallion, Alyx followed Raine back to the camp, where he went directly to a group of disreputable-looking men huddled about a fire. Raine, with his proud stance, his noble bearing, made these men seem even filthier than they were.

"Here, you three," Raine said in a low growl. "You take the first watch."

"I ain't stayin' out in them woods," one man said as he turned to walk away.

Grabbing him with one hand, Raine pulled the man back and administered a swift kick to his backside that sent him sprawling. "If you eat, you work," he said in a deadly voice. "Now get to your posts. I will come later, and if any of you are asleep, it will be the man's last sleep."

With his features set in a grim line, Raine watched the men as they left the camp, sulking like little children. "Those are your fine friends," he said in an undertone to Alyx as he turned away.

"They are no friends of mine!" she snapped.

"Nor is Pagnell a friend of mine!" he retorted.

Halting, she stared after his broad back. It was true, she knew. She had no right to hate him because of what another man had done.

"Blanche!" Raine grunted. "Food!"

With that, Alyx went tearing after him because she was very hungry. Inside the tent, Blanche placed roast boar, bread, cheese and hot wine before them, and Alyx tore into the food with gusto.

"That's the way, boy!" Raine laughed, slapping her on the back, making her choke. "Keep eating like that and you'll put some size on yet."

"Keep working me like today and I'll die in a week!" she gasped, trying to dislodge a piece of pork from her throat, ignoring Raine's laughter.

The meal finished, Alyx looked with longing toward the pallet along one wall of the tent. To rest, she thought, just to lie down and be still for a few hours would be heaven on earth.

"Not yet, boy," Raine said, grabbing her arm and pulling her upright. "There's still work before we can sleep. The guards need to be checked, I have animal traps set and we both need a bath."

That startled her awake. "Bath!" she gasped. "No, not me."

"When I was your age I had to be forced to bathe, too. Once my older brother scoured me with a horse brush."

"Someone forced you to do something?" she asked, incredulous.

Raine's pride seemed to be at stake. "Actually, it took both my older brothers, and Gavin came away with a blacked eye. Now, come on. We have work to do."

Reluctantly, Alyx followed him, but no matter how hard she tried, she could put no energy in her steps. Like someone dead, she followed Raine through the forest, occasionally bumping into trees, stumbling over rocks, as he went around the perimeter of the camp making sure the guards were on duty and awake and removing rabbits and hares from his traps. At first he tried to talk to her, explain what he was doing, how to toss a rock and see if the guards responded, but after a while he studied her in the moonlight, noting her exhaustion, and stopped talking.

At the stream outside the camp he told her to sit still and wait for him while he bathed. Half asleep, reclining on the bank, her head propped on her arm, Alyx watched with languid interest as Raine removed his clothing and stepped into the icy water. Moonlight silvered his body, caressed the muscles, played along his thighs, made love to those magnificent arms. Lifting herself on her elbows, Alyx unabashedly watched him. All her life had been given to music. While other girls were flirting with the boys at the town well, Alyx was composing a Latin lamentation for four voices. When her friends were getting married, she was inside the church organizing a boys' chorus. She'd never had time to talk to boys, to get to know them—actually, had never been interested in them, had always been too busy to even notice them.

Now, for the first time in her life, watching this nude man bathing she felt the first stirrings of . . . of what? She certainly knew about mating, had even listened to some of the gossip from the recently married women, but she'd never felt any interest in the process. This man standing before her, rising out of the water like some heavenly centaur, made her feel things she'd never thought possible.

Lust, she thought, sitting up farther. Pure and simple lust was what she was feeling. She'd like for him to touch her, to kiss her, to lie beside her, and she would very much like to touch that skin of his. Remembering how it felt when she'd straddled his back, she began to tingle, her legs seeming more alive, even her feet growing warm.

When he left the water and came toward her, she almost lifted her arms toward him.

"You look lazy," Raine commented, drying himself off. "Sure you won't take a bath?"

All Alyx could do was watch the course of the cloth he used for drying as it ran over his body and vaguely shake her head.

"I warn you though, boy, you start smelling so bad you drive me from the tent and I'll bathe you myself and it won't be a gentle bath."

Eyes wide, Alyx looked up at him, her breathing changing just slightly. To be bathed by this great god of a man, she thought.

"Are you all right, boy?" Raine asked, concerned, kneeling beside her as he frowned at her odd expression.

Boy! she grimaced. He thought she was a boy, and what if she were revealed as a girl? He was of the nobility and she was only a poor lawyer's daughter. "Aren't you going to get cold?" she asked flatly, rolling away from him to stand apart, not watching as he dressed.

When he was finished, she silently followed him back to camp, where she collapsed on her pallet but did not sleep until Raine had settled himself on his narrow cot. Content at last, she fell asleep.

Chapter Six

*L*EANING OVER THE edge of the water, Alyx studied her own reflection. She did look like a boy, she thought with disgust. Why couldn't she have been born beautiful, with lovely features that could never be mistaken for a male's no matter what she wore? Her hair, all a mass of curls, its color not sure of which way to go, changing with each strand, eyes turned up, lips like a pixie's, were not what a woman's should be.

Just as tears were beginning to blur her vision, Jocelin's voice startled her. "Cleaning more armor?" he asked.

With a sniff, she turned back to her task. "Raine is too hard on it. Today I had to hammer out a dent."

"You seem to care much for his things. Are you perhaps beginning to believe that a nobleman could be worth something?"

"Raine would be worth much no matter what his

birth," she said much too hastily, then looked away, embarrassed.

She'd been in Raine's camp for a week now, had spent nearly every second in his company and her opinions of him had completely reversed in that week. Once she'd believed he took over the camp, but now she knew it was that the outcasts forced him to take care of them. They were like children demanding that he provide for them, then acting rebellious when he did. He left his bed before anyone else and saw to the security of the people and always, late at night, he made sure the guard was alert and ready. He forced the people away from idleness and made them work for their own keep or else they'd sit and wait for him to provide for them, as if it were their due.

"Yes," she said quietly. "Raine is worth something, although he gets little reward for what he does. Why doesn't he leave this scurvy lot and leave England altogether? Surely a man with his wealth could make a decent home for himself."

"Perhaps you should ask him that. You are closest to him."

Close to him, she thought. That's where she wanted to be, even closer to him. Only now was she beginning to be able to function through her blinding fatigue, to live through the strenuous training sessions each morning, but as her muscles hardened and she began to feel better, she became more involved in the camp life.

Blanche occupied an exalted position in the camp, making everyone believe she shared Raine's bed and had his ear for anything they wanted. Alyx tried not to consider if Blanche ever had spent the night with Raine, but she liked to believe he had more taste than to use a slut like Blanche. And something else Alyx was able to find out about Blanche: she was terrified of Jocelin.

Jocelin, so incredibly handsome, so polite, so considerate, had every woman in camp panting after him. Alyx had seen women use every manner of enticement to lure him to their sides, but as far as she knew, Joss had never accepted an invitation. He preferred his duties and the company of Alyx to anyone else. And although he never mentioned her, he stayed well away from Blanche. When the woman happened to meet him she'd always turn tail and run.

Besides Joss, the only other decent outcast was Rosamund, with her beauty and the devil's mark on her cheek. Rosamund kept her head down, expecting people's hatred and fear. Once Raine had found a couple of men wagering on whether or not they'd be selling their souls if they took her by force. Twenty lashes each was his punishment for the men, followed by banishment, and Alyx felt a surge of jealousy that Raine so violently protected the flawed, beautiful healer.

"Alyx!" came a bellow through the trees that could only belong to Raine. At least now he called her by her name.

Using every ounce of power her voice contained, she yelled back at him, "I am working." The man was obsessed with work.

Coming through the trees, he grinned at her. "That voice of yours gives me hope that you'll grow, although it looks to me as if you're getting smaller." Critically, he eyed her legs stretched before her.

With a little smile, Alyx was glad to see that at least one part of her was unmistakably female. Her long legs and curvy little bottom had only been enhanced by the hard exercise of the last week. Perhaps now, at last, she would be revealed as a girl and then . . . what? She'd be tossed from Raine's tent and he'd once again only have that whore Blanche to care for him. Reluctantly, she slapped a steel leg sheath over her own legs.

"I'll grow," she snapped, "and when I do I'll pin you to the ground with your own sword." An upward glance at Raine saw that he seemed to be puzzled by something.

"You wanted Alyx for something?" Joss asked, his voice full of amusement as he interrupted the silence.

"Yes," Raine said quietly. "I need some letters written and some read to me. A messenger has come from my family. You can read, can't you?"

Curiosity made Alyx jump. She very much wanted to know about Raine's family. "Yes, of course," she said, gathering the armor and following Raine.

A man, dressed finely, his doublet embroidered with gold leopards, sat outside the tent, waiting patiently for Raine's command. With the wave of one hand, the young man was dismissed and Alyx wondered if all Raine's men obeyed so well and what a far cry from the outcasts they were.

There were two letters for Raine, one from his brother Gavin and one from his brother's wife, Judith.

The news from Gavin was bad. Bronwyn, Raine's other sister-in-law, had been taken prisoner by the same man who held Raine's sister, Mary. Bronwyn's husband was waiting, sitting and waiting, afraid to make a move for fear Roger Chatworth would kill his wife.

"Your brother Stephen," Alyx asked tentatively, "he loves his wife?"

Raine only nodded, his lips drawn into a tight line, his eyes focused on nothing.

"But it says here that she was in Scotland when she was taken. Why was she in Scotland? The Scots are coarse, vicious people and—"

"Hold your tongue!" he commanded. "Bronwyn is the laird of a clan in Scotland and there is no finer woman. Read me the other letter."

Chastised, Alyx opened the letter from Judith Montgomery, fully aware of the way Raine's eyes softened as she began to read. The letter was full of prayers for Raine's safety and entreaties for him to leave England until it was safe for him to return. She asked after his comfort, whether he had food and warm clothing, which made Raine chuckle and Alyx bristle at her wifely tones.

"Does her husband know she concerns herself so for her brother-in-law?" she asked primly.

"I'll not have you speak of my family so," he reprimanded and Alyx hung her head, embarrassed at her jealousy. It wasn't fair that she had to pose as a boy and never have a chance of gaining his attention. If she could wear a pretty dress perhaps he'd notice her, but then again she certainly was no beauty.

"Take your head from the clouds, boy, and listen to me."

His voice brought her to the present.

"Can you write what I say? I want to send letters back with my brother's man."

When she had pen, ink and paper, Raine began to dictate. The letter she was to write to his brother was one of anger and determination. He swore to stay as near as possible to his two sisters and he would wait as long as he could before bringing his fist to Chatworth's head. As for the King, he had no fear, since Henry's main source of income was from men he declared to be traitors. He told Gavin that Henry would pardon him as soon as he agreed to forfeit a goodly portion of his land.

Raine ignored Alyx's startled gasps at the insolent way in which he referred to their sovereign.

The letter to Judith was as warm and loving as hers had been, even once referring to his new squire, who thought he had no sense, not even enough to keep warm, and often covered him at night. With her head lowered, Alyx wrote, not allowing Raine to see her flushed cheeks. She'd had no idea he was aware of the many times she'd tiptoed about the tent, pulling the fur-lined coverlet about his bare shoulders.

The rest of the letter Alyx merely wrote, too embarrassed to even read what she wrote, and when she finished them she held them open, ready for Raine's signature. As he bent toward her, his face close to hers, she inhaled the smell of his hair, that thick, dark, curling mass and wanted to bury her face in it. Instead, she reached out and touched a lock of it, watched it curl about her fingertip.

Raine's head came up as if he'd been burned, his face inches from hers, his eyes wide as he looked at her. Alyx knew her breath had stopped and her heart had leaped to her throat. Now he'll know, she thought. Now he'll say that I am a girl, a woman.

Frowning, Raine stepped away from her, looking at her as if he couldn't quite decide what was happening. "Seal the letters," he said quietly, "and give them to the messenger." With that he left the tent.

Alyx gave a sigh that made one of the letters flutter to the floor and quick tears came to her eyes. Ugly, she thought. That's what I am—very, very ugly. No wonder no man ever even tried to contradict the priest and take me for his wife. Why fight for a prize not worth winning? Who wanted a flat-chested, boyish girl with a noisy voice for a wife? And no wonder Raine didn't see through her disguise.

With a sharp backhand swipe, she wiped her eyes and returned to the letters before her. No doubt his sisters-in-law and his sister were beautiful, beautiful women with chests . . .

With another sigh she finished the letters, sealed them and took them outside to the messenger, walking with him to his horse.

"Have you seen this Lady Judith or the Lady Bronwyn?" she asked the messenger.

"Aye, many times."

"And are they, perhaps, handsome women?"

"Handsome?" he laughed, mounting his horse. "God must have been happy the day he created those women. Lord Raine will not leave England nor would I if I had either of those women in my family. Go on, boy, try and find someone to console him," he said, motioning toward the tent. "The loss of such beauty even for a moment must make him a miserable man."

Console him! Alyx muttered as she went back to the tent, only to be greeted by some commotion, Raine standing at the heart of it.

"It is well for your life that you did not kill her," he was saying to two men, one a pickpocket, the other a beggar. Both had been on guard duty all morning. "Alyx," he said over their heads. "Saddle my horse. We ride."

Taking off at a run, Alyx had the big horse saddled and ready by the time Raine reemerged from the tent, a battle ax and a mace in his hand. He had mounted and pulled her up behind him before she could ask a question, and in seconds they were galloping through the forest at a breakneck speed.

After a good run, as fast as the trees permitted, Raine drew to a halt and jumped from his horse. Catching the reins, Alyx slid forward into the saddle and got her first glimpse of what was going on. A pretty woman with big brown eyes, wearing a beautiful dress such as Alyx had never seen before, was flattened against a tree, looking with terror at three men from the camp as they brandished knives and swords at her.

"Get out of here, you scum," Raine growled, tossing first one man, then the other aside.

The woman, shaking in fear, looked up at Raine in total disbelief. "Raine," she whispered before closing her eyes and starting to slide down the tree.

Raine caught her in his arms, lifted her, cradling her to him. "Anne," he whispered. "You are safe now. Alyx, fetch some wine. There's a pouch on my saddle."

Somewhat in awe of the scene before her, Alyx dismounted and took the hard leather container to him as he sat down on a fallen tree, holding this woman close to him.

"Anne, drink this," he said in a sweet, gentle voice, and the woman fluttered her lashes and began to drink. "Now, Anne," he said when she was fully awake. "Tell me what you were doing this deep in the forest."

The woman certainly didn't seem to be in any hurry

to remove herself from Raine's lap, Alyx thought, as she looked with absolute wonder at the woman's dress. It was of deep, deep red silk, a fabric she'd only seen in church, and it was embroidered all over with tiny hares, rabbits, deer, fish, all sorts of animals. The square neckline was very low, exposing a great deal of the woman's ample breasts, and about the neckline and waist were trims of gold and red, sparkling jewels.

"Alyx!" Raine said impatiently, handing her the bag of wine. "Anne," he said with great tenderness, holding the full-grown woman as if she were a child.

"What are you doing here, Raine?" she asked in a soft voice.

Can't sing, Alyx immediately thought. No strength in her voice and just a hint of a whine.

"King Henry has declared me traitor," Raine said, one dimple flashing.

Anne smiled at him. "After your money, is he? But what have you done to give him reason to take your lands?"

"Roger Chatworth has taken my sister Mary and Stephen's new wife."

"Chatworth!" she exclaimed. "Didn't that woman Gavin was so in love with marry a Chatworth?"

"My discreet brother," Raine said in disgust. "The woman is a whore and one of the worst sort, but Gavin could never see it. If nothing else, my brother is loyal. Even after he married Judith he still loved Alice Chatworth for a while."

"But what has this to do with why you are here?"

Why doesn't she stand on her own feet, Alyx thought. Why does she so calmly sit on his lap and talk as elegantly as if she were in some nobleman's hall?

"It's a long story," Raine said. "Through an accident, Alice Chatworth was badly scarred, and what little there was of her mind went with her beauty. Her brother-in-law cared for her since she was a widow, and perhaps the woman poisoned his mind, because later Roger challenged my brother to a fight, the winner to get the wife King Henry promised Stephen."

"Yes," Anne said. "I remember now. There was a great deal of property involved."

"Stephen's Bronwyn is a wealthy woman, yes, but Stephen wanted the woman as much as the land," he smiled. "But Chatworth could not stand losing and he has taken prisoner my sisters."

"Raine, how dreadful. But how did King Henry—"

"I was taking some of the king's men to Wales when I heard of Mary's being taken and I turned and went after Chatworth."

"Leading the King's army?" she asked, and when he nodded, she grimaced. "So Henry has some reason to declare you a traitor. Is that why you are dressed like a farmer and roaming about these dreary woods?"

"Aye," he said, looking at her. "You look well, Anne. It's been a long time since—"

With that she jumped off his lap, standing before him, smoothing her dress, a gown Alyx longed to touch. "You'll not seduce me again, Raine Montgomery. My father has promised to find me a husband soon and I'd like to go to him as pure as possible so I'll stand for no more of your lovely words." Turning, she looked at Alyx for the first time. "And who is this lad who stares at us with his mouth agape?"

Immediately, Alyx closed her mouth and looked away from the both of them.

"This is my squire," Raine said, his voice full of laughter from Anne's words. "I may have to live in this forest, but I do have some amenities. He works hard and can read and write."

"I take it no one was able to drive that knowledge into your thick skull," she snapped. "Raine! Stop looking at me like that. You'll get nowhere with me. Now you, boy, do you have a name?"

"Alexander Blackett."

"Blackett?" she said. "Where have I heard that name before?"

From the issue for my arrest, Alyx thought in a panic. Why hadn't she changed her last name? Now this odious woman would reveal her disguise to Raine.

"It's a common enough name," Raine said in dismissal. "Alyx, go back to the camp and wait for me."

"No, boy!" Anne said. "Raine, I'm serious. I'll not be used by you again, and I will not stay alone with you. You must lead me back to the other hunters. When they see that I am lost they'll try to find me."

"I have guards," he said, catching her about the waist, pulling her between his thighs. "We'll have all the time we need alone. Alyx, leave us."

"I want that pretty little squire of yours to stay," Anne said, her hands on his shoulders, pushing him away. "You've been so long in this woods perhaps you've come to prefer pretty boys over—"

She never finished her sentence as Raine drew her close to him, pulling her mouth down to his.

Unabashedly, Alyx watched them. Never had she seen anyone kiss someone like this, with bodies together, heads moving. More than anything in the world, Alyx wished it were she Raine was holding in his arms.

So engrossed was she in the scene before her that when the first arrow came sailing through the air, landing inches from Raine's leg, she stood still, not sure what was happening. Raine reacted instantly, in one motion flinging both Alyx and Anne to the forest floor.

"They are after me," Raine said calmly. "Alyx, you are small enough to move along the tree." He pointed with his head. "Try to make it to my horse and fetch the weapons."

"What about you?" she gasped as another arrow landed just above their heads.

"I must take Anne to safety. Obey me!" he commanded.

Without another thought, Alyx began crawling forward on her stomach, inching her way into the dense covering of the forest. Every time an arrow struck behind her, her body tightened in fear. Afraid to turn around, scared she'd see Raine lying dead, she struggled ahead. When she reached the end of the fallen tree she lifted to a crouching position and began to run. When the arrows sounded in the distance, she was able to halt and get her bearings.

The horse, that great angry stallion of Raine's, was prancing wildly from where it was tied, a man near it, trying to catch the reins. If they caught the horse, there would be no way of fighting, for most of the weapons were tied to the saddle. Damn Raine, she thought. He was so hot for the silk-clad woman he forgot everything.

After a moment's silent prayer, Alyx opened her mouth and let go of a bit of music she knew the horse liked. Instantly, it calmed, ears perked, and at that moment the man grabbed the reins, untied them and had the horse under control.

"The horse is as stupid as its master," she said under her breath before beginning another series of notes, high, sharp and discordant, something the horse hated. She was rewarded with the animal's bucking, loosing itself from its captors. When it galloped toward her, Alyx held her breath, afraid of the great animal for a moment before she once again began to sing and the horse calmed, allowing her to catch it and mount.

"Now, please do what I say," she whispered when it turned its great head toward her, its nostrils flaring, eyes wide, trained to help one heavy man in war and not liking this featherweight person in the saddle. "Go!" she commanded in the voice she used to control twenty-five active choirboys.

The horse took off in the wrong direction and Alyx used all her strength to pull back on the reins and guide the animal back where she came from.

"No, Raine! No!"

Alyx heard the woman Anne screaming as soon as she had the great beast under control, and when she broke through the trees, there stood Raine, sword drawn and bloodied over a dead man, facing two other men also with swords, Anne clinging behind the broad expanse of Raine.

"They are my father's men," she screamed. "They've come to find me. I told you they would." With that Anne left Raine to go to the man on the ground. "He's not dead. We can take him back with us," she said, tossing an angry look at Raine. "Why do you never listen to anyone?" she snapped. "Why do you draw sword and talk later?"

Alyx, feeling a great surge of anger tear through her, jumped down from the horse. It was obvious from his tight-lipped face that Raine was not going to defend himself. "My lord was attacked first!" she said, spitting rage at them. "When an arrow flies at him is he to stand and ask who sends the arrow before drawing sword? You, my fine lady, were well content when he protected your precious, plump body with his own, but now that it costs you the care of a man you do not remember how you tried to entice my master into the bushes."

"Alyx," Raine said from behind her, his hand on her shoulder. "Remember, it is not chivalrous to—"

"Chivalrous!" she yelled, whirling to face him. "The bitch—"

Raine clamped his hand over her mouth, drew her to him, her back pinned against his chest while she struggled to free herself. "Anne," he said quietly, ignoring Alyx, "forgive me and the boy as well. He has had little training. Take your men and go back to the stream. I will send someone to guide you out of the forest."

"Raine," she said, rising from the inert man. "I didn't mean . . ."

"Go now, Anne, and if you see any of my family, tell them I am well."

At that she nodded, a man helped her mount a horse behind him, the wounded man was thrown across the saddle and they left.

When they were out of sight, Raine released Alyx.

"They tried to kill you!" she gasped, glaring at him. "And that woman railed at you for hurting her man."

Raine shrugged. "Who can understand women? She's always been concerned with money and estates."

"And I take it you know her well," Alyx said, rubbing her jaw, aware of the touch of Raine's hand on her mouth.

"Her father once proposed that I marry her."

That made Alyx halt. "And you decided not to, or did she turn you down?"

He grinned crookedly, making one dimple show. "She accepted me in every way I asked but I did not ask her to marry me. She wavers from one moment to the next. She cannot even decide which dress to wear each day. I'm sure she would not like being a faithful wife, and I dislike beating women."

"You dislike . . ." Alyx sputtered.

"Now," he said, moving forward from the tree he'd been leaning against, "if we are through with your education about women for today, I'd like to do something about this leg of mine."

At that she glanced downward and for the first time saw the dark stain of blood soaking Raine's hose.

Chapter Seven

"YOU ARE WOUNDED," she said in a voice that sounded as if she meant he were dead.

"I don't think it's bad, but perhaps we should see to it."

Running to him, her arm about his waist, she leaned into him. "Sit down. I will fetch Rosamund and—"

"Alyx," he said, amused. "It isn't a mortal wound, and I can well ride back to camp. You know, you are the worst squire I have ever had."

"Worst!" she gasped as he sat down heavily on a tree stump. "You are an ungrateful—"

"What took you so long with the horse? I was fighting for my life and I could hear you in the woods singing. Were you hoping to entertain the enemy?"

Never, never was she going to speak to him again, she decided, as she turned her back on him and went for the horse. Hearing him chuckle behind her only made her lift her chin higher.

Even when he struggled to rise, she refused to help him and turned away so she could not see him.

"Alyx, I must mount on the opposite side and the horse will not like it. You must hold him steady. I don't wish to jar this leg more than I must."

At that she took the horse's head in her hands, looked it in the eye and began to sing, controlling it with her voice. Raine seemed to sit on the horse's back for some time before he spoke to her and offered her his hand to help her mount.

All the way back to camp, she held onto the saddle and watched Raine's blood seep down his thigh. The horse, smelling blood, began to prance, and, as a reflex, Raine clutched with his knees to control the animal. Alyx felt him stiffen at the pain that caused.

"Perhaps you could calm him with your songs," he said quietly.

"With my noise, don't you mean?" she answered, still hurt by his words.

"As you wish," he said stiffly.

Alyx had never heard this tone before, but she recognized it as a voice covering pain. He said his wound wasn't bad, but it showed no sign of ceasing to bleed. Now was no time to be angry. She began to sing and the horse calmed.

"I will have to show you to my brothers," he murmured. "They won't believe this unless they see it."

As they approached the camp, several people, sensing something was wrong, came out to greet them.

"It would be better if they did not see that I was

wounded," Raine said to her. "They're hard enough to control and I need no new problems now."

Quickly, she slipped off the horse and went to stand at Raine's side, her body blocking the people's view of his leg.

"We heard there was a fight," a black-toothed man said, his eyes greedy.

"Only in your mind, old man," Alyx yelled, startling everyone with the power of her voice. Visibly, the crowd jumped, and so did Raine's horse. "Stand back," she ordered. "The animal's gone wild. We had to take a whip to him to control him."

While the people were looking with fear at the great horse, its eyes rolling, smelling Raine's blood, Raine swung a mace from the saddle. "Have you no work to do?" he growled. "Joss, come to my tent. I have work for you."

Grumbling, the people began to go back to their fires and hovels.

When the horse was in front of the tent, they stopped and Alyx braced herself to help Raine dismount.

"For God's sake don't help me," he said through clenched teeth. "They will see you. Go and hold the horse's head. Sing good and loud and draw attention to yourself."

Alyx did as she was bid and did indeed draw much attention to herself, so much that she was nearly half an hour getting away from the people who wanted her to sing song after song. At last, feeling she'd covered Raine's awkward dismounting, she went into his tent.

He was propped on his cot, wearing his shirt and loincloth, Rosamund kneeling by his thigh, a basin of bloody water by her knees.

"There you are!" Raine growled. "Can't you do more than display that voice of yours? Heaven help us if you should go to war. Your enemy would ask you to sing and you would drop all weapons in order to perform like some mummer. Go now, Rosamund, and see to the man I hurt. Jocelin, show her the way. And you, my worthless songbird, see if you can bind this leg or mayhaps sing the wound closed."

Alyx opened her mouth to speak, but Joss put his hand on her shoulder, his back to Raine. "He is in pain, remember that," he whispered before leaving the tent.

One look at Raine's pale face made her realize the truth of Jocelin's statement.

"Do not stare at me! Make yourself useful," Raine spat at her.

She wasn't going to stand for this treatment. His anger and hostility could only hurt him. "Be quiet, Raine Montgomery!" she ordered. "I'll not take more of your insults. Lie still and I will tend to your wound, but there is nothing you can do to change the fact that you have been wounded. Growling at me will only make you feel worse."

He started to rise, but one look from Alyx made him lie back. "They'll kill each other," he said hopelessly, meaning the outlaws outside his tent.

"It doesn't matter if they do," she said callously, moving to the far side of the cot and Raine's wounded leg. "There aren't five of them worth their space on earth."

Kneeling, she went down beside Raine's thigh and lifted the cloth Rosamund had placed there. It was her first sight of such a wound, the skin cut, angrily inflamed from the puncture wound, blood still seeping out, and her stomach tightened.

"Are you planning to lose your dinner?" Raine taunted as he saw her pale. "I've had much worse wounds, only this one seems to be so deep."

His legs, with the heavy, muscular thighs stretched in front of her, had several thick ridges of scars. Tentatively, she touched one.

"An ax blade," he murmured, lying back, at last the loss of blood beginning to drain his strength.

As gently as she could, she cleaned the wound, frowned when she saw how dirty it was, as if the arrow had been filthy and had cleaned itself in Raine's flesh. When she was finished, she drew a stool near his bed and watched him, his eyes closed, his breathing shallow but even, and she hoped he was sleeping.

After a very long time, he spoke, his eyes staying closed. "Alyx," he whispered, and immediately she knelt by him. "Under the cot is a case. Would you get it?"

Instantly, she pulled the leather case out, smiled when she recognized it as containing a lute.

"Can you play it?" he asked.

Smiling confidently, she opened the case and withdrew the lute, her fingers already dancing in her anxiety to touch the strings. Softly she began to play and sing one of her own compositions.

It was hours later when she felt sure Raine was asleep, lying still and pale on the cot, and she put the lute aside. In the silence, with only his ragged breathing in the tent, she wished Rosamund would return. Raine seemed worse than he had been and she needed someone to tell her he was going to recover.

A glance about the tent showed her they needed water, and the side of her doublet was soaked with Raine's blood and needed to be washed. In the morning there would be questions from the outcasts as to where the blood came from.

Silently, buckets in both hands, she left the tent and headed for the river, avoiding all contact with the camp people. With a sigh of relief she saw Blanche engaged in a game of dice with several men and knew the woman would not leave to see to Raine.

It was almost dark by the time she reached the water, filled the buckets and began to wash the doublet. To her chagrin, her shirt was also soaked. After a moment's hesitation, she removed it and the binding on her breasts and began to wash everything, including her own dirty skin and hair. Nearly freezing, she dried herself with the binding cloth and gritted her teeth as she slipped into the very cold, very wet shirt and hose, tossing the doublet over her arm, grabbing the buckets and nearly running back to camp.

Inside the tent, she held her breath, listening, glad Raine was still sleeping. When she'd rid herself of the buckets, she quickly discarded her wet clothes and pulled on one of Raine's shirts, which covered her to her knees. She knew she was taking a chance, but, truthfully, she wasn't sure if she didn't hope he woke and found out she was a girl.

She'd no more put the shirt on than a groan from Raine made her turn.

"Mary," he said. "Mary, I'll find you."

With one leap she was beside him. He must stay quiet and not let the people in the camp know he was unwell. The idiots had some idea that Raine secreted jewels and gold inside his tent, and Alyx had no doubt they would love the opportunity to search.

"Mary," Raine called louder, one big arm waving, just missing Alyx's head.

"Raine, wake up," she whispered loudly. "You are having a bad dream." As she caught his arm and touched his skin, she realized immediately that he was feverish. His skin was hot to her touch.

"No," she gasped and cursed Rosamund for leaving the camp when Raine needed her. A fever! What could she do? Feeling totally useless, she dipped a cloth in one of the buckets of water and went to place it on his forehead, but one of Raine's arms hit her and sent the cloth flying. At the rate he was flailing his arms, he'd hit a tent pole and the whole canvas would come crashing down on their heads.

"Raine," she said fiercely, commandingly. "You must be still." She grabbed both his hands in hers and found herself lifted from the floor, pulled half across him.

"I must find Mary," he said, much louder, slurring his words, and as he moved, so did Alyx.

"You overgrown ox," she hissed. "Keep still!"

That seemed to register with him, for he opened his eyes and she could see the feverish glint even in the dark tent.

For just a moment he looked at her, unseeing, and then his eyes seemed to focus and he put one hand on the back of her head and pulled her mouth down to his.

Protest, even if Alyx had thought of such a thing, was not possible. The moment her lips touched Raine's all was lost. She was a woman of great passion, great feeling and, always, she'd spent that passion on music. At the first touch of Raine, music exploded throughout every pore of her body, angels singing, devils humming, choruses reaching new notes, happy songs, sad songs.

He turned her head as he nuzzled her lips apart, seeking the inner sweetness of her mouth, his tongue touching the tip of hers. It didn't take Alyx but a moment to learn how to kiss him back. One foot on the floor, the other waving about, in heaven, her body half across his, she put her arms around his head and pulled him closer to her, her tongue plunging deeper and deeper into his mouth. This was what she'd wanted ever since she'd first seen him, not to be treated as a boy but as the woman she was.

Raine reacted enthusiastically to her aggressiveness, his lips sucking at hers, biting them, pulling them between his teeth, running his tongue over the sweet swell of them.

When his hand slipped downward and touched the top of her calf, she drew her breath in sharply and began to kiss his cheek, her lips trailing down to his neck, that powerful, strong neck she'd looked at so many times, had watched with interest as sweat trickled down it.

His skin, so hot, broiling, left seared places on her legs as he moved to his side and began to run both hands up the sides of her legs, his fingers digging into the firm muscles at the backs of her thighs. When he reached her buttocks and cupped them, he gave a little chuckle of satisfaction. "Sweet wench," he murmured, moving his head so he again captured her lips, and the kiss strengthened as his fiery hands stroked her legs, kneading the flesh, exploring the curves and contours of her body.

But Alyx was not content to be a passive participant and her hands also began to explore him, pulling up his shirt, touching his feverish skin with her ardent, inquisitive hands. The hair on his chest, great curling piles of it, was as soft as she had imagined, and the muscles on his chest, undulating, curving, were exciting beyond her wildest imagination.

"Raine," she murmured, her lips following her hands, detesting the linen shirt. His hands stilled as he gave all his attention to what she was doing with her mouth. When the shirt would allow her to go no lower, she moved so that she could start at the bottom and work up.

Her lips touched the line of hair as it disappeared into his loincloth and Raine's breath quickened, his hands still as they clutched her firm, hard thighs. As her lips moved upward, so did her hands, taking the shirt with her until she reached his neck and, miraculously, the confining piece of cloth slipped off his body, exposing all of that sun-bronzed, hot skin to Alyx's view, and touch.

Raine, slow to move, slower to realize what was happening to him, that this nymphet from heaven was making love to him, easily, with a practiced gesture, divested the vision of her shirt, and in the same motion put an arm around the specter's tiny waist and pulled her to lie beside him.

It was Alyx's turn to gasp as her nude body touched Raine's flaming skin and his hot hands began exploring her body, stopping at her waist, loosely encircled by the gold Lyon belt. He seemed to think it was natural that she wore no clothes but this golden belt of her ancestors. As his hand moved upward toward her free breasts, she held her breath, afraid he'd reject her as too small for his taste, but as his hand encircled her and his lips nuzzled her neck, she forgot any imagined deformities. And when Raine's mouth burned a path down to her breast and touched the rosy tip with his tongue, she gasped and arched against him, her hips ungracefully banging against his.

A low, deep sensuous chuckle welled out of Raine's throat as his teeth nipped too hard on her nipple, causing her to squeal and move away from him. Raine quickly slipped a hand under her waist and easily pulled her back to him and all in one gesture caught her earlobe in his teeth. "You are mine, my sweet woodland fairy," he said between his teeth, and his breath, as hot as his skin, seemed to enter her ear and travel directly to the pit of her belly.

"No," she giggled in a tone that no one could mistake for a negative answer, her hands on his stomach, pushing against him. He let her move a few inches from him, but his hand pulled her back, treating her as if she were a child's toy on a string.

Caught up in the game, not liking his toying with her, Alyx brought her knees up to her chest and pushed out at him. She was pleased to see that at least it took two arms to hold her against the strength of her legs.

Seeming to enjoy her curled position, he held her and ran his hands down the back side of her, caressing her back and legs, curving around her buttocks, stroking and stroking, leaving a trail of heat until Alyx knew her body was as hot as his, and suddenly he turned serious again as his lips found hers and crushed her to him, hard, hard, his passion rising, a tangible thing, something she sensed in the air about them as well as felt through the crushing of his body on hers.

Impatiently, he pushed her legs down so they lay on their sides, facing each other and his hands were no longer gentle but demanding, pulling her slight body in to his larger one, seeming to attempt to fuse their skins.

Blinded, music, magnificent music, roaring in her head, Alyx tried to get closer to him, throwing one leg over his, wrapping it about his thighs, hooking her foot behind his knee.

Raine's hand descended down her back, slowly, feeling every nook and crevice until he reached the center of her being. Gasping, eyes wide, Alyx pulled back from him, saw his eyes were closed as he concentrated on feeling. When his finger entered her, she began to tremble, scared of this new experience, frightened of what was happening to her, of what her mind and body were feeling.

His hand moved, stroking her inner thighs, touching her ever so lightly, making her part her legs more and more widely, as she wrapped them about his hips, holding him so tightly she threatened to crush him.

When his hand left her she whimpered, but his mouth captured hers as he attempted to swallow her and Alyx, nearly in tears, pushed her body closer and closer to his. His loincloth disappeared and as his maleness touched her womanliness, she fairly jumped atop him. He held her back, entering her slowly, slowly, slowly, inch by inch by inch.

He held still, filling her, resting, allowing the sensations to flow from one body to the other until Alyx, eager, inexperienced, began to move, jerkily, ineptly.

Raine's hands cupped her buttocks and guided her, moving her in a fluid, slow motion, rhythmically, easily and with each stroke, pushing her higher and higher in her pain-pleasure.

When she began to move faster, he accommodated her, thrusting harder and faster, deeper and deeper until Alyx began to claw his back, bite at his neck, her whole body beginning to twist and turn, seeming to fight him and at the same time beg something of him.

With one twist, Raine slammed her on her back and lowered his magnificent, delicious, glorious weight on top of her, pressing her into the cot so hard she threatened to fall through and she clutched at him with her legs, locking her ankles, pushing her hips up to him as he came down for two penetrating, blindingly hard thrusts—and Alyx died.

White hot, intoxicating music exploded throughout her, blasted apart her skin, separating all the pieces of her as her body trembled and quaked, shivered until her strength turned to jelly.

Sticky, horribly weak, unsure of what her body had just done and she had done to it, she clung to Raine, letting herself feel all of his hot skin, his breath, uneven, in her ear. Moving one arm, and feeling as if she'd just rolled down a steep hill covered with stones, Alyx touched the damp hair along his neck. In a quick, fierce movement, Raine grabbed her hand as he rolled to his side, pulling her with him and clutched her hand in his, so tight he threatened to break her fingers.

"Mine," he whispered, bringing her hand to his mouth and kissing two fingers before sleep overtook him.

For several minutes Alyx dozed, half in sleep, half

out. Her body was exhausted, yet somehow she was more alive than she'd ever been. She felt no shame for mating with a man who was not her husband, and perhaps she should, but at this moment there was nothing in life she needed other than this dear man's leg across her, this wet stickiness holding more than their bodies together.

"I love you," she whispered to the man sleeping in her arms. "I know you can never be mine, but for this moment you are. I love you," she said again as she kissed one damp curl and fell asleep again, more happy than she'd ever been in her life.

Chapter Eight

$\mathcal{A}$LYX AWOKE TO a tent bright with early morning light, and Raine's skin touching hers was hotter than the night before. Asleep, he moved restlessly, rolling about, ignoring Alyx's presence as he rolled across her, threatening to break her bones. Pushing with all her might, she managed to get him off her and quickly began to don her clothes, which were wet in places, dry in others since they'd lain crumpled in a heap all night. She dearly wished she could put on a dress and give up the pretense of being a boy. Men's clothes and men's ways gave one a great deal of freedom, but if she were a boy she'd have missed a night such as she had had last night.

She had barely fastened her doublet when the tent flap opened and Jocelin, Rosamund behind him, entered.

"How is he?" Joss asked, watching Alyx intently.

Before she could answer, Rosamund interrupted them. "He has a fever and we must bring it down. Fetch some cold water while I get my herbs."

Immediately, Alyx grabbed the buckets and went to the river.

The next three days were torture for Alyx. She and Rosamund worked continuously to bring Raine's fever down. His big body was plastered with poultices and the women had to force noxious concoctions down his throat. This forcing was always accompanied by terrible commands from Alyx in which she called Raine everything from a worthless beggar to an overgrown strutting peacock, making Rosamund giggle and, at times, blush. Alyx sang to him constantly, played the lute often, anything to soothe him, to keep him from thrashing about so.

And while Raine was raging with fever, Jocelin tried to keep command of the outlaw camp, enforcing the daily training Raine had begun, trying to keep the cutthroats from murdering each other.

"I don't believe they're worth it," Joss said, sitting on the floor at the foot of Raine's cot. "Why does he," motioning to the sleeping man to his left, "feel he has to take on their problems?" He accepted a bowl of stew from Rosamund.

"Raine adopts everyone," Rosamund said quietly, her head lowered, as it always was. "He truly believes we are worth saving."

"We?" Alyx questioned as she looked up from Raine. She never left his side, slept sitting on a stool, her head propped on the edge of his cot. "I do not consider myself the same as a murderer."

"And you, Rose?" Jocelin asked. "What crime have you committed?"

Rosamund did not answer, but when Joss turned his head she looked up at him in such a way that Alyx gasped aloud, quickly covering the sound with a little cough. Rosamund was in love with Jocelin. As Alyx looked from one to the other, each with their extraordinary beauty, she saw how suited they were for each other. She knew why Rosamund was in this horrid camp, because people believed she was marked with the devil, but why was Joss here?

Early the next morning, Raine's fever broke. Alyx was sleeping, her head next to his bare arm when she sensed he was different. Looking up at him, she saw his eyes were open, looking about the tent and finally resting on her face.

Immediately, Alyx's heart began to pound and her betraying skin began to blush. How would he react to their having made love?

After a moment he turned away from her, his eyes telling her nothing. "How long have I been ill?"

"Three days," she answered, her voice catching in her throat.

"And you have held order in the camp? Or have they murdered each other?"

"They . . . they are well. Jocelin has held a sword over their heads and has kept the peace." When he didn't reply, she drew in her breath. Now he would speak of them, their passion.

Instead, he struggled to sit up, and when Alyx started to help him, he pushed her away as if she were of no consequence. Tossing the wool blanket aside, he tore the bandages off his thigh and impersonally inspected the wound on his leg, pushed at it.

"It's healing," she ventured. "Rosamund said the

wound was not bad, only the fever. We feared for your life."

Turning to her, he gave her a cold, hard look, and she could almost swear there was anger in his eyes. "Fetch me some food and a lot of it. I need to regain my strength."

Alyx didn't move.

"Damn you!" Raine bellowed, his voice shaking the walls of the tent. The explosion obviously depleted what little strength he had, and for a moment his hand went to his forehead. "Obey me," he said quietly, lying back. "And boy," he added as she reached the tent flap, water buckets in her hands. "Bring me hot wine."

"Boy!" Alyx gasped once she was outside the tent. "Boy!"

"Alyx?" Joss asked. "Was that Raine I just heard?"

Glumly, she nodded.

"Are you all right? What was he shouting about?"

"How should I know what that great ox was bellowing about?" she snapped. "How can a low being like myself know what a friend of the king thinks?"

To her consternation, Jocelin laughed aloud and left her, whistling what Alyx knew was a ribald little song.

"Men!" she cursed, tossing the buckets into the river, hauling up sand and rocks with the water and then having to repeat the process. The second time she paused, tears in her eyes. "Boy," she whispered to the cold, rushing water. Did she mean so little to him that he couldn't even remember their night together?

Perhaps he needed a few hours to remember, she thought as she went back to the tent, stopping to tell Blanche Raine wanted food.

"I should know," Blanche said, her voice sweet, insinuating. "He's already called me to him, and I must say that Raine Montgomery has lost none of his strength," she said loudly for the benefit of the people around her, ostentatiously fastening the top of the dirty shirt she wore. "I've taken him his food."

With her chin up, Alyx entered the tent, her shoulders dragged down by the heavy buckets.

"What took you so long?" Raine asked, his mouth full.

She whirled to face him. "I have more duties than fetching your food," she said angrily. "And it looks like that whore of yours can well provide for you."

"Fair enough," he said evenly, tearing into a leg of pork. "Perhaps we should work on your prudery. A woman is a woman, a fragile, helpless thing, someone to be protected and loved, no matter what her station in life. If you treat a whore like a lady, she'll be one, and a lady can become a whore. It all depends on the man. Remember that. You're a long way from reaching manhood yet, but when you do—"

"When I do I won't need any advice from you," she fairly shouted before turning toward the exit, where she slammed into Jocelin. With one angry glance at him, she pushed past him and left the tent.

Joss glanced at Raine, took a seat on a stool and idly began to strum the lute while Raine silently ate. After a moment, Joss stopped playing.

"How long have you known about Alyx?" Joss asked.

Only a hesitation in his eating showed that Raine had heard. "For a matter of hours, really," he said calmly. "And how long have you known?"

"Always." He laughed at Raine's expression. "I

was surprised no one else did. To me she was like a little girl dressed in her brother's clothes. When you called her a boy I couldn't believe you meant it."

"I wish the hell you'd told me," Raine said with feeling, a dimple appearing in his cheek. "A few days ago she was writing a letter for me and I nearly kissed her. I was sick for hours afterward."

"You've worked her harder than anyone else, you know."

"Perhaps I was trying to change her shape," Raine laughed. "I've been fascinated by her legs for some time."

"And now what do you plan to do with her?"

Pushing the tray away, Raine leaned back on the cot, feeling very weak, very weary. "Do you know how much of her story is true? What has Pagnell done to her?"

"Accused her of robbing him, declared her a witch, put a fat reward on her head."

Raine lifted one eyebrow at Joss, feeling foolish that he knew so little about what went on under his nose. "How do you think the filth of this camp would react to a young girl in their midst? One whose capture would bring them a reward?"

A snort from Joss was the only answer.

"I think it's best she stay a boy," Raine said thoughtfully, "and under my protection. The fewer people who know of her true identity the better."

"But you will tell Alyx you know she's a girl, won't you?"

"Ha!" Raine grunted. "Let the baggage suffer as I have. She's flipped that pretty little tail of hers at me at every opportunity, and this morning when I realized how she'd played me for a fool, I could have wrung her neck. No, let her stew awhile. She thinks I don't remember—" He glanced quickly at Joss. "She thinks I don't know she's female, let her stay that way."

Jocelin stood. "You won't be too hard on her, will you? Unless I'm mistaken, I think she believes herself to be in love with you."

Raine's grin was face splitting. "Good. No, I'll not harm her, but I will make her taste a bit of her own medicine."

An hour later, when Alyx returned to the tent, her chin pointed toward the sky, Raine and Jocelin were leisurely playing a game of dice, neither of them seeming to be much interested in the game.

"Alyx," Raine said, not bothering to look up. "Did you practice on the field today? You're scrawny enough without losing the little muscle you have."

"Practice," she gasped, then calmed herself. "For some reason I don't understand now, I was concerned about whether you lived or died and gave no thought to embellishing my puny body."

With an expression of astonishment and hurt, Raine looked up at her. "Alyx, how can you speak to me so? Are you truly angry that I lived? Go away, Joss, I'm too tired to play anymore. Perhaps I'll fetch myself some wine—as soon as I'm strong enough," he added, lying back on the cot with a great show of weariness.

Joss gave a choking cough before slipping the dice into his pocket, rolling his eyes at Raine and leaving the tent.

Alyx tried to remain aloof, but when she saw Raine collapsed on the cot, looking so pale, so helpless, she relented. "I will bring you wine," she sighed, and when she handed it to him his hand was trembling so that she had to put her arm around his shoulders, support him and hold the cup to his lips—those lips that even now made her breath come quick.

"You are tired," Raine said sympathetically. "And how long has it been since you've had a bath? No one in the world can get as dirty as a boy your age. Ah, well," he said, smiling, leaning back. "Someday when you've found the right woman you'll want to please her. Did I ever tell you of the time I was in a tournament outside Paris? There were three women who—"

"No!" she yelled, making him blink innocently at her. "I do not want to hear your dirty stories."

"A squire should have more of an education than just weapons. For instance, when you play the lute, the tunes you choose and the words you sing are more suited for a female. A woman likes a man who is strong, sure of himself, she'd never like a wailing youth who sounds more like a female."

"A wailing—!" she began, thoroughly insulted. She may not be beautiful, but she was sure of her music. "And what do you know of women?" she snarled. "If you know as little of women as music, you are as ignorant as you are—"

"As I am what?" he said with interest, propping himself on one elbow to face her. "As handsome? As strong? As lusty?" he asked, practically leering at her.

"As vain!" she shouted.

"Ah, would that the size of you matched the strength of your voice. Have you ever tried pulling down castle walls by screeching at them? Perhaps you could strike a note and an enemy's army of horses would follow you off into the wilderness."

"Stop it! Stop it!" she screamed. "I hate you, you great, stupid, cowering *nobleman!*" With that she turned toward the tent flap, but Raine, his voice low, commanding, called her back.

"Fetch Rosamund, would you? I don't feel well at all."

She turned one step toward him but recalled herself and left the tent. Outside many people stood, obviously having heard the argument inside the tent. Trying her best to ignore the people as they laughed and punched each other, Alyx went to the training ground and spent three hard hours practicing with a bow and arrow.

Finally, exhausted, she went to the river, bathed, washed her hair and ate before returning to the tent.

It was dark in the tent, and since no sound came from Raine she assumed he was asleep. Now, she thought, if she had the courage, she'd walk away from this camp and never return. Why did she think that what was special to her was anything at all to this lord of the realm? No doubt he was used to women slipping in and out of his bed and paid little attention to them. What did one more matter? If she revealed herself as his last conquest, would he laugh or perhaps try to establish her as one of his many women? Would she and Blanche take turns entertaining him?

"Alyx?" Raine asked sleepily. "You were gone a long time. Did you eat something?"

"A bucket full," she said nastily, "so I can grow to be the size of your horse."

"Alyx, don't be angry with me. Come and sit by me and sing me a song."

"I know no songs like the ones you like."

"I will manage," he said, and his voice was so tired

she relented, taking up the lute and playing quietly, humming with the tune.

"Judith will like you," he murmured.

"Judith? Your brother's beautiful wife? Why should a lady like her bother with a baseborn lawyer's . . . son?" She'd almost said "daughter."

"She will like your music," he said, his voice heavy with sleep, and Alyx resumed her playing.

When she was sure he was asleep she went to him, knelt by his bed and for a moment watched him, doing little more than assuring herself that he was alive. Finally, she went to her own hard bed and used all her strength to keep from crying.

In the morning Raine insisted on going to the training ground. No protest from Alyx or Jocelin could persuade him to rest for another day. As he walked, Alyx could see the sweat on his forehead, the dull look in his eyes as he forced himself to move.

"If you die, what use will you be to us?" Alyx tossed at him.

"If I die will you go personally and notify my family?" he said in such seriousness that her breath caught. Then a dimple flashed and she knew he was teasing her.

"I will throw your great carcass over a horse and go to meet your perfect family, but I will not kneel with your sisters to mourn you."

"There will be other women besides my sisters to cry at my passing. Did I ever tell you about Judith's maid Joan? I have never met a more enthusiastic woman in my life."

At that Alyx turned away, her back rigid against the sound of Raine's rumbling laugh.

After an hour's training, Alyx ran back to the tent

to fetch some of Rosamund's herb drink for Raine, and there she found Blanche sorting through his clothes.

"What do you think you're doing?" Alyx demanded, making Blanche jump guiltily.

"For . . . for laundry," she said, her eyes darting.

Alyx laughed at that. "Since when do you know what soap is?" With a quick movement she grabbed Blanche's arms. "You'd better tell me the truth. You know what the punishment for stealing is—banishment."

"I should leave here," Blanche whined, trying to twist away from Alyx. "There's nothing here for me anymore. Let me go!"

As Blanche pulled Alyx pushed, and Blanche went sailing across the room, her back hitting a tent pole.

"I'll repay you for this," Blanche sneered. "I'll make you sorry you ever took Lord Raine away from me."

"I?" Alyx asked, trying to keep the pleasure from her voice. "And how have I taken Raine?"

"You know he doesn't take me to his bed anymore," she said, rising. "Now that he has a boy—"

"Careful," Alyx warned. "It seems to me that you should worry about my anger toward you. What were you searching for when I came in?"

Blanche refused to speak.

"Then I guess I'll have to talk to Raine," Alyx said, turning to leave.

"No!" Blanche said, tears in her voice. "I have nowhere else to go. Please don't tell him. I'll not steal. I never have before."

"I have a price for not telling Raine."

"What?" Blanche asked, frightened.

"Tell me about Jocelin."

"Jocelin?" Blanche asked, as if she'd never heard the name before.

Alyx only glared at her. "I will be missed soon, and if I don't have the story by the time someone comes for me, Raine will hear of your stealing."

Immediately, Blanche began the tale. "Jocelin was a jongleur and all the highest-born ladies wanted him, not only for his music but for his . . ." She hesitated. "The man never grew tired," she said wistfully, making Alyx believe she had firsthand knowledge.

"He went to the Chatworth castle at the command of Lady Alice."

The name Chatworth made Alyx's head come up. Chatworth was the man who held Raine's sister and sister-in-law.

"Lady Alice is an evil woman," Blanche continued, "but her husband, Lord Edmund, was worse. He liked to beat women, watch their struggles as he took them. There was a woman, Constance, and he beat her until she died—or at least he thought she was dead. He gave the body to Joss to dispose of."

"And?" Alyx encouraged. "I haven't much time left."

"The woman was not dead and Joss hid her, nursed her back to health and he fell in love with her."

"Was this unusual for a man of Joss's . . . talents?"

Blanche suddenly began to look very nervous, her hands pulling on each other, standing on first one foot, then the other. "I don't believe he'd ever loved anyone before. When Lord Edmund found out the girl was still alive, he took her for his own again and threw Jocelin in an *oubliette*. And the girl . . . this Constance . . ."

"Yes?" Alyx said impatiently.

"She thought Joss was as good as dead and so she killed herself."

At that, Alyx crossed herself at such a sin. "But Joss did get out, and he came here," she finished.

"But first he killed Lord Edmund," Blanche said quietly, and with that she pushed past Alyx and ran from the tent.

"Killed a lord," Alyx whispered to no one. No doubt there was a huge reward for his head, and no wonder he wanted nothing to do with the women of the camp. Alyx knew very well what it was to love a man and to lose him.

"What are you doing in here?" Raine asked angrily from behind her. "You have been gone for at least an hour, and here I find you standing alone doing nothing."

"I'll work," she muttered, turning away.

He caught her arm but released her as quickly as he touched her. "Have you had some bad news?"

"None that would interest you," she snapped before leaving the tent.

Alyx's thoughts for the rest of the day were taken up with Jocelin. Joss was a sweet, kind, sensitive man, and he deserved someone to love him. She wished she could have fallen in love with Joss; how much easier everything would be. Someday, probably soon, Raine would leave the forest and go back to his rich family and she would be alone.

As she absently lifted a sword, trying to bring it straight down over her head, her eye caught a movement at the corner of the field. In the shadows, standing still, watching, was Rosamund. Following her glance, Alyx saw that the woman looked only at

Jocelin, that in her eyes blazed passion and fire and, as Alyx recognized it, lust. Her head wasn't bowed, and for the first time there was no subservience about her, no apology for having been born.

"Alyx! You slacken!" Raine yelled at her, and with a grimace she put her mind back on her training.

That night, Raine, exhausted, still very weak, went to his cot to rest, while Alyx sat outside in the cold night air and ate a bowl of beans. Beside her sat Jocelin.

"You tore your shirt," she commented. "Someone should sew it for you."

Before Alyx could breathe, three women cheerfully said they'd sew it.

"No," Joss muttered, looking at his bowl. "It does well enough as it is."

"Give one of them your shirt," Alyx said impatiently. "I will fetch one of Raine's to warm you. He has more than enough of them."

Reluctantly, Joss took off his shirt as Alyx hurried to the tent, cast one look at Raine's sleeping form and hurried out again, a shirt over her arm. Outside, she paused. Jocelin sat before the fire, his body bare from the waist up, women all around him, their eyes greedy as they looked at Joss, at his handsomeness, his obvious melancholy, and far to one side stood Rosamund. But Jocelin never looked at any of the women.

At the fire, Alyx handed Joss the shirt and dipped herself a mug of boiling cider, blowing on the liquid to cool it.

Suddenly, a noise just outside the circle of light made everyone's head turn in that direction.

Later, Alyx didn't really remember consciously planning what she did. No one was looking, she was standing next to Jocelin's bare body and holding the hot cider. All she thought of was that if Joss were hurt, he'd have to go to Rosamund, and the next moment she poured half the cider on Joss's arm.

Instantly, she was sorry. Jocelin jumped away from her, the shirt falling from his lap.

"Joss, I . . ." she began, looking in horror at the skin on his arm turning red.

"Rosamund," someone whispered. "Get Rosa-mund."

Within seconds Rosamund was there, her cool fingers on Joss's arm, and she was leading him away into the shadows.

Alyx wasn't aware of it, but there were tears in her eyes and her body was trembling from what she'd just done. It had all happened so fast and she'd had no time to think.

A great hand clamped on the back of her neck, paralyzing her.

"You will follow me to the river, and if you do not I will take a whip to your back now," Raine growled in her ear, his voice barely concealing his rage.

Her guilt over what she'd done to Joss was replaced by sheer terror. A whip to her back? Swallowing, she followed Raine into the dark forest. She deserved punishment, for she had no right whatever to hurt her friend.

Chapter Nine

$\mathcal{A}$T THE RIVER, Raine turned to her, his fine lips curled into a snarl. "I should beat you," he said fiercely as he pushed her once, lightly, sending her sprawling onto the cold earth.

"And what slight did you imagine Jocelin had done you?" he asked, teeth clenched. "Were you jealous of the cut of his doublet? Had he said something you disliked? Perhaps he played a better song than you."

That got her attention. "No one is better than I," she said firmly, her jaw jutted forward as she stared up at him.

"Damn you!" he said, grabbing the front of her shirt and pulling her upward. "I trusted you. I thought you were one of the few of your class who had a sense of honor. But you're like all the others—allowing your petty differences to override your honor."

The two of them were an odd couple, Raine twice Alyx's size, towering, looming over her, but Alyx's voice was second to no one's. "Honor," she yelled back at him. "You don't know the meaning of the word. And Jocelin is my friend. He and I have no differences." She made it clear who she had the differences with.

"So! Your low little mind poured boiling cider on him for the fun of it. You are like Alice Chatworth. That woman loves to give and receive pain. Had I known you were like her—"

With that Alyx doubled her fist and hit Raine in the stomach. While he was blinking at her, she grabbed his knife from the sheath at his side. "Spare me the history of your stupid family," she shouted, pressing the point to his stomach. "I will explain to Jocelin what I did and why I did it, but for you, you vain, arrogant braggart, you deserve nothing. You judge and condemn without one word of facts."

Impatiently, Raine brushed at her arm to knock the knife away, but Alyx's reflexes had quickened in the last weeks and Raine's were dulled from his fever. The blade cut the back and side of his hand and caused both of them to halt as they watched the blood well from the cut.

"You thirst for blood, do you?" Raine said. "Either mine or my friend's. I will show you how to receive pain." He reached for her, but she sidestepped him.

It took two tries to catch her, and when he did his hands clamped down on her shoulders as he shook her very hard. "How could you do that?" he demanded. "I trusted you. How could you betray me?"

It was difficult for the words to register when her head was about to fly off, but she finally began to understand what he was saying. Jocelin was Raine's responsibility, and he took his duties seriously. "Rosamund, Rosamund, Rosamund," she began to chant.

When at last he heard her, he stopped shaking her. "Tell me," he yelled in her face.

Her body was weak from the force of his shaking of her. "Rosamund is in love with Jocelin, and I thought she could replace Constance, but not if they were apart."

This made no sense to Raine. His fingers tightened on her shoulders, and she wondered if soon they'd come through. Quickly, she explained Joss's story about Constance, omitting the name of Chatworth.

Stunned silence from Raine filled the air. "You are matchmaking?" he croaked. "You wounded Jocelin because of some idiotic ideas of love?"

"What would you know of love?" she tossed at him. "You know so little of women that you don't know one when you see one."

"True," he countered quickly. "I am an innocent when it comes to the lying, deceiving ways of women."

"Not all women are liars."

"Name one who is not."

She was dying to mention herself but could not. "Rosamund," she blurted. "She is a good, kind person."

"Not when she uses such methods to snare a man."

"Snare! Who would want to catch such a loathsome specimen as a man?" She stopped her tirade when she saw Raine's eyes sparkling. "You know," she gasped. "You know."

She did not waste much time in speculating on the

truth of her assumptions but lifted herself from the ground and flew at him, her fists clenched. "You—!" she began in anger, but Raine stopped her. He caught her, clasping the slight body against him and drawing her mouth to his. Hungrily, he kissed her, his hand on the back of her head, his other hand about her waist, holding her off the ground.

"Remember that I am a weak man," he whispered. "And a long day on the training field has—"

Alyx bit him on the shoulder. "How long have you known?"

"Not as long as I would have liked. Why didn't you tell me from the start? I understand why you had to dress as a boy, but I would have kept the secret."

She nuzzled her face in his neck, such soft, sweet-tasting skin. "I did not know you. Oh, Raine, are you really, truly *very* weak?"

Raine's laugh rumbled through her body as he pulled her away from him, tossed her in the air. "Got your first taste of love and can't stop, is that it?"

"It is like music," she said dreamily, "the very best music."

"I'm sure I should take that as a compliment," he said, beginning to unbutton her doublet.

For a moment it flashed across Alyx's mind that he wouldn't like her flat-chested body now when no fever blurred his senses. "Raine," she said, her hand on his. "I look like a boy."

It took a while before he understood her words. "You drive me to distraction with those legs of yours, and now you say you look like a boy? I have done everything in my power to make a man out of you and failed. But I *have* made a woman out of you."

With her breath held, Alyx allowed him to undress

her, and when he looked at her slight body with hot, wanting eyes, she forgot any feelings of being unworthy.

With a laugh, she tore at his clothes, pulling whatever she could reach away from his skin.

Raine lowered her to the ground, kept his hands on her bare back while she had her way with him. Never had he encountered such enthusiasm.

"I do not hurt you?" he murmured as he held her small body.

"Only a little and only in the right places. Oh, Raine, I thought you would never recover from your fever." With that she jumped atop him, and after a look of astonishment, he put his hands on her slim hips.

"Sing for me, my little songbird," he whispered as he lifted her and lowered her onto his shaft.

Alyx's gasp was indeed musical, and it took her only minutes to catch the rhythm of Raine's movement as his big hands traveled upward to her breasts, warming her, exciting her. His hands traveled all over her body, halting just briefly at the gold Lyon belt, then down to her thighs that worked as she raised and lowered herself.

Raine's fingertips explored, caressed, until his urgency increased and his hands dug into her hips, holding her, manipulating her as he desired. With one violent upward thrust, he spent himself as Alyx shivered, shuddered and fell forward onto him.

"How could so much woman have disguised herself as a boy?" he murmured, his hands tangled in her hair, kissing her temple. "No wonder you threatened to drive me insane."

"Oh?" she asked, trying to hide her interest in his

answer. "When was that? I would never have guessed you knew I was alive except as someone to fetch for you."

"Perhaps when you bent over or tossed a leg before my face or other such unmanly things."

"Toss—! I did no such thing. And what about you? Having me climb on your back, to straddle you! Is that how you treat all boys?"

He laughed at her. "Boys would have been interested in my strength. Are you cold?"

She snuggled on top of him, her body touching only his. "No."

"Alyx!" His head came up. "How old are you?" There was fear in his face.

She gave him a haughty look. "I am twenty, and if you hope I will grow—"

Chuckling, he pushed her head back down. "God has given you the gift of music, what more could you want? I was afraid you were a child. You don't look more than twelve."

"Do you like my music?" she asked innocently, making her voice soft and seductive.

"You'll get no more compliments from me. It seems you've had too many already. Who has trained you?"

Briefly she told him of the priest and the monk.

"So that is how you come to be a virgin at twenty and Pagnell— Hush," he said when she started to speak. "He is a coward, and he will not harm you while you are near me."

"Oh, Raine! I knew you'd say that. I knew it! There are many advantages to being a nobleman. Now you can go to the king and beg his forgiveness, then you and I will go to your home. I will sing for you and play for you and we will be so very happy."

Raine, in one motion, pushed her off him and began to dress. "Beg the king's forgiveness," he said under his breath. "And what have I done to be forgiven? Do you forget that two of my family are being held prisoner? Do you forget *why* I am here? And what of those in that camp? One moment you preach about the Enclosure Acts and the next you demand the farmers leave this new home they have found."

"Raine," she pleaded, holding her shirt to her neck, "I didn't mean— Surely if King Henry heard your side of the story he'd help you. This man Chatworth should not be allowed to hold your family."

"Henry!" he snarled. "You talk of him as if he were a god. He is a greedy man. Do you know why he's outlawed me? For my lands! He wants to take all the power from the nobles and keep it for himself. Of course, your class wants him to do this since he does good things for you, but what happens when a bad king has the power? With the nobles, at least, a bad one controls only a small area. What if Pagnell were king? Would you wish to follow a man like him?"

Hastily she pulled on her shirt. She'd never seen Raine so angry. "I wasn't talking about all of England," she soothed. "I meant us. Surely you could do more good for your family if you were with them."

"And for that you wish me to go on bended knee to the king?" he whispered. "Is that what you want? You wish to see me groveling, forsaking my vows of honor?"

"Honor!" she said loudly. "What has honor to do with this? You were wrong to use the king's men."

For a moment she was sure he was going to strike

her, but he took a step backward, away from her, his eyes blazing. "Honor is all to me," he whispered before turning back to the camp.

As quickly as she could, she dressed and ran after him.

Standing before Raine's tent was one of his brother's men, a message in his hand. She was glad to see the man. Perhaps some good news from home would make Raine forget his anger.

Hurrying forward, she took the message and without a glance from Raine, slipped inside the tent. Smiling, she opened the message, and the next moment, her shoulders fell.

"What is it?" Raine growled. "Is someone ill?"

There were tears in Alyx's eyes when she looked up at Raine. As they locked gazes, his eyes hardened.

"What is it?" he demanded of her.

"Your . . . sister Mary is . . . dead," she whispered.

Raine's face betrayed no emotion except for a bit of white appearing at the corners of his mouth. "And Bronwyn?"

"Escaped from Roger Chatworth, but she has not been found yet. Your brothers are looking for her."

"Is there more?"

"No. Nothing. Raine—" she began.

He brushed her aside. "Go! Leave me to myself."

Alyx started to obey him, but as she looked back and saw his rigid back, she knew she couldn't leave him. "Sit!" she commanded, and when he turned to her his eyes were like black coals from hell.

"Sit," she said, quieter, "and we will talk."

"Leave me!" he growled, but he sat on a stool and dropped his head into his hands.

Immediately, Alyx sat at his feet, not touching him. "What was she like?" she whispered. "Was Mary short or fat? Did she laugh often? Did she rail at you and your brothers? What did she do when you were so obstinate she wanted to take a club to your head?"

He looked up at that, his eyes dark, angry. "Mary was good, kind. She had no flaws."

"It's a good thing," Alyx said. "She would have to be a saint to stand your mule-headedness, and no doubt your brothers are as bad."

Raine's hand fastened about her throat as he went for her, the stool flying. "Mary was an angel," he said into her face, pinning her body, his hands tightening.

"You will kill me," she said in a resigned voice, gasping. "And still Mary will not come back."

After a moment, his hands dropped and he pulled her close to him, twisting her body in impossible directions as his arms wrapped about her. Slowly, he began to rock her as he stroked her hair.

"Tell me about your angel. Tell me about your brothers. What is Judith like? And Bronwyn?"

It wasn't easy to get him to talk, but as the words began to come, she saw a close, loving family. Mary was the oldest of the five and adored by her younger brothers. Raine talked of her selflessness and, recently, how she and Bronwyn had risked their lives to save a serf's child. He spoke of Judith, how his brother had treated her badly yet Judith had loved him enough to forgive him.

Alyx, living in her small, walled village, had never thought about the family life of the nobles, had assumed they lived untroubled lives. Listening to Raine, she had a glimpse of heartache and sorrow, of life as well as death. She was glad that she had not read aloud Gavin's message to Raine. Roger Chatworth had raped the virginal Mary and, in horror, she'd thrown herself from a tower window.

"Alyx," Raine murmured. "Now can you see why I cannot go to the King? Chatworth is mine. I will have his head before we are finished."

"What!" she gasped, pulling away from him. "You're talking of revenge."

"He has killed Mary."

"No! He did not!" She looked away, damning herself for saying that.

Forcibly, he turned her face back. "You have not told me everything in Gavin's message. How did Mary die?"

"She . . ."

His fingers tightened on her jaw, the pain causing her tears. "Tell me!" he commanded.

"She took her own life," Alyx whispered.

Raine's eyes bored into hers. "She was of the Church, and she would not have done that if she had no reason. What was done to her?"

She could see that he had guessed, but he was pleading to be told he was wrong. She could not lie to him. "Roger Chatworth . . . took her to his bed."

Violently, Raine shoved Alyx across the room. As he stood, he threw back his head and let out a cry of such despair, such rage, such hate, that Alyx cringed at the foot of the cot.

Outside, everything was unnaturally quiet, even the wind having stopped.

Glancing up at him, Alyx saw that he was beginning to tremble, then shake, and as he lowered his head, she saw that pure hate was causing the convulsions.

Instantly, she left the floor to throw her arms around him.

"No, Raine, no!" she pleaded. "You cannot go after Chatworth. The King—"

He pushed her off him. "The man would be glad to have fewer nobles. He will take Chatworth's land as well as mine."

"Raine, please." She pressed herself against him again. "You cannot go alone, and your brothers are searching for Bronwyn. And what of the people out there? You cannot leave them to murder each other."

"Since when has your concern been for them?"

"Since I am in a terror of your being killed," she answered honestly. "How can you fight Chatworth? Your men are not here. You do have soldiers, don't you? Does Chatworth have knights?"

"Hundreds," Raine said through clenched teeth. "He is always surrounded by men, always protected."

"And if you went to him would he meet you fairly, one to one, or would you have to plow through his men first?"

Raine looked away from her, but she could see her words were making sense. How she wished she knew more about the nobility! Honor, think of honor and whatever you do, don't mention money, she warned herself.

"Chatworth is not honorable," she continued. "You cannot deal with him in the way of a knight. You must work together with your brothers." Silently she prayed they were not so hotheaded as Raine. "Please, wait until you are calmer. We'll write to your brothers and work out a plan together."

"I am not sure—"

"Raine," she said quietly, "Mary has been dead for days. Perhaps Chatworth has already been brought to justice. Perhaps he has escaped to France. Perhaps—"

"You try to coax me. Why?"

She took a deep breath. "I have grown to love you," she whispered. "I would die before I stood by and watched you be killed, and that is what would happen if you attacked Chatworth alone."

"I do not fear death."

She looked up at him in disgust. "Go, then!" she yelled. "Go and give your life to Chatworth. No doubt he'd like that. One by one he can destroy your family. And you will make it easy for him. Come, I will help arm you. You will wear your finest armor. We'll strap on every weapon you own, and when you are invincible, you can ride out to face this Chatworth's army of men. Yes, come on," she said, grabbing his armor's breastplate. "Mary will be pleased to look down from heaven and see her brother hacked to bits. It will give her soul great peace."

Raine's look was so cold she felt it piercing her skin.

"Leave me," he said at last, and she did.

Alyx had never known such fear as she felt at this moment. Even in the cold air outside the tent, she was sweating profusely.

"Alyx," came a whispered voice that belonged to Jocelin.

In seconds she was in his arms, her tears flowing. "Raine's sister," she sobbed. "Mary is dead and Raine wants to face the murderer's army alone."

"Ssh," Joss calmed her. "He is not like us. We were taught to be cowards, to turn tail and run, to live to fight another day. There are not many men like Raine. He'd rather die than face dishonor."

"I do not want him to die. He cannot die! I have lost everyone—my mother, my father. I know I have no right, but I love him."

"You have every right. Now be quiet and think what you can do to prevent his suicide. Surely his brothers know how hotheaded he is. Can you persuade Raine to write his brother and you can add a note?"

"Oh, Joss," she said, grasping his arms. At his wince, she stopped. "Your shoulder where I poured the cider. I am sorry, I—"

"Quiet," he said, placing his fingertips on her lips. "Rosamund is caring for me. It is a small wound. Now go to Raine and talk to him and do not lose your temper."

Silently, Alyx reentered the tent. Raine sat on the edge of the cot, head in his hands. "Raine," she whispered, touching his hair.

Fiercely, he grabbed her hand, kissed the palm. "I am useless," he said. "A man kills my sister and I can do nothing. Nothing!"

She sat by him, put her arms around him, her head on his arm. "Come to bed. It's late. Tomorrow we will write to Gavin. Perhaps he can do something."

Docilely, Raine allowed himself to be put to bed, but when Alyx started toward her own pallet, he caught her arm. "Stay with me."

There was no possibility that she was going to reject such an offer. With a smile, she glided into his arms.

All night, as she dozed fitfully, she was aware that Raine lay awake beside her.

In the morning there were shadows under his eyes and his temper was black. "Wine, I told you!" he bellowed at Alyx. "Then fetch pen and paper."

The letter Raine dictated to be sent to his brother was one of anger and revenge. He vowed to take Roger Chatworth's life, and if Gavin did not help him, he would go alone.

Alyx added her own message to the bottom, pleading with Gavin to talk some sense into Raine, that he was ready to take on all of Chatworth's men alone. Sealing the letter, she wondered what this great Lord Gavin would think of her presumption.

It was two days before replies came. The messenger, nearly dead from the pace he'd set, practically fell on Alyx. With trembling hands, she broke the seal.

King Henry was furious with both the Montgomerys and the Chatworths. He was placing a heavy fine on Roger Chatworth and renewing his issue for Raine being a traitor. He wanted both noblemen out of England and he was doing what he could to bring it about. He was angered by Raine's hiding in England, and it was rumored that Raine was raising an army to fight against the King.

With eyes filled with fright, Alyx looked up at Raine. "You would not do such a thing, would you?" she whispered.

"The man worries more as he grows older," Raine said in dismissal. "Who can train such scum as those to fight?"

"This is proof that you must stay in hiding. Your brother says King Henry would love to use you as an example of what would be done to others who do not believe he is the man with the power."

"Gavin worries about losing his land," Raine said in disgust. "My brother cares more for soil than he does for honor. Already he has forgotten our sister's death."

"He has forgotten nothing!" Alyx shouted at him. "He remembers he has other people in his family. Would it make you happier if he sent you to your death? He lost his unborn babe not long ago, he has lost his only sister, his brother's wife is missing and now he is to encourage you to willingly give your life for something as stupid as revenge?"

"For my sister's life!" he yelled back at her. "Do you expect me to stand still after what has been done to me? Is there no way one of your class can understand the meaning of honor?"

"My class!" she yelled back at him. "Do you think because of your high birth you are the only one with feelings? In one night one of your kind slashed my father's throat and burned my house. If that were not enough, I was declared a thief and a witch. And all this because of some man's lust. Now you talk to me of revenge, ask me if I understand it. I cannot step out of this forest for fear of my life."

"Alyx," he began.

"Don't touch me!" she shouted. "You with your superior ways. You ridicule us because we concern ourselves with money, but what else do we have? We scrape all our lives and give a big piece of our income to support you in your fine houses so you can have the freedom to spout about honor and revenge. If you had to worry where your next meal came from, I wonder how much you would talk of honor."

"You do not understand," he said sullenly.

"I understand perfectly and you damn well know it," she said before leaving the tent.

Chapter Ten

$\mathscr{I}$T WAS MANY hours before Alyx could calm herself. She sat alone by the river. Perhaps she was right in hating Raine because he was part of the nobility. There were barriers between them that could never come down. Everything he believed was the opposite of what she knew to be true. All her life she'd had to contend with work, chores before her music, chores after. There was always the worry that they were not going to have enough food. If it hadn't been for the priest, they would have gone without many winters. Sometimes Raine complained about the food in the camp, but the truth was she'd had more variety and quantity than she'd ever had.

When Pagnell had killed her father, she'd done what she could to survive. Survival! That meant nothing to someone like Raine and his powerful brothers. War, revenge, honor, these childish games of kidnapping each other were things that had never entered into her life.

"May I join you?" Jocelin asked. "Like to share your thoughts with me?"

Her eyes glistened. "I was imagining Raine behind a plow. If he had to worry about his fields growing he wouldn't have time to think of murdering this Chatworth. And if Chatworth were driving a team of oxen he wouldn't have had the energy to kidnap Raine's sister."

"Ah, make everyone equal," he said. "Rather like King Henry wants. Give all the power to one man and none to anyone else."

"You sound like Raine," she accused. "I thought you'd be on my side."

Jocelin leaned against a rock and smiled. "I am on no one's side. I have seen both ways of life and the poverty of the lower class doesn't appeal to me nor the . . . the decadence of the upper class. Of course, there are people in the middle. I think I should like to be a rich merchant, a buyer and seller of silks, and grow a fat belly."

"There were rich merchants in Moreton, but they weren't happy either. They were always worried about losing their money."

"Rather like Raine is worried about losing his honor?"

Alyx smiled at him, realized he was leading toward something. "What are you trying to tell me?"

"That all of us are different, that nothing is all good or bad. If you want Raine to understand your ways, be patient. Screeching at him will do little."

She laughed at that. "Screeching, is it? Perhaps I am a bit loud."

Jocelin gave an exaggerated groan. "You do realize that you are as stubborn as he is, don't you? Both of you are so sure you're right, that your way is the only one."

For a quiet moment, Alyx considered this. "Why do you think I love him, Joss? I know he's lovely to look at, but then so are you. Why would I love Raine when I know nothing can ever come of that love? The best I can hope for is to be made his family musician, to serve his . . . his wife and children."

"Who knows what makes us love?" Joss said, a faraway look in his eyes.

"It was almost as if I'd known Raine before I met him. All the way into the forest I kept thinking how I hated all the nobility, but as soon as I saw Raine—" She laughed. "I really did try."

"Come on, let's go back. I'm sure Raine will have work for us to do. And try to remember that he needs comfort now as much as lectures on what a mule he is."

"I will try," she said, taking his hand as he helped her up.

In the shadows of the trees stood a woman everyone seemed to have forgotten—Blanche. Her face contorted into ugliness when she saw Jocelin take Alyx's hand. For the last few days Alyx and Raine had been tearing at each other as only lovers can. They seemed to think the inside of the tent gave them privacy, but their two voices were so loud that stone walls wouldn't have sheltered them. The people in the camp wagered on who was going to win the arguments, saying the boy could hold his own. They cheered when Alyx said her class of people had too much work to do to talk about honor.

But there were things the people didn't hear, things that only Blanche heard as she fastened her ear to the tent wall: that Alyx had been declared a witch because of some man's lust, that Alyx loved Raine, and at night were the unmistakable sounds of lovemaking.

Once she'd had a good position in a castle, Edmund Chatworth's castle, and she'd had Jocelin for a lover. Now, in the rare times when Joss did look at her, his lips curled into a snarl and his eyes glowed with hatred. All because of that disgusting whore Constance! Constance had taken Joss away from Blanche, away from women everywhere. Jocelin, who used to laugh and sing, who took three women to his bed at once and made them all happy, was like a celibate priest now. Yet recently, he'd been looking at that devil-marked Rosamund with more than a little interest.

And now she was losing Raine—great, handsome, powerful, rich Raine. And to what? A skinny, short-haired, flat-chested boy/girl. If I were to wear men's clothes, Blanche thought, no one would mistake me for a boy. But that Alyx had no curves and her face looked like an elf's. So why was Raine panting after her? She was no highborn lady but of the same class as Blanche. Before Alyx came, Blanche was Raine's personal attendant and once, oh lovely night! she'd shared his bed. Now it was never likely to happen again—unless she could get rid of Alyx.

With a new, determined look on her face, she turned back to the camp.

For weeks Alyx worked to keep Raine from declaring war on Roger Chatworth. The letters that went from Montgomery Castle and back again began to be exchanged weekly. More than once, Alyx thanked the Lord Raine couldn't read, because at the bottom of her letters to Gavin, she added a postscript of her version of the truth. She told Gavin how Raine's anger grew each day, how he was driving himself harder and harder on the training field, preparing himself for battle with Chatworth.

In return Gavin wrote of Bronwyn's having been found, of her baby due in August. He wrote of their youngest brother's rage at his sister's death and how Miles had been sent to relatives on the Isle of Wight, in hopes that their uncle could cool Miles' temper. In a lighter vein, Gavin said that their uncle was the one in a rage now since his ward had fallen in love with Miles and was vowing to follow him to the ends of the earth.

"What is this brother of yours like?" Alyx asked, curious.

"Women like Miles," was all Raine would say. There was no humor about him these days. Even his lovemaking had a desperate edge to it.

Another brother, Stephen, wrote from Scotland. The letter, to Alyx's mind, was odd, filled with anger against the English, talk of the year's poor crops.

"Is your brother a Scotsman?" she asked.

"He is married to the MacArran and has taken her name."

"He has given up a good English name for a Scot's?" She was incredulous.

"Bronwyn could make a man do anything for her," Raine said flatly.

Alyx bit her tongue to keep from making a snide

comment about the idle, rich women Raine had always loved. Once she did say something of the sort and made Raine smile.

"Judith," he said with such longing that Alyx winced. "In my life I have never spent a day working as hard as she does each day."

"Chivalrous of you," Alyx had snorted, disbelieving what he said.

It was in April that things began to happen. The camp of outlaws seemed docile all through winter, but as the trees began to bud and there was a breath of fresh air about, they began to fight. Not fight each other head on, but sneak up quietly and club someone.

Raine's work increased a hundred fold. He was determined to keep order in the camp.

"Why do you bother?" Alyx snapped at him. "They aren't worth your time."

For the first time in a long while, she saw one of his dimples appear. "Can't teach honor to one of their class, is that it? Only we are privy to those feelings."

"We?" she snorted. "Since when have I become one of your satin-clad ladies? I'll wager I can handle a sword as well as your Judith can handle a needle."

For some reason this seemed to highly amuse Raine. "You'd win that bet," he laughed. "Now come here and give me a kiss. I know you're the best at that."

Gladly, she clung to him. "Am I, Raine?" she asked seriously. She tried to live each day as it came, but sometimes she thought of the future, of seeing Raine with his lady-wife, of herself in the shadows.

"Now, what's that look for?" he asked, tipping her chin up. "Am I so difficult to be around?"

"I'm just afraid, that's all. We won't always be in the forest."

"That is something to be thankful for!" he said passionately. "No doubt decay has set into my house in these last months."

"If you went to the King—" she began tentatively.

"Let's not argue," he whispered against her lips. "Is it possible to love a woman and hate her mind?"

Before Alyx could reply, he began to kiss her, and after that there was no thought of anything but the feel of him against her body. They were never very discreet; they couldn't be. Although Alyx still kept up the pretense of working on the training field, she was never quite serious. Whenever she felt Raine's eyes on her, she did everything she could to entice him to her. She teased him mercilessly.

And oh, what freedom the boy's clothes gave her! Once when they'd gone hunting and were quite some distance from the camp, Alyx turned around in the saddle to face him and untied the triangle in front of her tight hose. Raine, at first astonished, soon began to react to her creativity. Within seconds, he, too, was unfastened and he pulled her on top of him.

They had not counted on Raine's stallion. The horse, nostrils flaring, went wild at the smell of their lovemaking. Raine was fighting the horse and trying to hold onto Alyx's ardent little body. But the point came when he could no longer control anything. As his body exploded in Alyx's, the great beast reared, making Alyx's eyes fly open in wonder.

Raine laughed so hard at her expression she was insulted. "No, I will not do it again," he said, grinning. "And to think you spent most of your life

inside a church. Now you're"— he wiggled his brows
—"riding horses."

She made an attempt to snub him, but as she tried
to turn around, she realized the triangular patch on
her hose was missing. For an hour she had to bear
Raine's laughter while they scrounged in the leaves
looking for the bit of fabric.

But Alyx had the last laugh. The sight of her so
provocatively clad soon changed his words to honey.
She, with all the pride she'd learned from him, made
him fall to his knees and beg for her favors. Of course
she hadn't realized at what level his mouth would be
with him on his knees and her standing. In seconds, it
was Alyx begging for mercy.

After a long, leisurely lovemaking, Raine extracted
her hose patch from his pocket—where it had been all
along. As she pummeled his chest with her fists in
mock fury, he kissed her until she was breathless.

"Learn who is the master here, wench," he said,
nuzzling her neck. "Now we must return to camp.
That is, if my horse will let me ride him. No doubt he
is as in love with you as you are with him."

She tried not to, but she blushed furiously at his
jest. Raine gave her taut buttocks a friendly slap and
lifted her into the saddle. He shouted with laughter
when the horse danced in protest as Raine mounted.

"He protests your weight, most likely," she said
smugly.

"You do not protest my weight, so why should he?"

Alyx thought it was better to keep her mouth shut
because she knew Raine was going to win.

Now, holding onto him, she tried not to think of the
future, of the time when they would no longer be
equals.

A shout outside the tent made them start apart.

"What is it this time?" Raine growled. "Another robbery or another beating?"

There was a mob of people approaching the tent, all of them angry.

"We demand you find the robber," said the leader. "No matter where we hide our things, they are taken."

Rage swept through Alyx. "And what right do you have to make demands, you stupid oaf?" she yelled. "Since when is Lord Raine your protector? You should have gone to the gallows long ago."

"Alyx," Raine warned, clamping his hand onto her shoulder so hard she nearly fell. "Have you kept watch?" he asked the leader of the mob. "Have you hidden your goods?"

"Well!" he said, glancing hostilely toward Alyx. "Some of us have buried them. John here had his knife under his pillow and in the mornin' it was gone."

"Yet no one has seen this thief?" Raine asked.

Blanche stepped forward. "It must be someone small, someone light enough to slip about so easy." Her eyes darted to Alyx.

The mob turned their malevolent glances toward the boy next to Raine.

"It would have to be someone fearless," Blanche continued. "Someone who thought he was protected."

Involuntarily, Alyx took a step backward, closer to Raine.

"Blanche," Raine said quietly, "do you have someone you suspect? Get it out in the open."

"No one for sure," she said, loving the way everyone listened to her. "But I have me ideas."

Alyx, regaining her courage, started to step forward, but Raine stopped her.

"We'll catch the thief," one of the men said, "and when we do, is he gonna be punished?"

Alyx was so stunned by the look of hate in the man's eye that she didn't really hear Raine's answer. Somehow he was able to promise them enough that, grumbling, they finally dispersed.

"They hate me," Alyx whispered as Raine pushed her into the tent. "Why would they hate me?"

"You hate them, Alyx," Raine said. "They feel it even if you never say so. They think you put yourself above them."

She thought she was used to Raine's blunt way of speaking, but she was not prepared for this. "I don't *hate* them."

"They are people the same as you and me. We had the advantage of a family. Do you know the woman without a right hand? Maude? Her father cut off her hand when she was three so she'd get more money when she begged. She was a prostitute by the time she was ten. They are thieves and murderers, but it's only what they've known."

Alyx sat down heavily on a stool. "In these last months you've never mentioned this. Why?"

"It is your opinion. Each of us must do what we must."

"Oh, Raine," she cried, throwing her arms about his neck. "You are so good and kind, so noble. You seem to love everyone while I love no one."

"A saint is what I am," he agreed solemnly. "And my first act of sainthood is to declare my armor filthy and to deputize one scrawny angel to clean it."

"Again? Raine, in the next letter could I ask your brother for a *real* squire?"

"Up, you lazy child," he commanded, grabbing the pieces of steel, but as she stood at the door, loaded down, he gave her a fervent kiss. "To remember me by," he whispered before pushing her outside.

At the stream, Jocelin met her, five rabbits on a string across his shoulder. They spoke only briefly before Joss went back to the camp. He was spending more and more time with Rosamund.

Alyx tried her best to put the incident of the robberies out of her mind. Surely the people would not believe Blanche's insinuations.

Two seemingly uneventful days went by and then there was another robbery and again people looked at Alyx suspiciously. Blanche, Alyx thought. The woman had certainly been busy in the last few days.

Once, when she ladled herself a bowl of stew, someone jostled her and the hot broth burned her hand. It seemed to be an accident but she wasn't sure. Another time she heard two men loudly discussing people who thought they were better than others.

On the fourth day, as she was walking on the training field, a sword accidently cut her arm. At Raine's questioning, no one seemed to have had his hand on the sword, and when he made them all train an extra hour, they glowered at Alyx.

In the tent, Raine was quiet as he bound her wound.

"Say something!" she demanded.

"I don't like this. I don't like to see you hurt. Stay closer to me. Don't leave my sight."

She only nodded at him. Perhaps she had been too

hostile to these people. Perhaps they did deserve some of her time. She didn't know much about people really, only music. In Moreton she'd been popular because she gave people her music, but here they seemed to want something else. She knew Blanche was turning the people against her, but if she'd been kind over the last months Blanche wouldn't have had such an easy job.

That evening she borrowed Raine's lute and sat by the campfire and began to play. One by one, the people got up and left. For some reason this frightened her more than anything else.

For two days Alyx stayed close to Raine. The camp people now had someone to turn their hatred on, and they showed their feelings at every opportunity.

It was on the evening of the second day, while Alyx was just a few feet from Raine's side, that a man suddenly grabbed her and began searching her. Before Alyx could even cry out, the man yelled in triumph and held aloft a knife Alyx had never seen before.

"The boy took it," the man yelled. "We have proof."

Instantly, Raine was beside Alyx, pulling her behind him. "What does this mean?" he demanded.

The men grinned at the crowd gathering around them. "Your high-nosed little boy can't deny this," he said, holding the knife out for examination. "I found this in his pocket. I've had me suspicions for some time, but now we're all sure." He pushed his face close to Alyx's and his breath was foul. "Now you won't be thumin' your nose at us."

In seconds, he was picking himself up from the

ground where Raine had tossed him. "Get back to work!" Raine ordered.

The people, the crowd growing larger by the moment, refused to move. "He's a thief," someone said stubbornly. "Beat him."

"Tear the flesh off his back and then see how proud he is."

Alyx, eyes wide, moved behind Raine.

"The boy is no thief," Raine said stubbornly.

"You nobles talk about fair treatment," someone in the back yelled. "This boy steals from us and is allowed to go unpunished."

"No!" yelled at least five people.

Raine drew his sword, pointed it at them. "Get away, all of you. The boy is no thief. Now, who will be the first to lose his life over this lie?"

"We'll punish the boy," someone yelled before the crowd began to disperse.

Chapter Eleven

$\mathcal{I}$T WAS A very long while before Alyx could move away from the protection of Raine's solid form. Her knees were trembling and she clung to his arm.

"I didn't steal the knife," she finally managed to whisper.

"Of course not," Raine snapped, but she could tell from his expression that he wasn't dismissing the incident.

"What will happen now?"

"They will work to get what they want."

"And what is that?"

"A trial and your banishment. Before you came I promised them justice. I swore that all wrongdoers would be punished."

"But I have done no wrong," she said, on the verge of crying.

"Would you like to put that before a group of

them? They would find you guilty even if you were the Holy Mother."

"Buy why, Raine? I have done nothing to them. Last night I even tried to sing for them, but they turned away."

He was serious when he looked down at her. "Has your music always been enough for people? Has no one ever asked more of you than to sing prettily?"

She had no answer for him. For her there'd been no life except her music. To the people of her town all they'd expected of her was music, and it was enough for them as well as for herself.

"Come," Raine said. "We must make some plans."

Glumly, she followed him, her head down, not meeting an eye of anyone they passed. This anger directed toward her was something so new to her.

Once they were in the tent, Raine spoke quietly. "Tomorrow we will leave the forest."

"Leave? We? I don't understand."

"The people are poisoned against you, and it will no longer be safe for you to stay here. I cannot protect you every minute of the day and I cannot allow them to harm you. Tomorrow morning we'll leave."

Alyx, so aware of the hate of the people just outside the thin walls, could barely listen to him. "You cannot leave," she murmured. "The King will find you."

"Damn the King!" Raine said angrily. "I cannot stay here and worry that each day one of them will turn on you. You cannot sing your way out of this, Alyx. For all their look of it they are smarter than the horses you charm. They will do what they can to hurt you."

Alyx was beginning to listen to him. "You would go with me?"

"Of course. I couldn't very well let you leave alone. You wouldn't last a day outside in the world."

Tears blurred her eyes. "Because other people would also find out what I am? That I am a vain, arrogant person who cares for no one but herself?"

"Alyx, you are a sweet child and you care for me."

"Who could not love you?" she asked simply. "You have more kindness in your little finger than I have in all my body. And now you risk capture and imprisonment to save me."

"I will take you to my brother and—"

"And Gavin will risk the King's wrath because he harbors a woman wanted for witchcraft. Would you jeopardize all your family for me, Raine? Do you love me that much?"

"Yes."

Alyx's eyes flew to his, saw the love there, and instead of giving her pleasure it gave her pain. "I must be alone," she whispered. "I must think."

He followed her to the tent flap and as she left, he called Jocelin to him.

As Alyx made her way through the dark forest to the stream, her thoughts jumbled about in her mind. She sat on a rock, staring at the dark, sparkling water.

"Come out, Joss," she called. "You are a poor follower," she said despondently when he sat beside her. "Did Raine order you to protect me?"

Joss remained silent.

"He has to protect me now," she said. "He can't leave me alone for even minutes for fear someone will punish me."

"You have done no wrong."

"I have not stolen, true, but what good have I

done? Look at Raine. Now he could be in another country living in comfort, but he chooses to stay in this cold forest and help his countrymen. He protects them, sees that they are fed, works for them always. And yet there is a reward on his head and he must stay here while his family needs him. His sister is raped and commits suicide and in his grief he does not even stop work for an hour."

"Raine is a good man."

"He is a perfect man," she said.

"Alyx," Jocelin whispered, his hand on her arm, "Raine will protect you from the people, and what time he can't be near, I will be. Your love for him has helped him through his grief."

It came as no surprise to her that Joss knew she was a woman. "What good is my love? I am not worthy of him. Tomorrow he plans to leave this camp, to ride freely into the sunlight of a country where he is fair game for the King's wrath. He will leave the safety of the forest and risk prison or even death to protect me."

Again Jocelin was silent.

"Don't you have anything to say? No soothing words telling me Raine's life will be safe?"

"He will be in great danger if he leaves the forest. Raine is well-known and easily recognized."

A great sigh escaped Alyx. "How can I let him risk so much for me?"

"So what do you plan to do?" Joss asked sharply.

"I will leave by myself. I cannot stay and cause Raine worry, and he cannot leave with me. Therefore I will go alone."

Joss's laugh startled her. "I'm sure Raine Montgomery will be as obedient as a lap dog. You will inform him you plan to leave and he will meekly kiss you goodbye and wish you well."

"I am prepared for a fight."

"Alyx," Jocelin laughed. "Raine will toss you across his horse and carry you out of the forest. You can yell all you want, but when it comes to the point, muscle will win over words."

"You are right," Alyx gasped. "Oh, Joss, what can I do? He cannot risk his life for me."

"Love him," Joss said. "That's all he wants. Go with him, stay with him. See him through everything."

She jumped up from the rock, hands on hips, glaring at Jocelin. "What am I to do when he is killed because of me? Should I hold his cold hand and sing a sweet song to the Lord? No doubt I'll make magnificent music, and everyone will say how I must have loved him. No! I don't want cold hands. I want hot ones loving me—or loving anyone, for that matter. I'd rather give Raine back to Blanche than see him dead."

"Then how are you going to make him stay here?" Jocelin asked quietly.

She sat down again. "I don't know. Surely there must be something I could say. Perhaps if I insulted his family."

"Raine would laugh at you."

"True. Perhaps if I told him he were a . . ." She couldn't think of a single thing she hadn't already called him. Obviously names would not harm him. "Oh, Joss," she said desperately, "what can I do? Raine must be protected from himself. If he were to leave the forest no doubt he'd pursue Chatworth, and then the King would become involved in the quarrel and— I can't let it happen! What can I do?"

It was a long moment before Jocelin spoke and when he did, she barely heard him. "Go to bed with me."

"What!" She whirled on him. "I am talking to you of a man's safety, his possible death and you are trying to woo me to your bed? If you want a woman, get one of those hags who pant after you. Or take Rosamund to your bed. I'm sure she'd enjoy it more than I would."

"Alyx," he chuckled, hand on her arm. "Before you launch into me more fully, listen to me. If you are serious about Raine's staying here, there is nothing you can say to make him stay, but perhaps there is something you can do. He doesn't really know you very well, not enough to trust you, or perhaps no man ever trusts a woman. If Raine were to find you with another man there would be nothing you could say to make him take you back. He would let you go and he would stay here."

"He would hate me," she whispered. "He can have a violent temper."

"I thought you were serious about this. A moment ago you said you'd rather Blanche had him." He nearly choked on the woman's name. "Are you hoping that you can leave Raine now and later when he is again in the King's good graces, you can come back to him? That would only happen in a song you wrote yourself. The only way Raine Montgomery will let you leave this forest without him is if his feelings for you are totally reversed."

"To change his love to hate," she whispered.

"Do you dream of his standing and waving goodbye

to you, tears in his eyes?" Joss asked sarcastically. "Alyx, you love him too much to hurt him. Tomorrow let him take you out of here. His brothers will protect him until the King pardons Raine."

"No! No! No!" she shouted. "No one could protect him from an arrow. Even in this forest surrounded by guards, he was shot. To leave would risk death. How could I hurt him more than to kill him?"

She buried her face in her hands. "But to have him hate me! To change the way he looks at me from love to hate— Oh, Joss, that is a great price to pay."

"Do you want his love or his life? Would you rather sing over his grave or know he is alive but in another woman's arms?"

"I'm new to this idea of love, but right now the idea of another woman touching him makes me prefer his death."

Joss tried to keep from smiling. "Is that what you truly want?"

"No," she said softly. "I want him alive, but I also want him with me."

"You must choose one."

"And you believe the only way to get him to stay is to . . . to bed someone else?"

"I can think of nothing else."

Her eyes widened. "But what of you, Joss? Raine would be very angry with you."

"I daresay he will."

"What will you do? Your life here could be hell."

Joss cleared his throat. "If I want to keep my life, I think I should leave also. I wouldn't like to indulge in a duel with Raine after making love to his woman."

"Oh, Joss," she sighed. "I would be ruining your

life as well as mine. You're wanted for murder. What if someone recognizes you?"

She didn't see Joss start at her words. He had no idea she knew his history.

"I'll grow a beard and you, as a boy, will not be known. We'll sing together, play, and we'll be able to earn our keep."

Pagnell was her first thought, but she brushed it away. For the first time in her life she wasn't going to think of herself first. "Raine has had so much tragedy in his life. His sister's death was so recent, and now . . ."

"Make up your mind, Alyx, and get your clothes off. If I'm right, Raine is coming this way now."

"Now?" she gasped. "I need time to think."

"Choose," he said, close to her. "Dead and yours or alive and someone else's?"

The image of Raine quiet, forever silent, made her throw her arms about Jocelin's neck, her lips seeking his.

For many years, Jocelin had been an expert at removing women's clothes, and it was something he had not forgotten. Even if Alyx did wear boy's clothes, it was amazing how quickly Joss's skillful fingers rid her of them. Before she could come up for air, both of them were nude from the waist up, bare flesh against skin.

Jocelin entwined his hands in Alyx's hair and pulled her head back and kissed her hungrily as her eyes flew open in alarm.

She did not have a second to consider Joss's kiss because Raine's powerful hands pulled them apart, sending both of them flying across the stream bank.

"I will kill you," Raine said under his breath, his eyes boring into Jocelin's.

Alyx, dazed from the flight Raine's hands had sent her on, thrust her arms into her shirt as she saw Raine drawing his sword and bellowed, "No!" loud enough to make the trees drop their nighttime dew. Give me strength, she prayed as she stood.

She placed her body before Joss's. "I will give my life for this man," she said with feeling. As she saw the looks on Raine's face changing from bewilderment to hurt, to anger, to coldness, she felt them in her heart.

"Have I been a fool?" he asked quietly.

"Men are like music," she said as lightly as she could manage. "I cannot exist on a diet of love songs or alone on dirges. I need it all. I must have variety in men as well as in my songs. You, ah, you are a song of fury, of cymbals and drums, while Joss"—she fluttered her lashes—"Joss is a melody of flutes and harps."

For a moment, she thought perhaps Raine was going to tear her head from her body, and instead of feeling fear she was almost welcoming him. Her soul was praying that he wouldn't believe her. Could he truly believe that music meant more to her than he did?

"Go from my sight," he whispered from deep inside himself. "Let . . . your friend care for you from now on. Leave tonight. I do not want to see you again."

With that he turned to leave, and Alyx was several steps toward him before Joss grabbed her arm. "What can you say to him now except the truth?" he asked. "Leave him alone. Break the tie now. Wait here and I will return in a short while. Do you have any other clothes or other possessions?"

She shook her head and was barely aware that Jocelin left her alone.

There didn't seem to be any thoughts that went through her head as she waited for him to return. Raine believed her, believed that she thought her music was so very, very important. The people of the camp were willing to believe she was a thief and were eager to see her punished. Yet what had she ever done in her life to make anyone trust her, believe that she was a good person?

"Are you ready?" Jocelin asked from beside her, Rosamund a silent shadow behind him.

"I am sorry I have caused you—" she began.

"No more," Joss said firmly. "We must look to the future now."

"Rosamund, you will look after him? See that he eats? See that he doesn't train too hard?"

"Raine will not listen to me as he does to you," she said in her soft voice, her eyes devouring Jocelin.

"Kiss her," Alyx whispered. "Someone should give their love and not hide it." With that she turned away, and when she looked back she saw Rosamund clinging fiercely to Jocelin. When he returned to Alyx there was a look of surprise on his face.

"She loves you," Alyx said flatly before they started the long journey to reach the outer edges of the forest.

PART II

⚬

August 1502

Chapter Twelve

$\mathcal{A}$LYX PUT HER hand on the small of her back and eased herself down in a grassy patch just off the road, giving a grateful little smile to Joss when he handed her a cup of cool water.

"We'll rest here for tonight," he said, his eyes studying the tired lines on her face.

"No, we must play tonight—we need the money."

"You need rest more!" he snapped, then sat down beside her. "You win. You always do. Hungry?"

Alyx gave him a look that made him smile, and he glanced downward to her big belly as it pushed out the wool of her dress. The summer's heat and their constant walking made Alyx miserable.

It had been just over four months since they'd left Raine's camp, and in that time they'd barely stopped walking. At first it hadn't been difficult. They were both strong and healthy and they were popular musicians. But after a month on the road, Alyx became ill. She vomited so often people refused to travel with them, fearing the boy had some disease. And Alyx became so weak she could hardly walk.

They stayed for a week in a little village while Jocelin sat by the city gates and sang for pennies. Once Alyx came to him carrying bread and cheese, and as he watched her he thought how she'd changed since the time in the forest. Perhaps it was because he'd grown to care about her lately that she seemed to have grown lovelier, softer, prettier. Her boyish swagger had turned into a gentle, rolling, definitely female walk. And even though she'd been ill, she was gaining weight.

All of a sudden, it had hit Joss what was "wrong" with Alyx: she was carrying Raine's child. By the time she reached him he was laughing, and if they'd been alone, he'd have swirled her about in his arms.

"I will be a burden to you," Alyx said, but her eyes were alight. Before Joss could reply, she began chattering. "Do you think he will look like Raine? Would it be wrong to pray for a child to have dimples?"

"Let's save our prayers and wish for the means to dress you as a woman. If I travel with a pregnant boy I don't think I will live long."

"A dress," Alyx smiled, something soft and nice to make her feel like a woman again.

Once Jocelin was relieved of his feeling that Alyx was dying of some dread disease, he was more confident about allowing her to journey from castle to castle. And Alyx, after finding she had not lost all of Raine, was in much better spirits. She talked constantly about the baby, what it would look like, how

Raine's features would look on a girl and if she did have a girl, she hoped the child would not grow to be quite as big as her father. Alyx also laughed over the fact that she never did anything properly. Instead of being ill the first three months, she was ill the second three.

Joss listened to everything over and over again. He was so pleased she was no longer silent and sullen as she'd been for months after they left the forest. At night, sleeping on pallets on the floor of whatever house they were performing at, he often heard her crying, but she did not mention her sorrow during the day.

Once they played and sang at a large manor house belonging to one of Raine's cousins. Alyx had again become very silent, but he could almost feel her straining to hear any bit of news.

Jocelin had dropped a few hints to Montgomery's wife and the woman had told him much. Raine was still in the forest and King Henry, in his grief over the death of his eldest son, had nearly forgotten the outlawed nobleman. The King was much more worried about what to do with his son's wife, the Princess Katherine of Aragon, than what to do about a private feud. He ignored the petitions of the Montgomery family to punish Roger Chatworth. After all, Chatworth had not killed Mary Montgomery, only raped her. He had harmed her in no way. It was on the girl's soul that she committed suicide.

There was news that in July Judith Montgomery had borne a son and later in August Bronwyn Mac-Arran had also been delivered of a son. The Montgomery cousins were still incensed over Stephen's adoping the Scot's name and ways.

Alyx listened avidly to everything Jocelin reported to her.

"It's good that I'm no longer with him," she said quietly, strumming a lute. "His family is full of ladies while I am a lawyer's daughter. If I had stayed with him I don't believe I could have been docile or polite to his lady-wife and she wouldn't have wanted me near, though some of these ladies I see are cold-blooded wenches. Perhaps he could have used a little warmth."

Jocelin tried to show her that what was different between her and the ladies could be solved with a silk dress, but Alyx wouldn't see it. He knew she brooded not only over Raine but over the hatred of the people in the forest.

As Alyx's pregnancy advanced she grew quieter, more thoughtful, and she seemed much more aware of the world than she had been when he first met her. Once in a while, not often, really, she'd stop practicing to help someone do something. On the road they always traveled with a group rather than risk the highway robbers alone, and Alyx sometimes took a few children for a walk to give the mothers some peace, and once she shared her food with a toothless old beggar. Another time she prepared a meal for a man whose wife was lying under some trees giving birth to her eighth child.

The people smiled in gratitude and as a result they'd made friends wherever they traveled. A child once gave Alyx a little bouquet of wildflowers, and there'd been tears in Alyx's eyes.

"These mean a great deal to me," she'd said, clutching them tightly.

"She was repaying you for helping her yesterday.

The people here like you." He motioned to the travelers beside them.

"And not music," she whispered.

"Pardon?"

"They like me for something besides my music. And I have given them something besides music."

"You have given of yourself."

"Oh, yes, Joss," she laughed. "I have tried to do things that were difficult for me. Singing is so very, very easy."

Jocelin laughed with her. That anyone could say that music such as Alyx produced was easy was amazing.

Now, in August, when the burden of the heavy child was dragging on her, her steps were slower and slower and Joss wished they could afford to stay in one place for a length of time.

"Are you ready to go?" she asked, trying to heave herself upward. "We'll make the castle by nightfall if we hurry."

"Stay here, Alyx," he urged. "We have food."

"And miss the lady's betrothal celebration? No, once we're there we'll have plenty to eat, and all we have to do is create a divine bit of music celebrating the heiress's slender charms. I do so hope this one is pretty! The last one was so ugly I confessed the severity of the lies I sang to the priest."

"Alyx!" Joss said in mock chastisement. "Perhaps the lady was beautiful inside."

"Only you would think such a thing. Then, of course, with your face you can afford to be generous. I saw the way the ugly girl's mother threatened to devour you. Did she make you an offer after the singing?"

"You ask too many questions."

"Joss, you can't keep cutting yourself off from people and life. Constance is dead."

It had taken Alyx a long time to get him to tell her about the woman he'd once loved.

Jocelin set his jaw in such a way that Alyx knew he was refusing to speak of himself. Between them, her problems were common property while his were his own.

"Of course, none of the women have been as lovely as Rosamund. Except for her devil's mark, that is. That hideous thing makes it difficult to see any beauty at all. I wonder if it really is Satan's sign."

Jocelin whirled on her. "It is more likely a mark of God's favor because she is a good, kind, passionate woman."

"Passionate, is she?" Alyx teased as he turned away.

"You are cruel, Alyx," he whispered.

"No, I only want you to see that there is no reason for you to bury yourself with me. You cannot hold yourself inside. You have so much to give, yet you stay inside yourself."

When he looked at her, his eyes were cold. "Raine is not here, so why don't you find someone else to love? I've seen many men, from noblemen down to stable boy, give you looks. They'd take you even with your big belly. Why not marry some merchant who will give your child a home and who will make love to you every night?"

After his attack, she was quiet for a few moments. "Forgive me, Joss. I had hoped Rosamund could replace Constance, but I see she cannot."

Jocelin turned away because he didn't want Alyx to

see his face. Too often in the last months the face he remembered at night was Rosamund's, not Constance's. Rosamund, so silent, almost apologizing for her existence, was quite often the woman he saw, not as the quiet, gentle woman he knew but as the woman who'd kissed him goodbye. For the first time since Constance's death, a spark had shot through him. Not that there hadn't been a few women here and there, but before he'd met Constance and since then he'd been detached, always apart from the women. Only that one brief time when he'd held Rosamund had he felt even a flicker of real desire, real interest in a woman.

Joss took Alyx's hand in his and together they started toward the castle that loomed ahead of them. It was an old place, one tower crumbling, and Alyx knew they'd have another drafty sleeping place. In the last months of traveling she'd learned a great deal about the nobility. Perhaps the most significant thing was that noble women had as little freedom as women anywhere. She'd seen great ladies with blackened eyes from their husband's beatings. She'd seen weak, cowardly noblemen who were treated with contempt by their wives. There were matches of great love, couples who hated each other, households of great decadence and some based on love and respect. She'd begun to realize that nobles had problems very similar to those of the people in her own small town.

"Daydreaming?"

"Thinking about my home, what a protected childhood I had. I almost wish my music hadn't set me apart from everyone else. It makes me feel as if I don't quite belong anywhere."

"You belong wherever you want."

"Joss," she said seriously, "I don't deserve either you or Raine. But someday I hope I can do something worthy."

"Did you know you talk more like Raine every day?"

"Good!" she laughed. "I hope I can rear his child to be even half as good as he is."

As they approached the old castle, they had to wait to be admitted, since there were hundreds of people entering before them. The betrothal was to join two powerful, rich households and the guests and entertainment were to be sumptuous.

Joss kept his arm around Alyx's shoulders as he led her through the crushing crowds.

"Are you the singers?" a tall woman shouted down at Alyx.

Alyx nodded up at her, awed by the dark, steel-banded hair, the richness of her gown.

"Follow me."

Gratefully, Alyx and Jocelin followed her up a narrow, winding stone stairway to a large round room at the top of the tower, where several women were pacing and showing signs of agitation. In the center of the room was a young woman wailing loudly.

"Here she is," a woman beside Alyx said.

Alyx looked up at an angelic face, blonde hair, blue eyes, an ethereal, delicate smile.

"I am Elizabeth Chatworth."

Alyx's eyes widened at the name, but she said nothing.

Elizabeth continued. "I'm afraid our little bride-to-be is terrified," she said in a tone of exasperation and disgust. "Do you think you could calm her enough so that we could get her downstairs?"

"I will try."

"If you can't, then I'll have to put my hand to her cheek and see if that music will quieten her."

Alyx had to smile at this sweet-looking woman's words. They did not fit her face at all. "What is she frightened of?" she asked, trying to decide what music to play.

"Life. Men. Who knows? We have both just come from the convent, and you'd think Isabella was going to her death."

"Perhaps her betrothed—"

"He's manageable," Elizabeth said with a wave of dismissal. Her eyes went to Jocelin, who was staring openly at Elizabeth. "You're pretty enough to not frighten the rabbit," she said. A loud wail from Isabella sent Elizabeth to her side.

"My goodness," Alyx said, feeling as if she'd just left a storm. "I don't believe I've ever met anyone quite like her before."

"And I pray we don't again," Joss said. "She calls us. Heaven help the man who dares disobey that one, although . . ."

Alyx looked up at him, saw the speculative gleam in his eye. "She'll have your hair if you disobey her."

"It's not my hair she'd remove, and damned if I'd mind letting her."

Before Alyx could reply, Joss pushed her toward the crying bride.

It took an hour to calm the woman, and all the while Elizabeth Chatworth paced behind the chair, now and again narrowing her eyes at the weeping Isabella. Once she opened her mouth to say something but Alyx, fearing the woman would ruin what she and Joss had accomplished, sang even louder to cover the beginning of Elizabeth's sentence.

When at last Isabella was ready to go downstairs, all of her maids went with her, leaving Jocelin and Alyx alone with Elizabeth Chatworth.

"You did well," Elizabeth said. "You have a magnificent voice, and unless I miss my guess you are well trained."

"I have spent some time with a few teachers," Alyx said modestly.

Elizabeth's eyes fixed on Jocelin in a piercing gaze. "I have seen you before. Where?"

"I knew your sister-in-law, Alice," he answered softly.

Elizabeth's eyes turned hard. "Yes," she said, with a brief, insolent look up and down Joss's form. "You would be her type. Or perhaps any man with the proper equipment is pleasing to her."

Jocelin had an expression on his face Alyx had never seen before. She wished he'd say no more. After all, it was Joss who'd killed Edmund Chatworth, Elizabeth's brother.

"And how are your brothers?" Joss asked, and there was challenge in his voice.

For a long moment Elizabeth's eyes bored into his, and Alyx held her breath, praying Elizabeth would not know who Joss was.

"My brother Brian has left my home," she said quietly, "and we do not know where he is. There is rumor that he is held by one of the filthy Montgomerys."

Jocelin's hand clamped down on Alyx's shoulder brutally. "And Roger?" he asked.

"Roger . . . has changed. Now!" she said smartly.

"If we are through discussing my family, I am sure you are wanted below." With that, she swept from the room.

"Filthy!" Alyx yelled before the door was closed. "Her brother kills my Raine's sister and she dares call us filthy!"

"Alyx, calm yourself. You cannot take on a woman like Elizabeth Chatworth. She'd eat you alive. You don't know what kind of brother she grew up around. Edmund was mean, vicious, and I've seen Elizabeth stand up to him at times when even Roger backed down. And she adores her brother Brian. If she thought the Montgomerys caused him to be taken from her home, she'd be full of hate."

"But she has no right! It was the Chatworths' fault."

"Quiet! and let's go downstairs." He eyed her sharply. "And none of your tricks of writing songs about feuds. Do you understand me?"

She nodded once, but she didn't like making such a promise.

It was late at night, and most of the guests were lying drunken on the floor or sprawled across the tables when a servant whispered to the man sitting in the corner. With a smile, the man rose and went outside to greet these newly arrived guests.

"You'll never believe who is here," the man said to the one dismounting.

"What! no greeting?" he asked sarcastically. "No concern for my safety? Come, John, you're letting your teeth show."

"I have remained sober to tell you this. That should be enough."

"True, that is a great sacrifice." He gave the reins of his horse to a waiting servant. "Now, what is so important that it can't wait until I've had some wine myself?"

"Ah, Pagnell, you're too impatient. Remember that little songbird this winter? The one who knocked you over the head?"

Pagnell stiffened, glaring at John. It was all he could do to keep from fingering the ugly scar on his forehead. He'd had headaches ever since that night, and although he'd tortured to death some of the people from her town, no one would tell him where she was. Every time a pain shot through his head, he vowed he'd see her burn for what she'd done to him. "Where is she?"

John laughed deep in his throat. "Inside and swelled out with a brat. She's traveling with a pretty lad and the two of them are singin' as pretty as you please."

"Now? I thought everyone would be asleep."

"They are, but I marked where the lad and the songbird stretched out."

Pagnell stood still for a moment, contemplating his next move. When he and his friends had gone over the town wall looking for Alyx, he'd been drunk and so had bungled the job. Now he mustn't make that mistake again.

"If she cried out," Pagnell said, "would she receive help?"

"Most of them are dead drunk; the snoring's so loud a charge of gunpowder might not be heard."

Pagnell looked up at the old stone walls. "Does this place have a dungeon, some place for keeping prisoners before they're executed?"

"Why wait? We'll tie her to a stake and burn her as the sun rises."

"No, some people frown at that, and with the King in this melancholy mood, who knows how he'll react? We'll do this legal. A cousin of mine is conducting court not far from here. We'll toss the slut in the cellar, then I'll talk to my cousin and when I return, we'll have a trial. *Then* we'll watch her burn. Now show me where she is."

Alyx was lying in an uncomfortable sleep, trying her best to position her big stomach, when a hideous whisper sounded in her ear. The voice, one she had never forgotten, and never would, sent shivers down her spine, made her skin tighten.

"If you want your little play fellow to live, you'll be quiet," came the voice.

Pressed against her throat was the sharp steel of a knife. She didn't need to open her eyes to see Pagnell's face leering into hers. It was a face that had haunted her dreams for months.

"Have you thought about me, sweetheart?" he whispered, his face very, very close to hers. His hands went down to caress her hard stomach. "You gave to somebody else what you fought me for. You're going to die for that."

"No," Alyx whispered as the knife pressed forward.

"You going to go peacefully, or do I have to slip a knife into his heart?"

She knew well who he meant. Jocelin was asleep not a foot from her, his breath coming even and deep, not even aware that her life was in danger.

"I'll go," she managed to say.

Trembling, too frightened to cry, Alyx heaved

herself upward, Pagnell's knife scraping, cutting the skin of her throat once. It wasn't easy to make her way through the bodies sprawled on the floor. Each time she stumbled, Pagnell twisted her arm behind her back, almost pulling it from the socket.

When they came to the dark, cold, stone stairs leading downward, he pushed Alyx so hard she slammed into the wall and tripped down four steps until she caught her balance. Pausing for a moment, her hands protectively on her belly, she tried to catch her breath.

"Go on," Pagnell sneered, pushing her again.

Alyx managed to get down to the bottom without falling again. The room they were in was cold and totally dark, the ceiling very low. Barrels and sacks of stores crowded the floor. She whirled when she heard the door creak open.

Pagnell stood in front of a heavy door, open to reveal a yawning black nothingness. "In here," he growled.

"No." She backed away, but the room was so crowded there was nowhere to go.

He grabbed a handful of her hair and with one shove, slammed her into the blackness.

Crouching in a corner, surrounded by the cold blackness, she saw the door shut, blocking off the last ray of light, and heard the heavy iron bolt shoot into place.

Chapter Thirteen

THE HIDEOUS LITTLE room seemed to be the epitome of every nightmare, every bad thought, every horrible story she'd ever heard. There was no light, and even after an hour she still could not see her hand before her face. For a very long time she remained huddled in the corner where Pagnell had tossed her, afraid to move.

If she could not see, she could certainly hear the noises of insects on the walls and floor, sounding loud and treacherous. What made her finally move was something scampering across the soft leather of her shoes. With a little squeal, she came upright, her hands trying to clutch the stones of the wall behind her.

"Calm yourself, Alyx," she said aloud, and her voice echoed off the walls. It would be morning before long and Jocelin would be looking for her—if he were still alive. No, she couldn't depend on anyone getting her out of here. She had to try to find her own means of escape.

Cautiously, hands out like a blind person, she took a step forward and nearly fell across a low bench. Kneeling, she ran her hands over it and was glad to see that she could make out the shadow of it. When she'd finished her exploration of the bench, she moved to the walls, feeling her way to the door. For all the door gave when she pushed against it, she might have been trying to move the stone walls.

The room was about six feet square with stone walls and a dirt floor, and the only furniture was the short bench. There was no window in the door and no light came in around the corners. The low ceiling allowed her to explore every inch of the room. There were no windows, no gratings, no weak places anywhere. When she finished, the upper half of her body was covered with spiderwebs, and there were tears on her face. Angrily, she tried to brush the sticky things from her face and clothes, all the while crying and cursing Pagnell and men of his kind.

After several hours she sat down on the bench, knees drawn up, and put her head down. Absently, she pushed the baby's foot down from where it was kicking her in the ribs, and as her child became more active, restless, she started to sing to him. Gradually, he quietened and so did Alyx.

Overhead, she heard people walking and knew the ceiling was the castle floor. Somewhere up there Jocelin was trying to find her. She began to imagine ways to escape and wished she could start a fire, thinking that perhaps she could burn her way out.

But, of course, the smoke would probably kill her before the fire burned the door.

When the door opened, the sound, so loud in the quiet room, startled her so badly she nearly fell off the bench. Candlelight flooded the room and nearly blinded her.

"There you are," came a voice she knew was Elizabeth Chatworth's.

Alyx gave no thought to her class as she threw her arms about Elizabeth. "I am so very, very glad to see you. How did you find me?"

Elizabeth gave Alyx a one-arm hug. "Jocelin came to me. It's that idiot Pagnell, isn't it? That man is as vicious as any man created. Now, come on before the dunce returns."

"Too late," came a drawling, half-amused, half-angry voice from the doorway. "You haven't changed much, Elizabeth, you're still giving orders to everyone."

"And you, Pagnell, are still tearing wings off butterflies. What has this one done to you? Refused your advances as any woman with any sense would do?"

"Your tongue is too sharp, Elizabeth. If I had time I'd teach you softer ways."

"You and how many other men?" Elizabeth spat. "You're scared to death of me because what I say is true. Now get out of the way and let us pass. We've had enough of your nasty little games. Go find someone else to play with. This child is under my protection."

He planted himself in front of Elizabeth and Alyx, not letting them out of the little cell.

"You go too far!" Elizabeth hissed. "You're no

longer threatening a helpless servant. My brother will have your head if you harm me."

"Roger is too busy plotting against the Montgomerys to give a thought to anyone else. I hear he stays drunk all the time now that dear, sweet, crippled Brian has gone off sulking somewhere."

Alyx didn't see the little eating dagger Elizabeth pulled from the sheath at her side, but Pagnell did. With a sidestep he dodged her, caught her arm and, twisting it, pulled her to him. "I'd like to feel you under me, Elizabeth. Do you bring as much fire to your bed as you do to everything else?"

Alyx saw that now was her chance. On the wall outside the cell, to her left, was a heavy ring of keys. In one swift motion she flung them at Pagnell's head, catching him on the temple.

He released Elizabeth, staggered back one step and put his hand to his head, stared at the blood on his hand. By the time he regained his senses, Elizabeth and Alyx were halfway up the stairs.

Pagnell caught Elizabeth's skirt and jerked so hard she came tumbling backward, slamming into his chest. "Ah, my dear Elizabeth," he drawled into her ear, his arm about her waist, the other hand going to her ample breast. "I've dreamed of this moment for a long time."

Alyx knew Pagnell's attention was on Elizabeth and she could have escaped, but she couldn't leave Elizabeth alone because it was obvious what he planned for the young noblewoman. She could think of nothing else but to throw her body weight onto both of them.

Pagnell stumbled backward, still clutching Elizabeth, while Alyx rolled away, her hands protecting her stomach. Elizabeth saw her opportunity and slammed her elbow into Pagnell's ribs, making him grunt in pain. With one swift motion she grabbed a small oaken cask and brought it down with considerable force on Pagnell's head.

Oak staves broke away and dark red wine ran down his face, over his clothes as, after one startled look, he lapsed into unconsciousness.

"Such a waste of good wine," Elizabeth said, looking across the inert man to Alyx. "You haven't harmed your baby, have you?"

"No, he's secure enough."

"Thank you," Elizabeth said. "You could have run away, but you stayed to help me. How can I reward you?"

"Excuse me," came a voice from the doorway.

They turned to see a tall dark man, sword drawn.

"I hate to interrupt this little meeting, but unless you revive my friend and quickly, I shall take pleasure in killing the both of you."

Elizabeth made the first move, jumping away from Pagnell's body to the dark man's right side. "Go to his other side, Alyx," she directed. "He cannot take both of us at once."

Immediately, Alyx obeyed, and the man moved his head back and forth like a baited bull, watching the two women. A groan from Pagnell made the man look at his friend. As he did, Alyx made a quick move toward him. He backed into the opening of the stairway, guarding the entrance.

"God's teeth!" Pagnell cursed, trying to clear his vision. "You'll be sorry for this, Elizabeth," he groaned. "Hold them there, John. Don't let them get nearer. Neither of them is human. Pity to man the day woman was created."

"You wouldn't know what a woman was," Elizabeth hissed. "No female worth her salt would let you near her."

Shakily, Pagnell stood, looking in disgust at his wine-stained doublet. Suddenly, his head came up and he began to smile at Elizabeth in a nasty way. "Last night when I rode in I saw the camp of Miles Montgomery." He grinned broader at the way Elizabeth stiffened at the name. "I wonder if Miles would like a guest? I heard he was so angry at the death of his sister that his brother sent him to the Isle of Wight to keep him from declaring open war on the Chatworth family."

"My brother would annihilate him," Elizabeth said. "No Montgomery—"

"Spare me, Elizabeth, especially since from the story I heard, Roger attacked Stephen Montgomery's back."

Elizabeth leaped for him, hands made into claws, and Pagnell caught her to him.

"I hear Miles is a great lover of women and has many bastards. Would you like to add yours to his stable, my virginal little princess?"

"I would die first," she said with feeling.

"Perhaps. I'll leave that up to Miles. I would take care of you myself, but first I have a debt owed me by that one." He motioned his head toward Alyx, who stood quietly, John's sword in her back.

"And how do you get me out of here?" Elizabeth asked, smiling. "Do you think there won't be a protest if you carry me through the hall?"

Pagnell seemed to consider this for a moment as he looked about the dark cellar. With a smile, he looked back at her. "How do you think Miles will like playing Caesar?"

Puzzled, Elizabeth had no reply.

Pagnell grabbed her arm behind her. "John, watch that one carefully while I take care of Elizabeth. My head hurts too much to tussle with both of them again."

"More than your head will hurt if you harm me," Elizabeth warned.

"I'll leave that worry to Miles. The Montgomerys are altogether too high above themselves. I'd like to see all of them brought down, their land dispersed."

"Never!" Alyx shouted. "No slime-infested carrion such as you will ever destroy a Montgomery."

The full power of Alyx's voice made all of them stop and stare at her. Elizabeth stopped struggling against Pagnell and her gaze on Alyx turned speculative. Pagnell's look was calculating.

John gave Alyx a nudge with his sword tip. "Raine Montgomery is said to be hiding in the forests somewhere, king of a band of criminals."

"This bears investigation," Pagnell said, giving Elizabeth's arm a twist. "But first we must deal with this one." Pulling her with him, he grabbed a length of hemp rope from atop a pile of wine barrels and began to tie Elizabeth's hands behind her back.

"Think what you're doing," Elizabeth said. "I'm not some—"

"Shut up!" Pagnell commanded, clipping her on the shoulder with his fist. When her hands were bound, he pushed her onto grain sacks and bound her ankles. With his knife he cut a piece of red silk from her dress. "A kiss, Elizabeth?" he teased, holding the gag close to her lips. "Just one before Miles Montgomery takes them all?"

"I'll see you in hell first."

"I'm sure you'll be there with me if some man doesn't dull the edges of that tongue of yours."

Before she could speak again, he tied the cloth tightly over her mouth. "Now you look almost appealing."

"What do you do with her now?" John asked. "We can't very well carry her out like that."

From a far corner of the cellar Pagnell picked up a dirty, moth-eaten piece of canvas and, after a couple of shakes which sent dust flying, he spread it at Elizabeth's feet. "We shall roll her in this and carry her out sight unseen."

Alyx watched Elizabeth, her eyes widening with fear now, but all Alyx could think of was that Elizabeth would be much better off with Miles than anyone else. "You'll be safe with Miles," she said, trying to reassure Elizabeth.

Again, they all stared at Alyx, but she ignored them. Elizabeth needed her help now.

Not at all gently, Pagnell pushed Elizabeth onto the filthy canvas and rolled her in it, hiding her completely.

"Can she breathe?" Alyx asked.

"Who cares? If she dies she can tell no tales. As it is, after Miles finishes with her she won't even remember me."

"Miles won't harm her," Alyx said passionately. "He's good and kind like his brother."

Pagnell laughed at that. "No one has ever had a temper to match Miles's. As soon as he finds she's a

Chatworth . . . oh, I almost envy him, but I'm not a fool like Miles. He won't care about Roger Chatworth, and when Roger hears what Miles has done to his beloved baby sister— The King will have all the Montgomery lands to award to him who does favors for the King. And I shall be there to collect."

"You are a vile pig of a creature."

The back of Pagnell's hand slammed into Alyx's jaw, sending her reeling. "I'll ask for the advice of an underling like you when I want it. Is it Raine Montgomery who's put ideas into your head? The man thinks he can reform all of England. He hides in the forest and sneers at anything material, spouting about the old ways of honor and nobility while the people of your class grow fat and rich."

Alyx wiped blood from the corner of her mouth. "Raine is worth a hundred of you," she said.

"Raine is it? No 'Lord Raine'? Do you carry his brat? Is that what makes you think you're so high and mighty? When the flames lick up your legs we shall see if the name of Montgomery is so gentle on your lips. John!" he said sharply. "Take Elizabeth away. Give her to Miles Montgomery and see what he wants to do with her. And John," he warned, "Elizabeth's virginity is a known fact, and I want her to arrive at Miles's feet intact. Let all of Roger Chatworth's wrath come onto the Montgomery heads and not mine. Do I make myself clear?"

John gave him an insolent look as he tossed the bundle containing Elizabeth across his shoulder. "Montgomery will receive her in the best possible condition."

"But make sure he is inclined to forget she is a

high-born lady. See if you can rearrange her clothing to stir his blood."

With a parting grin, John left the cellar.

"What do you want from me?" Alyx asked, backing away from Págnell as he came closer to her. "I have done you no wrong."

He glared at her big belly. "You have given to another man what should have been mine." He grabbed her arm and pushed a small, sharp dagger to her ribs. "Now, go up the stairs and out the door and then to the stables. If you make a single sound it will be your last."

Her breath held, Alyx had no choice but to obey him. Once in the great hall there were guests milling about, but no one paid the least attention to Pagnell and the cheaply clad girl. They were nursing swollen heads and bruised bodies from where they'd slept across stools and tables.

Alyx searched for Jocelin, but she saw no sign of him. Every time she attempted to move her head, Pagnell's knife pushed harder against her until she kept her head straight. Perhaps Jocelin didn't know she was in trouble. Perhaps he was with a woman and hadn't yet discovered she was missing from the hall. For all their closeness, they respected each other's privacy. There were whole days when they didn't see each other and no questions were asked later.

Outside, Pagnell pushed her toward the stables, where he bellowed to a servant to saddle his horse. Before Alyx could think, she was slammed into the saddle, Pagnell behind her, and they set off at a pace that made Alyx's teeth jar.

It was nightfall when they finally stopped before a

tall stone house at the edge of a small village. Pagnell pulled her from the horse, grabbed her arm and dragged her to the door.

A short, fat, balding man greeted them. "You took longer than I thought. Now what is so important I must wait for you this late at night?"

"This," Pagnell said, pushing Alyx into the room before him. It was a large, dark room, a few candles on a table at one end.

"What do I care for a dirty, pregnant lowling like that? Surely you could have found a tastier bit than that for your sport."

"Get over there," Pagnell commanded, pushing her toward the table. "If you say one word I'll slit your throat."

Too tired to reply, Alyx moved, sank down to the floor before an empty fireplace in a shapeless heap.

"Explain," the fat man said to Pagnell.

"What, uncle, no welcome, no wine?"

"If your news is good enough, I will feed you."

Pagnell sat down in a chair before the table, studying the sputtering candles. It wasn't that his uncle was so poor that made him use such cheap tallow but that for the last three years the man had done little except wait for his own death.

"What are your feelings toward Raine Montgomery?" Pagnell asked softly, watching with interest as his uncle's face turned from white to red to purple.

"How can you say that man's name to me in my own house?" he gasped. Three years before, in a tournament, Raine had killed Robert Digges's only child. No matter that the son had been trying to kill Raine rather than just unhorse him or that his son had already killed one man and severely wounded another that day. It had been Raine's lance that had taken Robert's son's life.

"I thought you felt the same way," Pagnell smiled. "Now I have a way to repay the man."

"How can you? The man hides in the forest and not even the King can find him."

"But our good king doesn't have the bait that I do."

"No!" Alyx shouted, getting to her feet with what strength she had left.

"See," Pagnell said, amused, "with every breath she takes she defends the man. Whose child do you carry?"

Alyx gave him a stubborn look. If she hadn't tried to reassure Elizabeth about the Montgomery men, Pagnell wouldn't know about her relationship with Raine, but Elizabeth had helped her.

"Pagnell," Robert commanded, "tell me all of your story."

Briefly, Pagnell told his version of the story, that Alyx had used her voice to entice him. Then, when he'd gotten close, she'd disappeared into thin air. Later, he'd gone looking for her and she'd leapt on him with the force of demons. He showed his uncle the scar on his head. "Could a little thing like that have left such a scar unless she were helped by the Devil?"

Robert gave a weak laugh, a snort of derision. "It sounds to me like she outsmarted you."

"She's a witch, I tell you."

Robert waved his hand in dismissal. "All women are witches to some extent. What does the girl have to do with Raine Montgomery?"

"I believe she's spent the last few months in his

camp and it's his child she carries. If we were to let it be known that we mean to burn her as a witch, he'd come after her. And when he does, we'd be ready for him. You could have him, and we could share the King's reward."

"Wait a minute, boy," Robert interrupted. "Look at her! You mean to use that as bait? Raine Montgomery can have his pick of women. No doubt there are lean pickings in the forest and she probably does carry his child, but why would he risk his life to come after *that?* And why would you spend so much time searching for a flat-chested, hipless, plain-faced child such as her?"

Pagnell gave his uncle a look of contempt before turning to Alyx. "Sing!" he commanded.

"I will not," she said firmly. "You plan to murder me anyway, so why should I obey you?"

"You will die," he said evenly, "but the question is whether you will burn before or after the child's birth. If you disobey me I will see that the child dies with you. Now sing for your child's life."

Alyx obeyed him instantly, her hands on her stomach as she lifted her voice in a plea to God for her child's life.

There was a long silence when she finished, both men watching her intently.

Robert, rubbing away the chills on his forearms, spoke first. "Montgomery will come after her," he said with conviction.

Pagnell smiled in satisfaction, glad his uncle could see why he'd spent so many months searching for the girl. "In the morning we begin the trial, and when she's found guilty we will tie her to a stake. Montgomery'll come for her and we'll be ready for him."

"How can you be sure he'll hear of this in time? And if he does come, are you sure you can take him?"

"I tossed the chit in a cellar for a few hours and let it be known to the pretty boy she was with what I planned to do with her. He rode away like a shot and I'm sure he was headed south toward the forest where Montgomery hides. And as for men, there won't be time for him to collect them. Now he's surrounded by criminals and out-of-works. None of them can ride a horse, much less wield a sword."

Alyx bit her lower lip to keep from defending Raine. It was much better that Pagnell thought Raine defenseless; perhaps then Pagnell would send only a few men to capture Raine.

What was she thinking about? Raine would never come after her after what she'd done to him. She doubted very much if he'd speak to Jocelin. The forest guards reported to Raine whenever someone approached, and all Raine had to do was refuse Joss entrance—which he'd surely do. If Jocelin tried to sneak into the forest, Raine could order the guards to kill him. No! Raine wouldn't do that, would he? And what if Jocelin did somehow get to Raine? Would Raine believe Joss? Would he care what happened to Alyx?

"He'll come," Pagnell repeated. "And when he does, we'll be ready for him."

Chapter Fourteen

ALYX LOOKED OUT the window of the small stone-walled room and into the courtyard below, watching with horrified fascination as the carpenters built the gallows for her burning. It had been eight long, terrifying days since she'd been taken by Pagnell, and during that time she'd been subjected to a fiasco of a trial.

The men who ran the trial had been some of Pagnell's relatives, and he'd easily persuaded them to his views. Alyx listened to it all, for they talked about her as if she weren't there, and her head echoed with Raine's words.

Raine and she had argued so many times about the rising middle class. Alyx had always adored King Henry, loved the way he was taking away the power from the nobles, was forcing the nobles to pay wages and no longer own serfs. But Raine said the King was turning the nobles into fat merchants, that if the ruling class had to count pennies they would forget their knightly virtues, would no longer know the meaning of honor. She talked of people being more equal, but Raine asked who would do the fighting if England were attacked. If there weren't a class of people freed from money making to stay strong and practice warfare, who would protect England?

As Alyx sat through the "trial," she began to see more clearly what Raine meant. The judges didn't for a minute believe she was a witch, and Alyx marveled at this because the people in her town believed quite strongly in witches, and had a multitude of ways to protect themselves from evil curses.

All the judges cared about was winning the King's favor and reaping the rewards that came with the King's pleasure. Pagnell told them that she carried Raine Montgomery's child and, like vultures, they jumped on this fact. Raine had been declared a traitor, and with a little more pushing, he could have his lands given to someone else. King Henry loved to create his own nobles, to give out titles to anyone rich enough to buy one. The judges hoped he would give some of the Montgomery lands to them if they delivered Raine—or his head—to the King.

Alyx sat silently through the whole proceedings as they plotted and planned, laughed and argued. At the end, they pushed her into a cart and drove her through the little town—she didn't even know its name—a man walking before her declaring her to be a witch.

As if she were someone else, Alyx watched the people cross themselves, make crosses of their fingers, turn away lest she look on them with an evil eye, and the bolder ones threw food and offal at her. She wanted to cry out that what was being done to her had nothing to do with witchcraft but greed—the greed of men already rich. But as she looked at the fascinated/scared expressions of the dirty, diseased people, she knew she could not reason with them. She was not going to do away with centuries of ignorance in a few minutes.

When the cart ride was over she was dragged to the ruins of an old stone castle, one tower standing, and pushed up the stairs. Many hours later she was given a small bowl of water and Alyx washed the stench from her body as best she could.

They kept her there for days, guards on the floor below and more on the roof. At night the townspeople gathered to circle the tower and chant exorcisms to guard themselves against her evil. Alyx merely sat in the center of the cold little room and tried to listen to the music that ran through her head. She knew the judges delayed her execution to give Raine time to arrive to rescue her. She prayed with all her might for his safety, pleaded with God to let him realize he was walking into a trap. The judges and Pagnell had been so right when they said that Raine could not go for his own knights. In fact, Pagnell had taken his own men north to Raine's home to guard that Raine did not ride there first.

Alyx sat and thought over the men in Raine's camp, what poor soldiers they were, how lazily they trained —and how much they hated her. "Please," she prayed, "do not let Raine come alone. If he comes, let him have a guard and let the men protect him."

Before daylight on the ninth day, a fat, stinking old woman came bearing a plain white linen sheath for

Alyx to wear. Without a protest, calmly, Alyx slipped it on, leaving it loose over her stomach. At the proceedings she'd pleaded for her child's life, but the men had only given her a blank look, totally uninterested in her. One of the judges told Pagnell to silence her and one slap from him had made Alyx hold her tongue. There was nothing she could say to sway them anyway. They figured they had to burn her now while Raine was still hot for her and the child must also be endangered. Pagnell laughed and said he'd hold Raine and make him watch while Alyx burned.

With her chin high, using all her strength to control the shaking in her knees, Alyx descended the stairs before the old woman who carried Alyx's dress over her arm—pay for risking being in the same room with the witch.

A priest waited at the foot of the stairs, and quickly, Alyx made her confession, denying that she was a witch or that she carried the Devil's child. With an air of disbelief, he blessed and sent her on her way.

It must have looked strange, Alyx thought, for someone of her size to be escorted by so many large men: one in front, one in back, two on each side. The clanking of the full armor they wore was the only thing louder than the pounding of her heart as she fixed her eyes on the platform in front of her. A tall stake reached skyward and all around it was a pile of brush and dried grasses.

The crowd was joyous as they watched her approach, jubilant at the special treat that awaited them. Not many witches were burned nowadays.

As Alyx climbed the stairs, the guards kept her circled, their backs to her as their eyes scanned the horizon. Involuntarily, Alyx also looked at the landscape. Hope and fear mixed together within her. She feared for Raine's life should he try to save her, yet she hoped she would not have to die.

A guard grabbed her arm, pulled her to the stake and tightly tied her wrists behind her.

Alyx lifted her eyes skyward, fully aware that this would be the last time she'd see the day. The early morning sunlight was just lightening the day and she looked across the high brush and into the crowd. It was bad, very bad, that these were the last faces she'd ever see, that she'd go to Heaven—or Hell—with these faces on her mind.

Closing her eyes, she tried to picture Raine.

"Get on with it," came a voice that made Alyx open her eyes. Voices were life to her; she'd more likely remember a voice than a face or a name. Scanning the crowd, she saw no one she knew. They all seemed to be an especially dirty, scarred lot.

"Let me light the fire," came the voice again, and this time Alyx looked into Rosamund's eyes. A chill went all over her skin, her scalp tightening and a tiny flame of hope surged through her.

The guards, all around her, were taking their time in lighting the fire as they studied the country around them, looking for some sign of a knight and his men.

Not sure whether to trust her eyes, she looked at the crowd again.

"What're ye waitin' for?" came a voice Alyx knew as well as her own. There, in the forefront, with blackened teeth and a dirty, bloody bandage over one eye was Jocelin. Beside him stood a man Alyx recognized from the forest camp, one of the men who'd accused her of stealing. They were changed, some looking dirtier than she remembered, but the whole forest camp was there, gazing up at her with half-smiles of conspiracy as they saw she recognized them.

In spite of all she could do, tears began coursing down her cheeks, but through her blurred vision she could see that Joss was trying to say something to her. It took a long moment to understand what he was mouthing.

"This fire should make the witch sing loudly," he said, and Alyx recognized exasperation in his voice.

Surreptitiously, she glanced at the guards as they frowned at the bare distance, never even glancing at the crowd at the foot of the platform.

"We've waited long enough," said one of the black-robed judges from behind Alyx. "Let the witch burn."

One of the guards lowered a flaming torch toward the bracken and as he did so, Alyx filled her lungs to capacity with air. Desperation, fear, hope, joy, all combined in her voice and the note she emitted was so strong, so loud, that for a moment everyone was paralyzed.

Jocelin was the first to move. With a cry much like Alyx's, he leaped to the top of the platform and behind him came twenty men and women. One confessed murderer threw his weight onto the guard holding the torch, sending the flames backward, to land in the pile of branches behind Alyx, where they went up instantly.

There were six guards and four judges on the platform. The judges ran away at the first sign of trouble, their robes raised to their knees, flying out behind them.

Smoke curled around Alyx's body as she watched the men and women fight the steel-clad knights. With each blow that hit flesh she felt it in her own. These people she had treated so badly were risking their lives to save her.

The smoke grew thicker, making her cough and her eyes water. Heat, like the hottest sun, hurt the back of her. Trying to see, she looked at the people around her, fully aware how fragile they were compared to the knights in their heavy armor. Her only consolation was that Raine had been sensible enough not to risk his life in this fight. At least he'd stayed away somewhere safe.

It was some time before she became aware that one of the knights was not being attacked by the forest people. It was only when she heard his roar, hollow from inside the helmet, that she realized that one of her guards was Raine.

"Jocelin! Cut her loose!" Raine commanded as he brought a double-edged ax down on the shoulder of an armored knight, sending the man to his knees. A woman jumped on the fallen knight, pulled his helmet off, while a one-eyed man slammed a club into the head of the dazed knight.

The smoke was so thick Alyx could see no more and her throat was raw from coughing. More tears flowed as Joss cut the ropes about her wrists, grabbed her hand and pulled her away from the burning brush.

"Come with me," he said, pulling her by the hand.

She'd halted, looking back at the platform. Raine fought two men at once, swinging mightily at them with a steel-studded mace, sidestepping, moving with slow grace in the heavy armor. Behind blazed the fire, flashing off the men's armor, turning it to a frightening, bloody red.

"Alyx!" Jocelin shouted at her. "Raine gave me

orders of where to take you. He's angry enough at both of us. For once, obey him."

"I can't leave him!" she tried to say, but her raw throat and the lump there made it come out as a croak.

One strong pull from Joss and they were running together. After a very long time she saw horses coming toward them.

"He's late," Joss yelled, panting from the run. "Come on, Alyx!"

At least the running kept her mind from the danger Raine was in. Carrying the extra weight of her unborn child made her awkward, and she needed every bit of her wind.

When they reached the horses, Jocelin mounted and pulled her up behind him and, to her chagrin, they headed away from where Raine and the others fought. Alyx tried to protest, but again her voice failed her. Her silence was so uncharacteristic that Joss turned to look at her, and his snort of laughter showed he understood her predicament.

They rode hard for two hours and when they stopped at last, it was at a monastery. Alyx, exhausted from her fear during the last several days, could hardly stand when Joss helped her down.

"Is your voice really gone?" Joss asked, half amused, half in sympathy.

She again tried to speak, but only a rasp that hurt her throat came out.

"Maybe it's better this way. Raine is angry enough to tear the tongues out of both of us. Are you all right, though? They didn't harm you while you were a captive?"

Alyx shook her head.

Before Joss could speak again, a tonsured, brown-robed monk opened the heavy wooden door.

"Won't you come in, my children? We are ready for you."

Alyx touched Jocelin's arm and frowned in question. What did the monk mean by "ready"?

"Come inside. You'll find out," Joss said, smiling.

Inside the wall was a large, lovely courtyard, green and shady in the early morning August sunlight. There were doors off three sides of the courtyard, a thick stone wall behind them.

"We have a few rooms for women visitors," the monk said, glancing down at Alyx's soot-covered coarse white gown. "Lord Raine has made arrangements for your comfort."

Moments later Alyx was in a spacious room off the courtyard and given a mug of thick buttermilk to drink. She was only halfway through it when the sound of clanging steel came through the door.

"Alyxandria!" came a bellow that could only be Raine's.

Out of habit, Alyx opened her mouth to answer him in kind, but only a painful yelp came out. With her hand at her throat, she opened the door.

Raine whirled to look at her and for a moment their eyes locked. There were shadows under his eyes and his hair was sweat-plastered to his head in black curls. Dents in his armor were numerous. But what was frightening was the fury in his eyes.

"Come out here," he growled, and his tone left no room for disobedience.

When she stood before him he clutched her shoulders, stared for a moment at her stomach, then looked back into her eyes. "I should beat you soundly for this," he said.

Alyx tried to speak, but the rawness of her throat made tears in her eyes.

He looked puzzled for a moment, then one dimple flashed in his cheek. "The smoke take your voice away?"

She nodded.

"Good! That's the best news I've heard in months. When we get through with this I have a few things to say to you and for once you're going to listen." With that he grabbed her shoulder and pushed her toward a small gate in the wall. Outside was a tall, deeply recessed door that obviously belonged to a chapel. Not waiting for her to enter on her own, Raine opened the door and pushed her inside. Before the altar stood Jocelin and a tall, slim man whom Alyx had never seen before.

"In your armor?" the stranger asked, looking at Alyx curiously.

"If I took time to change no doubt she'd slip through my fingers again. You have the ring, Gavin?"

Alyx's eyes opened wide at the name. So this was Raine's older brother, the man she'd written to and begged to help control Raine's anger at Roger Chatworth. As she looked up at Gavin, thinking he wasn't at all like Raine physically and Raine was so much more handsome, she was barely aware of a priest before them, talking.

"Pay attention, Alyx," Raine commanded, and Gavin coughed to cover a laugh.

In consternation, Alyx looked at the men surrounding her. Jocelin's eyes danced with laughter, Raine's smouldered with barely controlled rage and Gavin seemed to be amusedly tolerant of everything. The priest was waiting patiently for something from her.

"Alyx!" Raine growled. "I know you can't speak, but you could at least nod your head—unless of course you'd rather not marry me. Perhaps you'd rather have Jocelin . . . again?"

"Marry?" she mouthed.

"For the Lord's sake, Raine! Sorry, Father," Gavin said. "Have pity on her. She's had a shock. One minute she's about to be burned at the stake and the next she's getting married. She needs a moment to adjust."

"And since when have you known so much about women?" Raine asked hostilely. "You dumped Judith on your doorstep hardly minutes after you married her, and if I hadn't broken my leg, she'd have been alone."

"If you hadn't been there she might have come to me sooner. As it was—"

"Quiet!" Jocelin shouted, then stepped backward when the two Montgomery brothers turned their wrath on him. He took a deep breath. "Alyx was looking at Lord Gavin and I'm not sure she realized she was marrying Lord Raine. Perhaps if it were explained to her, she'd answer the questions properly, even without her voice."

The full realization of what was going on hit Alyx and, with her usual ladylike finesse, her eyes widened and her mouth dropped open.

"Is that horror at the idea?" Gavin laughed.

Raine looked away from Alyx, obviously not sure

what her expression meant. "She carries my child. She will marry me," he said flatly.

Alyx couldn't speak, but she could hiss at him through her teeth, and when Raine still wouldn't look at her she looked about for other means of getting his attention. He didn't ask her to marry him, didn't allow her the sweet pleasure of throwing herself at him and telling him she loved him, but instead stood sullen and angry and announced she would marry him.

"Would you like to borrow my sword?" Gavin asked, and his voice was so full of laughter he could hardly speak. "Oh, Raine." He slapped his brother's shoulder, making the armor clank, but Raine didn't move. "I hope she leads you a merry chase. Judith's going to like a sister-in-law who looks daggers at her husband. It'll make her feel less alone in the world."

Raine didn't bother to look at Gavin and Alyx sensed there was some old argument involved. Never in her life had she wished more for the power of her voice than she did at this moment. She'd make Raine look at her if she could speak.

"My lady," the priest said, and it took Alyx a while to understand that he was speaking to her. "It is not the church's place to encourage unwanted marriages. Is it your desire to marry Lord Raine?"

She looked up at Raine's profile, furious that he wouldn't look at her. With two steps, she planted herself in front of him, his eyes focused somewhere over her head. Slowly, she reached out and took his hand, held it in hers. His hand was cut in several places, bloody, bruised, and as she looked down at it she knew he'd been hurt saving her. She raised it to her lips and kissed his palm, and when she looked up, his eyes were on her. For a moment they seemed to soften.

"She will marry me," he said as he glanced back at the priest.

Alyx wanted to curse at him for his self-assurance and for his refusal to weaken in his anger at her. Silently, she moved back beside him and the marriage was completed, a gold ring slipped onto her finger.

Raine gave no one time to congratulate her. "Come, Lady Alyx," he said, fingers digging into her upper arm. "We have a great deal to discuss."

"Leave her alone, Raine," Gavin said. "Can't you see she's tired? And besides, this is your wedding day. Rail at her some other time."

Raine didn't bother to even look at his brother as he ushered Alyx from the chapel back through the courtyard and into her room. The moment the door was closed, Raine leaned against it.

"How could you, Alyx?" he whispered. "How could you say you cared for me then put me through the last few months of hell?"

It was very frustrating not to be able to talk. She looked about for a pen and paper but remembered Raine couldn't read.

"Do you know what it's been like the last few months?" He tossed his helmet on the bed. "For years I've searched for a woman I could love. A woman with courage and honor. A woman who wasn't afraid of me or after money or land. A woman who made me think."

He began unbuckling the leather straps that held his armor in place, tossing piece after piece in a heap on the bed. "First you drive me nearly insane in those tight hose, flipping about in front of me, looking up at me with big eyes so full of hunger you frightened me."

With one movement, he pushed all the armor to the side, sat down on the edge of the bed and began unfastening his leg coverings. Alyx knelt before him and helped. Raine leaned back on his elbows, never stopping his tirade.

"When I found you were a female I had a fever and wasn't sure I wasn't dreaming, yet that night I found more joy than I ever had. There was no coyness about you, no holding back, just exuberance, pleasure given, pleasure received. Later I was furious at you for having played such an ugly trick on me, but I forgave you."

He said the last as if he were the most magnanimous person alive, ignoring Alyx's look of disgust as he raised his leg for her to unbuckle the second leg sheath.

A knock on the door made him pause. Several servants, dressed more costly than Alyx had ever been, entered the room bearing a large oak tub and several buckets of steamy hot water.

"Put it there," Raine said distractedly.

Standing, Alyx watched the procession with disbelief. A tub full of hot water, brought by servants and set before them as if they were royalty. Never in her life had she had a full, hot bath. In Moreton she'd bathed from a basin and in the forest there'd been the icy stream.

"What is it, Alyx?" Raine asked when they were alone again. "You look as if you'd seen a ghost."

Silently, she pointed at the steaming tub.

"You want to bathe first? Go ahead."

Cautiously, she knelt by the tub, put her hands into the water and smiled up at Raine as he began to remove the leather padding he'd worn under his armor.

"Don't try to distract me," he said a little too sweetly. "I am still considering blistering your behind. Do you know how I felt after I found you with Jocelin?"

She looked away from him, remembering the hurt in his eyes that night.

"It took me years to find you, then to have you tell me your . . . your music meant more than I did. Close your mouth! You did in effect say that. You know, Alyx, I rather like your not being able to talk. My brother wouldn't believe that a little thing like you could outshout fifty grown men. I offered for him to put some money on his big mouth, but he declined.

"Alyx," he warned, "don't look so offended. You have no right to be offended. No! I am the one who's gone through hell these last months. I never knew where you were, how many men you were sleeping with."

At that, she sent him a look of blackness.

"You were the one who made me believe you lacked virtue—that is the kindest way I can say it. At camp I drove the people nearly insane. Some of them rebelled and refused to go near the training field."

He frowned for a moment at the way she was pointing at him. "I spent a great deal of time there, if that's what you mean. I was trying to wear myself out so I wouldn't remember you and Joss."

Alyx narrowed her eyes at him, used her hands to form a large curving mound over her chest.

"Oh, Blanche," he said, understanding so easily

that Alyx hissed at him. "It would serve you right if I had invited her into my bed, but after you I wanted no other woman. Damn you, Alyx! Stop looking so pleased with yourself. I was miserable while you were gone."

She pointed at herself and all her love showed in her eyes.

He looked away and his voice was hoarse when he spoke again. "I nearly killed Joss when he came to me. I refused to see him and the guards wouldn't let him pass, but he knows his way about the forest too well. One night I'd had a little too much to drink and when I woke in the morning Joss was sitting on a stool by my bed. It took a while before I would listen to him."

Alyx heard the understatement in his words and rolled her eyes so exaggeratedly that Raine pointedly ignored her.

"I can tell you that it didn't help my sore head any to hear of Pagnell's capture of you, nor that the loathsome man planned to set a trap for me."

Alyx, sitting by the tub, reached up and grabbed Raine's hand. He wore only a loincloth now. To think that he had risked his life for her.

"Alyx," he said softly, kneeling before her. "Don't you realize yet that I love you? Of course I'd come for you."

She tried to show him, with her hands and expressions, how she'd worried about Pagnell harming him.

"What?" Raine said, standing. "You thought I didn't know about the trap?" He was obviously insulted. "You thought some mosquito like Pagnell could maneuver a Montgomery into his clutches?"

With a swift gesture, he tore off the loincloth and

stepped into the tub. "The day a bit of filth like that—Alyx, you didn't *really* believe that Pagnell—?"

She threw up her hands, bowing before him with mock humility.

"Well, perhaps you should be forgiven. You don't know what the man is like. Maybe to you all noblemen are alike."

Now she was the one insulted. By "you" he meant people of her class, lowlings who believed in witches and the goodness of the King, who thought the trials were honest and fair and other stupid things. She slammed her fist into the water, splashing it into Raine's face.

He grabbed her wrist. "Now what was that for? Here I've forgiven you for leaving me, saved your skin from a fire and married you and you aren't even grateful."

Oh how very, very much she wished she could talk. She'd tell him in a voice that'd pin his ears back that she left him to keep him safe from the King's wrath and she was facing being burned because she carried *his* child. As for marrying her, he'd no doubt done it out of his stupid sense of honor.

"I don't like what you're thinking," he said, pulling her closer to him. "Gavin laughed at me when I said you'd be grateful for what I'd done. He said women never reacted the way they should, I mean with logic. Now what have I done?"

She'd doubled her fist and threatened to smack him in the nose.

"Alyx, you really are trying my patience. Don't you have even one kind thought for me? I've been through an awful couple of days. I had to scale that tower wall at night, kill the guard on the roof and put on his armor, all so quietly the other man wouldn't hear me."

As he held both her wrists, she could feel herself melting. No matter that it was his fault that she was facing being burned; he had risked a great deal to rescue her.

"Aren't you pleased with me just a little?" he murmured against her lips. "Aren't you just a little bit glad to be married to me?"

As Alyx felt her body dissolving, disappearing under his strong will, she wasn't aware of how he was pulling her across the tub. With a great loud splash, he pulled her onto his lap, water sloshing over the sides.

"Now I have you," he laughed as she tried to sit up. "Now I'll make you pay for your lack of gratitude." He laughed again as Alyx tried to protest, her voice croaking, but as he began to kiss her, she forgot about speaking.

Chapter Fifteen

$\mathcal{A}$LYX'S ARMS WENT about Raine's neck and all thoughts of anger were gone. It had been so long since she'd seen him, and her hunger for him was overwhelming. Eagerly, she pulled him closer to her, her mouth clinging to his, her tongue invading his mouth, seeking as much of him as she could reach.

"Alyx," he whispered into her hair, and there were tears in his voice. "I saw you as I went up the wall, sitting alone in that tower room, crying softly, so little, so sad. Right then I wanted to kill all the guards, but I knew I couldn't rely on the men from the forest to help me. If my brothers had been free, I would have tried it, but I wouldn't risk injuring you."

Her head came up at the mention of brothers. Elizabeth!

"What is it, Alyx? What's wrong?"

She tried to get out the word "Elizabeth," but it

was unintelligible. After several more attempts she managed to say "Miles."

"Did you meet my little brother? No, you couldn't have. He's been on the Isle of Wight. After Mary . . . died, Miles nearly went crazy and Gavin persuaded him to go visit Uncle Simon. He left the Isle a few weeks ago."

Raine was puzzled at Alyx's vigorous shaking of her head. Miles, she kept mouthing. "Has something happened to Miles? Is he in danger?"

Alyx nodded yes, and before she had made one more nod, Raine was out of the tub, Alyx under his arm. Hastily, he set her down, wrapped a cloak around her and pulled on his loincloth. "We'll go see Gavin and you can write what you have to say."

Alyx's face was red the instant they left their room. She wore only a wet sheath under the cloak while Raine wore practically nothing as he pulled her through the holy monastery. They found Gavin in the stables.

"You aren't ready to ride so soon, are you, brother?" he teased. "Surely your bride deserves some attention."

Raine ignored his jibe. "Alyx says Miles is in trouble. She'll write for you what's happened."

Gavin's face immediately turned serious. "Come to the monk's study."

He led the way with such long strides that Alyx would not have been able to keep up if Raine hadn't grabbed her arm and pulled her behind him. He'd better enjoy this time while she had no voice, she thought.

The monk in the study protested a woman's presence, but the men ignored him.

"Here!" Gavin said, thrusting paper, pen and ink before her.

It took her several minutes to write the story of Pagnell's tying of Elizabeth Chatworth and his plan to deliver her to Miles. Raine and Gavin hung over her shoulder until her palms began to sweat.

"Elizabeth Chatworth," Gavin said, "I thought she was still a child."

Alyx shook her head.

"What does she look like?" Raine asked seriously.

Alyx's expression was enough to make them understand.

"The King isn't going to like this," Gavin said. "He has placed a heavy fine on the Chatworth estates and ordered Roger away from all Montgomery land."

"Land!" Raine shouted. "Is that all you care about? Chatworth kidnapped Bronwyn and killed Mary. What does it take to make you consider people instead of land?"

"I care more for my brothers than *any* land. What will happen if Miles rapes this Chatworth girl? It will look as if we are disobeying the King, and who will suffer then? You! He will never pardon you and you will have to spend your life in that forest with that army of cutthroats. And how will the King punish Miles? By outlawing him, too? I'm worried about losing two of my brothers because of Pagnell's nasty tricks."

Raine was still glaring at his brother while Alyx looked at Gavin with new respect.

"It's been days," Raine said finally. "I'd put my life on it that the girl is virgin no longer, and I'll wager that Miles raped no one. Perhaps if he knew who she was, he released her, and all we can do is pray she doesn't bear his child."

Gavin's snort said a great deal. "I'll take half my men and leave now and try to find Miles. Maybe I can talk some sense into him. Perhaps the girl's fallen in love with him and won't demand his head."

Alyx grabbed Gavin's arm and shook her head vigorously. Elizabeth Chatworth was never going to fall in love with a Montgomery in less than a fortnight.

"A hellion, is she?" Gavin asked, then paused and raised Alyx's hand to his lips. "Raine is going to take you home and you'll meet my Judith. I'm sorry your wedding has been such a hurried affair. When this is all settled we'll give a tournament in your honor."

Still holding her hand, he looked back at his brother. "You'll be safe at the Montgomery castle for a while. Take her there, let her rest. You haven't seen my son yet, either. And buy her some clothes!"

Alyx was sure Raine would take offense at Gavin's tone, but Raine was smiling. "It's good to see you again, brother," he said softly, his arms open. The brothers clasped each other fiercely for a long moment.

"Give Miles my best and try to keep him out of trouble," Raine smiled. "And when he returns he can meet my wife."

With one flashing grin, Gavin left them.

Raine turned back to Alyx. Her cloak had fallen open and the damp gown clung to her. "Now, if I remember correctly, we were just starting something when my little brother's problems interrupted us."

Alyx took a step away from him, gesturing toward the room they were in.

With a laugh, Raine swept her into his arms, carried

her through the courtyard and back to their room. Heedless of the piles of dirty armor on the bed, he tossed her in the midst of it and in one gesture stretched out on top of her.

"Will I hurt the child?" he murmured, biting her earlobe. Her headshaking was so vigorous that he gave a warm, seductive laugh as his hand trailed downward and pulled at the linen gown. The coarse, poorly sewn garment came away from her body with one easy tear.

Alyx had never been very proud of her body, always wishing for more curves, but now, bloated with child as she was, she didn't want him to see her in daylight. Her attempts to cover herself were brushed away by Raine.

Moving off her, he kissed her stomach, caressed it. "It's my child who distorts you, and I love it as well as his mother."

"Daughter?" she managed to say, hurting her raw throat.

"I only ask for your safety and, if God wills, the life of the child. I would love to have a daughter. With you for a mother, Bronwyn and Judith for aunts, I will gladly leave her all my estates. I'm sure she'll run them better than I do."

She tried to speak again, but he didn't let her as he began kissing her neck again. When she felt him remove his loincloth, knew his skin was next to hers, she forgot her worries about how she looked.

She had no idea how much she'd missed him physically, how much she needed the caress of his hands. He touched her body all over, running his hard fingertips over her skin from toes to head, making her feel cherished, loved. Even now when she could feel the power of his hunger for her, he took his time, loved her, touched her.

She lay on her back, eyes closed, her arms lightly about his neck as he ran his hands over her. When he touched her inner thighs, she opened her eyes, met his and the deep, dark blue piercing through her made chills run along her spine. The power of this man, the strength, the size of him, all held in leash as he fondled her, excited her horribly.

With an upward thrust of her body, she pressed against him, kissed his mouth hungrily, making him laugh deeply as he rolled onto his back and pulled her on top of him. The armor surrounding them clanged and a couple of pieces fell to the floor.

Alyx ran her teeth down Raine's neck, her hands sinking into the mass of muscle of his upper arms. Glorious! she thought, such a magnificent, splendid man—and all hers!

The laughter that came from her burned throat wasn't pretty, but the deep, raspy quality of it was seductive. She ran her thumb down Raine's ribs so hard he pushed her arm away as he sought her mouth. But Alyx applied her thumb to his other side, laughed again when he twisted away from her.

"Hellion!" he murmured, grabbing her by the hair and pulling her head back as he lifted his head and bit into her stomach.

Gasping, Alyx brought her feet forward, attempted to get away from him. Raine caught her left foot and proceeded to bite each one of her toes. The sensation that ran up her made her stop all movement.

She lay on top of him, stretched out, her feet in his face, his in hers. Two can play this game, she thought as she raked her teeth across the soft underpad of Raine's toes. She was quite pleased to feel him jump beneath her, and another piece of armor went crashing to the floor.

Raine's arms, longer than hers, slid up the sides of her legs, caressing and kneading so provocatively that after a moment she could think of nothing else but his hands on her body.

She began to tremble, shiver, and her skin seemed as hot as when the fire had been licking at her back.

Raine grabbed her hips and as if she had no weight at all, picked her up and set her down on his manhood with such an accurate thrust that Alyx let out a raspy squeal.

"Swordplay," Raine laughed. "I'm very accurate with a sword."

Alyx leaned forward and with her strong thighs began a rhythm that left Raine too busy to speak again. He lay still, his face a mask of almost pain as he held back, all his senses given over to the enjoyment of what Alyx was doing.

When he could stand no more, he grabbed her to him, rolled her over and with two hard, almost violent thrusts, they ended together, shaking, quivering, clutching as if they might get even closer.

After several moments, Raine raised his head and gave Alyx a smile that said more than all the words in the world. With a grunt of satisfaction, he rolled off her, pulling her close to him, their sweaty skin glued together. And together they slept.

It was early evening when they woke and Raine made an awful sound as he pulled a sharp, hard knee

VELVET SONG

up from under the small of his back. "How can anything so small be so dangerous?" he asked a sleepy Alyx.

With one sharp smack on her buttocks, he moved away from her to stand and stretch. "Up!" he commanded. "We've stayed here too long already. It'll take us two days to get home as it is."

Alyx didn't relish moving to ride on a horse and her expression said so. She'd much rather stay here—in bed—with Raine for a few more days.

"Alyx, don't tempt me. Get out of there this minute or I shall return to the forest and send some of Gavin's men to escort you to the Montgomery estates."

That made her jump. Within seconds she was out of bed and had pulled the torn white sheath over her head.

"Filthy thing," Raine said, fingering it. "Judith will find you dresses fit for a Montgomery. It will be nice to see you dressed as you should be, although I must say I like your hair like this." He rubbed her curls as if he still thought of her as his squire.

There was no time for anything else as he pushed her out the door and tossed her into the saddle of a horse. Except for messengers, Alyx had never seen knights as they were with their lord master. Raine had only to hint at a command and Gavin's men jumped to obey. Quickly, efficiently, they cleared the armor Raine had taken from Pagnell's man from the room while Raine dressed in the dark green wools he'd worn in the forest. One of the knights gave such a look of astonishment that Raine laughed.

"They itch, too," he said. "Ready, Alyx?"

Before she could answer, they were off, galloping at a pace that she should have been used to. It was no surprise to her when Raine rode through half the night. But what did surprise her was the way Gavin's men treated her. They asked after her health, if she were tired. When they stopped to eat and rest the horses, some of the men presented her with flowers. One man spread his cloak for her to sit on. No one seemed to notice that the fur-lined cloak was of far better quality than the sack she wore.

With surprise and disbelief in her eyes, she looked up at Raine but saw that he thought nothing of the way the men treated her. A knight asked permission to play the lute for her, and as three men sang together, Raine raised one eyebrow at her, for the men were not very good. Alyx looked away, because to her, the knights, so kind, so polite, were perfect.

When Raine lifted her back on her horse, he said, "They are practicing their chivalry on you. I hope you can bear with them."

Bear with them! she thought as they started riding again. She felt as if she'd just seen a glimpse of heaven and, indeed, she could withstand it.

At night they stayed at an inn and Alyx was embarrassed by the way she was dressed. There was no need to be. The innkeeper took one look at Raine and the twenty men in their rich green and gold and he practically lay down to be their carpet. Food such as Alyx had never seen before was set before them in a quantity that made her gasp.

"May they sit with you?" Raine asked.

It took her a moment to realize he was asking permission for these lovely men to sit at the same long oak table with her. With a large smile, she gestured to them and the chairs.

The men's table manners were so good that Alyx

was overly cautious about her own. All through the meal they offered her prize tidbits of meat and fruit. One man peeled an apple, placed a sliver on a plate and asked if she'd accept it.

They expressed sympathy about her lost voice, which made Raine laugh and say they were missing more than they knew. Formally, they asked Lord Raine to explain this. He said they'd not believe what he said, which made Alyx blush.

In their room was a large, soft bed, sparkling clean, and Alyx immediately snuggled under the light blanket. In seconds, Raine joined her there, pulling her close to him, his hands caressing her stomach, smiling when the baby jumped.

"Strong," he murmured, falling asleep. "A good, strong child."

In the morning the landlord tapped on their door and delivered fresh baked bread and hot wine, along with twenty red roses from Gavin's knights.

"That's Judith's doing," Raine said, dressing. "They're all half in love with her, and it looks like you've won their hearts, too."

Alyx shook her head at this and indicated that they only cared for her because of her relationship to him.

He kissed her nose. "Perhaps all men fall in love with women who can't speak."

Alyx grabbed a pillow and threw it at him, catching him in the back of the head.

"Is that any way for a lady to act?" he teased.

In spite of his light manner, Alyx worried about his words all day. She wasn't a lady and she didn't know how one should behave. How could she possibly meet this paragon, Judith Montgomery, dressed in a sooty, scorched, shapeless sack?

"Alyx, what's wrong with you? Are those tears I see?" Raine asked from beside her.

She tried to smile and indicate that there was something in her eye and she would be fine in a moment. After that, she tried to control herself better, but by the time they rode into sight of the Montgomery castle, she was ready to turn tail and run.

The massive stone fortress, centuries old, was even more formidable than she had imagined. As they rode closer to it, the old stone walls seemed to be crushing down on her.

Raine led them to the back entrance, to announce their arrival to as few people as possible. The path to the gate was lined with high stone walls and as they rode, men called down in joyful greeting to Raine. He seemed so at home here that the man she knew began to seem far away. The men who obeyed him without question, the whole vast scope of this place, was closer to the real man than the artificial outlaw camp.

They rode into a courtyard and, to Alyx's astonishment, houses, looking comfortable, with many windows, were inside the walls. In the few castles where she and Jocelin had sung, the people still lived in the towers, which were so uncomfortable most castles had been abandoned.

They had barely stopped when out of a little walled garden came running a breathtakingly beautiful woman wearing a gown of flashing red satin.

"Raine," she called, running, arms open.

She can't sing, Alyx thought defensively, watching her husband leap from his horse and run toward the woman.

"Judith," he said, grabbing her, twirling her about,

feet off the ground, kissing her mouth, in Alyx's opinion, much too exuberantly.

"My lady," came a voice to Alyx's left. "May I help you down?"

Her eyes never leaving Raine and the exquisite Judith, she let herself be lifted down.

"Where is she, Raine?" Judith was saying. "Your message was so garbled we could hardly understand it. We must have misheard because it seemed the messenger was saying your wife was about to be burned at the stake."

"True. I rescued her at the very last moment." His voice held a great deal of pride. With one arm around Judith, he led her to Alyx, whom he casually embraced. "This is Alyx and this vision is my unworthy brother's wife."

Alyx nodded once, openly staring at her sister-in-law. She'd never seen anyone who looked like this before: gold eyes, auburn hair barely visible under a pearl embroidered hood, a small voluptuous figure.

Judith pulled away from Raine. "You must be tired. Come with me and I'll have a bath brought for her." She took Alyx's hand in hers and started toward the house.

"Oh, Judith," Raine called from behind them. "Alyx lost her voice because of the smoke."

Beside her, Alyx felt Judith stiffen and knew it was because Raine dared to marry someone like her. Rapidly, she tried to blink back tears.

"You are tired," Judith said sympathetically, but there was an edge to her voice.

Alyx had no time to look at the house as Judith led her up the stairs and into a large paneled room. Alyx's house in Moreton could have been set in the room at least four times.

Heavy footsteps on the stairs made Judith turn. Raine stood just inside the doorway, grinning. "She's pretty, isn't she?" he said fondly, looking at Alyx. "Too bad her voice is gone, but I'm sure it's only temporary."

"No thanks to you," Judith said, leading Alyx to a chair.

"What does that mean?" Raine asked, bewildered. "I rescued her."

Judith whirled on him. "From what? From Pagnell's trap? She was used as bait to lure you to him. Raine," she calmed, "I think you should leave now. I don't think your sweet little wife wants to hear what I plan to say to you."

"Sweet!" Raine snorted. "And what reason do you have to be angry with me?" He was offended.

"You are trying my patience, Raine," she warned. "Alyx, are you hungry?"

"Look, Judith, if you have something to say, say it."

"All right, then we'll leave this room. Your wife needs her rest."

Alyx was beginning to get an idea of what Judith had to say. She grabbed her sister-in-law's hand and with her eyes urged her to continue. There were so many things she would like to say to Raine.

Judith blinked in understanding and whirled back to face Raine. "All right, I shall tell you what I have to say. You men, all of you, all four of you brothers, think nothing of dragging a woman all over England with no thought to her safety or comfort."

Raine's jaw jutted out. "We stayed in a very comfortable inn last night."

"You what! You took your lady wife into a public place dressed like that? How dare you, Raine? How dare you treat any woman like that?"

"What was I supposed to do, shop for clothes? Perhaps I should have ridden to London and asked the King for a bit of silk."

"Don't try to gain sympathy from me for being declared a traitor. It was your own Montgomery hotheadedness that caused all your problems."

At this Alyx began to clap her hands.

Judith flashed an understanding half-smile at her while Raine glared.

"I can see I'm not needed here," Raine said.

"You're not running away from this," Judith said. "I want you to run downstairs, pull Joan from whatever corner—or bed—she's lounging in, then order a bath sent up here. Oh, Raine, how could you do this to this poor child? The mother of your baby? It's been days since the fire and she's still covered with soot, and how you must have ridden to get here so fast! Now go along and get yourself cleaned up and dressed properly."

With his jaw still out, refusing to speak, Raine left the room, the door slamming behind him.

With a sigh, Judith looked back at Alyx. "You have to stand up for yourself or men will take advantage. Are you well? Raine didn't harm you in his haste, did he?"

Alyx only shook her head, looking at Judith with admiration and the beginnings of love.

"It's a good thing the three of us are all sturdy and strong or else we'd be dead by now."

Alyx held up three fingers, frowned in question.

"Bronwyn, Stephen's wife. You'll have to meet her. She is lovely, absolutely lovely, but Stephen drags her everywhere, makes her sleep on the ground rolled up in a wool blanket. It's really dreadful."

A knock on the door interrupted Judith, and seconds later servants arrived with a tub and pails of hot water. "I should send Raine more often," Judith said. "He certainly gets things done quickly."

Alyx gave a little giggle and Judith smiled back.

"They are good men. I wouldn't trade Gavin for anyone, but sometimes you have to raise your voice a bit. Someday you'll get over your awe of your husband and you'll find yourself shouting right back at him. You may not think so now, but you will."

Alyx merely smiled and allowed herself to be led to the tub.

Chapter Sixteen

RAINE, UP TO his neck in a tub of hot water, his
eyes still blazing with anger, looked up hostilely as the
door to his room opened. Gavin burst in.

"Miles has taken the Chatworth girl to Scotland,
and from what I can gather he had to drag her there
while she screamed curses at him. Damn him!" he
said passionately. "Why do I have so much trouble
with my younger brothers? Only Stephen—"

"You'd better stop," Raine warned. "I'm in a mood
to drive a sword through someone's belly."

"And what has happened now?" Gavin asked tiredly, sitting down across from Raine. "I have more
problems than I need. Has your wife said an unkind
word to you?"

"Not *my* wife." He stopped. "What do you plan to
do about Miles? Do you think he's taking her to
Stephen?"

"I can only hope so. Sir Guy is with him, so perhaps he can talk some sense into Miles."

"Do you have a reason why Miles should keep the girl? Other than for his own pleasure, that is? I can't imagine our little brother forcing a woman to do anything, nor can I imagine one refusing him. I've never seen him have any trouble with women."

"One of Miles's men broke his arm right after Lady Elizabeth was delivered and so stayed behind when Miles went to Scotland. I caught him on the road."

"And what was his bad news? It couldn't be as bad as the look on your face."

"There were four men in Miles's tent at the time. Pagnell's man was allowed to enter, all the men holding swords on him. He was carrying a long carpet in his arms. He paused just inside the entrance, tossed it to the floor, gave it a push with his foot and unrolled it."

"Well?" Raine demanded.

"It unrolled at Miles's feet, uncovering Elizabeth Chatworth wearing nothing but several feet of blonde hair."

"And what did our little brother do?" Raine asked, torn between laughing and groaning at the picture he'd conjured.

"From what I found out, all the men stood and stared without moving until Lady Elizabeth jumped up, grabbed a cloth from a cot and an ax from a corner and took after Miles."

"Was he harmed?"

"He managed to dodge her blows and sent the other men from the tent. When the lady started cursing worse than what anyone had heard before, Sir

Guy took the men out of hearing distance of the tent."

"And no doubt she was purring the next morning," Raine said, smiling. "Our little brother has a way with women."

"I don't know what happened after that. An hour later the man I spoke to broke his arm and was sent back to Miles's house."

"Then how did you know they went to Scotland?" Raine asked.

"I went to Miles's campsite and when no one was there, I asked some of the tradesmen in the area. Over a week ago Miles and his men left, and several people heard them say they were going to Scotland."

"No clue as to why?"

"Who can say what goes on in Miles's mind? I know for sure he wouldn't harm the girl, but I'm afraid he'll hold her to punish Chatworth."

"Miles would fight a man, many men, but he wouldn't take his grudges out on a woman. That's Chatworth's game," Raine said grimly. "I'm sure he had a reason to take her from England. What do you plan to do now?"

Gavin was quiet for a moment. "I'll leave him to Stephen and see what he can do with Miles. And Bronwyn has a level head on her. Perhaps she can do something with Miles."

Raine stood in the tub. "I doubt if anyone can reason with him where women are concerned. If the woman took more than ten minutes to fall in love with him, it would be the first time such a thing has happened. Maybe Miles saw it as a challenge."

Gavin snorted. "Whatever his reasons, he's tempting the King's wrath. King Henry's changed since his eldest son died."

Drying himself, Raine stepped from the tub, gave a kick to his clothes heaped at his feet. "It will be good to get out of these for a while."

"How long do you think you can stay?"

"Three, four days at most. I need to get back to the camp."

"Are your outlaws so important?"

Raine considered for a moment. "They aren't all outlaws, and perhaps if you'd lived their life you would have different ideas about right and wrong."

"Stealing is wrong no matter what," Gavin said firmly.

"Would you sit by quietly and let Judith and your new son starve to death? If they were hungry and a man pushing a cart of bread walked by, would you sit on your high morals and let it go?"

"I don't want to argue with you. Does Alyx know you plan to return?"

"No, not yet. I'm not sure I'll tell her, but just slip away. If I don't I'm sure she'll try to go with me. I want her here with you and Judith. I want her to live the way she never has before."

With one sweep he picked up his old clothes, flung them into a corner and reached for the silver embroidered, black velvet gown on the bed.

"What's this?" Gavin asked, moving to lift something from Raine's dirty clothes. He held up a gold belt.

"It's Alyx's Lyon belt, as she calls it, but for the life of me I can't make out anything like a lion on it. One of the guards at the trial took it from her, and I had a devil of a time getting it from him."

With a frown on his face, Gavin took the belt to the window and studied it in the sunlight. "It looks very old. Is it?"

"I guess. Alyx says it's been handed down from mother to daughter in her family for as long as anyone can remember."

"Lions," Gavin muttered. "There's something familiar about this belt. Come downstairs with me to the winter parlor."

When Raine was dressed, he followed his brother to the paneled room. On one wall hung an old and faded tapestry. It had been there for ages and was so familiar to Raine it was nearly invisible.

"Did Father ever tell you about this tapestry?" Gavin asked. When Raine shook his head, Gavin continued. "It was woven in the time of Edward the First, and the subject was a celebration of the greatest knight of the century, a man called the Black Lion. See, here he is atop the horse and this lovely lady was his wife. Look at her waist."

Raine looked, somewhat bored by Gavin's recitation of the family history, but saw nothing special. He was always a man concerned with today and now, not centuries ago.

Gavin gave his brother a look of exasperation. "I saw a drawing of this belt—" he pointed to the tapestry—"long ago. The Black Lion's wife's name was something to do with a lion, and for a wedding gift the Lion gave his wife a belt of a lion and his lioness."

"You don't think Alyx's belt could be that one. It would have to be a couple of hundred years old."

"Look at the way this thing is worn down," Gavin

said, holding Alyx's belt aloft. "The links have been wired together with iron and the design is almost gone, but from what I can see of the clasp it could be lions."

"How would Alyx have gotten the belt?"

Gavin didn't need to be reminded of his new sister-in-law's origins. "The Black Lion was a fabulously wealthy man, but he had one son and eight daughters. He gave all his daughters enormous dowries, and to his eldest daughter went the lion belt to pass on to her eldest daughter."

"You don't think Alyx—" Raine began.

"The Black Lion's eldest son was named Montgomery, and it's through him that all our family has descended. Don't you remember Father saying you were like the Black Lion? The four of us were tall, slim and fair while you were always shorter, sturdier."

Raine remembered all the teasing he'd taken as a child and sometimes wondered if he was a full brother to his sister and three brothers. But he'd been twelve when his father had died, and there were many things he didn't remember.

"Father said you were like him." He pointed to the massive black-haired man atop the rearing stallion in the tapestry.

"And you think this belt Alyx has could have belonged to the man's wife?" Raine took the belt from his brother. "She cherishes it, never lets it out of her sight. I knew it would be taken from her at the trial. She hasn't mentioned it to me, but last night she must have been dreaming and she cried out about this bit of gold."

"Did you know the Black Lion married a woman

well beneath him? Not quite Alyx's status, but compared to him, the Montgomerys are as poor as gamekeepers."

Raine rubbed the worn belt between his fingers. "It's too farfetched to believe. But sometimes I feel as if I've known Alyx longer than just a few months. I've been with women more beautiful than her, and certainly women who treated me with more respect, but when I first looked at her—" He stopped and laughed. "When I first saw her I thought she was a boy and I thought that if I had a son he would look like Alyx. There was something about her . . . I don't know how to explain it. Was it the same with you and Judith?"

"No," Gavin said flatly, looking away. He hated any reminder of how he'd treated Judith when they were first married.

"Speaking of your wife," Raine said. "She gave me a tongue-lashing when I arrived."

Gavin laughed at that. "And what had you done? If I remember correctly, she usually fawns over you to no end."

"She said I was mistreating my wife by bringing her here."

"Because of the King?" Gavin asked. "We discussed it and she agreed that you would be safe for a few days. It will take that long for someone to recognize you and get word to the King."

"No, it wasn't that." Raine was truly puzzled. "It was something about not buying her enough dresses. Perhaps she thinks I carry dresses on my saddle."

"I'm certainly glad I arrived in time to defend myself," Judith said from the doorway, smiling. Immediately, she went to her husband and kissed him. "You are safe? Well?"

"As well as can be," he said, holding her close to him. "And what is this I hear about your berating my brother? I hope you did not hurt him. He's not as strong as I am."

"Delicate," Judith said sweetly. "All of your brothers are as delicate as spring flowers." She smiled up at Raine, both men overpowering her slight form. "I merely said that Raine should not have dragged his wife across the country when she is carrying his child and she is ill from the fire's smoke and all the while dressed worse than the lowest menial."

Judith started to say more but turned as in the doorway stood Alyx, but an Alyx no one had seen before. She wore a gown of deep, dark purple velvet, the low, square neckline hung with a heavy silver chain, a large purple amethyst in the center. The back of her head was covered with a simple hood of silver cloth embroidered with purple flowers. Her violet eyes sparkled brilliantly.

Raine moved toward her, lifted her hand and kissed it. "I am overwhelmed with such beauty," he said sincerely.

"You are different," she whispered.

"And you can talk. Can you sing yet?"

"Don't rush her, Raine," Judith said. "I've given her honey and herbs, but I think she'll heal much faster if she doesn't use her voice. Dinner is ready. Is anyone hungry?"

Alyx was glad she couldn't speak because she didn't believe she could have anyway. Raine had always seemed so much more than the people around him even when he dressed in his forestry clothes, but now, in his black and silver, he was awesome. He fit so well into this magnificent house, and he saw nothing unusual about so many people bowing toward him.

As Raine led her to the tables set in the Great Hall, she had to work to keep her mouth from dropping open. The meal she'd seen at the inn had seemed like a feast, but on these tables was food enough for a village.

"Who are these men?" she whispered to Raine beside her. There were over a hundred people eating with them.

Raine glanced up, noticing the people as if from her eyes. "They're Gavin's men, a few of mine, some of Stephen's. Those men are Montgomerys, cousins, I think. You'll have to ask Gavin for the exact relationship." He pointed toward the end of the table where they sat. "Some of them are castle retainers. You can ask Judith. I'm sure she knows who everyone is."

"Yours so big?" she rasped.

"No," he grinned. "My estates are small compared to this. Judith is the rich one. She brought great wealth when she married into our family, and she has to support many people. She's always buying and selling and counting grain in the storerooms."

"Me?" Alyx asked, scared.

Raine took a while to understand her. "You mean will you have to run my estates? I don't see why not. You can read and write. That's more than I can do." He looked away as one of his cousins spoke to him.

Alyx had difficulty eating more of the meal and after a while sat quietly as course after course was brought into the room. Most of the food she'd never seen before, and new names and flavors were beginning to run together.

After a long while, Raine stood and introduced her and the people shouted a welcome to her.

Judith asked Alyx if she'd like to rest, and together they went back to Alyx's room.

"Is it all a bit bewildering?" Judith asked.

Alyx nodded her head.

"Tomorrow there's a fair in the village, and I'll see if Raine will take you to it. You'll have some fun and not have so many new people to deal with. But now, why don't you rest? Gavin and Raine are preparing a message to send to Miles, and you'll have hours to rest because I'm sure they'll argue for that long."

When Alyx had removed her dress and slipped beneath the covers, Judith took her hand. "You have nothing to fear from us. We are your family from now on and whatever you do will meet our approval. I know that all this"—she motioned to the elegant room—"is new to you, but you'll soon learn and we're here to help you."

"Thank you," Alyx whispered and was asleep before Judith was out of the door.

Nothing could have prepared Alyx for the fair set up in Montgomery pastureland. She'd slept soundly and long and when she woke, her voice was at least half restored. The sound was there and she was glad, even if the tones were gone.

"Do you think I'll be able to sing again?"

Raine laughed at the fear in her voice and helped her button the purple dress Judith had altered to fit Alyx. "I'm sure that in another few days the birds will fly into the room just to hear you."

Laughing, she whirled about the room, the bell-shaped skirt swirling around her. "Isn't it lovely? It is the most beautiful dress on the earth."

"No," Raine laughed, grabbing her. "It is you who makes it lovely. Now stop turning about before you make my child dizzy. Are you ready for the fair?"

The fair was like a city, a city composed of people from all over the world. There were stalls for animals, stalls of lead and tin from England, booths of Spanish wines, German commodities, Italian cloths, toy shops, wrestling matches, games of skill, butchers, fishmongers.

"Where do we begin?" Alyx asked, clinging to Raine's arm. They were surrounded by six of Gavin's knights.

"Perhaps my lady is hungry?" asked one knight.

"Or thirsty?"

"Would my lady like to see the jugglers or the acrobats?"

"I hear there's a fair singer just this way."

"The singer," Alyx said firmly, making Raine laugh.

"To see what you have to compete with?" he teased.

She smiled at him, too happy to let his teasing bother her. After a brief visit to the singer, who was no good at all in Alyx's opinion, they stopped at a gingerbread stall and Raine bought her a spicy fresh-baked lady.

Eating her treat, looking this way and that, she was hardly aware when Raine stopped before an Italian's booth.

"What do you think of this?" Raine asked, holding up a length of violet silk.

"Lovely," she said absently. "Oh, Raine, there is a bear doing tricks."

"Your bear of a husband is going to do tricks if you don't listen to him." When she looked up, he continued. "I have had enough of Judith's berating me. Choose the colors you want and I'll have them sent to the castle."

"Choose?" she asked dumbly, looking at the wealth before her.

"Give us everything you have in purple," Raine said quickly. "And those greens. You'll look good in those, Alyx." He turned back to the merchant. "Cut off enough of each one for a dress and send it to the castle. A steward will pay you." With that he took Alyx's arm and pulled her away.

Like a child, Alyx looked backward, her gingerbread in her mouth. There must have been three shades of purple, four of green in each type of fabric, and the types included silks, satins, velvets, brocades and others Alyx didn't recognize. Raine stopped before the performing bear, but when he saw Alyx wasn't watching, he pulled her to another booth—a furrier's.

This time he didn't wait for her to choose but ordered a cloak lined with lambskin and another with leopard from Asia. He told the furrier to see the cloth merchant and send some bits and pieces for trim for the dresses he'd ordered.

By now Alyx was recovering herself. She was being dressed without even so much as a consultation as to what she wanted. If she had any idea of what she did want, she'd protest Raine's highhandedness.

"Do you choose your own clothes like this?" she

ventured. "Do you leave the choices up to the merchants?"

He shrugged. "I usually wear black, saves time that way. Miles is the one who knows clothes."

"And what about Stephen? What does he know?"

"He keeps Gavin and me apart and all he wears are the Scots' clothes, leaving most of him bare."

"Sounds interesting," Alyx murmured, making Raine give her a sharp look.

"Behave yourself. Look at this. Have you seen this before?"

What Alyx saw was a woman working with hundreds of wooden spools on a fat little pillow. "What is it?" The finished product looked to be white silk cobwebs.

"It's lace, my lady," the woman said and held up a collar for Alyx's inspection.

Gently, Alyx touched it, almost afraid it would fall apart.

"Here," Raine said, pulling a bag of gold from under his doublet. "Let me have three of those. Take your pick, Alyx, and we'll give one to Judith and send the other to Bronwyn."

"Oh, yes," she breathed, pleased at the idea of a gift to Judith.

The lace collars were carefully laid in a thin wooden box and given to one of the knights to carry.

The next few hours were the happiest Alyx had ever known. Seeing Raine in his natural environment, seeing him get the respect he deserved, was a joy to her. Yet this man who was so honored could sit down with the lowest beggar and listen to the man.

"You're looking at me oddly," Raine said.

"I am counting my blessings." She looked away from him. "What are all those people looking at?"

"Come on and we'll see."

The crowd in front of them parted to let the seven big men and the small woman through. Inside the circle were four half-dressed women, their flat bellies bare, their legs visible through transparent silks, undulating to some strange music. After her initial shock, Alyx glanced up at her husband, saw he was completely captivated by the women, as were the guards around them. And to think that moments before she'd been thinking Raine was close to the Lord's angels!

With an exclamation of disgust, which Raine didn't even hear, Alyx began backing out of the crowd, leaving the men to their obsession.

"My lady," said someone beside her. "Let me lead you out of this crush. You're so small that I fear for your safety."

She looked up into the dark eyes of a very handsome man. He had blond hair streaked by the sun, an aquiline nose over a firm mouth. There was a curved scar by his left eye and shadows under his eyes. "I'm not sure—" she began. "My husband . . ."

"Let me introduce myself. I am the Earl of Bayham and your husband's family and mine are well acquainted. I've traveled a long way to speak to Gavin, but when I saw the fair I hoped to find one of the family here."

A heavy-set man who'd had more than a little to drink lunged toward them, and the earl put out a hand, protecting Alyx.

"I feel it's my duty to protect you from this mob. Let me lead you out of here."

She took the arm he offered. There was something about him that seemed both sad and kind at the same time, and she instinctively trusted him.

"How did you hear of my marriage?" she asked. "It was so recent and I haven't come from the same people as my husband."

"I have a special interest in what the Montgomery family does."

He led her away from the noise of the fair, to a bench just inside a small grove of trees. "You must be very tired since you've not sat down all morning. And surely the child must be a heavy burden."

Gratefully, she sat down, rested her hands on her stomach, and looked up at him. "You have indeed been watching us. Now, what do you want to talk to me about that you needed me away from my husband?"

At that the earl smiled slightly. "The Montgomerys choose their women well, for brains as well as beauty. Perhaps I should reintroduce myself. I am Roger Chatworth."

Chapter Seventeen

$\mathcal{A}$LYX, FEELING SO smug because she thought she'd guessed that this man wanted her to use her influence on her husband, suddenly felt very frightened. Clumsily, her fear showing on her face, she started to stand.

"Please," he said softly. "I don't mean to harm you. I only want to talk to you for a moment." He sat down on the end of the bench, feet away from her, his head down, hands clasped. "Leave. I won't stop you."

Alyx was already past him when she turned back. "If my husband sees you, he will kill you."

Roger didn't answer and Alyx, frowning, telling herself she was a fool, went back to the bench. "Why have you risked coming here?" she asked.

"I would risk anything to find my sister."

"Elizabeth?"

Perhaps it was the way she said the name, but Roger's head came up sharply. "You know her? What do you know?" His hands made fists.

"Pagnell, the earl of Waldenham's son—"

"I know the piece of slime."

Quickly, Alyx told the story of how Elizabeth had helped her and how Pagnell had punished Elizabeth.

"Miles!" Roger said, standing. He was richly dressed in dark blue velvet, a satin brocade doublet, his long, muscular legs tightly encased in dark hose. This was not the man Alyx would have imagined as anyone's enemy.

"And what has Miles done with my innocent sister?" Roger demanded, his eyes flashing.

"Not what you did with the Lady Mary," Alyx shot back.

"The woman's death is on my soul, and I have paid for it with the loss of my brother. I do not plan to lose my sister as well."

Alyx had no idea what he was talking about. What did Roger's brother have to do with Mary's death? "I don't know where Miles and Elizabeth are. I have not been well. Perhaps while I was resting Raine found out about Miles, but I know nothing."

"What of the Lady Judith? I don't think much is done that she doesn't know about. Did she tell you something?"

"No, nothing. Why are you free when my husband has to hide, yet it was you who killed Mary?"

"I did not kill her!" he said vehemently. "I—no! I don't want to discuss it, and as for being free, the King has taken all my rents for the next three years. Most of my men have left me because I cannot pay them. I have only one small estate to house what is left of my family, which now consists of one vicious sister-in-law. My brother hates me and has vanished from the earth, and now my lovely, sweet sister is held prisoner by a boy who is notorious for his deflowering of women. I have not been punished? Your husband still retains his lands, his own steward runs them while a King's man runs mine. Do you know what will be left in three years' time? Your husband has all of his family. He even has the leisure to fall in love and marry while I have no one left—one brother killed, one turned against me, my sister a prisoner. And you say I am not punished? That I am free?"

He stopped after this speech and looked away, unseeing, into the distance.

"I don't know what has happened to Elizabeth. Gavin went after Miles, but he came back right away. I didn't speak to him when he returned."

"I will kill him if he harms her."

"And what will that gain?" Alyx shouted, hurting her sore throat, but at least her voice made him blink. "Will any of you rest until all of you are killed? Miles did not take Elizabeth; she was given to him. He is innocent. Pagnell is the one who should bear your wrath. But you are too used to hating the Montgomerys and blaming them for all your problems."

"What could I expect from a Montgomery?" he asked sullenly. "Already you believe them to be gods on this earth."

"Stupid man!" she spat. "I only want this war of yours to end. Raine has to live in a forest surrounded by criminals and all because of you."

"Gavin started this by playing with my sister-in-law. One woman wasn't enough for him. He also wanted Alice."

Alyx put her hands to her head. "I don't know any of this. You must go now. Raine will be looking for me."

"Do you mean to protect me?"

"I plan to protect my husband from a fight and me from his wrath."

"I cannot leave until I find out about Elizabeth."

Alyx gritted her teeth. "I don't know where Elizabeth is."

"Will you find out and tell me?"

"Absolutely not!" She was astonished that he'd ask this. "Miles is with her, and I'll not do anything to endanger him."

Roger's mouth made a grim line. "You are a fool to come out here with me. I could take you now and demand Elizabeth's release while I hold you."

Swallowing once, Alyx knew she must brave this out and not let him see her fear. "You have no guards near you. Will you strike a pregnant woman? How far will you get alone with me? Elizabeth still believes you are a good man. Would she still if you took yet another Montgomery prisoner?" Alyx could tell by his face that she was striking a nerve. "How did you explain Mary's death to her?"

Alyx paused a moment, watching him. "You must go."

Before either of them could react, through the trees burst Raine and his guards. Instantly, four swords were at Roger Chatworth's throat.

Raine grabbed Alyx, held her with one arm, his sword drawn in the other. "The bastard has not harmed you?" Raine growled. "Kill him," he said in the next breath.

"No!" Alyx screamed at the top of her lungs and successfully made the men halt. Instantly, she placed herself before Roger. "He has done me no harm. All he wants to know is where his sister is."

"In the grave beside mine," Raine said, eyes narrowed.

"She's not dead," Alyx said. "Raine, please, let's end this feud now. Swear that you'll see that Elizabeth is returned to Roger."

"Roger, is it?" Raine breathed in through his teeth, glaring at her until she took a step backward, closer to Roger. "How long have you known him?"

"How—?" she began, bewildered. "Raine, please, you're not making sense. He's a man alone and I don't want to see him killed. He wants his sister. Do you know where she is?"

"Now you ask me to betray my brother for this filth. Has he told you of Mary's last moments alive?" He looked at Roger, a snarl curling his lip. "Did you enjoy the sound of her body breaking on the stones?"

Alyx could feel herself becoming ill at the images Raine conjured, and she almost wanted to turn Roger over to him. But the King would only have another excuse to keep Raine's lands. He'd never pardon Raine if an earl were killed by him.

"You have to release him," she said quietly. "You cannot kill him in cold blood. Come, Roger. I will walk with you to your horse."

Without a word, Roger Chatworth walked before her back into the fair where his horse waited. Neither Raine nor his guards followed.

"He will never forgive you," Roger said.

"I didn't do it for you. If Raine killed you, the King

would never forgive him. Go now and remember that a Montgomery was good to you when you didn't deserve it. I want no harm to come to Miles or Elizabeth and I will do what I can to see that she is returned to you."

With a look of disbelief, awe and gratefulness, he turned his horse and rode away from the Montgomery estates.

Alyx stood still a moment, her heart beating wildly as she thought about facing Raine again. Of course he'd be angry, but when she explained why she'd helped his enemy, he'd understand. Slowly, dreading the coming argument, she walked back toward the trees where the guard stood.

It took only seconds to see that Raine wasn't there. "Where is he?" she asked, sure he had gone to some private place for their coming battle.

"My lady," one of the guards began. "Lord Raine has returned to the forest."

"Yes, I know," she said. "Where we can be alone. But which direction did he take?"

For a moment Alyx only looked at the man, and after a long while she came to realize what the man meant. "The forest? You mean the camp of the outlaws?"

"Yes, my lady."

"Fetch my horse! I'll go after him. We can catch him."

"No, my lady. We have orders to return you to Lord Gavin. You are not to follow Lord Raine."

"I must go," she said, looking up at the men pleadingly. "Don't you see that I had to keep Raine from killing Chatworth? The King would put Raine on the block if he killed an earl. I must explain this to my husband. Take me to him at once!"

"We cannot." The guard hardened his jaw against the look of sympathy in his eyes. "Our orders come from Lord Raine."

"Perhaps if my lady were to speak to Lord Gavin," another guard suggested.

"Yes," she said eagerly. "Let's return to the castle. Gavin will know what to do."

Once mounted, Alyx set a pace that the knights had difficulty keeping up with. As soon as the horse's hooves touched the pavement of the courtyard, Alyx was off and running into the house.

She slammed into one empty room and started for another, then stood still and bellowed, "Gavin!"

In seconds, running down the stairs came Gavin, his face a mask of incredulousness. Judith was close behind him.

"Was that you calling?" Gavin asked, awed. "Raine said you had a strong voice but—"

Alyx cut him off. "Raine has returned to the outlaw camp. I must go to him. He hates me. He doesn't understand why I did it. I must explain."

"Slow down," Gavin said. "Tell me what's happened from the beginning."

Alyx tried to breathe deeply. "Roger Chatworth—"

The name was enough to make Gavin explode. "Chatworth! Has he harmed you? Has Raine gone after him? Fetch my men," he said to one of his men standing behind Alyx. "Full armor."

"No!" Alyx shouted, then put her face in her hands. The tears were finally starting.

Judith put her arm around Alyx. "Gavin, talk to the men while I take care of Alyx." She led Alyx to a cushioned niche under a window, took her hands in her own. "Now tell me what has happened."

Alyx's tears and her sense of urgency made her nearly incoherent. It was only by careful questioning that Judith was able to piece the story together.

"I didn't understand," Alyx sobbed. "Roger kept talking about things I didn't understand. Who is Alice? Who was his brother? What did he have to do with Mary's death? Raine was so angry. He ordered Roger killed and I had to stop him. I had to!"

"It's a good thing you did. Now I want you to sit here quietly while I go find Gavin. I'll tell him your story and Gavin will be able to reason with Raine."

Judith found her husband and twenty knights in the courtyard, looking as if they were preparing for war. "Gavin! What are you doing?"

"We're going after Chatworth."

"Chatworth? But what about Raine? He believes Alyx sided with Chatworth. You have to go to Raine and make him understand. Alyx was protecting Raine —not Chatworth."

"Judith, I don't have time to solve a lovers' quarrel now. I have to find Miles and warn him about Chatworth or else find Chatworth and see that he can't gather an army and go after my brother."

"Get Miles to release Elizabeth. That's what Chatworth wants," Judith said. "Give him back his sister."

"Like he returned mine? Across a horse, face down?"

"Gavin, please," Judith pleaded.

He stopped a moment and pulled her to him.

"Raine is safer in the forest. No doubt Chatworth will let the King know of Raine's threats and that will renew the King's wrath. And Alyx was to stay here anyway, so it's worked out well. Now Miles is of more concern to me. I don't believe he's harmed the girl, but I'd hoped we'd have time before Chatworth found out where she was. I have to warn my brother and give him protection if he needs it."

"And what of Alyx? Raine believes she betrayed him."

"I don't know," Gavin said, dismissing the subject. "Write him and send a messenger. Raine is safe—angry perhaps, but anger won't harm him. Now I must go. Look after Alyx while I'm gone and feed my son."

She smiled up at him and he kissed her lingeringly. "Take care," she called after him as he and his men rode out.

Judith's smile didn't last long as she reentered the house and saw Alyx sitting alone on the window seat.

"Is Gavin going to Raine?" Alyx whispered, hope in her voice.

"Not now. Perhaps later he will go. Now he has to warn Miles that Roger Chatworth knows a Montgomery holds Elizabeth."

Alyx leaned back against the stone casing. "How could Raine believe I'd betray him? Chatworth asked me to find out where Elizabeth was, but I refused. I only wanted to help Raine, to help the whole family. Now I have worsened all of it."

"Alyx," Judith said, taking her sister-in-law's cold hands. "There are things you don't know, things that happened before you were part of our family."

"I know about Mary's death. I was with Raine when he found out."

"Before that there were events—"

"Having to do with this Alice Roger mentioned and his brother?"

"Yes. Alice Chatworth started it all."

Alyx was amazed at the coldness in Judith's eyes, at the way her lovely features changed. "Who is Alice?" Alyx whispered.

"Gavin was in love with Alice Valence," Judith said in a small voice. "But the woman would not marry him. Instead she caught herself a rich earl, Edmund Chatworth."

"Edmund Chatworth," she said. The man Jocelin had killed.

"Edmund was killed one night by a singer who was never caught," Judith continued, not knowing Alyx's knowledge.

"I always believed Alice Chatworth knew more about what happened than she told. As a widow she decided she could afford to marry Gavin, but Gavin refused to put me aside and marry her. Alice did not take losing very well." Judith's voice was heavy with sarcasm. "She took me prisoner and threatened to pour boiling oil on my face. There was a scuffle and the oil scarred Alice."

"Roger said his household consisted of one vicious sister-in-law. Surely he cannot have harmed Mary because of the scarring?"

"No, later Roger was in Scotland and met the woman King Henry had promised Stephen for a bride. Bronwyn is rich and well worth a fight. Roger claimed her for his and he and Stephen fought. Roger is a proud man and a renowned knight, but Stephen bested him and in a rage, Roger attacked Stephen's back."

"Stephen was not hurt, was he?"

"No, but Roger's reputation was destroyed. All over England people laughed at him and began calling a back stabbing a 'Chatworth.'"

"And so Roger retaliated by taking Mary. He must have seen the Montgomerys as the cause of all his humiliations," Alyx said.

"He did. He begged Stephen to kill him on the battlefield, but Stephen wouldn't and Roger felt further insulted. So Roger held Mary and Bronwyn prisoners for a while. I don't believe he'd have harmed Mary if it weren't for Brian."

"And who is Brian?"

"Roger's young brother, a crippled, shy boy who fell in love with Mary. When Brian told Roger he planned to marry Mary, Roger got drunk and climbed in bed with Mary. You know what Mary did. Brian brought her body back to us."

"And now Miles has Elizabeth," Alyx said. "Raine is outlawed. Roger has lost his family and his wealth and now Miles's life may be in danger. Is there no way to stop this hatred? What if Roger kills Miles? What will happen then? Who will be next? Will any of us ever be safe again? Will our children grow up to hate Chatworths? Will my child fight Roger's?"

"Quiet, Alyx," Judith said softly, pulling Alyx into her arms. "Gavin has gone to warn Miles and he will be safe. Besides, Bronwyn is there with her men, and even if Chatworth were to raise an army, he won't be able to fight the MacArrans."

"I hope you're right. And Raine will be safe in the forest."

"Let's go and write letters to Raine now. We'll send a messenger tonight."

"Yes," Alyx said, sitting up, brushing tears away. "As soon as Raine knows the truth I'm sure he'll forgive me."

Chapter Eighteen

$\mathscr{R}$AINE RETURNED ALYX'S letters unopened. Although he read Judith's explanation of what had happened, he made no comment in the verbal messages he sent back. He had no squire now, so Judith had to be careful to send only messengers who could read.

Alyx seemed to accept all that was happening stoically, yet each morning her eyes were red and her appetite was all but gone.

When Gavin returned from Scotland, he gasped at the sight of Alyx, nearly skin and bones except for her stomach sticking out in front.

"What is your news?" Judith asked before he could say anything about Alyx's appearance.

"We found Chatworth and detained him for a while, but he escaped."

"Did you harm him?" Judith asked.

"Not one hair!" Gavin snapped. "When he was gone we went to Scotland, but he hadn't appeared there. My guess is Chatworth went to King Henry."

"Did you see Miles?"

Gavin nodded his head in frustration. "He has always been stubborn, but now he goes too far. He refuses to release Elizabeth, and nothing anyone could say made him see reason."

"And what about Elizabeth?"

"She fights him constantly. They would argue over the color of the sky, but sometimes I see her looking at him with something besides hate. Now, how is Alyx?"

"Raine returns her letters unopened and I've had no mention of her, although my letters plead with him to listen. The messenger says Raine has him skip the passages dealing with Alyx."

Gavin's frown said a great deal. "My brother would forgive a triple murderer, but if he thinks his honor is besmirched he is remorseless. I'll write to him and tell him of Alyx's condition. When's the child due?"

"In a few weeks."

Raine did not answer Gavin's words about Alyx either.

In November, Alyx was delivered of a large, healthy baby girl who smiled seconds after her birth and showed that she had Raine's dimples. "Catherine," Alyx whispered before falling asleep.

But in the next weeks, the child was not so happy. Catherine cried constantly.

"She cries for her father," Alyx said bleakly, and Judith almost shook her.

"If I didn't know better," Judith said, "I'd think she was hungry."

Judith's words were prophetic because as soon as a wet nurse was found, Catherine quieted.

"What good am I?" Alyx wailed.

Judith did shake her. "Listen to me! You have to think of your child. Perhaps you can't feed her, but there are other things you can do. And if the child isn't enough, I can find work for you to do."

Alyx nodded numbly and before she knew what was happening, Judith gave her more work than she knew existed. Alyx was given ledgers to read, columns of figures to add, bushels of grain to count and record. There were storerooms to clean, meals to oversee and hundreds of people to care for.

Alyx was given the care of the hospital for two weeks and learned she was good at cheering the patients. Judith was pleased with Alyx's musical ability, but she saw no reason for Alyx to spend the day alone working on music. She composed songs as she bandaged a wounded leg or as she was riding to the village below the Montgomery castle.

It was a bit of a shock to Alyx when neither Judith nor Gavin was awed by her talent but took it in stride. They, too, had talents, but they did not indulge them to the exclusion of work.

Alyx wasn't sure when she started to realize how selfish her life had been. She'd been set apart from the people of her village by her talent. Everyone had been reserved toward her, had treated her as if she were someone touched by Heaven. In her smug sureness she'd decided she hated the nobles because of what one man had done. But in truth she was jealous. She'd always felt she was the equal of anyone, but actually, what had she ever given to anyone? Her music? Or was her music really for herself?

She realized that Gavin's men and the servants were kind to her because of her relationship to Raine, but she wanted to give something that wasn't so easy for her.

She set up a school for the many children in the castle complex and began to teach them to read and write. There were many days when she wanted to quit, but she kept on and was rewarded once in a while when a child learned a new word.

In the afternoons she worked with the wounded and ill. Once a man's leg was crushed under a wine barrel and it had to be taken off. Alyx took his head in her hands and used all her training, and all her feeling, to hypnotize him with her voice. Afterward, she cried for hours.

"It hurts to become involved," she said to Judith. "One of my children, a lovely child, fell off the wall yesterday and she died in my arms. I don't want to love people. Music is safer."

Judith held her and soothed her and they talked for a long time. In the morning Alyx went back to her school. Later, the man who'd lost his leg asked for her and there were tears of gratitude on his face for Alyx's help.

Judith was behind Alyx. "Did God give you your talent to help men who need you or should you save it for prettily dressed people in church?"

At Christmas, Judith's mother came to visit them. Helen Bassett didn't look old enough to be anyone's mother. At her side was her husband John, who looked as content as any man could. Together they smiled at their eleven-month-old daughter, who was just learning to walk.

Judith's son was six months old, Alyx's daughter

two months. Everyone tried to make the festivities merry and no one mentioned how many of the family were missing.

"We were all together last year," Gavin muttered into his ale cup.

There was no word from Raine.

In January, everything seemed to happen at once. Roger Chatworth had indeed gone to King Henry—but not alone. Whether by chance or contrivance, Pagnell had appeared at the same time.

Roger said Miles was holding his sister prisoner in Scotland and Pagnell said he had proof, not just the vague rumors of before, that Raine was training non-nobles to fight as knights, that he was attempting to raise an army against the King.

King Henry said he was heartily sick of the feud between the Chatworths and the Montgomerys and he wanted Lady Elizabeth released. If Miles did not do so, he would be declared a traitor and his lands confiscated. As for Raine, if he put more weapons in those outlaws' hands, the King would burn the forest and all of them together.

Gavin sent a messenger to Scotland, pleading with Stephen to force Miles to obey the King. Before there was a reply, it was heard that Pagnell had been found dead and it was whispered that the Montgomerys were responsible. The King added this to a long list of grievances.

"He wants what we've held for centuries," Gavin said. "Other kings have tried to take it and have failed. This one will, too." He grabbed a mace from the wall. "If Stephen cannot reason with Miles, I can."

Within an hour he was off again for Scotland.

"And what about Raine?" Alyx asked quietly as she held Catherine. "Who is going to warn him about the King's threats?"

"King Henry won't burn the forest," Judith said practically. "There are too few of them left. Raine wouldn't really march on the King with his band of cutthroats, would he?"

"Perhaps. Raine would dare anything if he saw some injustice. If he thought his brother were in danger there is no predicting what he might do."

"Miles will listen to Gavin this time—I hope," Judith said. "Roger will get his sister back and everything will be settled."

They looked at each other for a long moment, neither of them believing Judith's words.

"I'm going to Raine," Alyx said softly, then opened her eyes in surprise.

"Will he allow you into the forest? Oh, Alyx, I'm not sure you should do that. The Montgomery men can get terribly angry."

"Has Gavin's anger ever kept you from doing what you had to do? If Gavin were in danger would you hesitate helping him in any way you could?"

Judith was quiet for a moment. "I once led Gavin's men against a man who held him captive."

"I merely ride into a forest. Would you care for Catherine? She's too young to take with me. It will be cold there."

"Alyx, are you sure?"

"I might be able to distract Raine. I'm sure he's brooding over all that has happened and no doubt contemplating all manner of horrors to commit against Roger Chatworth. Sometimes I can outshout him and force him to listen to me. He probably won't know what Gavin is doing to persuade Miles to release Elizabeth."

She stood, clutching her baby tightly. "I must prepare. I'll need a tent, for I can't see Raine willingly sharing his with me."

"He might forgive you the moment he sees you," Judith said, eyes dancing.

"Forgive me!" Alyx said, then saw she was teasing. "I'll make him sorry he accused me of betraying him. And I'll need medicines. I owe something to those outlaws Raine leads. They helped me once, but I never helped them. I want to make up for some of my neglect and my arrogance."

"How soon do you want to leave?" Judith asked.

"Before Gavin returns or we may have trouble. How soon can we gather things together?"

"A day if we hurry."

"Judith," Alyx said. "You are an angel."

"Perhaps I just want to see my family safe. Come along now, we have work to do."

Silently, Alyx groaned. Raine had once said Judith did twice as much in a day as anyone else. Alyx guessed it was closer to three times as much. Quickly, she handed Catherine to a maid and hurried after her sister-in-law.

Chapter Nineteen

"I DON'T LIKE like this place," Joan said from the horse beside Alyx's. "It's too dark. Are you sure Lord Raine lives in a place like this?"

Alyx didn't bother to answer. Judith had said her maid, Joan, would be an asset in this venture, that Joan could keep Alyx looking good enough to make Raine notice and Joan could ferret out all sorts of information. Judith had also warned that Joan was much too familiar and must be constantly reminded of her place.

"Hello," Alyx called up into a tree.

Joan looked at her as if she'd lost her mind. "Is the tree expected to answer you?" She added, "My lady" when Alyx gave her a sharp look.

From the tall branches of the tree dropped what Joan saw as a divine man.

"Joss!" Alyx laughed, and before she could dismount Jocelin had grabbed her about the waist and pulled her into his arms.

For a moment they just laughed and hugged until Alyx pulled away and looked at him. "You've changed," she said quietly. "There are roses in your cheeks."

Joan coughed loudly. "Perhaps the gentleman would like roses elsewhere than his cheeks."

"Joan!" Alyx warned. "I'll leave you overnight alone in this forest if you don't behave."

"Is that the voice of command I hear?" Joss asked, holding her hands at arms' length. "You have more than changed. I have never seen such a lovely lady. Walk with me and let's talk."

When they were away from Joan and the loaded horses, he asked, "You have a child?"

"A daughter with Raine's dimples and my eyes. She is sweet and perfect in every way. How is he?"

Jocelin knew who she meant. "Not well. Wait! He is physically well, but he is sad, never smiles and when a messenger comes from his brother he is angry for days." He paused. "What happened after your marriage?"

Briefly, she told him of Roger Chatworth.

"So, you have left your child and come back to Raine."

"No doubt he will welcome me with open arms." She grimaced. "There are several reasons why I've returned. I owe the people here something for saving me from the burning. How many . . . died?"

"Three, and a fourth one later."

Her hand tightened on Joss's arm. "The King's

anger at the Montgomerys and the Chatworths is increasing daily. Gavin has gone to Scotland to reason with one brother while Raine is mine to deal with."

"Do you know that he won't let any messenger read anything concerning you in a letter?"

"I guessed as much. Damn Raine and his honor! If he'd just listen for ten sentences he'd find out I'm not a traitor. The best I can hope for is to distract him for a while. I'm afraid he may decide to go after Roger Chatworth on his own, and no doubt he will if he thinks his baby brother is in danger. If his 'little' brother weren't such a seducer of women perhaps none of this would be happening. But the Montgomery brothers stand up for each other no matter what."

"Distract him?" Joss asked, smiling. "I think you'll do that. Do you know how good you look? The violet of your dress makes your eyes glow."

"Speaking of seducers," she teased, looking him up and down. "I thought I'd wear simple clothes more suited for the forest, but Judith planned my wardrobe, saying beautiful gowns would make me more visible to Raine. Have I really changed?"

"Yes, you've filled out. Now, who is that greedy wench you brought with you?"

For a moment Alyx studied Joss. In all the time she'd known him, she'd never seen him so full of laughter or tease so much. "How is Rosamund?" she asked tentatively.

Jocelin tossed his head back and laughed. "You are too clever. She's magnificent and getting better. Now, let's go into camp. Raine will be glad to see you no matter what he says."

* * *

Although Alyx thought she was prepared for her first sight of Raine, she wasn't. He'd lost weight and the striations in his muscles were standing out. He was standing by a campfire looking down at two men who talked to him earnestly.

For a moment Alyx stood completely still, watching him, remembering every inch of him, wanting to run to him, launch herself into his arms, feel him welcoming her.

But when he turned, her breath caught in her throat. Hate she could have dealt with, but Raine's eyes did not show the warm fires of hate. Instead there was nothing there but a frigid wasteland of ice: blue so cold it sent slivers of ice through her body. There was no flicker of recognition and especially none of welcome.

Without moving, Alyx watched as Raine turned his back on her and walked toward the training field.

"A mite angry, isn't he?" Joan said from behind Alyx. "Those Montgomerys do have tempers. Did I ever tell you about the pit Lady Judith climbed into to save Lord Gavin? Of course, any woman in her right mind would risk all for such a man as Lord Gavin. And Miles, too. I've never been to bed with Lord Raine, though. Is he pleasing?"

"You go too far!" Alyx snapped, spinning around.

Joan gave a catlike grin. "At least I got you to quit feeling sorry for yourself. Now where do you want the tent? You decide while I fetch a few men to help us."

With that she was off, silently slipping into the group of people who were slowly gathering about Alyx and the four loaded horses.

"We see you didn't get much of you burned," one man said, looking Alyx up and down insolently.

"Can't burn real witches," a woman said.

"Fancy dressin'," came another voice. "Who'd you sleep with to get that?"

Alyx put her chin up. "I want to thank all of you for coming to my rescue when I needed help. I'm sure I didn't deserve it, but thank you."

This seemed to take the crowd back for a moment.

"Nobody meant to help you," said a man with a scarred face. "'Twas for Lord Raine that we went. And now, from the looks of him, he wishes we'd let you burn."

This caused a great roar of laughter from everyone and, shaking their heads, slapping one another's backs, they went back to the camp, leaving Alyx alone.

"You plannin' to cry?" Joan asked nastily in Alyx's ear. "They'd like that. Here, come see what I found."

With one deep sniff, Alyx turned away from the forest camp. Had she expected them to see that she'd changed? She looked up at Joan, who was flanked by four large, good-looking young men.

"They'll help us set up the tent," Joan said, slipping her arms through two of the men's.

Alyx had to smile at Joan, who could be made happy so easily. Judith had said Joan was a cat slipping from bed to bed. With amazement, Alyx watched as Joan began to give the young men orders, all the while giving them a caress here and there. Once Joan looked up and winked at Alyx. Insolent girl! Alyx thought, turning away to hide a smile.

At the horses she began to unload the bundles she and Judith had packed.

"Need any help?" asked one of Joan's young men from behind her as he took the bundle from her.

"Thank you," she said, smiling up at him. "Are you new in the camp?"

At that he laughed and his brown eyes sparkled. "I was here before Raine, was here when you were a boy. You've changed some," he teased, watching her.

"I don't . . ." she began before looking away.

"I don't guess you looked at any of us. It was always him you watched." He jerked his head toward Raine's tent. "I don't guess I blame you, seein' as how he's a rich nobleman and you are—were—a . . ." He stopped.

"Is that how it looked?" Alyx said, mostly to herself.

"It did explain a great deal when Lord Raine told us we were to rescue you."

"Told you, did he?" she asked. "No doubt everyone was quite cheerful at the prospect of saving *me*."

The young man cleared his throat and shifted his burden. "I'll take this to the camp for you."

"Wait!" she called. "What is your name?"

"Thomas Carter," he said, grinning.

Thoughtfully, Alyx finished unloading the horse. She'd spent months in this camp and to her knowledge she'd never even seen Thomas Carter, yet he'd been here all along and had even risked his life to rescue her.

Frowning, she went back to the camp and was very pleased when Thomas smiled at her.

Joan and the young men had the tent erected in a very short time and the goods stored inside. Outside blazed a warm campfire.

"Come up in the world, ain't ya?" asked a woman

from across the fire, her eyes glaring at Alyx. There was an enormous goiter on her neck, making her hold her head to one side.

"Could we share what we have with you?" Alyx asked quietly, then turned to glare at Joan, who'd gasped in protest.

The woman shook her head, her eyes wide, and left them.

"You can't let that diseased scum near us!" Joan hissed. "Would you like to have one of those things on your neck? All she has to do is sit by us and—"

"Quiet!" Alyx said, seeing herself in Joan. "I'll not have you snubbing these people. They saved my life and for all their filth and disease they deserve more than I can repay. And as for you, you will treat them well—and not just the men."

Joan set her jaw firmly, muttering something about Alyx betraying her class, that she was becoming more like Lady Judith every day. Without a sound, she slipped off into the darkness.

Like Lady Judith, Alyx thought, and knew she'd never had such a compliment before. Smiling, she stood and went into her tent. Alone on the little cot, she was reminded of her nights with Raine. At least now she was close to him, and for the first time in months she was able to sleep well. Her last thoughts before falling asleep were of Catherine.

In the morning, Alyx awoke refreshed, smiling. The clean, cold, forest air felt good to her and even somewhat like home. Joan was not in sight, so Alyx dressed alone in a dress of emerald green wool trimmed with gold braid. A little cap on the back of her head did nothing to conceal the curls about her face. Her hair was longer now, and no longer did she hate the unusual color that made every strand seem to be an individual.

Outside the tent, she was greeted by an exhausted-looking Joan sitting lifelessly on a tree stump of a stool. Her hair was down her back, the shoulder of her dress torn. There was a bruise on her neck. She looked up at Alyx with bright eyes staring out of bluish eye sockets. "They are lusty men," she said wearily, yet so happily, that Alyx worked to keep from laughing.

"Go and rest," Alyx said sternly. "And when you awaken we'll talk of your disgusting conduct."

Heavily, Joan rose and walked toward the tent.

Alyx caught her maid's arm. "All four of them?" she asked curiously.

Joan only nodded, her eyelids drooping wearily, as she went inside the tent.

Alyx was contemplating this—four men at once?—when Raine presented himself before her, his eyes blazing angrily. She gulped twice. "Good morning," she managed to say.

"Damn your mornings!" he growled, glaring at her. "That harlot you brought with you has worn out four of my men. They're no good to me at all this morning. Can't even lift a sword. I don't know why you came here, but I think it's time you returned."

She smiled at him sweetly. "What a charming welcome, my husband. I apologize for my maid, but as you may remember I haven't had much practice in handling underlings. We can't all be born to the nobility. As to why I came here, I have a debt to pay."

"You owe me nothing."

"You!" Alyx spat, then calmed herself, forcing a smile. "Perhaps I do owe you something, but I owe more to these people."

"Since when have you cared?" He narrowed his eyes at her.

"Since they risked their lives to save me," she said calmly. "Would you care to join me for a bit of food to break your fast? I can offer you a cold meat pie."

He seemed to want to say something but turned on his heel and left her.

Alyx kept smiling, her heart pounding as she watched his broad back retreat.

"Pleased with yourself?" Jocelin asked from behind her.

Alyx laughed aloud. "Am I so transparent? Raine Montgomery is an arrogant man, isn't he? He thinks I'm here only because of him."

"And aren't you?" Joss asked.

"I shall drive him insane," Alyx said happily. "Would you like something to eat? Do you have time to sit with me and answer some questions?"

The questions Alyx asked were about the camp people, questions she should have known the answers to, since she'd lived with them for months. But she felt like an outsider.

"They won't be easy to win," Jocelin said. "They have many grudges against you. Blanche has blamed many problems on you."

"Blanche!" Alyx said, sitting up straight. Pieces of the puzzle were falling into place.

"Blanche was the woman who caused Constance's death. How else would she have known about Edmund Chatworth? You must hate Blanche."

"I am through with hating." He stood. "Would you

like to see Rosamund? If you want to help the people, she can tell you how to start."

Alyx wasn't prepared for the changes in Rosamund. Her eyes shone so brightly when she looked at Jocelin that the birthstain on her cheek almost disappeared. Joss's eyes were no less bright.

"Alyx would like to help you," he said in a soft, sweet voice, taking Rosamund's hand.

Rosamund gave Alyx a tolerant smile that made Alyx stiffen her back, and she thanked heaven for Judith's training.

"I'm sure we can find something for you to do," Rosamund said in her soft voice.

It took Alyx a week to make Rosamund realize she meant business. During that time Alyx worked early and late and no job was beneath her. She washed and bandaged running sores. She delivered a child to a woman eaten with the French pox and when the blind baby died, she buried it; no one else would touch the poor thing. She sang to an old woman who screamed incoherently at ghosts only she could see.

"Her ladyship's doin' us low ones a favor," a man said to her as she went through the dark to her tent. "Afraid to dirty her hands, she was, and now nothin's dirty enough for her. But I don't see Raine bowin' before her."

In her tent, Alyx put her hands to her temples. Her head ached from noises and ugly smells. The sick allowed her to touch them, but the healthy people ignored her except to taunt her. And as for Raine, she rarely even saw him.

"Did you come here to win Raine or these diseased scum?" Joan asked frequently.

"Raine," Alyx had whispered, rubbing her temples. Now the tent was empty, Joan obviously sleeping somewhere else. Alyx wasn't used to having servants and was a failure at controlling Joan. Seeing that the water buckets were empty, Alyx grabbed them and went to the river.

Kneeling at the bank she looked about her, at the sparkling surface of the water, broken diamonds in the moonlight. A sound made her turn and her heart leaped to her throat at the sight of Raine, his big body—a body she knew so well—blocking the moon.

"Have you proven what you wanted?" he asked quietly, his voice as smooth and hard as steel. "Did you expect to bandage one nasty wound and the people would fall at your feet in gratitude? They are better judges of people than I am."

"And pray tell me what that means," she said, aghast.

"You are a good actress. Once I believed you were . . . honest, but I learned the hard way. I hope they do not fall as far as I did."

She stood, hands into fists at her side. "Spare me your self-pity," she said through her teeth. "Poor Lord Raine lowered himself to fall in love with a commoner, and then when she did her best to save him from the King's wrath, he knew at once she'd overstepped her bounds."

Her voice rose. "I want to tell you something, Raine Montgomery. It doesn't matter if these people do hate me. I damn well deserve it. And as for their falling at my feet, I don't expect them to. At least they are the honest ones. You hold yourself up like some martyr and won't listen to anyone. Instead you'd rather believe yourself wronged and to think that only you has a sense of honor."

"And what do you, a woman, know of honor?" he sneered.

"Very little. In fact I know very little about anything except music. But at least I'm willing to admit I have faults. I have wronged these people, and I'm trying to right my wrong. You, my high lord, have wronged me—and your daughter whom you don't even ask about."

"I have heard of her," Raine said stiffly.

Alyx let out a sound that ran across Raine's skin like a steel rasp. "How big of you!" she spat. "The great, lordly Raine, lord of the forests, king of the outlaws, has heard of his own daughter."

She quietened. "I came here to win you back, but now I'm not sure I want you. Stay away from me. Take your cold honor to bed with you."

"There are other women willing to share my bed," he said, eyes hard.

"My pity goes to them," Alyx forced out. "As for me, I prefer a different sort of man, one who is not so stiff and cold, one who is still alive."

She did not see his arm shoot out. He was always faster, stronger, than she remembered. His strong fingers bit into the back of her waist and as her eyes locked with his, he smiled slightly, humorously, as he pulled her close to him.

Bending his head, his lips hovered above hers. "Cold, am I?" he said, and his voice sent chills down her spine.

Some small part of Alyx's brain could still reason.

He meant to teach her a lesson, did he? she thought, as she stood on tiptoe and slipped her arms about his neck.

When their lips touched, both of them drew in their breaths sharply and pulled away from each other, violet eyes staring into blue. Alyx blinked once, twice, before Raine's mouth descended on hers with the hunger of a dying man. He straightened, his arms about her, and her feet came off the ground as he grabbed the back of her head in his strong hand and turned her head sideways. His tongue thrust inside her mouth, sending sparks so hot through her body that they seemed to burn away her strength. Her body went limp against his, allowing him to support her full weight.

His lips began working against hers, pulling her closer, his hand massaging, kneading her head, his fingers playing with the muscles in the back of her neck.

Alyx began to tighten her grip in her attempt to get nearer. Her legs moved upward until they were about his waist. She turned her head, taking the initiative as her tongue tangled with his, her teeth hard against his lips.

The sound of approaching riders, many horses strong, came through to Raine's sense of danger. Slowly, groggily, he came out of the red fog and roughly, angrily, set Alyx away from him.

For a moment, his expression was soft; then it turned cold again. "Did you hope to entice me back to you?" he whispered. "Did you use the same weapons on Chatworth?"

It took Alyx a moment to understand what he

meant. "You are a fool, Raine Montgomery," she said softly. "Does your hate override your love?" With that, she lifted her skirts, forgetting the water buckets at her feet, and turned back to camp. Behind her she heard Raine talking to the riders, his voice unnecessarily angry.

Chapter Twenty

$\mathcal{F}$OR WHAT GOOD it is," Joan was saying as she combed Alyx's curls, "the people are less angry with you." There was no congratulation in Joan's voice. "When are you going to stop wasting your time and go after Lord Raine? We've been here two whole weeks and still he only glares at you. You should strip off your clothes and climb into bed with him."

"He'd gloat too much," Alyx said, buttoning the purple wool of her sleeve. "I'll not give him the satisfaction of winning so easily. He's said some awful things to me."

At this, Joan laughed. "What does it matter what men *say?* They have brains only for killing each other. Put a sword in a man's hand and he's happy. A woman must work to teach him there are things in life besides war."

"Perhaps you're right. Raine worries more about whether I have betrayed him than he does about how his child fares alone without its mother. Perhaps I should return to my Catherine and leave Raine to his brooding."

"Brooding is correct," Joan said. "Did you know that he has slept with no woman since he returned from Lord Gavin's?"

Alyx's smile started small and stretched very wide.

"He loves you, Alyx," Joan said softly.

"Then why doesn't he show it! Why does he sneer and glower at me? When I am with Rosamund I'll look up and there he'll be, watching me with his cold looks. I feel as if I've had the icy river water tossed on my body."

Joan laughed delightedly. "He *is* showing you that he cares! What do you expect him to do—apologize?" Joan laughed even harder at this idea. "The Lord made women stronger so they could put up with men's weaknesses. You say you were wrong to treat the forest people as you did, so you admitted it and set about changing your error. Do you think any man could be so strong?"

"Raine has accused me of being a traitor," she said stubbornly.

"The King has said Lord Raine is a traitor. The King is wrong, but will he admit it? No more so than your husband will come to you and ask you to forgive him."

"I don't like this," Alyx said, her lower lip thrust out. "I have done no wrong to Raine. Roger Chatworth—"

"Damn Chatworth!" Joan said. "Raine's pride is

hurt. You stayed beside some other man instead of your husband. Above all else, men expect blind loyalty."

"I am loyal, it is—"

She cut herself off when a breathless Jocelin burst into the tent unannounced.

"You should come," he said to Alyx. "Maybe you can prevent a death."

"Whose?" Alyx asked, standing immediately and following Joss before he could answer.

"Brian Chatworth has just begged entrance into the camp. Raine is donning armor to meet him."

"But Judith said Brian loved Mary, that Brian brought her body back to them."

"Maybe it's the name Chatworth. That alone would send Raine into a rage."

Jocelin pulled Alyx onto a horse and set out quickly, dodging tree branches as they rode. When at last they stopped, the sight ahead of them surprised Alyx. In a small clearing, lit by the early morning sun, stood a young man. He was small, slight, even delicate. Yet he had the facial features of Roger Chatworth. Had Alyx seen him elsewhere she would have guessed this near boy was Roger's son.

Alyx slid off the horse before Joss could dismount. "May I welcome you?" she said, walking toward the boy. "I am Alyxandria Montgomery, Lord Raine's wife. I have met your brother."

Brian pulled himself to his full height. "I have no brother," he said in a surprisingly masculine voice. "I come to join Lord Raine in his fight to avenge his sister's death."

"Oh, my," Alyx said, astonished. "I had hoped you offered some solution to this feud."

"We're all wishing that," came a voice from above Alyx's head.

She looked up but could see no one. "Who are? You're not one of Raine's guards."

"Oh, but I am, and are you truly Raine's wife?"

Alyx listened to the voice, sure she'd never heard it before, yet something about it was familiar. It was definitely a voice full of humor. She glanced at Brian and Jocelin. Brian's face was immobile, too hard for one so young, while Joss gave a shrug.

Her attention was suddenly given to the appearance of Raine riding his great heavy war horse, wearing full armor, covered from head to foot in steel.

Dismounting, he walked toward Brian Chaworth, and the young man did not flinch. One blow from Raine's hand would have been enough to send him sprawling. "Do you plan to hide behind my wife's skirts?" Raine said in a low voice. "She is known to protect Chatworths."

Alyx put herself between Brian and Raine. "And do you make war on children?" she yelled up at him. "Can't you listen to him? Or are you too pig-headed to give the boy a chance?"

Raine never said a word to Alyx because laughter coming from the trees made him halt.

Alyx watched, openmouthed, as a man dropped to the ground. He was wearing the most extraordinary clothes she had ever seen: a big-sleeved shirt, a soft yellow color, was covered by a bright blue tartan blanket wrapped about his waist in such a way that it formed a skirt and then was tossed over one shoulder, a heavy belt holding it in place. His knees were bare, his calves encased in heavy wool socks, thick shoes on his feet.

"Stephen," Raine breathed, his eyes softening.

"Aye, 'tis me," this oddly dressed man said. He was tall and slim with dark blond hair, a very handsome man. "I've brought this boy to you. He wants to share your exile and would like to learn from you."

"He's a Chatworth," Raine said, his eyes hardening again.

"Yes, he's a Chatworth," Alyx said. "And you'll not forgive him, will you? No doubt you'll hate this man for daring to bring him here. Go," she said to Stephen. "It's no use trying to reason with him. He has a piece of wood for a brain."

To her surprise, Stephen began to laugh, a great, deep, joyful laugh.

"Oh, Raine," he cried, slapping Raine on his armored shoulder, making the steel rattle. "How Gavin and I have prayed for this time. So you've fallen head over heels for a woman who fights you at every step? Gavin had written us what a sweet, helpful, congenial little thing our new sister was." He turned to Alyx. "Judith said you had a strong voice, but a moment ago you nearly knocked me from the tree."

"You are Stephen Montgomery," Alyx said in wonder. He did look a bit like Gavin, but besides his clothing, his accent was strange.

"MacArran," Stephen corrected, smiling at her. "I am married to the MacArran and my name is hers. Now do I get a kiss or would you rather fight with my brother?"

"Oh, a kiss!" Alyx said so enthusiastically that Stephen laughed again before drawing her into his arms. His kiss was less than brotherly. "Can you help me talk some sense into him?" she whispered. "He is obsessed with the Chatworths."

Stephen winked as he released her, turning back to Raine. "I've come a long way, brother. Will you offer me no refreshment?"

"And what about him?" Raine motioned toward Brian.

"He may come, too," Stephen laughed. "He can help me disarm you. And you, Alyx, will join us?"

"If I am invited," she said, looking directly at Raine.

"*I* invite you," Stephen said, as he threw an arm around Alyx's shoulders and started forward. "Follow us, Brian," he called over his shoulder.

"Are you always so courageous?" Alyx asked, looking up at Stephen.

Stephen's face was serious. "How long has he been like this?"

"I'm not sure I know what you mean."

"Unsmiling, angry, glaring at everyone. This isn't like Raine."

She thought a moment before she answered. "He has been this way since Mary's death."

Stephen nodded once. "Raine would take it hard. That's one reason why I brought Brian. They are very much alike. Brian is eaten with hatred for his brother. And what of you? My brother's black moods don't frighten you?"

"He thinks I've betrayed him."

"Yes, Gavin and Judith told me."

Her voice became louder. "He won't listen to me. I tried to explain, but he sent my letters back unopened. And he won't listen to Gavin, either."

Stephen squeezed her shoulders. "Gavin will always think of Raine and Miles as children. Raine and Gavin can't be in a room two minutes without arguing. Stay with me and I'll see if I can make him listen."

Alyx gave him such a radiant smile that Stephen laughed. "My Bronwyn will have your heart on a platter if you keep looking at me like that. Can you really sing as well as Judith says?"

"Better," Alyx said with such confidence that Stephen laughed again.

They stopped before Raine's tent and Stephen muttered something about wasting money that Alyx didn't understand. Rather like a sulky boy, Raine followed them inside and, after one malevolent look cast at Alyx, turned to Stephen. "What has caused you to travel so far south? Have those Scots tossed you out?"

"I came to meet my new sister-in-law, of course."

"She would prefer that you were a Chatworth."

Stephen paused, Raine's helmet in his hand. "I cannot allow you to say such things," he said quietly. "Don't cause a quarrel between us. Do you plan to disown me because I have brought a Chatworth to your camp?"

"You are my brother," Raine said flatly.

"Meaning that you trust me?" There was laughter under his voice. "Tell me, brother, what bothered you the most, that your wife talked to a Chatworth or that she dared to talk to any handsome man?"

"Chatworth!" Raine said loudly, with a glance at Alyx, who was studying her fingernails.

"Did I ever tell you the trick Hugh Lasco played on me?" Stephen knelt to unbuckle Raine's leg protectors.

As Stephen began to tell some long-winded, slightly unbelievable tale, Alyx watched Raine. After a while she began to understand Stephen's point. Stephen had believed all manner of low-minded things about his wife, and as a result of his mistrust, he'd almost lost her.

"Alyx," Stephen turned to her suddenly. "Are you in love with Roger Chatworth? Are you contemplating leaving Raine for him?"

The idea was so ridiculous that Alyx laughed—until she saw the smoldering light in Raine's eyes. "Roger Chatworth deserves to die for what he did to Mary but *not* at my husband's hands. He's not worth seeing Raine hanged for his murder."

For a moment Alyx thought Raine might be listening to her, but the moment passed as he sat down on the cot and began removing the cotton pads that protected his skin from the steel armor. "Women have glib tongues," he murmured.

Stephen glanced at Alyx, saw her eyes shoot fire. "You have my permission to take an ax to him," he said amiably. "Alyx, could you fetch us some food? I may die of hunger soon."

As soon as they were alone, Raine turned to his brother. "Why have you come? Surely you want more than to step between my wife and me."

"Someone should," Stephen snapped. "Her heart is in her eyes. Can't you forgive her? She doesn't know our ways, and women have such strange ideas about honor. I hear you haven't seen your daughter. She looks like you."

Raine refused to be swayed. "Why did you bring Chatworth?"

"For the reason I said: he wants to train with you.

The King won't like your training one nobleman to fight another. And what is this I hear of your raising an army of criminals to overthrow the King?''

Raine guffawed at this idea. "What liar told you this?"

"Pagnell of Waldenham told King Henry this. Hadn't you heard? I thought Alyx came to warn you of this. The King's ears are being filled with lies against the Montgomerys."

"Alyx hasn't seen fit to warn me," Raine said.

"And I'm sure you sat down and asked her nicely why she deserted her child and the comfort of Gavin's house to come live near you in this cold forest."

"I neither need nor want your interference in my life."

Stephen shrugged. "I remember a few kicks I received when Bronwyn and I had problems."

"And now all is sweetness and light with you, is it?" Raine asked, one eyebrow raised.

Stephen cleared his throat. "We do have . . . ah, a few disagreements now and then, but generally she learns the true way."

"I'd like to hear Bronwyn's version of that," Raine said before changing the subject. "Have you seen Miles?"

Stephen was saved from answering by the appearance of Alyx bearing a tray, Joan behind her with a second tray. Stephen didn't want to tell Raine that his problem with women was mild compared to Miles's.

As soon as Alyx realized that Joan was going to make a fool of herself over Stephen, she sent the maid out. The meal was an awkward one, the first Raine and Alyx had shared since she returned to the forest.

Stephen did nearly all the talking, entertaining them with stories of Scotland.

"And you should see my son," Stephen boasted. "Already Tam has taken him riding and he can't really sit up yet. You and I weren't on a horse until we could walk. And how is your daughter, Alyx?"

For the first time in two weeks Alyx let herself think completely about her daughter. "She is strong," she said dreamily, "short and healthy with a lusty cry that made Judith's son cry, too."

"Protective of his cousin, no doubt," Stephen said. "She has your eyes."

"You saw her?" Alyx came off her stool. "When? Was she healthy? Had she grown any?"

"I doubt if she's changed much since you've seen her, but I agree about her voice. Do you think she'll be able to sing?" He turned to Raine. "She has those dimples you got from Mother's family."

"I must see to the camp." Raine stood so suddenly he nearly upset the food Alyx had brought. Quickly, he left the tent.

"He'll come around," Stephen said confidently, smiling at Alyx's tearing eyes.

Alyx tried not to think of Raine's constant anger and instead turned her attentions to Brian Chatworth. He was a miserable young man, his eyes black with a deep, burning hatred, and he never smiled nor seemed to find pleasure in anything. Alyx could not persuade him to talk or to confide in her about any subject. Her questions about where he'd been for the last several months since Mary's death were met by silence.

Alyx gave up after a while and left him to the men on the training field. As for Raine, he neither looked at nor spoke to the boy and spent most of his time with Stephen.

After Stephen had been in camp for three days, Joan came to Alyx.

"I think they're fighting," Joan said excitedly.

"Who? Not Raine and Brian Chatworth?"

Joan's voice was impatient. "Of course not! Lord Raine and Lord Stephen have gone deeper into the forest, and one of the guards has reported loud voices coming from there. Everyone's planning to go and watch."

"You will not!" Alyx said, pushing past her maid and out into the cool air. "Jocelin," she shouted when she saw her friend. "Stop them. Leave Raine in private. And you," she turned to Joan. "Help keep the men in camp. Do what you must. But nothing lewd," she called over her shoulder as she hurried forward.

Jocelin enlisted the aid of some ex-soldiers to help him while some of the wounded helped Alyx, and Joan had her own methods of making men obey her. Together they managed to keep the camp people away from where Raine and Stephen were having their "discussion."

"They're just settin' now," said a guard as he was replaced by someone else.

Alyx walked away, not wanting to hear any more of the facts. Raine was so much heavier than his brother, obviously so much stronger. Stephen couldn't possibly win a fight between them, and Alyx prayed Raine would hold back and not truly hurt his slim brother.

At sundown, Alyx took the water buckets to the river, hoping to escape the gleeful voices of the people in the camp. They were all huddled about campfires listening to the guards with rapt attention.

She stood beside the river, motionless, glad for the quiet, when a sound made her whirl. Coming toward her, walking heavily, wearily, was Raine. Perhaps she should have listened to the people's comments so she would have been prepared for her first sight of him. The left side of his face was swollen and turning purple. There were bruises on his jaw, his eye a flamboyant mixture of unnatural colors.

"Raine," she whispered, making him look up and away from her as he knelt by the water. She forgot any memories of anger between them but ran to him, knelt beside him. "Let me see," she said.

Docilely he turned his head to her and she placed cool fingers on his misshapen face. Without a word, she raised her skirt, tore away linen petticoat, dipped it in cold water and touched his face.

"Tell me all of it," she said in a half-command. "What sort of club did Stephen use on your face?"

It was a long moment before Raine spoke. "His fist."

Alyx paused in her washing of Raine's face. "But a knight—" she began. She'd heard Raine shout a hundred times about how unchivalrous, how unmanly it was to fight with one's hands. Many honorable men had died rather than lose their honor by using their fists.

"Stephen has learned some strange ways in Scotland," Raine said. "He says there is more than one way to fight."

"And no doubt you stood there like a great ox and let him beat you rather than do an unknightly thing such as hit his face in return?"

"I tried!" Raine said, then winced and calmed himself. "He danced about like a woman."

"Don't insult my sex. No woman did this to your face."

"Alyx." He grabbed her wrist. "Have you no feeling for me? Will you always side with others against me?"

She took his face gently in her hands, her eyes searching his. "I have loved you since the first moment I saw you. Even then, when I had planned to hate you, I was drawn to you. I fought against loving you, but it was as if some great power controlled me and I had no say in what I did. Don't you realize that I'm always on your side? That day at the fair if you'd killed Roger Chatworth you could have been hanged. I pretended to bed Jocelin to keep you from leaving the safety of the forest. What more can I do to prove my loyalty and love?"

He pulled away from her. "Perhaps it's your methods I don't like. Why can't you tell me what you're doing? Why must you fight me all the time?"

"Fighting is the only way you'll listen to me," she said in exasperation. "I told you you could not leave the forest when the people accused me of stealing, but you wouldn't listen. I told you not to kill Roger Chatworth, but you stood there like a bull with veins standing out on your neck." Her voice was rising.

"I don't know who unmans me most—my brother or you."

His tone was so little-boy, feel-sorry-for-himself

that Alyx tried not to laugh. "What did you and Stephen quarrel about?"

Raine rubbed his jaw. "Stephen suggested I consider that perhaps you weren't disloyal when you saved Chatworth's miserable life."

Raine turned and looked at her. "Have I been wrong? Have I treated you very badly? Is there any love in your heart left for me?"

She touched his cheek. "I will always love you. I sometimes think I was born loving you."

A single dimple appeared in his cheek and she caught her breath as she thought he was going to pull her into his arms. Instead, he reached under his doublet and rummaged in his pocket. "Perhaps I can purchase a smile or two," he said as he dangled the Lyon belt before her eyes.

"My belt!" she gasped. "How did you find it? I thought it was lost forever. Oh, Raine!" She threw her arms around him and began kissing his face so enthusiastically that she caused him great pain, but he didn't mind.

"You are the best husband," she whispered, kissing his neck. "Oh, Raine, how I have missed you."

She didn't say anymore because his hands twisted in her hair and pulled her head backward as his lips came down on hers. Alyx was sure she would burst apart into little pieces. She catapulted all her weight against him, and as he was in a precarious position, he fell backward, caught himself, then changed positions on her mouth and let himself fall, pulling Alyx with him.

Mouths attached, they rolled sideways, then changed directions, and in one quick movement landed themselves in the icy river water, Alyx on bottom.

"Raine!" Alyx screeched in pain as his heavy body rolled atop her arm, scraping it against a rock. "You're breaking me!" Already, her teeth were beginning to chatter.

"It would be small payment for what you've done to me," he said, lying in the water as if it were a feather bed. "Before I met you my life was peaceful and calm. Now my own brother beats me."

"Which you deserved!" she spat. "It's the only way to make you listen. Now let me up and let me get dry before I freeze to death."

"I know a way to keep you warm." He began to nuzzle her neck.

"You great stupid boar," she yelled into his ear, making him move away and shake his head to clear the ringing. "I'm cold and wet, and if you don't let me up I'll bring the whole camp to my rescue."

"You think they'd come to rescue you or would they side with me?"

She pushed at him. "They wouldn't recognize you with your great purple face."

He chuckled at that and easily moved off her. "You look good, Alyx," he said, his eyes alight, looking at her wet dress, which clung to her.

Alyx put her arms behind her and started to push herself up and found the wet dress to be very heavy. With another chuckle, Raine stood, lifted her and started toward the darkest part of the forest.

"The camp is that way," she pointed.

"Alyx, someone should teach you that you shouldn't always give orders. Perhaps you are right now and then, but sometimes you should listen and leave the commands to the men."

"I have to do what is right, and if you need to be saved from yourself, I will," she said arrogantly.

"You are leading up to a paddling such as you've never had before—if you've ever had one, which I doubt. That priest who trained you should have applied a lute to the bottom half of you now and again and perhaps you'd have a little humility."

"I have as much humility as you do," she said, watching him. "If you do foolish things, am I to stand aside and not raise my voice?"

"Alyx, you are going too far," he warned.

"And how will you punish me for speaking the truth?"

"Not in a way that you'll like."

"How can you threaten me after all I've done for you? I've saved you from Roger Chatworth. I was nearly burned at the stake because the judges wanted your lands. I left with Jocelin to keep you safe in the forest."

Raine grabbed her shoulders and held her at arms' length, her feet off the ground. One half of his face was swollen purple, but the other half was red with rage. "You've gone too far," he said through his teeth.

Before Alyx could take a breath, Raine had seated himself on a stump, pulled Alyx across his lap, bottom end up and tossed her skirts over her head. He gave her one strong, painful whack across her buttocks.

"You were not tried as a witch because of *me*," he said. "You had your quarrel with Pagnell before I ever met you."

Alyx didn't have a chance to answer as Raine

smacked her bottom again. "True, I was angry and perhaps should not have ordered Chatworth to be killed, but as we were in a secluded place, who would have known to tell the King? I am not as stupid as you seem to think and would not have left the body near my brother's estate."

Again, his hand came down. "I don't like having my orders countermanded and especially not before my men. Is that clear?" Again he punctuated this with a blow.

Alyx, tears in her eyes, nodded silently.

"Good! Now, as for you and Jocelin, I don't like games and jests at which I'm the butt. It hurt too much to see you with another man, and later when I found out it'd all been a trick, as if I were a dunce to be made a fool of, I could have killed you. And you risked the life of my daughter with your stupid jests."

A very hard blow hit her. "You nearly lost my daughter to the fire as well as to the hazards of the road while you and Jocelin wandered about the country. I want no more of it, Alyx." He struck her again. "Do you understand me? You are my wife and you damn well better start acting like it."

With one more painful spank, he pushed her off his lap.

Alyx sat up, wincing with pain when her bottom hit the forest floor. There were so many tears in her eyes that she could hardly focus.

Raine stood, towering above her. "When you're through sulking," he said, "come back to the tent and I'll make love to you so passionately you'll forget who you are." With that, he walked away from her.

For a moment, Alyx sat staring after him, then she closed her mouth and stood. No sulking in the world was worth missing a bout of lovemaking. As quickly as her stiff legs could carry her, she ran after Raine.

Chapter Twenty-one

$\mathcal{A}$LYX LAY ON her back on Raine's cot, a bare leg dangling over the edge, one soft leather shoe hooked over two happy toes. All of her was immensely happy, from toes up to the roots of her hair. Raine had made good his promise. All last night he'd been insatiable, never letting her sleep, tossing her around like a rag doll. She'd be on top, then on bottom, then he'd stretch her sideways and pull her between his legs. One minute he was sweet and gentle, the next fierce, driving, and the next he'd be almost bored, as if he'd forgotten she was there. At those times Alyx would do something naughty to get his attention back to her. His sensuous laugh would make her aware that he was manipulating her and was far away from being bored.

The sun was coming up when she finally pleaded with him to halt. He'd merely kissed her nose, smiled lopsidedly with his battered face, rose, washed, dressed and left the tent. Alyx settled her sore, bruised, exhausted body to a few hours' sleep.

Now, awake at last, she lay still, humming to herself and remembering last night.

"Looks like you finally learned what to do with a man," Joan said, slipping inside the tent. "I wondered if all the brothers were as good as Lord Miles. It looks like you think so. Did you know you were smiling in your sleep?"

"Be quiet, you insolent woman," Alyx said in such a friendly way that Joan only laughed.

"You'd better get up. Lord Stephen has had some news from Scotland and he's leaving very soon."

"It's nothing bad, is it?" Alyx asked, reluctantly sitting up, wincing at a pain in her back. Sometimes Raine seemed to think she was a piece of cloth the way he wrapped her about his body, one leg here, another one there, an arm over there. There was a crick in her neck and the memory of what Raine had done to hurt *that* area made her grin.

Joan was looking at her with unconcealed interest. "My four men together could not have made me look as you do now. Is Lord Raine really such a lover?"

Alyx shot her a dangerous look. "I'll have your heart on a platter if you so much as look at him."

Joan only grinned. "I've been trying for years and he's not interested. What will you wear today?"

Alyx dressed carefully in a dress of palest lavender, trimmed in rabbit fur dyed a deep, luscious purple.

"Ah," Stephen said when he saw her, "such beauty in the midst of such a wilderness." He took her hand and kissed it.

Alyx caught his hand, examined his knuckles, which were raw, cut, not yet beginning to heal. "May you lose your hand if you strike my husband again," she whispered passionately.

Stephen blinked once before he laughed. "And my brother worries about your loyalty. You must come and meet my Bronwyn. She will like you."

"I've heard you have news."

Stephen's face darkened. "Roger Chatworth found Miles and Elizabeth alone and has run a sword through Miles's arm. Lady Elizabeth has returned to England with her brother."

"Then perhaps soon this feud can end. Roger has his sister safe. All that's left is to make the King forgive Raine."

"Perhaps," Stephen said. "Now I must go home and help my clan. My little brother is in a rage and wants to ride on Chatworth."

"Go!" she said. "Stop him."

He kissed her hand again. "I will do what I can, and now I know I leave Raine in good hands. He is a stubborn man."

Alyx laughed at that. "In your . . . talk yesterday, did you by chance mention Brian Chatworth? Now that Roger has harmed Miles, will Raine take it out on Brian?"

"No, I don't think so. This morning Raine and Brian talked for a long time and I believe Raine's heart has gone out to the boy. I don't believe there'll be more problems. In fact, they're on the training field now. I must go. My men wait for me."

"Your men?" Alyx asked, astonished. "I saw no one. I assumed you were alone."

Stephen seemed pleased by this. "There are six MacArrans with me, all stationed about the forest, keeping watch."

"But we have guards. They should have come into the camp near the fires and had some hot food. They'll freeze out there."

Stephen laughed hard at this. "The English are a soft lot. Our summers aren't as warm as your winters. You'll have to come to the Highlands someday. Douglas says your singing will make his brothers cry."

There were so many questions Alyx wanted to ask, but she had no idea where to start. Her emotions showed on her face.

"You'll have to come," Stephen smiled, kissed her cheek and disappeared into the trees, the short plaid swirling about his thighs.

What followed for Alyx were three days of relative peace. Raine seemed to grow an attachment for the crippled Brian and was impressed by Brian's eagerness to learn.

"The hate is eating him," Raine said as he and Alyx lay in bed. "He thinks that if he trains hard enough he'll be able to fight his brother, but Roger is formidable. He would slay Brian in one thrust."

"Brother against brother," Alyx whispered and shuddered.

Alyx felt sorry for Brian, who slept apart from the people of the camp.

"I don't trust him," Joan said. "He says too little and he has nothing to do with anyone."

"He's been hurt. He'll get over it," Alyx defended the boy.

"He's planning something. He's been gathering the down from thistles and yesterday he paid a man to send a message to someone."

"To whom?" Alyx demanded, immediately concerned. Perhaps Brian was actually loyal to his brother and was planning to lead Roger Chatworth to Raine, or worse, to send the King's men in.

"I don't know who it went to."

"We must tell Raine," Alyx said, grabbing her maid's wrist and dragging her toward the training area.

"I know of the message," Raine said when Alyx told him. "Brian wishes to find out the condition of his sister."

"Have you had a reply?"

Raine jabbed a sword at a quintain. "My little brother's seed has taken and Lady Elizabeth carries his child."

Alyx thought of the lovely Elizabeth—and her sharp tongue. "She'll not like that. She'll not like any man taking her to bed, then discarding her."

Raine gave her a hard look. "You seem to give my brother all the credit. Perhaps this Elizabeth is a wayward wench and seduced my brother. Then, when he loved her, she left him. If Chatworth struck Miles, it would seem that Miles fought to keep the woman."

"Perhaps, but Miles—" She broke off at the sound of trumpets in the distance. "What is it?"

Raine turned to some ex-soldiers near him. "Find out what that is."

Within seconds, the men were on their horses and away into the forest. Long minutes later, they returned. "Roger Chatworth is accepting your challenge, my lord."

"Raine!" Alyx bellowed at him.

After one quelling look, he ignored her. "I have issued no challenge. Perhaps Chatworth means to make the first move."

"No, my lord. He—"

"I sent the challenge," Brian Chatworth said from behind them and they all turned. "I knew my brother would not respond to a challenge from me, so I sent it in the name of Raine Montgomery."

"You can just go and tell him what you've done," Alyx said, as if talking to a child.

In the distance, the trumpets sounded again.

"Go now," Alyx said, "and explain."

"Alyx," Raine said in a low voice. "Go to the tent. This is not business for women."

She looked up at him, still bruised from Stephen's beating, and what she saw there frightened her. "Raine, you can't be thinking of accepting the challenge? You didn't issue it. You surely have more sense than to—"

"Jocelin," Raine ordered. "Take Alyx away."

Alyx waited for her husband inside the tent, pacing back and forth, snapping at Joan until the maid left her.

When Raine finally appeared and their eyes met, Alyx gasped. "No, Raine," she said, wrapping her arms around his middle. "It wasn't you who made the challenge."

He pulled her away from him, his hands on her arms. "You must understand that it's a matter of honor and it's been a long time coming. When Chatworth is dead, perhaps then my family can live in peace again. If I don't kill him now he'll go after Miles for impregnating his sister. He swears Miles took her by force."

"Let Miles fight Chatworth!" Alyx yelled. "I don't care. Let all your brothers fight, but not *you*."

"Alyx," Raine said gently. "I realize you're a woman and more, you haven't been raised to our

285

ways of honor, but now I must ask you not to insult me more. Help me dress."

"*Help* you! Honor! How can you talk to me of such things? What do I care for honor when the man I love may die? I have fought long and hard to keep you safe, but now because of some foolish games of a boy you must pay the price. Let Brian fight his brother."

Color was rising in Raine's neck. "Brian is no match for Roger Chatworth. And it's the Montgomery family who has been insulted. Do you forget my sister who died because of what Chatworth did to her? I don't fight for Brian but for Mary and for Miles and for future peace."

She dropped to her knees in front of Raine as he sat on the edge of the cot. "Please don't go. If you aren't killed, you'll be hurt badly."

"Alyx." He nearly smiled at her as he touched her hair. "Perhaps you don't know, but the estates I have I purchased with money I'd won in years of tournaments. I've been through hundreds of these challenges."

"No," she said with feeling. "Not like this one. The hatred that you and Chatworth have for each other wasn't involved in those fights. Please, Raine."

He stood. "I'll listen to no more. Now, will you help me arm myself or must I get Jocelin?"

She also stood. "You ask me to help prepare you for your death? Should I be the dutiful wife and murmur soft words about honor? Or should I talk of Mary and how she died and add fuel to your hate? If Mary were alive would she want you to fight for her? Wasn't her whole life an attempt at peacemaking?"

"I don't want us to part with angry words between us. This is something I must do."

She was so angry she was shaking. "If we part now as you walk off to answer a challenge that wasn't made by you, then it will be with angry words—and it will be final."

Their eyes held each other's for a long while.

"Think carefully on what you say," Raine said quietly. "We've quarrelled before over this matter."

"Raine, can't you see how this hatred is eating at you? Even Stephen saw how it had changed you. Forget Roger Chatworth. Go to the King, beg his forgiveness and let us live, not this constant talk of death and dying."

"I am a knight. I am sworn to avenge wrongs."

"Then do something about the Enclosure Acts!" she screamed. "They're wrong. But cease this hideous feud with Roger Chatworth. His sister will bear a Montgomery. A new life for Mary's. What more could you want?"

Outside, the trumpets sounded, and the noise went through Alyx.

"I must dress," Raine said. "Will you help me?"

"No," she said quietly. "I cannot."

"So be it," he whispered. With one last look at her, he turned toward his armor.

"You are choosing between me and Roger Chatworth today," she said.

He didn't answer her but kept at his armor. Alyx left the tent.

"Go to him, Jocelin," she said once she was outside. To Joan, she said, "Come, we must pack. I'm going home to my daughter."

Alyx had every intention of being out of the forest before any fighting began. Of course Raine could win, she thought, but could she stand by and watch bits and pieces hacked off him? She was sure Roger Chatworth would be as filled with hatred as Raine was.

It was two hours before she heard the first sounds of steel against steel as they echoed through the forest. Slowly, she dropped the gown she was folding and left her tent. Whatever he did, whoever he fought, for whatever reason, he was hers.

She was almost to the clearing where the men fought when Joan stopped her.

"Don't look," Joan said. "Chatworth is merciless."

Alyx stared at her maid a moment, then started forward.

"Joss," Joan called. "Stop her."

Jocelin grabbed Alyx's arms, held her in place. "It's a slaughter," he said, catching her eyes. "Perhaps Roger's hatred was greater and has given him more strength. But whatever the reason, Raine is losing badly."

Alyx pushed away from Joss. "Raine is mine in death as well as alive. Let me go!"

With one look at Joan, Jocelin released her.

Nothing could have prepared Alyx for the sight in front of her. The two men fought on foot, and Raine's armor was so covered with blood that the gold Montgomery leopards were nearly hidden. His left arm seemed to be hanging by a thread, but he kept fighting, swinging valiantly with his right. Roger Chatworth seemed to be toying with the weakened, bloody man as he circled him, teased him.

"He's dying," Alyx said. Raine always believed in honor so much, but now, to die like this, as an animal in a cage, at the mercy of Chatworth's torments.

She started forward, but Joss caught her. "Raine!" she yelled.

Roger Chatworth turned toward her, looked at her, although his face couldn't be seen beneath the helmet. As if understanding her misery, he circled once more and plowed his ax into the small of Raine's back.

Raine hesitated for a moment then fell forward, face down, Roger standing silent over him.

Instantly, Alyx pulled away from Joss and ran forward. Slowly, she knelt beside Raine's torn body and pulled his head into her lap. There were no tears, only a deep numbness, a feeling that her blood was also pouring onto the ground.

With great reverence, she lifted his head and removed his helmet.

The gasp she let out at the sight under the helmet made Roger Chatworth turn back. After one long moment of disbelief, he threw back his head and let out a horrible cry—a cry very much like the one Raine had given when he heard of Mary's death.

"A life for a life," whispered Brian from Alyx's lap. "Now Mary can rest."

With a trembling hand, Alyx touched Brian's sweaty cheek, watched as he gave his last breath and died in her arms.

"Leave him," Roger said as he bent and picked up his brother's body in his arms. "He is mine now."

Alyx stood in her blood-soaked gown and watched as Roger carried Brian toward the waiting Chatworth men and horses.

"Alyx," Joss said from beside her. "I don't understand. Why is Chatworth taking Raine's body?"

Her body was shaking so much she could hardly speak. "Brian wore Raine's armor and Roger has killed his young brother."

"But how—?" Joss began.

Joan held up thistle down, the ends of it soaked in blood. "He must have planned this for a long while. No doubt he used the down to pad a hauberk so Lord Raine's armor would fit."

Alyx turned to them with wide eyes. "Where is Raine? He wouldn't have docilely allowed Brian to take his armor."

It took them some time to find Raine, his armor missing, lying in his leather padding, soundly asleep under a tree. Joan laughed when she saw him, but Alyx didn't. The unnatural position of Raine's body alarmed her.

"Poison!" Alyx screamed and ran to her husband. The warmth of him showed he wasn't dead, but he might have been for all the notice he paid her.

"Fetch Rosamund at once," Jocelin ordered Joan.

Alyx started to slap Raine's cheeks when her voice couldn't rouse him. "Help me stand him up."

It took all Joss's strength and Alyx's to lift Raine's inert form, but still he slept on.

Rosamund came running and after only a glance at Raine she looked at Joss with fear in her eyes. "I hoped I was wrong. My opium was stolen two days ago, and I hoped the thief knew how to use it."

"Opium?" Alyx demanded. "Isn't that a sleeping drug? My sister-in-law used it."

"It's common enough," Rosamund answered, "but what most people don't know is that if too much is taken, the victim could sleep until death."

Alyx's eyes widened. "You don't think Brian Chatworth gave Raine a great deal, do you?"

"A thimbleful is too much. We must assume Lord Raine has taken too much. Come, there is much, much work to be done."

It took a full day to clean out Raine's system. Rosamund gave him vile-tasting concoctions that made him vomit, that emptied his bowels. And constantly, men took turns walking him.

"Sleep, let me sleep," was all Raine would mumble, his eyes closed, his feet dragging.

Alyx allowed no one to stop walking him nor would she let him turn away from the liquids that were forced down his throat. After many hours, he began to regain control of his feet and started walking somewhat under his own power. His body was empty of all solid matter and Rosamund began to make him drink buckets full of water, hoping to flush him more. Raine was waking enough to protest more loudly.

"You didn't leave me," he said once to Alyx.

"I should have, but I didn't," she snapped. "Drink!"

At noon of the second day, Rosamund finally allowed Raine to sleep and gratefully, she and Jocelin also rested. Tired beyond belief, Alyx went to each of the people of the camp and thanked them personally for helping her with Raine.

"You ought to sleep yourself," came a gruff voice, and Alyx recognized one of the men who'd accused her of stealing. "We don't want to save one of you just to lose the other."

She smiled at him so gratefully that he turned red and looked away. Still smiling, she staggered into Raine's tent and fell asleep beside him.

Alyx stayed with Raine for another week—until he found her holding a woman's baby and crying silently.

"You must go back to Gavin," Raine told her.

"I can't leave you."

He raised one eyebrow. "You've seen that your presence here won't prevent what's going to happen. Chatworth will lay his brother to rest, then we shall see what will happen. Go home and see to our daughter."

"Perhaps a visit," she said, her eyes alight. "Maybe just for a week or so, then I'll return to you."

"I don't think I can live long without you. Go now and tell Joan to pack for you. You can see our Catherine in three days' time."

Alyx's thanks, her joy at the thought of seeing her daughter again, made her leap into Raine's arms. And her kisses soon led them elsewhere. Before either of them realized what was happening, they were rolling on the floor on top of a Saracen carpet, tossing pieces of clothing here and there.

Gleefully, they made love and Raine was pleased to see so much happiness in his wife's eyes. Afterward, he held her close. "Alyx, it meant a great deal to me that you stayed during the fight with Chatworth. Whether you admit it or not you have a high sense of honor—not the honor I believe in but your own special sort. Yet you forgot it for love of me. I thank you for that."

He smiled when he felt her tears wet his shirt. "You are going to see our daughter, yet all I get are tears."

"Am I selfish for wanting everything? I want you to see our daughter, for the three of us to be together."

"I will soon. Now give me a smile. Do you want me to remember you in tears or with your own special impish smile?"

At that she smiled and Raine kissed her. "Come on, let's start getting you ready."

Alyx kept telling herself the parting was only for a

month or so, but she had a sense of permanence, as if she'd never see the forest camp again. The people seemed to think the same thing.

"For your baby," said a man as he handed her a toy whittled out of a bit of green oak. There were more gifts, all homemade, all simple, and each one brought fresh tears to her eyes.

"You stayed up with my baby when she was sick," said one woman.

"And you buried mine," said another.

When it was time to leave, Raine stood quietly behind Alyx, his hand on her shoulder, and he was radiating his pride in her. "Don't stay away too long," he whispered, giving her one last kiss before setting her on her horse.

Alyx rode away, her head twisted back over her shoulder, watching all the people waving at her until the trees hid them.

Chapter Twenty-two

$\mathcal{F}$OR TWO WHOLE weeks, Alyx was content to play with her child, to create lullabies for Judith's son and Catherine. She sent long, glowing messages to Raine describing the perfections of their daughter and parcels of medicines to Rosamund. A messenger returned with the news of the camp saying that Blanche had been caught stealing and had been banished from the forest. Alyx felt no joy at the announcement.

After two weeks of bliss, she began to miss Raine, and she left the children's nursery in search of his family.

"I'd heard you were with us again," Gavin teased, "but I wasn't sure. Come and join us. Judith is with the falconer and I was about to join her."

"Do you think the King will like this hawk, Simon?" Judith was asking the grizzled old falconer.

"Aye, my lady. There's no finer in the land."

Judith held the big, hooded bird on the end of her gloved arm, studying the hawk, frowning.

"Are you planning a gift for the King?" Alyx asked.

"I'll try *anything*," Judith said vehemently. "Since Brian Chatworth's death and Elizabeth's pregnancy, the King despises the name of Montgomery."

"And now since the Queen's death—" Gavin began.

"Queen Elizabeth died!" Alyx said loudly, and the hawk fluttered its great wings until Judith soothed it. "I'm sorry," she said. She knew nothing of hawks and hawking. "I hadn't heard the Queen had died."

"He's lost his eldest son and his wife in under a year and his son's widow's family threatens to take her dowry back. The man does little but brood now. Once I could have gone to him and talked to him."

"And what would you ask him?" she asked, hope in her voice.

"I want this feud ended," Gavin said. "There has been a life taken from the Montgomerys and one from the Chatworths. Perhaps if I could speak to the King I could persuade him to pardon Raine?"

"And what about Miles?" Alyx asked. "He has heartily used Elizabeth Chatworth. I don't think her brother will forgive him that."

Gavin and Judith exchanged looks and Judith spoke. "We have corresponded with Miles, and if the King gives permission, he is willing to marry Elizabeth."

"No doubt Roger Chatworth will welcome a Montgomery into his family with open arms," Alyx smiled. "So! You'll use the gift of the hawk to persuade the King. Does he like to go hawking?"

Again, Gavin and Judith exchanged looks.

"Alyx," Gavin began, "we've been waiting to speak to you. We knew you wanted to spend some time with Catherine, but now there's no more time to lose."

For some reason, Alyx began to feel a sense of dread. Absurd, of course, but still, cold little fingers went up her spine. "What did you want to talk to me about?"

"Let's go inside," Judith said, handing the hawk to Simon.

Once the old man was inside the stone falconery, Alyx stood her ground. "Tell me what I should know," she said flatly.

"Gavin!" Judith said. "Let me tell her. Alyx, the King doesn't particularly care for hawking. Right now he cares for nothing or no one—except one thing." She paused a moment. "Music," Judith said quietly.

Alyx stood still a moment, staring. "You want me to go to the King of England, sing him a song and while I'm there casually beg him to forgive my husband and to give the hand of a wealthy heiress to her sworn enemy?" She smiled. "Never have I said I was a magician."

"Alyx, you could do it," Judith encouraged. "No one in the country has a voice or talent to match yours. He'll offer you half of his kingdom if you but make him forget for an hour or so."

"The King?" Alyx sputtered. "What do I care for the King? I would love to play and sing for him. My concern is Raine. He's spent a year trying to make me understand his sense of honor and now I do—at least to the extent that I know he wouldn't thank me for begging before the King."

"But if you could get a pardon for Raine . . ." Judith argued.

Alyx turned to Gavin. "Were you in Raine's place, would you want Judith to go to the king for you or would you expect to fight your own battles?"

Gavin's face was serious. "It would not be easy for me to swallow such a humiliation."

"Humiliation!" Judith said. "If Raine were free, he could come home and we could be a family again."

"And our strife would be internal," Gavin said. "I can see Alyx's point. I don't think she should go against her husband. We will all fight our own battles and keep the King out of this."

Judith seemed to want to reply, but as she looked from Gavin to Alyx, she remained quiet.

But what made Alyx change her mind was Roger Chatworth's growing anger. Gavin sent out spies and they came back with the news that Roger was vowing death to both Miles and Raine to revenge his young brother and the loss of his sister's virtue.

"Raine has no men to fight Chatworth," Alyx said. "And will Miles last against a seasoned warrior such as Roger?"

"He has the backing of all the Montgomery forces," Gavin said quietly.

"You are talking about war!" she yelled. "A private war which will cause you all to lose your lands and the King—" She stopped. Everything seemed to go back to the King.

With tears in her eyes, she fled the room. Was she the only one who could possibly prevent a private war? She'd once told Jocelin she'd do *anything* to keep Raine alive, that she'd rather see him with another woman than dead. Yet he'd been so very, very angry when she did what she felt she had to. He did not want her to interfere in his life and especially in what he considered his honor.

What if she kept quiet now, didn't try to win a pardon from the King and there was a war? Would she be happy knowing Raine died with his honor intact? Or would she curse herself for all eternity for not at least trying to prevent the battles?

With quiet dignity, she stood, smoothed her dress and went downstairs to the winter parlor where Judith and Gavin sat over a game of draughts.

"I will go to the King," Alyx said quietly. "I will sing with all my might and I will ask, plead, beg, whatever I have to do, to get him to pardon Raine and to arrange the marriage of Elizabeth and Miles."

Alyx stood outside the King's chamber, her body trembling so badly she feared her dress would fall off. What was she, a common lawyer's daughter, doing here?

A shout from inside the chamber and a sound of something breaking made her gasp. After a moment, a slim man tiptoed out of the room, a red mark on his cheek, a flute in his hand.

He gave Alyx an insolent look. "He's in a bad mood today. I hope there's more to you than appears."

Alyx pulled herself up to all of her small height and glared at him. "Perhaps it's the music he hasn't heard today that's put him in a bad temper."

The man grunted and left her alone.

Alyx adjusted her dress again, a wonderful concoction of deep green velvet with sleeves and skirt inset so heavily embroidered with gold thread that the fabric was stiff. The dress had been Judith's design and the embroidery was a fanciful arrangement of centaurs and fairies playing many musical instruments. "For luck," Judith had said.

"Come in and wait," said a dark-clad man, just his head sticking out of the door. "His Majesty will hear you in a moment."

Alyx picked up her cittern, a magnificent thing of rosewood and inlaid ivory, and followed the man.

The King's chamber was a large room paneled in oak, richly done, but certainly no better than the rooms at Montgomery Castle. This surprised Alyx. Perhaps she'd expected the King's rooms to be made of gold.

She took the seat the man pointed to and watched. The King sat on a red-cushioned chair and Alyx wouldn't have known he was the King except that occasionally someone would bow before him. He was a tall, somber, tired-looking man, and as he drank from a silver goblet, she saw he had few teeth and they were blackish. He frowned at the singer before him, and the young man's nervousness was apparent in every word he sang. The air was charged with tension as the musician tried to please him.

With the big room echoing as it did and everyone being so stiff, it was no wonder he was displeased, Alyx thought. None of the music made him forget for a moment his sadness. If I were in charge, I'd put the musicians together, challenge them with some new music. When they were enjoying themselves, the King would find pleasure.

Alyx sat still for a moment longer. There were eleven musicians auditioning for the King today.

Lately, he'd been staying alone in his rooms, refusing even to attend the Queen's funeral. Alyx had had to wait a week to get this chance to play and sing for him. And would she shake and quiver before him as these others were doing?

Think of Raine, she told herself. Think of all the Montgomerys.

She took a deep breath and stood, offered a silent prayer of hope, then let her voice take over.

"Here!" she said loudly to the singer. "You'll have us all in tears. What we need is laughter and no more tears."

Someone put a cautioning hand on her arm, but Alyx looked straight at King Henry. "With your permission, Your Majesty." She curtsied, and the King gave her a nonchalant wave.

Alyx's heart was in her throat. Now if she could just get the musicians to cooperate. "Can you play a harpsichord?" she asked a man who gave her a hostile look.

"Wait your turn," he hissed.

"I have more to lose than you do. Perhaps together we can work some magic." She cocked her head. "Or is your talent too limited?"

The man, after one considering look, went to the harpsichord.

As if they were all the choirboys she'd taught at Moreton, she began ordering the men about, giving them different instruments that were abundant in the room.

Once they were seated or standing, she flew about, giving melody here, rhythm there. About halfway through she began to sing and two of the musicians were immediately won to her side. Grinning, they picked up the melody and stayed with her.

It seemed to Alyx everything was taking so long and she only felt encouragement when the man on the harpsichord added his voice to hers. The man on the harp caught the melody and showed his talent with those heavenly strings.

Alyx had chosen an old song, hoping they'd all know it, but perhaps it was her rendition of it that made them awkward. The man she'd given a tambourine moved to a kettledrum hidden in a shadowy corner and the sound began to make the floor vibrate.

Finally, finally, everyone seemed to have caught the song, and Alyx dared to turn and look at the King. His face was impassive, silent, but the men behind him looked astonished. At least she knew now that what she was doing wasn't an everyday occurrence.

They repeated three choruses of the song and Alyx started them on something new, church music this time, and when that was done she went to a folk song.

It had been an hour since she'd started and she quieted the musicians. This time, she'd sing alone, unaccompanied. Once, four years ago, a singer had come to Moreton and the villagers had said Alyx at last had some competition from someone. Alyx, frightened of looking bad, stayed up all night and composed a song that would be difficult for even her to sing, a song that covered the entire range of her abilities. The next day, she'd sung the song and the visitor, an older woman, had looked at Alyx with tears in her eyes and kissed Alyx on both cheeks, saying Alyx should give thanks daily for her gift from God.

Now, Alyx planned to sing that song. She'd hated it ever since she wrote it because the woman she'd meant to humble had actually humbled her. But now she needed to do what she could to win the King's favor.

The song showed the heights and depths of Alyx's voice, as well as the controlled softness and extraordinary volume. She built up to the total power of her voice slowly, liltingly, and just when it seemed she could go no further, she put everything into one note and held it—and held it until there were tears in her eyes and her lungs were dry.

When she finished, she dropped to a deep curtsy and there was total, absolute silence about her, the sound of Alyx's last note still reverberating off the walls, swirling about the people like blue and yellow lights.

"Come here, child." The King broke the silence.

Alyx went to him, kissed his hand, kept her head bowed.

He leaned forward, lifted her chin. "So you are the newest Montgomery wife." He smiled at her startled look. "I try to keep up with what happens in my realm. And I find the Montgomery men marry the most entertaining women. But this . . ."—he motioned to the musicians about the room—". . . this is worth a king's ransom."

"I am pleased to give you pleasure, Your Majesty," Alyx whispered.

He gave the first indication of a smile. "You have more than pleased me. Now, what do you ask in return? Come, you didn't leave Gavin's home for no reason."

Alyx tried to gather her courage. "I would like to

end the feud between the Montgomerys and the Chatworths. I propose a blood bond between them, Miles to marry Lady Elizabeth Chatworth."

King Henry frowned. "Miles is a felon by the Act of 1495. He abducted the Lady Elizabeth."

"He did not!" Alyx bellowed in her usual manner. "Forgive me, Your Majesty." She fell to her knees before him. "Miles did not abduct her, but it was because of me that Lady Elizabeth has suffered."

"You! Fetch a stool," King Henry commanded and when Alyx was seated, he said, "Now tell me all of the story."

Alyx told of Pagnell accusing her of using her voice to seduce him, of her hiding in the forest, of falling in love with Raine. She watched his eyes, saw that he was interested in her story and went on to tell of her capture by Pagnell and Elizabeth's abduction.

"You say he meant to roll her in a carpet and hand her to Lord Miles?" King Henry asked.

She leaned forward. "Please don't repeat this, but I heard she was delivered without a stitch of clothing on and that she attacked Lord Miles with an ax. Of course the story could be wrong."

The King gave a sound very like a laugh. "Go on with your story."

She told him of the witchcraft trial, how the men had used her to entice Raine to her rescue.

"And he saved you at the last moment?"

"A little after the last moment. The smoke was so bad I lost my voice for days."

He took her hand in his. "That," he said with great gravity, "was a tragedy. And what happened after this magnificent rescue?"

Her voice changed as she told of her child and her

return to the forest and meeting Brian Chatworth. She told the way Brian had dressed in Raine's armor and how Raine had nearly died from the opium.

"So now you'd like Lord Miles to marry Lady Elizabeth."

"And . . ."

"Yes?" he encouraged.

"Please pardon Raine," she said. "He's so good. He isn't trying to raise any army against you. The people in the camp are outlaws and out-of-works. Raine only trains them to give the criminals something to do and to keep the others from dying of melancholia."

"Melancholia," the King sighed. "Yes, I know of that disease. But what of Lady Elizabeth? Is she willing to marry Lord Miles?"

"She is intelligent and she'll no doubt see the sense of the marriage and if Miles is like his brothers, how could she refuse him?"

"Someday I'll have to learn the secret of the Montgomery men and the loyalty they can inspire. If Lady Elizabeth is willing, I'll allow the marriage if for no other reason than to give the child a name."

"And Raine?"

"For that you will have to work. What say you to spending a week here with me and singing for me night and day?"

"I will dedicate my life to your pleasure if it will save my husband," Alyx said fiercely.

"No, do not tempt me, child, I have enough problems. Now go and sing and I'll have the papers drawn." He waved to one of the men behind him who quickly left the room.

Alyx sang for the rest of the day, until her throat

was raw. It was only after the sun had long ago sunk that the King fell asleep in his chair.

"Go and rest now," said one of the King's retainers. "Lord Gavin waits outside for you and he'll show you to your rooms. I'm sure His Majesty will call you early in the morning."

As soon as Alyx saw Gavin, her weariness left her. Grinning from ear to ear, she flung herself into his arms. "He agreed! He agreed!" she croaked.

Gavin held her tightly, spun her around. "Let's tell Judith and do something about your voice. Besides, we're about to start some ugly gossip."

Alyx stiffened as soon as Gavin released her and formally he escorted her through long drafty corridors hung with riotously colorful tapestries and into the set of rooms reserved for them.

Alyx drank the honey concoction Judith prepared for her and sat down to wait—a waiting which took days. King Henry kept Alyx at his side constantly and, like a trained dog, showed her off to his son Henry and to his late son's widow, Catherine. Alyx was involved in the court gossip, hearing that the King himself planned to marry the young princess. She very much liked the big, good-looking twelve-year-old Prince Henry. If ever anyone seemed like a King, he did.

Instead of the week King Henry had asked for, Alyx remained at court for two weeks before the papers for Raine's pardon and an order for Miles and Elizabeth's marriage were drawn up. Both Gavin and Judith were pleased at leaving court, but Alyx was very worried at seeing Raine again. What would be his reaction to her interference?

It took days to pack all their belongings that they'd

needed at court and more days to return to Montgomery Castle. With a pounding heart, Alyx dismounted
and waited, hoping Raine would be there.

He wasn't, but messages awaited them. Roger
Chatworth had refused to release Elizabeth, but Miles
wrote that he'd found her. Gavin groaned at this,
lamenting his little brother's disregard for the law.
They'd been married not far from the Chatworth
estate and immediately after the ceremony, Elizabeth
had returned to her brother. This puzzled them, but
Miles gave no hint of explanation.

A week went by and there was no word from Raine.
At the end of the second week, Gavin sent messengers to the forest, but the men came back saying they
were not greeted by guards as usual but had wandered
for two days, finding no one.

The next day Gavin and his men rode out and it was
a week before they returned.

"Raine's at his own estates now," Gavin reported.
"And he's brought all the forest people with him. He
must have five farmers in every field and he insists on
paying them all. He'll be a beggar himself in three
years."

"Gavin—" Alyx began.

Gavin touched her cheek. "He's angry now, but
he'll get over it."

Quietly, Alyx left the room, Gavin and Judith
watching her.

"Tell me the truth," Judith said.

"Damn that brother of mine!" Gavin shouted,
pounding his fist on the table. "Raine says Alyx has
insulted him for the last time, that he can bear no
more. He says he's warned her repeatedly but she
won't listen to him and he knows she never will."

"Perhaps Stephen could talk to him—" Judith began.

"Stephen tried, but he won't listen. He's spending all his time with those criminals . . ." He stopped and laughed. "The oddest thing has happened. Alyx always complains that she owes those people in the forest so much and could never repay them. There's a singer with the band, Jocelin, I believe he traveled with Alyx, and this Jocelin met a man who'd been in the room the day Alyx first performed for the King. I'm not sure what happened that day, but according to the witness, Alyx was magnificent and one of the things she asked for was security for the people under Raine."

"I don't remember Alyx saying anything about that."

"I don't think she did—directly, anyway. But she did mention that later she told the King stories about her life in the forest. I heard King Henry had her dress as a boy once to prove she'd actually done it."

"You think Alyx told King Henry about how some of the people had been unjustly treated?"

Gavin smiled. "Sometimes Alyx is so innocent. With her background I doubt if she had any idea of the power she held. Men have killed to be able to hold the King's ear for as long as she did each day. If she'd had an enemy she could have sent him to the gallows."

Judith gave her husband a speculative look. "Or she could have saved several hundred people. By any chance were more pardons issued?"

Gavin grinned. "Raine was allowed to pardon anyone he thought fit for forgiveness. According to Jocelin, Alyx sang songs of Raine's loyalty and honor until King Henry was ready to declare him a saint. She twisted things until it seemed Raine was doing the King a favor when he attacked Chatworth."

"Clever girl! She can do so much with that voice of hers. The people know that it was she who obtained their pardons?"

"This man Jocelin made sure they knew. When it comes to singing praises, he's as bad as Alyx. All of them sent greetings to Alyx and said they wished her well. The lot of them are as bad as Stephen's Scots— the world is losing respect for its betters."

Judith laughed at that. "We must tell Alyx she's done some good and now we'll start working on Raine. He must see that Alyx has not insulted him by going to the King."

"I hope you can reason with him."

"I pray that I can, too."

Chapter Twenty-three

$\mathcal{A}$ MONTH PASSED and there was no word from Raine—and all correspondence sent to him was ignored. For the first weeks Alyx was sad but her sadness soon turned to anger. If his pride meant more than their love and their daughter, so be it.

Her anger fed itself for an entire summer. She watched Catherine grow, saw that the little girl had indeed inherited her father's sturdiness.

"There'll be no chance for a slim, elegant lady," Alyx sighed, looking at Catherine's chubby legs as she took her first steps.

"All babies are fat," Judith laughed, tossing her son into the air. "Catherine looks more like Raine every day. Too bad he can't see her. One look at those violet eyes and her dimples and he'd melt. Raine could never resist a child."

Judith's words haunted Alyx for days and at the end of the fourth day she made a decision. "I'm going to send Catherine to her father," Alyx announced one evening as Judith was weeding the roses.

"I beg your pardon?"

"He may not forgive me, but there's no reason Catherine should be punished. She's almost a year old now and he's never even seen her."

Judith stood, wiping her hands. "What if Raine doesn't return her? Could you bear losing both your husband and your daughter?"

"I'll say I'm sending her until Christmas, then Gavin will fetch her. Raine will honor the agreement."

"If he agrees."

Alyx didn't answer. She hoped with all her heart that Catherine would win her father's heart, melt it.

Days later, when Catherine was ready to leave, Alyx almost changed her mind, but Judith held her shoulders and Alyx waved goodbye to her daughter, who was escorted by twenty of Gavin's men and two nurses.

Alyx waited breathlessly for the next weeks. No message came from Raine, but one of the nurses wrote regularly, sending her letters via a complicated network arranged by Gavin through Jocelin.

The nurse wrote of the turmoil that had been caused by Lady Catherine's arrival and how brave the little girl had been. Raine's house, his men and Raine himself had frightened her badly. At first the nurse thought Lord Raine was going to ignore his daughter but once, while playing in the garden, Raine had retrieved Catherine's ball and he'd sat a few moments on a bench watching her. Catherine had begun rolling her ball toward her father and he had played with her for an hour.

The letters of the nurse began to describe more and more incidents. Lord Raine took Catherine for a ride. Lord Raine put his daughter to bed. Lord Raine swears his daughter can talk, that she is the smartest child in all of England.

Alyx was glad to hear the news but she was unhappy at being so alone. She wanted to share the pleasure of their daughter with her husband.

In the middle of November, the letters stopped and it wasn't until nearly Christmas that she heard any more news. Gavin came to her and said that Catherine had been returned and waited below in the winter parlor.

Alyx flew down the stairs, tears blurring her eyes as she saw her daughter in an elaborate dress of gold silk standing quietly before the fire. It had been months since they'd seen each other and Catherine took a step away from her mother.

"Don't you remember me, sweetheart?" Alyx whispered pleadingly.

The child took another step backward and as Alyx moved forward, Catherine turned and ran, grabbing her father's legs.

Alyx turned startled eyes up at Raine's intense blue ones. "I . . . I didn't see you," she stuttered. "I thought Catherine was alone."

Raine didn't say a word.

Alyx's heart jumped into her throat and threatened to choke her. "You look well," she said as calmly as she could.

He bent and picked up his daughter and, jealously, Alyx saw the way Catherine clung to him.

"I wanted you to meet your daughter," she whispered.

"Why?" he asked and his voice, that deep rich voice she knew so well, nearly made her cry.

But Alyx refused to cry. "Why?" she hissed. "You hadn't seen your daughter in her entire life and you ask me why I sent her to you?"

His voice, quiet, low, interrupted her. "Why would you send her to a man who deserted you, who left you alone to fight his battles?"

Alyx's eyes widened.

Raine stroked his daughter's hair. "She is a beautiful child, kind and giving like her mother."

"But I'm not—" Alyx began, then stopped as Raine started walking toward her. He passed her, opened the door and handed Catherine to the waiting nurse. "Could we talk?"

Silently, Alyx nodded her head.

Raine walked to the fireplace and studied the blaze for a moment. "I think I could have killed you when you went to the King," he said with feeling. "It was as if you were announcing to the world that Raine Montgomery couldn't handle his own problems."

"I never meant—"

He put up his hand to silence her. "This isn't easy for me, but it must be said. While we were in the forest it was easy for me to see why people disliked you. You put yourself so above them and they resented you so much. When you came to understand what you were doing you set about to do something about it. You changed, Alyx."

He paused for a long moment. "It's not so . . . comfortable to look at myself, to judge myself."

His broad back was to her, his head low, and her

heart went out to him. "Raine," she whispered. "I understand. You don't have to say anymore."

"But I do!" He turned to face her. "Do you think it's easy for me—a man—to realize that a little bit of a child/woman such as you can do something I can't?"

"What have I done?" She was genuinely astonished.

At that he paused and smiled, and there was much love in his eyes. "Perhaps I thought I should have my way because I was sacrificing all I had for some filthy beggars. Maybe I liked being a king of criminals."

"Raine." She reached out her hand to touch his sleeve.

He caught her hand, raised her fingertips to his lips. "Why did you go to King Henry?"

"To ask him to pardon you. To persuade him to let Elizabeth and Miles marry."

"It hurt my pride, Alyx," he whispered. "I wanted to march into King Henry's chamber wearing silvered armor and talk to the King as an equal." A dimple appeared in his cheek. "But instead, my wife went and pleaded for me. It hurt very much."

"I didn't mean to . . . Oh, Raine, I would beg anyone to save you."

He didn't seem to notice that his hand was nearly crushing hers. "I have been distorted with pride. I want to . . . ask your forgiveness."

Alyx wanted to shout that she'd forgive him anything, but now was not the time for flippancy. "In the future I am sure I will do other things to wound your pride."

"I'm sure you will."

Her chin raised a fraction. "And what will you do when I offend you?"

"Rage at you. Get very, very angry. Threaten to murder you."

"Oh," Alyx said in a small voice, blinking back tears. "Then perhaps—"

"Alyx, I want *you*, not someone who will agree with my every word." He swallowed, grimaced. "You were right to go to the King."

"And what about Roger Chatworth?"

For a moment, Raine's eyes shot fire. "You were *wrong* about him. If I'd killed him, then Miles wouldn't—"

"If you'd killed him, then King Henry would have killed you!" Alyx shouted up at him.

"I could have done away with his body. No one—"

"You would have probably felt the need to confess your sins in public," she said with disgust. "No, I did the right thing."

Raine started to say something but stopped. "Perhaps you're right."

"I'm what?!" Alyx said, aghast, then saw Raine's dimple. "You're teasing me." She set her jaw.

Raine, with a deep laugh, pulled her into his arms, held her when she tried to pull away. "It seems we'll never agree on everything, but perhaps we can agree to work *together*. Will you just discuss what you plan before you do it?"

She considered that for a moment. "And what if you tell me not to do something? I think perhaps I should do it the way I have done."

"Alyx," he said in almost a growl, then began to laugh. "Alyx, Alyx, Alyx." Laughing, he tossed her into the air, caught her. "I think we shall always quarrel. Are you willing to live with that?"

"We wouldn't quarrel if once in a while you'd think

before you acted. Just once you should think about tomorrow. If you'd stopped to consider what you were doing maybe you wouldn't have led the king's men against . . ." She trailed off because Raine was nibbling her neck.

"I am a man of passion," he murmured. "Would you like me to change that?"

She tilted her head to allow him better access. "I might be able to stand your passion. Raine!" She pulled away to stare at him and she was very serious. "Will you leave me again? If I do something you dislike will you leave me and our children alone?"

His eyes too turned serious. "I will make a vow to you, Alyxandria Montgomery, a vow as sacred as any oath as a knight. I will never again leave you in anger."

For a moment she watched him, searched his face and finally she smiled, threw her arms about his neck. "I love you so very much."

"Of course I may lock you in your room, put you under guard, whatever I must. But I will never again ship you off to my brother to let him deal with my problems."

"Problems!" she bellowed beside his ear. "I am a joy to your family. You are the one who has broken their hearts. You are a great, stubborn—"

Raine rubbed his battered ear. "Ah, the delicate voice of a woman, as soft as a spring morning, as gentle as a—"

He stopped because Alyx planted her mouth on his and he forgot about words.

Velvet Angel

To Joan Schulhafer, who started as my publicist and became my friend. Thank you for all the love and laughter, and most of all, for all you taught me.

Velvet Angel

Chapter 1

THE SOUTH OF ENGLAND

August 1502

ELIZABETH CHATWORTH STOOD ON THE VERY EDGE OF THE
steep cliff, gazing toward the sea of tall barley grasses.
Below her, seemingly tiny men walked with scythes on
their shoulders, a few rode horses and one drove a team
of oxen.

But Elizabeth didn't really see the men because her
chin was held too high and it was locked into place so
rigidly that nothing was going to bring it down. A warm
gust of wind tried to force her away from the edge but
she braced her legs and refused to move. If what had
already happened to her today and now what she faced
did not sway her, no mere wind was going to break her
stance.

Her green eyes were dry but her throat was swollen
shut with a lump of anger and unshed tears. A muscle

in her jaw flexed and unflexed as she breathed deeply, trying to control her pounding heart.

Another gust of wind blew her tangled mass of honey blonde hair away from her back and, unbeknownst to Elizabeth, one last pearl disentangled itself and slid down the torn, dirty red silk of her dress. The finery she'd worn to her friend's wedding was now shredded beyond repair, her hair loose and flowing, her cheek smudged—and her hands were crudely tied behind her back.

Elizabeth lifted her eyes toward heaven, unblinking at the bright daylight. All her life, she'd had her looks referred to as angelic and never had she looked so delicate, so serene, so much like a celestial being as she did now with her heavy hair swirling about her like some silken cloak, her ragged gown giving her the look of a Christian martyr.

But the farthest thoughts from Elizabeth's mind were ones of sweetness—or of forgiving.

"I will fight to the death," she murmured skyward, her eyes darkening to the color of an emerald on a moonlit night. "No man will best me. No man will make me submit to his will."

"Pleadin' with the Lord, are you?" came the voice of her captor from beside her.

Slowly, as if she had all the time in the world, Elizabeth turned to the man, and the coldness in her eyes made him take a step backward. He was a braggart like the hideous man he served, Pagnell of Waldenham, but this underling was a coward when his master wasn't present.

John gave a nervous cough, then boldly stepped

forward and grabbed Elizabeth's upper arm. "You may think you're the great lady but for now I'm your master."

She looked him squarely in the eyes, showing none of the pain he was causing her—after all she'd had more than enough physical and mental pain in her life. "You will never be anyone's master," she said calmly.

For a moment John's hand released its pressure on her arm, but the next second he pulled her forward and pushed her roughly.

Elizabeth nearly lost balance, but by a supreme concentration she managed to stay upright and began to walk forward.

"Every man is any woman's master," John was saying from behind her. "Women like you just haven't realized it yet. All it'll take is one good man slamming away on top of you and you'll learn who's your master. And from what I hear this Miles Montgomery is the man to give you what you need."

At the name of Montgomery Elizabeth tripped, falling to her knees.

John's laugh was disproportionately loud as he acted as if he'd succeeded in some great feat. He stood by, watching insolently as Elizabeth struggled to stand, her feet tangled in her skirt, her bound hands making her awkward.

"Excited about Montgomery, are you?" he taunted as he jerked her to her feet. For a moment he touched her cheek, the soft ivory skin, running a dirty fingertip over her delicate lips. "How can a woman as lovely as you be such a termagant? You and I could be nice to each other and Lord Pagnell would never know. What would it matter who's first? Montgomery will take your virginity anyway, so what difference does a day or so make?"

Elizabeth gathered the saliva in her mouth and spit it all into his face. It cost her a great deal of pain in her sore body as his hand came out to strike her face, but she ducked expertly and began to run. Her tied hands made speed impossible and John caught her easily, grabbing what was left of her skirt and causing her to fall, face down, on the ground.

"You vicious little slut!" he gasped, turning her over, straddling her. "You'll pay for that. I've tried to be fair with you but you deserve to be beaten."

Elizabeth's hands and arms were pinned under her and in spite of all she could do, the pain was causing tears to gather in her eyes. "But you won't beat me, will you?" she said confidently. "Pagnell would find out what you'd done and he would beat you. Men like you never risk harm to their own precious selves."

John put his hands on her breasts and his lips on hers, grinding his mouth against hers, but Elizabeth showed no emotion whatsoever. In disgust, he moved away from her and angrily walked back toward the horses.

Elizabeth sat up and tried to regain her calm. She was quite good at not showing her inner emotions and now she wanted to save all her strength for the ordeal to come.

Montgomery! The name rang in her head. Of all her fears, of all her terrors in life, the name Montgomery seemed to be the cause of them all. A Montgomery had caused her sister-in-law to lose her beauty and most of her sanity. A Montgomery had caused her older brother's disgrace and her brother Brian's disappearance. And indirectly, a Montgomery had caused her own capture.

Elizabeth had been an attendant at a friend's wedding and by accident she'd overheard an odious man she'd known all her life, Pagnell, planning to turn a pretty little singer over to his corrupt relatives to be tried as a witch. When Elizabeth tried to rescue the girl, Pagnell had caught them and, as a joke, had decided to have Elizabeth delivered to her enemy, a Montgomery. Perhaps things wouldn't have been so bad if the singer, in a generous but not wholly intelligent gesture, had not given the information that she was somehow connected with a Montgomery.

Pagnell had bound and gagged Elizabeth, rolled her in a filthy piece of canvas and ordered his man, John, to deliver her to the notoriously lecherous, satyric, hot-blooded Miles Montgomery. Of all the four Montgomery men, Elizabeth knew that the youngest, a boy of only twenty years, just two years older than Elizabeth, was the worst. Even in the convent where she'd spent the last several years, she'd heard stories of Miles Montgomery.

She'd been told that he'd sold his soul to the devil when he was sixteen and as a result he had an unholy power over women. Elizabeth had laughed at the story but she'd not told the reason for her laughter. She thought it much more likely that Miles Montgomery was like her dead brother Edmund and had ordered women to his bed. It was a pity that this Montgomery's seed seemed to be so fertile, for it was rumored that he had a hundred bastards.

Three years ago a young girl, Bridget, had left the convent where Elizabeth often lived to go and work at the ancient Montgomery fortress. She was a pretty girl with big dark eyes and swaying hips. To Elizabeth's disgust, the other residents alternately acted as if the girl were going to her wedding or to be a human sacrifice. The day before Bridget left, the prioress spent two hours with her and at vespers the girl's eyes were red from crying.

Eleven months later, a traveling musician brought them the news that Bridget had been delivered of a large, healthy boy who she named James Montgomery. It was freely admitted that Miles was the father.

Elizabeth joined in the many prayers offered for the girl's sins. Privately she cursed all men like her brother Edmund and Miles Montgomery—evil men who believed women had no souls, who thought nothing of beating and raping women, of forcing them to do all manner of hideous acts.

She had no time for more thoughts as John grabbed a handful of her hair and pulled her to her feet.

"Your time for prayers is over," he said into her face. "Montgomery has made camp and it's time he got a look at his next . . ."—he smiled—"mother of his next bastard."

He laughed aloud when Elizabeth struggled against him, and when she realized he enjoyed her struggles, she stopped and gave him her coldest look.

"Witch!" he flung at her. "We'll see if this devil Montgomery can capture the angel you look like—or will he find your heart as black as his own?"

Smiling, his hand twisted in her hair, he brought a

sharp little dagger to rest against her throat. When she didn't flinch at the feel of the cold steel against her skin, his smile changed to a smirk.

"Sometimes the Montgomery men make the mistake of talking to women instead of using them as God meant them to be used. I plan to see that this Montgomery has no such ideas."

Slowly, he trailed the tip of the blade down her throat to the high square neck of what was left of her gown.

Her breath held, her eyes on his, her anger held under rigid control, she stood very still. She would not goad him to use the knife on her.

John did not cut her skin, but the blade easily parted the front of her dress and her tight corset under it. When he'd exposed the full curve of her breasts, he looked back into her face. "You've been hiding a great deal, Elizabeth," he whispered.

She stiffened and looked away from his face. It was true that she dressed conservatively, flattening her breasts, thickening her waist. Her face attracted more men than she wanted, but aside from covering her hair she could do nothing about her face.

John was no longer interested in her face as he concentrated on slicing away the rest of her gown. He'd seen very few women nude and never one of Elizabeth Chatworth's station—or her beauty.

Elizabeth's spine was so stiff it could have been made of steel and when her clothes fell away and her bare skin felt the warm August sun, she knew that this was more painful than what had heretofore been done to her.

An ugly expletive from John, uttered from deep within him, made her blink.

"Damn Pagnell!" he cursed and reached for her.

Elizabeth stepped backward and tried to muster her dignity as she glared at John, saw he was practically foaming at the mouth. "You touch me and you're a dead man," she said loudly. "If you kill me, Pagnell will have your head—and if you do not, I will see that he finds out what you have done. And have you forgotten my brother's rage? Is your life worth one coupling with *any* woman?"

It took a moment for John to sober and bring his eyes to her face. "I hope Montgomery causes you endless misery," he said with great feeling and stalked away to the carpet slung across his horse's rump. Without a glance at her, he unrolled it on the ground.

"Lie down," he commanded, his eyes on the carpet. "And let me warn you, woman, that if you disobey me I will forget Pagnell and Montgomery and your brother's wrath."

Obediently, Elizabeth lay down on the carpet, the short woolen nap pricking her skin, and when John knelt over her, she held her breath.

Roughly, he pushed her to her stomach, cut the bindings on her wrists, and before Elizabeth could even blink, he tossed the edge of the carpet over her and began rolling her in it. There were no more thoughts. Her only concern was a primitive instinct to continue breathing.

It seemed an eternity that she lay still, her head tilted back as she sought the air coming from the top of the carpet roll. When she was at last moved, lifted, she had to struggle to find air, and when she was tossed across the back of the horse, she thought her lungs would collapse.

John's muffled words came through the layers of carpet. "The next man you see will be Miles Montgomery. Think on that while we ride. He won't be as kind to you as I have been."

In a way, the words were good for Elizabeth because the idea of Miles Montgomery, of his evil ways, gave her some incentive to work hard at breathing. And when the horse jolted her, she cursed the Montgomery family, their house, their retainers—and she prayed for the innocent Montgomery children who were part of this immoral clan.

The tent of Miles Montgomery was a splendid affair: deep green sendal trimmed in gold, the gold Montgomery leopards painted along the scalloped roof border, pennants flying from the crown. Inside, the walls were lined with pale green silk. There were several collapsible stools, cushioned with blue and gold brocade, a large table carved with the Montgomery leopards and, against opposite walls, two cots, one abnormally long, both draped with pelts of long-haired red fox.

Four men stood around the table, two dressed in the rich uniform of the Montgomery knights. The attention of the other two men was given to one of the retainers.

"He says he has a gift for you, my lord," the knight was saying to the quiet man before him. "It could be a trick. What could Lord Pagnell have that you would want?"

Miles Montgomery raised one dark eyebrow and it

was enough to make his man back down. Sometimes men newly in his service thought that since their master was so young, they could take liberties.

"Could there be a man rolled in the carpet?" asked the man beside Miles.

The subdued retainer craned his neck to look up at Sir Guy. "A very small one, perhaps."

Sir Guy looked down at Miles and there passed a silent communication between them. "Send him and his gift in," Sir Guy said. "We will meet them with drawn swords."

The knight left and within seconds he returned, his sword pointed at the small of the back of the man carrying the carpet. Insolently, smirking, John half tossed his bundle to the carpeted ground and with his foot pushed it very hard, sending it, unrolling, toward Miles Montgomery's feet.

When at last the carpet stopped, there were four stunned faces as they gaped at what lay before them: a nude woman, her eyes closed, long thick lashes soft on delicately colored cheeks, great massive torrents of honey blonde hair wrapped and twisted about her, curls tickling her waist and the tops of her thighs. She was outrageously curved with large firm breasts, a tiny waist, long, long legs. And her face was something men expected to see only in heaven—delicate, ethereal, not quite of this world.

Smiling triumphantly, John slipped out of the tent unnoticed.

Elizabeth, half dazed from the lack of air, opened her eyes slowly and looked up to see four men standing over her, their swords drawn but aimed toward the ground. Two of the men were obviously retainers and she dismissed them. The third man was a giant, several inches over six feet, steel gray hair, a scar running diagonally across his entire face. Although the man was indeed frightening, she somehow sensed he was not the leader of this group.

Beside the giant was another man dressed resplendently in deep blue satin. Elizabeth was accustomed to seeing strong, handsome men, but something about this one with his leashed power held in check so easily made her stare. The other men's eyes were fastened on Elizabeth's body, but this man turned and she looked for the first time into the face of Miles Montgomery, and their eyes locked.

He was a handsome man, very very handsome, with dark gray eyes under heavy, arched brows, a thin nose with slightly flaring nostrils and a full sensual mouth.

Danger! was Elizabeth's first thought. This man was dangerous to women as well as men.

She broke eye contact with him and in seconds she stood, grabbing a pelt from one of the cots near her and a war ax from the top of the table. "I will kill the first man who comes near me," she said, holding the ax with one hand while she tossed the pelt over one shoulder, leaving the other bare, one leg exposed from waist to bare foot.

The giant took a step toward her and she raised the ax, both hands on the handle.

"I know how to use this," she warned, looking up at the man with absolutely no fear.

The two knights took a step closer toward her and Elizabeth backed away, looking from one to the other.

The back of her knees hit the edge of the cot and she could go no farther. One of the knights smiled at her and she snarled at him in return.

"Leave us."

The words were quiet, uttered in a low voice, but it held command and all of them looked at Montgomery.

The giant of a man gave Elizabeth one last look, then nodded at the two knights and the three of them left the tent.

Elizabeth tightened her grip on the ax, her knuckles already white, as she glared across the space toward Miles Montgomery. "I will kill you," she said through her teeth. "Do not think that because I'm a woman I won't enjoy hacking a man to pieces. I would love to see the blood of a Montgomery spilled upon the earth."

Miles didn't move from his place by the table, but kept watching. After a moment he lifted his sword and Elizabeth drew in her breath, preparing for the battle to come. Very slowly, he placed his sword on the table and turned away from her, presenting his profile. Again slowly, he removed the jeweled dagger he wore at his side and placed it on the table beside the sword.

He turned back to her, his face expressionless, his eyes giving nothing away, and took a step toward her.

Elizabeth lifted the heavy ax and held it in readiness. She would fight to the death, for death was preferable to the beating and rape she knew this devil-man planned.

Miles sat down on a stool, several feet in front of her; he did not speak, but only watched her.

So! he did not think a woman a worthy opponent, but disarmed himself and sat down while she held a weapon of death over his head. With one lunge, she leaped forward and swung the ax at his neck.

Effortlessly, he caught the handle in his right hand, easily held it and looked into her eyes as she stood close to him. For a moment she was paralyzed, hypnotized by his eyes. He seemed to be searching her face for something, as if he asked silent questions of her.

She jerked the ax away from his grip and nearly fell when she found he released it freely. She caught herself at the edge of the table. "Damn you!" she said under her breath. "May the Lord and all His angels curse the day a Montgomery was born. May you and all your descendants writhe in the fires of hell forever."

Her voice had risen almost to a shout and outside she could hear movement.

Miles still sat there, watching her silently, and Elizabeth could feel her blood beginning to boil. When she saw her hands starting to shake, she knew she must calm herself. Where was the cool detachment she'd cultivated over the years?

If this man could remain calm, so could she. She listened and if her guess were correct, the sounds she heard outside were the men moving away. Perhaps if she could get past this one man, she could escape and get home to her brother.

With her eyes on Miles, she began to walk backward, circling him as she made her way toward the tent flap. Slowly, he turned on the stool and watched her. Outside she heard the whinny of a horse and she prayed that if she could just make it outside she'd be free.

Even though her eyes never left Miles's, she still never saw him move. One moment he was sitting, relaxed, on the stool and the next, just as her hand touched the tent flap, he was beside her, his hand around her wrist. She brought the ax straight down toward his shoulder but he caught her other wrist and held her.

She stood still, imprisoned lightly, painlessly, by his grip, and glared up at him. He was so close she could feel his breath on her forehead. As he looked down at her, he seemed to be waiting for something and then he looked puzzled.

With eyes as hard as the emeralds they resembled, she glared up at him. "And now what comes next?" she asked, hatred in her voice. "Do you beat me first or rape me? Or perhaps you like them both at the same time. I am a virgin and I've heard it hurts most the first time. No doubt my added pain will give you much pleasure."

For just a second, his eyes widened as if in astonishment and it was the first unguarded expression Elizabeth had seen on his face. His gray eyes locked into hers so hard that she looked away.

"I can endure what you deal out," she said quietly, "and if your wish is to see me beg, you will fail."

His hand released her wrist holding the tent flap and he cupped the left side of her cheek, gently turning her back to look at him.

She stiffened at his touch, hating his hands on her.

"Who are you?" he half whispered.

She straightened her spine even more and hatred flamed in her eyes. "I am your enemy. I am Elizabeth Chatworth."

Something passed quickly across his face and then was gone. After a long moment, he removed his hand from her cheek and, after a backward step, he released her other wrist. "You may keep the ax if it makes you feel safer but I cannot let you leave."

As if dismissing her, he turned his back and walked toward the center of the tent.

Immediately, Elizabeth was through the tent flap and out of the tent and, just as quickly, Miles was beside her, his hand once again encircling her wrist.

"I cannot let you leave," he repeated, this time more firmly. His eyes traveled downward to her bare legs and up again. "You aren't dressed for running away. Come inside and I'll send my man to purchase clothes."

She jerked away from him. The sun was setting and in the twilight he looked even darker. "I want no clothes from you. I want nothing from any Montgomery. My brother will—"

She broke off at his look.

"Do not mention the name of your brother to me. He killed my sister."

Miles recaptured her wrist and gave a light tug. "Now I must insist that you come inside. My men will be returning soon and I don't think they should see you dressed like this."

She held her ground. "What does it matter? Isn't it the custom of men like you to throw female captives to their knights when they've finished with them?"

She wasn't sure but she thought she saw just a flicker of a smile on Miles's lips. "Elizabeth," he began, then paused. "Come inside and we'll talk there." He turned toward the dark trees near them. "Guy!" he bellowed, making Elizabeth jump.

Immediately, the giant stepped into the clearing.

After only a cursory glance at Elizabeth, he looked at Miles.

"Send someone into the village and find some suitable women's clothes. Spend what you need." The voice Miles used to his man was quite different from the one he used with her.

"Send me with him," Elizabeth said quickly. "I will talk to my brother and he will be so grateful that you've released me unharmed that it will end this feud between the Chatworths and Montgomerys."

Miles turned back to her and his eyes were hard. "Don't beg, Elizabeth."

Without thought but with a cry of rage, she lifted the ax again and aimed for his head. In one seemingly practiced motion, he pulled the ax from her hand, flung it away and swung her into his arms.

She wasn't about to give him the pleasure of struggling against him and instead she stiffened, hating the feel of his clothes against her skin. The fox pelt hung to one side, baring the leg against his body.

He carried her inside the tent and gently laid her on one of the cots.

"Why do you bother with clothes for me?" she hissed. "Perhaps you should do your coupling in the fields like the animal you are."

He walked away, his back to her, and poured two goblets of wine from a silver vessel on the table. "Elizabeth," he said, "if you keep asking me to make love to you, I will eventually succumb to your temptations." He turned, walked toward her and sat on a stool a few feet away. "You've had a long day and you must be tired and hungry." He held out a full wine goblet to her.

Elizabeth swept it away, the wine spilling, staining one of the luxurious carpets that comprised the floor of the tent.

Miles glanced at it, unconcerned, and drank his wine. "And now, Elizabeth, what am I to do with you?"

Chapter 2

ELIZABETH SAT UPON THE COT, HER LEGS WELL COVERED, only her head and one shoulder bare, and refused to look at Miles Montgomery. She would not lower herself to try and reason with him as he seemed to consider her ideas begging.

After a time of silence, Miles rose and stepped outside the tent, his hand holding the flap doorway open. She heard him order a basin of hot water.

Elizabeth didn't respond to his momentary absence but thought that he had to sleep sometime and when he did, she would escape. Perhaps it would be better to wait until she had some proper clothes.

Miles didn't let his man enter with the water, but carried it in himself and set it at the side of the cot. "The water is for you, Elizabeth. I thought perhaps you'd like to wash."

She kept her arms folded across her chest and her head turned away from him. "I want nothing from you."

"Elizabeth," he said and there was exasperation in his voice. He sat down beside her, took her hands in his. He waited patiently until she turned her angry glare toward him. "I am not going to hurt you," he said gently. "I have never beat a woman in my life and I don't plan to start now. I cannot allow you to jump on a horse wearing practically nothing and ride across the countryside. You wouldn't last an hour before you'd be attacked by hordes of highway-men."

"Am I to believe you're any better?" Her hands clasped his for a moment and her eyes softened. "Will you return me to my brother?"

Miles's eyes looked into hers with an almost frighten-ing intensity. "I . . . will consider it."

She thrust his hands from hers and looked away. "What could I expect from a Montgomery? Get away from me!"

Miles rose. "The water grows cold."

She looked up at him with a slight smile. "Why should I wash? For you? Do you like your women clean and fresh smelling? If so, then I'll never wash! I will grow so dirty I will look like a Nubian slave and my hair will crawl with lice and other vermin that will soil your pretty clothes."

Miles looked at her a moment before speaking. "The tent is surrounded by men and I will be outside. If you try to leave, you will be returned to me." With that, he left her alone.

As Miles knew he would be, Sir Guy was waiting for

him outside the tent. Miles nodded once and the giant followed him into the trees.

"I sent two men for the clothes," Sir Guy said. When Miles's father died, Miles was nine and the elder Montgomery's dying wish was that Sir Guy take care of the young boy who was sometimes like a stranger even in his own family. Miles talked as much to Sir Guy as he did to anyone.

"Who is she?" Sir Guy asked, his hand on the bark of an enormous old oak tree.

"Elizabeth Chatworth."

Sir Guy nodded once. The moonlight cast eerie shadows on the scar across his face. "I thought as much. Lord Pagnell's sense of humor would run to delivering a Chatworth to a Montgomery." He paused, watching Miles for a long moment. "Do we return her to her brother on the morrow?"

Miles walked away from his man. "What do you know of her brother, Edmund Chatworth?"

Sir Guy spit lustily before answering. "Compared to Chatworth, Pagnell is a saint. Chatworth loved to torture women. He used to tie them up and rape them. On the night he was killed—and bless the man who did the killing—a young woman cut her wrists in his chamber."

Sir Guy watched as Miles clenched and unclenched his fists, and Guy regretted his words. More than anything else in the world, Miles loved women. Hundreds of times Guy had had to pull Miles off a man who'd dared to wrong a woman. As a boy he'd attacked grown men and when his temper was aroused it was all Guy could do to hold him. Last year, Guy had not succeeded in keeping Miles from killing a man who'd slapped his sharp-tongued wife. The king'd almost refused to pardon Miles for that fracas.

"Her brother Roger isn't like Edmund," Sir Guy said.

Miles whirled on him, his eyes black. "Roger Chatworth raped my sister and caused her suicide! Do you forget that?"

Guy knew that the best way to handle Miles's temper was to remain silent on the subject that angered him. "What do you plan to do with the girl?"

Miles turned away, ran his hand down the trunk of a tree. "Do you know that she hates the Montgomery name? We have been innocent in all the hatred between the Montgomerys and Chatworths yet still she hates us." He turned to face Sir Guy. "And she seems to hate me in particular. When I touch her she is repulsed. She wipes where I have touched her with a cloth, as if I'd defiled her."

As soon as Sir Guy closed his open mouth, he almost laughed. If possible, women loved Miles more than he loved them. As a child, he'd spent most of his time surrounded by girls, which is one reason why Miles was put in Sir Guy's charge—to make sure he turned into a man. But Guy had known from the first that there was no doubt of young Miles's masculinity. He just liked women. It was a quirk, rather like the love of a good horse or a sharp sword. At times, Miles's absurdly gentle treatment of women was a bother, such as his lethally enforced rule of no raping after a battle, but on the whole, Sir Guy'd learned to live with the boy's affliction—he was all right otherwise.

But Sir Guy had never, *never* heard of a woman who wasn't willing to lay down her life for Miles. Young, old, in between, even newborn girls clung to him. And Elizabeth Chatworth wiped away his touch!

Sir Guy tried to put this information into perspective. Perhaps it was like losing your first battle. He reached out and put a big hand on Miles's shoulder. "We all lose now and then. It doesn't make you less of a man. Perhaps the girl hates all men. With her brother for an example—"

Miles shrugged the hand away. "She's been hurt! *Badly* hurt! Not just her body that's covered with bruises and scratches, but she's built a wall around her of anger and hatred."

Sir Guy felt that he was standing on the edge of a deep ravine. "This girl is a highborn lady," he said quietly. "You can't keep her prisoner. The king has already outlawed your brother. You don't need to provoke him anymore. You must return Lady Elizabeth to her brother."

"Return her to a place where women are tortured? That's where she learned to hate. And if I return her now, what will she think of the Montgomerys? Will she have learned that we aren't evil as her brother was?"

"You can't think to keep her!" Sir Guy was aghast.

Miles seemed to be considering this. "It will be days before anyone learns where she is. Perhaps in that time I can show her—"

"And what of your brothers?" Sir Guy demanded. "They're expecting you home. It won't take Gavin long to find that you hold Elizabeth Chatworth prisoner." He paused, lowering his voice. "The girl will have only

22

good to say about the Montgomerys if you return her unharmed."

Miles's eyes sparkled. "I believe Elizabeth would say she used an ax to force me to return her." He gave a slight smile. "My mind is made up. I will keep her for just a little while, long enough to show her that a Montgomery isn't like her dead brother. Now! I must return and"—he smiled more broadly—"give my dirty little captive a bath. Come on, Guy, don't look like that. It's just for a few days."

Sir Guy kept quiet as he followed his young master back to camp, but he wondered if Elizabeth Chatworth could be conquered in just a few days.

The moment Elizabeth was sure Miles was gone, she ran to the far side of the tent and, lifting the heavy fabric, saw men's feet just outside. She checked the entire perimeter of the tent and there was practically no space between the guards' feet, almost as if they were holding hands to protect themselves against one small woman.

She was scratching her dirty scalp when Miles returned carrying two buckets of steaming water. Instantly, she stiffened her spine, folded her arms across her chest. Even when he sat beside her on the cot she didn't look at him.

Not until he took her hand and began to bathe it with a warm, soapy cloth did she look at him. After a moment's astonishment, she jerked away from him.

He caught her chin in his hand and began to wash her face.

"You'll feel much better when you're clean," he said gently.

She knocked his hand away. "I don't like to be touched. Get away from me!"

Patiently, he recaptured her chin and resumed washing. "You are a lovely woman, Elizabeth, and you should be proud of your looks."

Elizabeth looked at him and decided at that moment that if she didn't already hate Miles Montgomery, she would now. Obviously, he was a man used to women falling over their feet for him. He thought all he had to do was touch a woman's cheek and she would be panting with desire. He was handsome, true, and his voice was sweet, but many men were more handsome and had years of experience behind them—and several of these men had tried unsuccessfully to seduce Elizabeth.

She gazed into his eyes, let hers go liquid and when she saw the little gleam of satisfaction creep into his eyes, she smiled—and then sunk her teeth into the side of his hand.

Miles was so astonished that it took him a moment to react. He grabbed her jaw and buried his fingers into the muscles, forcing her to open her mouth. Obviously still astonished, he flexed his hand, studied the deep teeth marks in his skin. When he looked back at Elizabeth, there was triumph in her eyes.

"Do you think I'm stupid?" she asked. "Do you think I don't know what game you're playing? You hope to gentle the tigress and when you have me eating from your hand, you'll return me to my brother, no doubt carrying another of your bastards. It will be a great triumph for you, both as a Montgomery and as a man."

His eyes held hers for a moment. "You are a clever

woman, Elizabeth. Perhaps I would like to prove to you that men are capable of more than savagery."

"And how shall you do that? By holding me prisoner? By forcing me to endure your touch? You can see that I don't tremble with lust every time you get near me. Is it that you hate to admit defeat? Pagnell likes rape and violence. What stirs you? The chase? And once you have the woman do you discard her as used goods?"

She could see that she'd asked him questions he couldn't answer and it disgusted her that her own species had always succumbed to him so easily. "Can't a man, just once, do something decent? Send me to my brother!"

"No!" Miles shouted into her face, then his eyes widened. Never had a woman made him angry before. "Turn around, Elizabeth. I'm going to wash your hair."

She gave him a calculating look. "And if I refuse, will you beat me?"

"I am close to considering it." He grabbed her shoulder and spun her about, pulling her down onto the cot so her long hair hung over the edge.

Elizabeth was quiet while he soaped and rinsed her hair and she wondered if she'd pushed him too far. But his manner infuriated her. He was so quiet, so sure of himself, that she longed to find his feet of clay. She'd already seen that he merely had to hint at an order to his men and they obeyed him. Did women come to him so easily, too?

Perhaps she was wrong to try to anger him. Perhaps he'd release her if she pretended to fall madly in love with him. If she wept prettily on his shoulder he might do as she asked, but besides the disgusting ordeal of voluntarily touching him, she refused to beg to any man.

Miles combed her wet hair with a delicate ivory comb and when he was finished, he left the tent and returned in moments with a lovely gown of red samite, a mixture of silk and wool. There were also underclothes of fine lawn.

"You may finish bathing or not, as you like," he said, "but I would suggest you put the clothes on." With that he left her alone.

Elizabeth did wash, hurriedly, wincing a few times at bruises but hardly noticing them. She was glad for the clothes because they gave her more freedom to carry out her plans to escape.

Miles returned with a loaded tray of food, and he lit candles in the dark tent. "I brought a bit of everything as I have no idea what you like."

She didn't bother to answer him.

"Does the gown please you?" He was watching her closely but she looked away. The gown was an expensive one, trimmed with embroidery done in gold wire. Most women would have been pleased with it, but Elizabeth didn't seem to notice whether she wore silk or russet.

"The food grows cold. Come and eat here at the table with me."

She looked at him. "I have no intention whatsoever of eating anything at your table."

Miles started to speak but closed his mouth instead. "When you grow hungry enough, the food will be here."

Elizabeth sat on the cot, her legs stretched before

her, her arms folded, and concentrated on the tall, ornate candlestand in front of her. Tomorrow she would find a way to escape.

Ignoring the smells of the food Miles was eating, she lay down and forced her body to relax. She would need her strength for tomorrow. The long ordeal of the day made her exhausted body quick to fall asleep.

Elizabeth woke in the middle of the night and instantly she tensed, sensing some sort of danger but too sleep-befuddled to remember it. Within minutes, her mind cleared and quietly she moved her head to look at Miles, asleep in the cot on the other side of the tent.

As a child living in a household filled with horrors, she'd learned the art of moving about soundlessly. Stealthily, not allowing the noisy dress to make a sound, she tiptoed toward the back of the tent. No doubt guards were stationed all around, but at the back they'd be less alert.

It took her many minutes to lift the back of the tent enough to crawl under it. She compressed her body into a thin line and rolled, not in one movement, but inch by cautious inch. A guard walked past her but she clung to a bit of shrubbery and faded into its outline. When the guard had his back turned, she ran for the forest, seeking out and using every deep shadow. Only through years of practice, of dodging her brother Edmund and his "friends," was she able to slip away so silently. Roger had chided her, saying she would make an expert spy.

Once inside the forest, she allowed herself to breathe and used her will to calm her racing heart. Forests at night were no stranger to her and she began walking at a brisk, easy pace. It was amazing how little noise she made.

When the sun rose, Elizabeth had been walking for about two hours, and her pace was beginning to slow. She hadn't eaten in over twenty-four hours, and her energy was flagging. As her feet dragged, her skirt caught on shrubs, branches caught in her hair.

After another hour, she was trembling. She sat on a fallen log and tried to compose herself. Perhaps it was understandable that she didn't have a great deal of strength, since the combination of lack of food and the ordeal of the previous day had taken nearly all of it. The thought of rest made her eyes heavy and she knew that if she didn't, she'd never be able to continue.

Wearily, she lowered herself to the forest floor, ignoring the little crawly things on the underside of the log; it wasn't the first time she'd spent the night in a forest. She made a feeble attempt to cover herself with leaves but was only half finished when she fell back, asleep.

She woke to a sharp poke in the ribs. A big, burly man dressed in little more than rags grinned down at her, one of his front teeth missing. Two other men, filthy men, stood behind him.

"Told you she wasn't dead," the burly man said as he grabbed Elizabeth's arm and pulled her upright.

"Pretty lady," said one of the other men, putting his hand on Elizabeth's shoulder. She went one way and his hand stayed where it was; the dress tore, exposing her shoulder.

"Me first!" gasped the third man.

"A real lady," said the burly man, his hand on Elizabeth's bare shoulder.

"I am Elizabeth Chatworth and if you harm me the Earl of Bayham will have your heads."

"'Twas a earl that tossed me off my farm," said one man. "Me wife and daughter died of the winter cold. Froze to death." His expression was ugly as he looked at Elizabeth. She would have backed away but the log behind her imprisoned her.

The burly man put his hand to Elizabeth's throat. "I like my women to beg."

"Most men do," she said coolly and the man blinked at her.

"She's a mean one, Bill," said another man. "Let me have her first."

Suddenly, the man's expression changed. He gave a strange gurgle and fell forward onto Elizabeth. Deftly, she sidestepped his falling form and barely gave a look to the arrow protruding from his back. As the two men were gaping at their dead companion, Elizabeth lifted her skirts and leaped over the log.

Out of the forest came Miles. He grabbed Elizabeth's arm and his face made her breath catch. It was contorted with rage, his lips a single line, his eyes black, his brows drawn together, his nostrils flared. "Remain here!" he ordered.

For a moment she obeyed him and because of her hesitation she saw why Miles Montgomery had been awarded his spurs on the field of battle before he was eighteen. The men he faced were not unarmed. One held a spiked ball on a chain and expertly swung it at Miles's head. Miles ducked while wielding his sword at the other man.

29

Within seconds, he had destroyed both men while barely quickening his own pulse. It did not seem possible that this killer could have washed her hair without so much as creating a single tangle.

Elizabeth didn't waste time contemplating the complexities of her enemy but started running away from the battle area. She knew she could not outrun Miles but she hoped she could outsmart him. At the first low hanging branch, she caught it and swung herself upward.

Within seconds, Miles appeared below her. There was blood on his velvet doublet, blood on his drawn sword. Like a baited bear, he swung his head from side to side, then stopped and listened.

Elizabeth held her breath and didn't make a sound.

After a moment, Miles suddenly turned on his heel and looked up at her. "Come down here, Elizabeth," he said in a deadly voice.

Once, when she was thirteen, this same thing had happened. Then she'd leaped from the tree, straight onto the hideous man pursuing her, knocked him down and before he'd recovered his wind, she escaped. Without another thought, she threw herself onto Miles.

But he did not fall. Instead, he stood steady and held her tightly to him.

"Those men could have killed you," he said, seemingly unaware of her attempt to knock him down. "How did you slip past my guards?"

"Release me!" she demanded, struggling against him, but he held her easily.

"Why didn't you obey me when I told you to wait for me?"

That idiot question stopped her struggles. "Should I have waited for one of those ruffians if he'd commanded me to do so? What's the difference between them and you?"

His eyes showed anger. "Damn you, Elizabeth! What do you mean that I'm like those scum? Have I harmed you in any way?"

"So you found her," came Sir Guy's voice and there was a hint of amusement in it. "I am Sir Guy Linacre, my lady."

Elizabeth, her hands pushing hard against Miles's shoulders, nodded at Sir Guy. "Are you finished mauling me?" she snapped at Miles.

He released his grip on her so suddenly she almost fell. The quick change of motion was too much for Elizabeth's empty stomach. At once, she put her hand to her forehead and as things grew black, she put out her hand in search of something to steady herself.

It was Sir Guy who caught her and swung her into his arms.

"Do not touch me," she whispered from inside the fog she was experiencing.

As Miles took her from Sir Guy, he said, "At least it isn't *only* me she repulses." When Elizabeth opened her eyes, Miles was giving her a look of disgust. "How long has it been since you've eaten?"

"Not long enough to make me welcome you," she answered tartly.

At that Miles laughed, not one of his little half-smiles but a deep-down laugh, and before Elizabeth could react, he bent his head and kissed her lips soundly. "You are utterly unique, Elizabeth."

She wiped her mouth with the back of her hand so hard she threatened to remove her skin. "Put me down! I am perfectly capable of walking."

"And let you try and run again? No, I think I'll keep you chained to me from now on."

Miles put Elizabeth on his horse before him and together they rode back to the camp.

Chapter 3

SHE WAS SURPRISED TO SEE THAT THE TENTS HAD BEEN taken down and mules were packed and ready to leave. Elizabeth wanted to ask where he was taking her but she kept rigid in the saddle, touching Miles as little as she could, refusing to speak to him.

He led the horse away from the waiting men and into the woods, Sir Guy remaining behind. Inside the forest was set a table laden with several steaming dishes. A small, old man hovered over the array, but left when Miles gave a dismissing motion of his hand.

Dismounting, Miles held up his arms for Elizabeth, but she ignored him and slid to the ground without aid. She did this slowly so as not to repeat her ridiculous act of half fainting.

"My cook has prepared a meal for us," Miles said as he took her hand and led her forward.

She jerked from his touch and glanced at the food.

Tiny roasted quails lay upon a bed of rice, surrounded by a cream sauce. A platter contained raw oysters. There were sliced hard-cooked eggs in a saffron sauce, sliced salted ham, fish eggs on twice-baked bread, flounder stuffed with onions and nuts, poached pears, cream tarts, a pie oozing blackberries.

After a look of astonishment, Elizabeth turned away. "You travel well."

Miles caught her arm and when he spun her around, Elizabeth again felt dizzy and clutched at a stool at her feet. "The food is for you," he said, helping her to sit down. "I will not allow you to starve yourself further."

"And what will you do?" she asked wearily. "Put hot coals to the bottoms of my feet? Or perhaps you have your own special ways of forcing women to do what you want."

A frown crossed Miles's face, drawing his brows together. He grabbed her upper arms and pulled her to stand before him. "Yes, I do have my own forms of punishment."

Elizabeth had never seen this look of his, with his eyes just this shade of gray, looking as if tiny blue fires burned behind the gray. Bending, he put his lips to her neck, ignoring her when she stiffened and tried to pull away from him.

"Do you have any idea how desirable you are, Elizabeth?" he murmured against her neck. His lips nibbled upward, barely touching her skin, just enough to impart warmth to her, while his right hand played with the shoulder exposed by her torn dress. His fingers moved inward slowly, caressing the top of her breast while his teeth gently touched her earlobe.

"I would like to make love to you, Elizabeth," he whispered, so low that she felt more than heard his words. "I would like to thaw your cool exterior. I'd like to touch and caress every morsel of you, to look at you, to have you look at me with all the desire I feel for you."

Elizabeth had stood quite still during Miles's touching of her and, as always, she felt nothing. He did not truly repulse her as his breath was not foul and he didn't hurt her, but she felt none of the blood-quickening rush the girls in the convent had giggled about.

"If I swear to eat will you stop this?" she asked coolly.

Miles pulled away from her, studied her face for a moment, and Elizabeth prepared herself for the coming abuse. All men, when they found she was not overwhelmed by their lovemaking, responded by calling her many ugly names.

Miles gave her a quiet smile, caressed her cheek one more time, and offered his arm to lead her to the table. Ignoring his arm, she went to the table alone, not allowing Miles to see her confusion.

He served her himself, placing choice tidbits upon an ornate silver plate, and smiled when she ate her first bite.

"And now you are congratulating yourself on having kept me from starving myself," she said. "My brother will thank you for returning me to him in good condition."

"I am not returning you yet," Miles said softly.

Elizabeth refused to allow him to see how he upset

her, but continued eating. "Roger will pay you whatever ransom you ask."

"I will take no money from my sister's murderer," Miles said, the sound coming from a closed throat.

She threw the quail leg she was eating to her plate. "You have said this before. I know nothing of your sister!"

Miles turned toward her and his eyes were the color of steel. "Roger Chatworth tried to take the woman who was promised in marriage to my brother Stephen, and when Stephen fought for his bride, your brother attacked his back."

"No!" Elizabeth gasped, standing.

"Stephen bested Chatworth but refused to kill him, and in retaliation, Chatworth kidnapped my sister and, later, Stephen's bride. He raped my sister and, in horror, she cast herself from a window."

"No! No! No!" Elizabeth shouted, her hands over her ears.

Miles stood, grabbed her hands, held them. "Your brother Brian loved my sister and when she killed herself, he released my sister-in-law and brought the body of my sister to us."

"You are a liar! You are evil! Release me!"

Miles drew her closer, held her loosely in his arms. "It's not pleasant to hear that someone you love has done so much wrong."

Elizabeth'd had much experience in getting away from men and Miles'd had no experience in women struggling against his grasp. Quickly, she brought her knee up between his legs and instantly he released her.

"Damn you, Elizabeth," he gasped, leaning against the table, cupping himself.

"Damn you, Montgomery," she shot back as she grabbed a pitcher of wine and flung it at his head just before she turned to flee.

He ducked the pitcher and caught her arm in the same motion. "You'll not escape me," he said, pulling her toward him. "I'm going to teach you that the Montgomerys are innocent in this feud, even if I have to die proving it."

"The idea of your death is the first pleasant notion I've heard in days."

For a moment Miles closed his eyes as if in a silent prayer for help. He seemed recovered when he looked back at her. "Now, if you have finished eating, we must ride. We are going to Scotland."

"To—!" she began, but he put a finger to her lips.

"Yes, my angel"—his voice was heavy with sarcasm —"we are going to spend time with my brother and his wife. I want you to get to know my family."

"I know more than enough about your family. They are—"

This time, Miles kissed her and, if she did not react to his touch, when she turned away she was silent.

They rode for many hours at a slow, steady pace. The many baggage mules behind them bearing furniture, clothing, food, armor, weapons, made their progress ponderous.

Elizabeth was given her own horse but a rope was tied to the saddle and attached to Miles's horse. Twice he tried to make conversation but she refused to speak to him. Her mind was too busy thinking about, and trying not to think about, what Miles had told her about her brother.

For the last two years the only contact she'd had with

her family was through Roger's letters and snatches of gossip from traveling musicians. Of course the musicians were aware she was a Chatworth and so had said little either way about her family.

But the extensive Montgomery family was another matter. They were a favorite subject of songs and gossip. The oldest brother, Gavin, had jilted the beautiful Alice Valence and on the rebound she'd married Elizabeth's brother Edmund. Elizabeth had begged Roger to stop the marriage, saying that the poor woman didn't deserve to be shackled to the treacherous Edmund. Roger said there was nothing he could do to prevent the marriage. Only a few months later, Gavin Montgomery had married the magnificently wealthy Revedoune heiress, and after Edmund's murder, the jealous heiress had tossed boiling oil on poor Alice Chatworth's face. Elizabeth had written from the convent and begged Roger to care for her brother's widow and Roger had quickly agreed.

Less than a year later, Roger had written that the Scottish heiress, Bronwyn MacArran, had pleaded to be allowed to marry Roger but Stephen Montgomery was forcing the poor woman to become his bride. Roger had challenged Stephen in an attempt to protect the MacArran woman, and during the fight, Montgomery had cleverly made it appear that Roger attacked his back. As a result, Roger was disgraced.

She wasn't sure why Brian had left his home; Roger would never say. But she was sure it had to do with the Montgomerys. Brian was sensitive and gentle. Perhaps he could no longer stand all the horrors that had been done to his family because of the Montgomerys. But whatever made Brian leave had nothing to do with the lies she'd heard today. She doubted if Roger even knew the Montgomery men had a sister.

All during the long ride, she'd idly been tucking the torn shoulder of her dress inside the high neckline. When Miles called a halt to the procession, she was startled to see that it was growing dark. Her thoughts had kept her occupied for hours.

Before them was an inn, half timbered, old but prosperous-looking. The landlord stood outside, his big red face split by a welcoming grin.

Miles stood beside her. "Elizabeth"—he held up his arms for her—"do not embarrass yourself by refusing me," he said, a twinkle in his eye as he glanced at her raised foot.

Elizabeth considered for a moment, then allowed him to help her from her horse, but she stepped away from his touch as soon as she was on the ground. Two of his men entered the inn first while Miles caught Elizabeth's arm.

"I have something for you." Watching her closely, he held out a lovely, intricately wrought gold brooch of a pelican, its beak tucked under its outstretched wing, standing on a band of diamonds.

Elizabeth's eyes didn't flicker. "I don't want it."

With a look of exasperation, Miles pinned the shoulder of her gown together. "Come inside, Elizabeth," he said flatly.

Obviously, the innkeeper was expecting them, for the bustle of activity within was enormous. Elizabeth stood to one side as Miles conferred with Sir Guy while the landlord waited for their commands.

It was a large room set with tables and chairs, a big fireplace to one side. For the first time, Elizabeth really looked at Miles's men. There were an even dozen of them and it seemed they gave remarkably little trouble. Now they walked about, opening doors, quietly checking for any hidden danger. Did Miles Montgomery have so many enemies he must always be wary—or was he just cautious?

A pretty young maid curtsied before Miles and he gave her his little half-smile. Elizabeth watched curiously as the maid blushed and preened under Miles's gaze.

"Yes, my lord," she said, smiling, bobbing up and down. "I hope ye like the meal I've cooked."

"I will," Miles said so matter-of-factly that it made his enjoyment seem a sure fact.

With another blush, the girl turned back to the kitchen.

"Are you hungry, Elizabeth?" Miles asked, turning back to her.

"Not for what you seem to inspire." She nodded toward the maid's retreating back.

"How I wish there were jealousy in those words. But I have patience," he added with a smile and gave her a little push toward the table before she could answer.

Miles and she sat at a small table, apart from his men but in the same room. Dish after dish was brought to them but Elizabeth barely ate.

"You don't seem to have a big appetite at best."

"If you were held prisoner would you gorge yourself on your captor's food?"

"I would probably not lose a moment in planning my captor's death," he answered honestly.

Elizabeth glared at him in silence and Miles concentrated on his food.

Halfway through the long, silent meal, Miles caught the hand of one of the maids placing a dish of fresh salmon on the table. As Elizabeth looked up in surprise, she saw that the maid's hands were scratched and raw.

"How have you injured yourself?" Miles asked gently.

"The berry brambles, milord," she answered, half frightened, half fascinated by Miles's attention.

"Landlord!" Miles called. "See that the girl's hands are cared for and she's not to put them in water until they heal."

"But my lord!" the man protested. "She's only a scullery maid. She's serving tonight because my regular girl has the pox."

Sir Guy slowly rose from the head of the table of Miles's retainers, and all that was needed was the size of the giant and the landlord took a step backward.

"Come, girl," the landlord said angrily.

"Thank . . . thank you, my lord," she bobbed a curtsy before she fled the room.

Elizabeth cut herself a slice of French cheese. "Did Sir Guy come to your defense for the girl's sake or his own?"

Miles's expression went from amazement to amusement. He caught her hand and kissed the palm. "Guy doesn't like fights over scullery maids."

"And you do?"

Smiling, he shrugged. "I prefer to avoid fights about anything. I am a peaceful man."

"But you would have fought a fat, congenial landlord over the scratched hands of a worthless girl." It was a statement.

41

"I do not consider her worthless. Now"—he dismissed the subject—"you must be tired. Would you like to retire?"

Miles's men all bid her goodnight and she nodded toward them, following Miles and the landlord up the stairs to the single room—and single bed—that awaited them.

"So! You have waited until now to force me to your bed," she said when they were alone. "Perhaps the tent walls were too thin to muffle my cries."

"Elizabeth," he said, taking her hand. "I will sleep on the windowseat and you may have the bed. I cannot allow you to have a room alone because you'd find some way to leave."

"Escape, you mean."

"All right, have it your way, escape. Now come here. I want to talk to you." He pulled her to the windowseat, sat down and pulled her to sit beside him. When he drew her back against his chest, she began to protest.

"Relax, Elizabeth. I will leave my hands here about your waist and not move them, but I'll not let you up until you relax and talk to me."

"I can talk sitting up, away from you."

"But I cannot keep from touching you," he said with feeling. "All the time I want to caress you, to soothe away your hurt."

"I am not hurt." She pushed at his arms holding her to him. He was a large man, tall and broad, and the outward curve of his chest just fit the arch of her back.

"But you are hurt, Elizabeth, probably more than you know."

"Ah yes, I see now. There is something wrong with

me because I don't salivate with adoration whenever you are near me."

Miles kissed her neck, chuckling. "Perhaps I deserved that. Hold still or I'll kiss you more." Her abrupt stillness made him wince. "I want you to tell me what you like. Food does not interest you, nor pretty dresses. Gold and diamonds don't even make you blink. Men don't rate a glance from you. What is your weakness?"

"My weakness?" she asked, thinking about it. He was stroking her hair at her temple and in spite of herself, she was beginning to relax. The last two days of tension and anger were draining her strength. His long legs were stretched out on the windowseat and she was between them. "What is your weakness, Montgomery?"

"Women," he murmured, dismissing the question. "Tell me about you."

The muscles in her neck were relaxing and her weight was easing against him. It wasn't a bad feeling to be held so safely by such strong arms when the man wasn't pawing at her, tearing her clothes, hurting her. "I live with my two brothers, both of whom I love and who love me. I am far from being a pauper and I have but to hint at a jewel or gown I'd like and my brother Roger purchases it for me."

"And . . . Roger"—he tripped over the name—"is good to you?"

"He protects me." She smiled and closed her eyes. Miles was massaging the tight muscles in her neck. "Roger has always protected Brian and me."

"Protected you from what?"

From Edmund, she almost said but caught herself.

Her eyes flew open and she sat up. "From men!" she spat. "Men have always liked my looks but Roger kept them away from me."

He kept her hands imprisoned. "You know many tricks for repulsing men and you have wrapped yourself in steel. You are obviously a naturally passionate woman, so what has killed your passion? Was it that perhaps Roger was not always near enough to protect you?"

Elizabeth refused to answer him and she cursed her momentary trustfulness. After a while, Miles gave an exaggerated sigh and released her. Immediately she sprang away from him.

"Go to bed," he said tiredly as he stood, turning his back on her.

Elizabeth didn't trust him to keep his word about not sleeping with her, but she would do nothing to entice him. Fully clothed except for her soft leather shoes, she slipped into the big bed.

Miles blew out the single candle and for a long moment stood silhouetted before the moonlit window.

When Elizabeth heard no sounds from him she quietly turned on her back to watch him. All her body was tense with fear of what was to come. With resignation she watched him undress, and when he was nude she held her breath. But Miles lifted the thin blanket on the windowseat and stretched out—or tried to. He cursed once when his feet hit the paneling at the end of the cushion.

It was some minutes before Elizabeth began to realize that Miles Montgomery was not going to force himself on her. But she suspected that as soon as she was asleep he would pounce. She dozed lightly but every noise woke her. When Miles tried to turn on his narrow bed, he woke her and for a moment she would tense, but when she heard his even breathing of sleep, she'd relax again and sleep—until the next noise woke her.

Chapter 4

"DIDN'T YOU SLEEP WELL?" MILES ASKED THE NEXT morning as he pulled on his clothes. Tight black hose gripped his powerful legs, an embroidered jacket barely reaching the tops of his thighs.

"I never sleep well in the presence of my enemies," she retorted.

With a chuckle, he brushed her hands away and braided her hair for her, tying the tail with a bit of ribbon. When he finished, he kissed her neck, causing her to jump away while rubbing her neck.

He held out his arm to her. "I know you will be sad to leave my company but my men wait below for us."

She ignored his arm and left the room ahead of him. It was very early yet, the sun only a warm glow on the horizon. Miles murmured that a meal was waiting for them some distance down the road, and that they would ride for a few hours first.

Miles and Elizabeth stood together on the little porch of the inn, Sir Guy before them, Miles's knights waiting with the horses and baggage mules behind the giant.

"Everything is ready?" Miles asked Sir Guy. "The innkeeper has been paid?"

Before Sir Guy could answer, a little girl, about four, raggedly dressed, came running out of the inn, swerved to miss Miles and fell down the two steps. Instantly, Miles was on his knees, pulling the child into his arms.

"Hush, sweetheart," he whispered, standing, the child clinging to him.

To Sir Guy and the knights, this was a familiar sight, and they waited patiently, with a bored air, while Miles comforted the child. Elizabeth didn't concern herself with Miles. Her one and only thought was for the injured child. She stretched out her arm, put her hand on the back of the crying child's head.

The child pulled her face away from the hollow in Miles's shoulder, and through tear-blurred eyes she looked at Elizabeth. With a fresh burst of tears she lifted her arms and lunged forward into Elizabeth's grasp.

It was difficult to tell who was more astonished: Miles, Sir Guy or the Montgomery knights. Miles gaped at Elizabeth and for a moment his pride took a beating.

"Hush now," Elizabeth said in a gentle voice such as Miles had never heard before. "If you stop crying Sir Guy will give you a ride on his shoulders."

Miles coughed to cover the laugh that threatened to

choke him. Between Sir Guy's size and the hideous scar on his face, most people, and especially women, were terrified of him. He'd never seen anyone dare to volunteer the giant to be a child's horse.

"You'll be so tall," Elizabeth continued, swaying with the child, "you'll be able to reach up and catch a star."

The child gave a sniff, pulled away from Elizabeth and looked at her. "A star?" she hiccuped.

Elizabeth caressed the child's wet cheek. "And when you get the star, you can give it to Sir Miles to repay him for the new dress he's going to purchase for you."

The eyes of Miles's men went to their lord to watch his reaction—and no one dared laugh at his look of indignation.

The child sniffed again and twisted to look at Lord Miles. She gave him a smile, but when she looked at Sir Guy she clung to Elizabeth.

"There's no reason to be afraid of him," Elizabeth said. "He likes children very much, don't you, Sir Guy?"

Sir Guy gave Lady Elizabeth a hard, assessing look. "In truth, my lady, I like children a great deal but they have little use for me."

"We shall remedy that. Now, child, go with Sir Guy for your ride and bring back a star."

The child, a bit hesitant at first, went to Sir Guy and clung to his head when he set her on his shoulders. "I'm the tallest girl in the world," she squealed as Sir Guy walked away with her.

"I've never seen you smile before," Miles said.

Elizabeth's smile disappeared instantly. "I will reim-

burse you for the child's dress when I am home again."
She turned away.

Miles caught her hand and led her away from his
men's listening ears. "The child was only a beggar's."

"Oh?" she said offhandedly. "I thought perhaps she
was one of yours."

"Mine?" he asked, bewildered. "Do you think I'd
allow one of my children to run about in rags, with no
supervision?"

She turned on him. "And how do you know where all
your children are? Do you keep ledgers full of their
names? Their whereabouts?"

Miles's face showed several emotions: disbelief,
some anger, amusement. "Elizabeth, how many children do you think I have?"

She put her chin into the air. "I neither know nor
care how many bastards you have."

He caught her arm, turning her to face him. "Even
my own brothers exaggerate about my children so why
should I expect more from outsiders? I have three sons:
Christopher, Philip and James. And any day I expect to
hear word of another child of mine. I am hoping for a
daughter this time."

"You are hoping—" she gasped. "It doesn't bother
you about their mothers? That you use the women,
then discard them? And what of the children? They
must grow up with the label of bastard! Outcasts
because of some hideous man's one moment of pleasure."

His grip tightened on her arm and there was anger in
his eyes. "I do not 'use' women," he said through
clenched teeth. "The women who have given me

49

children came to me freely. And all my children live with me, are cared for by competent nurses."

"Nurses!" She tried to pull away from him, but couldn't. "Do you toss the children's mothers into the street? Or do you give them a little money like you did Bridget and send them on their ways?"

"Bridget?" Miles searched her face for a moment. His rising temper calmed. "I assume you mean the Bridget who is the mother of my James?" He didn't wait for her answer. "I will tell you the truth about Bridget. My brother Gavin sent a message to St. Catherine's convent to ask for some serving girls. He wanted girls of good reputation who wouldn't be tantalizing his men and causing fights. From the moment this Bridget entered our house she pursued me."

Elizabeth tried to pull away from him. "You are a liar."

Miles caught her other arm with his hand. "Once she told me that she'd heard so much about me that she felt like a child who'd been told not to play with fire. One night I found her in my bed."

"And you took her."

"I made love to her, yes, that night and several other nights. When she realized she was going to have my child, I took a lot of ribbing from my brothers."

"And you cast her out—after you took her child away, that is."

He gave her a small smile. "Actually, she cast me aside. I was away for four months and she fell in love with Gavin's second gardener. When I returned I talked with them, told them I'd like to have the child and would raise him to be a knight. Bridget agreed readily."

"And how much money did you give them? Surely you must have offered some consolation to a mother giving up her child."

Miles released her arms, glaring at her. "Did you know Bridget very well? If you did you'd know she was more interested in her pleasures than motherhood. The gardener she was marrying didn't want Bridget or the child and later he asked for money for 'what he was giving up.' I gave him nothing. James is mine."

She was silent for a moment. "And what of your other children's mothers?" she asked quietly.

He walked away from her. "I fell in love with the younger sister of one of Gavin's men when I was just a boy. Christopher was born when both Margaret and I were only sixteen. I would have married her but her brother sent her away. I didn't know about Kit until Margaret died of smallpox a month after Kit's birth."

He looked back at Elizabeth and grinned. "Philip's mother was a dancer, an exotic creature who shared my bed for two"—he sighed—"two very interesting weeks. Then nine months later she sent a messenger with Philip. I've never seen or heard from her since."

Elizabeth was fascinated with his stories. "And this new child?"

Miles ducked his head and if he'd been a woman she would have thought he blushed. "I'm afraid this child may cause some problems. The mother is a distant cousin of mine. I resisted her as long as I could but . . ." He shrugged. "Her father is very angry with me. He says he'll send the child to me but . . . I'm not sure he will."

Elizabeth could only shake her head at him in

disbelief. "Surely there must be other children." Her voice was sarcastic.

He frowned slightly. "I don't think so. I try to keep track of my women now and watch for children."

"Rather like gathering eggs," she said, eyes wide.

Miles cocked his head to one side and gave her an intense look. "One moment you condemn me for leaving my children in rags, strewn about the country like so much refuse, and now you damn me for caring for them. I am not a celibate man nor do I intend to be, but I take my responsibilities seriously. I love my children and I provide for them. I should like to have fifty of them."

"You have a good start," she said, sweeping past him.

Miles stood still, watching her walk back toward his men and the horses. She stood a little apart from the men, with that stiff-backed carriage of hers. She wasn't like either of his sisters-in-law, used to authority, at ease with the people who worked for them. Elizabeth Chatworth was rigid whenever she was near men. Yesterday, by accident, one of his men on horseback had brushed against her and Elizabeth had reacted so sharply, pulling her horse's reins so unexpectedly, that her horse had reared. She'd controlled the animal and held her seat but the experience had disgusted Miles. No woman—or man for that matter—should be so frightened of another human's touch.

Sir Guy returned, alone, to the men and at once he searched for Miles, walking toward him when he saw him. "It's getting late. We should ride." He paused. "Or perhaps you've reconsidered about returning the lady to her brother."

Miles was watching Elizabeth, who was now talking to the mother and the little girl who'd fallen earlier. He turned back to Guy. "I want you to send a couple of men to my northern estate. They are to bring Kit to me."

"Your son?" Sir Guy questioned.

"Yes, my son. Send his nurse with him. No! On second thought, bring him alone but with a heavy guard. Lady Elizabeth will be his nurse."

"Are you sure of what you're doing?" Sir Guy asked.

"The Lady Elizabeth likes children so I will share one of mine with her. If I can't reach her heart one way, I will use another."

"And what will you do with this woman once you've tamed her? Once, when I was a boy, there was a cat that had lived wild and it claimed the area around a certain shed as its own. Whenever anyone went near the shed, the cat scratched and bit. I set myself the job of taming it. It took many weeks of patience to gain the cat's trust but I felt triumphant when it began to eat from my hand. But later the cat began to follow me everywhere. I tripped over it constantly and it became a major nuisance. After several months I was kicking the cat, hating it because it was no longer the wild thing I'd loved at first, but only another cat, just like all the others."

Miles continued to study Elizabeth. "Perhaps it *is* the chase," he said quietly. "Or perhaps I'm like my brother Raine, who can't stand any injustice. All I know now is that Elizabeth Chatworth fascinates me. Maybe I do want to have her eat from my hand—but maybe when she does, it will be because I'm her slave."

He turned back to Sir Guy. "Elizabeth will like Kit

and my son can only benefit from knowing her. And I'd like to see my son as well. Send the message."

Sir Guy nodded once in agreement before leaving Miles alone.

Minutes later they were mounted and ready to leave. Miles didn't try to talk to Elizabeth but silently rode beside her. She was beginning to look tired and by midday, he was of half a mind to return her to her brother.

A half-hour later, she suddenly sprang to life. While Miles had been feeling sorry for her, she'd worked loose the rope attaching their horses. She kicked her horse forward, used the loose end of her reins to slap the rumps of two horses in front of her, and with the rearing horses as a shield, she gained precious seconds to escape. She was half a mile down the rutted, weed-infested road before Miles could get around his men and follow her.

"I will bring her back," he shouted over his shoulder to Sir Guy.

Miles knew the horse Elizabeth rode had little speed in it but she got what she could out of it. He was close enough to catch her when the girth of his saddle slipped and he was sent sliding to one side. "Damn her," he gasped, knowing very well who'd loosened the saddle, but, at the same time, he smiled at her ingenuity.

But Elizabeth Chatworth wasn't prepared for a man who'd grown up with three older brothers. Miles was used to practical jokes such as loosened cinches and he knew how to handle them. Expertly, he shifted his weight to the front of the horse, in essence riding bareback but sitting on the horse's neck, the saddle behind him.

He lost some speed when the horse threatened to revolt at this new position, but Miles controlled the animal.

Elizabeth turned her mount into a corn field when the primitive road disappeared and she was disconcerted to see Miles close on her heels.

He caught her in the corn field, grabbing her about the waist. She fought him wildly and Miles, with no stirrups to anchor himself, started falling. When he went down his arm was still fastened around Elizabeth's waist.

As they both fell, Miles twisted and took most of the jolt, cushioning Elizabeth, putting his arm up to protect her back from a flying hoof. The horses ran for a few more feet then stood, sides heaving.

"Release me," Elizabeth demanded when she caught her breath. She was sprawled on top of Miles.

His arms held her to him. "When did you loosen the cinch?" When she didn't answer he hugged her until her ribs threatened to break.

"At dinner," she gasped.

He moved his hand to the back of her head, forcing it to his shoulder. "Elizabeth, you are so clever. How did you manage to sneak past my men? When did you leave my sight?"

His neck was sweaty and his heart was pounding against her own. The exercise had done away with her tiredness and she was glad for it even if she hadn't succeeded in her escape.

"You gave me a good run," he said, amused. "If my brothers hadn't thought it a great joke to send me out with a loosened cinch, I wouldn't have known how to handle it. Of course *they* were careful that I was on a slow mount so if I fell I wouldn't kill myself." He moved to look at her face. "Would you have been terribly glad to see me break my neck?"

"Yes, very," she said, smiling, practically nose to nose with him.

Miles laughed at that, kissed her quickly, pushed her off him and stood, frowning as she wiped the back of her hand across her mouth. "Come on, there's an inn not far from here and we'll stop for the night." He didn't offer to help her up.

When they returned to the men, Sir Guy gave Elizabeth a quick look of admiration and she guessed that he'd be more vigilant from now on. She wouldn't have more chances to toy with the men's gear.

It wasn't until they were mounted again that Elizabeth saw that Miles's forearm was cut and bleeding. She knew it had happened when he'd put his arm between her and the horse's hoof. Sir Guy inspected the cut and bound it while Elizabeth sat on her horse and watched. It seemed odd that this man, a Montgomery, would protect a Chatworth from harm.

Miles saw her watching. "A smile from you, Elizabeth, would make it heal faster."

"I hope it poisons your blood and you lose your arm." She kicked her horse forward.

They didn't speak again until they arrived at the inn at which, as before, Miles had sent someone ahead to prepare for them. This time, Miles and Elizabeth were given a private dining room.

"Tell me more about your family," he said.

"No," she answered simply, reaching for a dish of snails in garlic sauce.

"Then I will tell you of mine. I have three older brothers and—"

"I know about them. You and your brothers are notorious."

He raised one eyebrow at her. "Tell me what you've heard."

"With pleasure." She cut into a beef and chicken pie. "Your brother Gavin is the eldest. He was to marry Alice Valence but he rejected her so he could marry the rich Judith Revedoune, who is a vicious-tempered woman. Between your brother and his wife they succeeded in driving Alice—now Chatworth—insane."

"Do you know your sister-in-law?"

Elizabeth studied the food on her plate. "She wasn't always as she is now."

"The bitch was born a whore. She rejected my brother. Now, tell me of Stephen."

"He forced a woman who wanted my brother to be his bride."

"And Raine?"

"I know little of the man, except that he's magnificent on a battlefield."

Miles's eyes burned into hers. "After your brother raped my sister and Mary killed herself, Raine led some of the king's men to attack your brother Roger. The king has declared Raine a traitor and my brother lives in a forest with a band of criminals." He paused. "And what of me?"

"You are a lecher, a seducer of young girls."

"I am flattered that my virility is so overrated. Now let me tell you the truth about my family. Gavin had to take over the raising of three brothers and the managing of estates when he was but sixteen. He barely had time to find out about women. He fell in love with Alice Valence, begged her to marry him, but she refused. He married Judith Revedoune and only after a long while did he realize he loved Judith. Alice tried to scar Judith with hot oil but Alice was the one scarred."

"You lie constantly," Elizabeth said.

"No, I do not lie. Stephen is the peacemaker in our family and he and Gavin are close. And Raine—" He paused and smiled. "Raine believes the world's burdens rest upon his big shoulders. He is a good man but unbelievably stubborn."

"And you?" Elizabeth asked softly.

He took his time answering. "I am alone. My brothers seem so sure of what they want. Gavin loves the land, Stephen is a crusader about his Scots, Raine wants to change the world, but I . . ."

She looked up at him and for a moment there was a silent exchange. She too had felt alone in her life. Edmund was evil, Roger was always angry and she'd spent her life escaping Edmund and his friends while trying to protect Brian.

Miles took her hand in his and she didn't pull away. "You and I have had to grow up quickly. Do you remember being a child?"

"All too well," she said flatly, pulling her hand away.

For a while they ate in silence. "Was your home . . . happy?" she asked, as if it didn't matter.

"Yes." He smiled. "Each of us was fostered but we still spent a great deal of time together. It's not easy being the youngest son. You get knocked about a bit. And were you happy?"

"No. I was too busy running from Edmund to think

of anything as silly as happiness. I would like to retire now."

Miles followed her to their room and she saw that tonight a cot had been set along one wall.

"No windowseat," he said cheerfully, but Elizabeth didn't laugh. He took both her hands in his. "When are you going to trust me? I am not like Edmund or Pagnell or any other of the disgusting men you know."

"You are holding me prisoner. Do men as good as you think you are hold innocent women captive?"

He kissed her hands. "But if I returned you to your brother, what would you do? Would you wait for Roger to find you a husband and then happily settle down to wedded bliss?"

She pulled away from him. "Roger has given me permission to never marry. I have considered taking vows of the church."

Miles gave her a look of horror. Before she could protest, he pulled her into his arms, stroked her back. "You have so much love to give. How could you think to hide it? Wouldn't you like to have children, to watch them grow? There's nothing like a child looking at you with complete adoration and trust."

She lifted her head from his shoulder. She was growing almost used to his touching and holding of her. "I've never before met a man who loved children. All the men I know care only for fighting, drinking, raping women."

"There's something to be said for a good rousing fight now and then and I've been drunk before, but I like willing women in my bed. Now, let's get you out of this dress."

She jerked away from him, her eyes hostile.

"I plan to sleep on that cold, hard, lonely cot but I think you must be sick of that gown. You'd be more comfortable sleeping without it."

"I am more comfortable *in* my clothes, thank you."

"All right, have your own way." He turned away and began to undress while Elizabeth fled to the protection of her bed.

The single candle was still burning and when Miles wore only his loincloth, he bent over her, pulling the blanket from over her face. She lay stiff, rigid, while he sat on the edge of the bed, his hand caressing the hair at her temple. Not speaking, he simply looked at her, enjoying the feel of her skin.

"Goodnight, Elizabeth," he whispered as he planted a soft kiss on her lips.

Her hand shot out to wipe it away but he caught her wrist. "What would it take to make you love a man?" he murmured.

"I don't think I could," she replied honestly. "At least not as you mean."

"I'm beginning to think I want to test that. Goodnight, my fragile angel."

He kissed her again before she could protest that she was far from fragile, but this time she was able to wipe the kiss away.

Chapter 5

MILES, ELIZABETH, SIR GUY AND THE MONTGOMERY knights traveled for two more days before reaching the southern border of Scotland. Elizabeth tried once more to escape—at night while Miles slept close to her—but she didn't reach the door before he caught her and led her back to bed.

Elizabeth lay awake a long time after that, thinking about how she was a prisoner and yet not a prisoner. She had never been treated with as much courtesy as Miles Montgomery treated her. He did insist upon touching her at every opportunity but she was growing used to that. It certainly was no pleasure but it was no longer as vile as it'd seemed at first. Once, at an inn where they'd stopped for dinner, a drunk had fallen toward Elizabeth and, as a reflex, she'd stepped nearer to Miles for protection. He had been inordinately pleased by that.

Today he'd told her that from now on they'd be using his tent as the inns were not as abundant in Scotland. He hinted that once they crossed the mountains, there could be trouble since the Highlanders didn't like the English.

All through supper, he'd seemed preoccupied and had conferred with Sir Guy several times.

"Are the Scots as bloodthirsty as all this?" she asked after he'd left the supper table the second time.

He didn't seem to understand what she was talking about. "I'm meeting someone here and he's late. He should have been here by now."

"One of your brothers—or is it a woman?"

"Neither," he said quickly.

Elizabeth asked no more questions. As she crawled into her bed, wearing the same dress Miles had given her, she turned to her side to watch him on his cot. He tossed and turned every moment.

When a loud knock came on the door, Elizabeth sprang out of bed almost as quickly as Miles. Sir Guy entered, a little boy behind him.

"Kit!" Miles cried, grabbing the child, hugging him fit to crush him. The boy didn't seem to mind as he also clung to Miles.

"What took them so long?" Miles asked Sir Guy.

"They were caught in a rainstorm and lost three horses."

"No men?"

"Everyone was saved but it took a while to replace the horses. Young master Kit held onto his saddle when two knights couldn't," Sir Guy said with pride.

"Is that true?" Miles asked, turning the boy around.

Elizabeth saw a small replica of Miles but with brown eyes instead of gray, a handsome boy, his face solemn.

"Yes, Papa," Kit answered. "Uncle Gavin said that a knight always stays with his horse. Afterward, I helped the men pull the baggage from the water."

"You're a good boy." Miles grinned, hugging Kit once again. "You may go, Guy, and see that the men are fed. We'll leave first thing in the morning."

Kit smiled goodbye to Sir Guy, then whispered loudly to his father. "Who is she?"

Miles stood Kit on the floor. "Lady Elizabeth," he said formally, "may I present Christopher Gavin Montgomery."

"How do you do?" she said, taking the child's extended hand. "I am Lady Elizabeth Chatworth."

"You are very pretty," he said. "My papa likes pretty women."

"Kit—" Miles began, but Elizabeth interrupted him.

"Do you like pretty women?" she asked.

"Oh yes. My nurse is very, very pretty."

"I'm sure she is if your father hired her. Are you hungry? Tired?"

"I ate a whole sackful of sugared plums," Kit said with pride. "Oh Papa! I have a message for you. It's from someone named Simon."

A frown crossed Miles's face, but as he read the message he broke into a grin.

"Good news?" Elizabeth asked, not able to hide her curiosity.

Miles sobered himself as he tossed the note to his rumpled cot. "Yes and no. My cousin has been delivered of my daughter but my Uncle Simon is threatening my life."

Elizabeth wasn't sure whether to laugh or be disgusted. "You have a little sister, Kit," she said at last.

"I have two brothers already. I don't want a sister."

"I believe your father makes those decisions. It's late and I think you should be in bed."

"Kit can take the cot and I'll . . ." Miles began, eyes twinkling.

"Kit will sleep with me," Elizabeth said loftily, offering her hand to the child.

Kit accepted readily and he yawned as she led him around the bed.

Miles watched, smiling a bit triumphantly, as Elizabeth undressed the sleepy little boy down to his underwear. He readily went into her arms as she lifted him into bed. Elizabeth crawled in beside him, pulled Kit to her.

For a moment Miles stood to one side, watching them. With a smile, he bent and kissed both foreheads. "Goodnight," he whispered before going to his cot.

During the next day, it didn't take Miles long to see that Elizabeth's interest extended only to Kit. And the child took to Elizabeth as if he'd known her forever. All Elizabeth would say was, "I have always liked children and they seem to know this." Whatever the reason, Kit seemed perfectly at ease with Elizabeth. In the afternoon, he rode with her, fell asleep against her. When Miles suggested he take the heavy child, Elizabeth practically snarled at him.

At night they curled up with each other on a single cot and slept peacefully. Miles looked down at them and felt like an outsider.

They traveled for three more days and Elizabeth knew they must be getting close to the MacArrans' land. Miles had been in deep thought all day and twice she'd seen him arguing with Sir Guy. From the frown on Sir Guy's face, Miles was obviously planning something the giant didn't like. But whenever Elizabeth got within hearing distance the men stopped talking.

At midday Miles stopped the entourage of men and mules and asked if she and Kit would like to dine with him. Usually they all ate together, within sight and protection of each other.

"You seem pleased with yourself about something," Elizabeth said, watching him.

"We're within a day's ride of my brother and his wife," Miles said happily, lifting Kit from Elizabeth's horse.

"Uncle Stephen wears a skirt and Lady Bronwyn can ride a horse as fast as the wind," Kit informed her.

"Stephen wears a plaid," Miles amended as he pulled Elizabeth from her horse, ignoring her attempts to brush his hands away. "My cook has laid a meal for us inside the forest."

Kit took Elizabeth's hand and Miles held the child on the other side and together they walked into the forest.

"What do you think of Scotland?" Miles asked as he held her arm as she stepped over a fallen log.

"It's as if the place has been untouched since the beginning of time. It's very rough and . . . untrimmed."

"Rather like its people." Miles laughed. "My brother has let his hair grow to his shoulders and his clothing . . . no, I'll let you see for yourself."

"Aren't we going a bit far from your men?" The

primitive forest closed around them and the under-growth was making it more difficult to walk.

Miles drew an ax from where it was slung across his back and began to hack away a wider path.

With a look of puzzlement, Elizabeth turned to him. He was wearing somber clothes of dark green, a brown cloak about his shoulders—and he was heavily armed. There was a longbow with a quiver of arrows on his back, as well as the ax, his sword on his hip and a dagger at his waist. "Something is wrong, isn't it?"

"Yes," he said, looking about her. "The truth is, Elizabeth, I was given a message to meet someone here, but we've gone too far."

She raised one eyebrow. "You would risk your son's life in this secret meeting?"

He slipped his ax back into its sheath. "My men are all around us. I wanted you close to me rather than leave you and Kit with any of my men."

"Look, Papa!" Kit said excitedly. "There's a deer."

"Shall we go and see the deer?" she said calmly. "Run ahead of us and we'll catch you." Keeping Kit in her sight, she turned to Miles. "I will stay with Kit and you go look for your men. I feel there's been some trick to separate us."

Miles's eyes widened at her ordering of him, but within moments he disappeared into the forest while Elizabeth hurried after Kit. When Miles seemed to take forever before he returned, she looked about with anxious eyes.

"Are you unhappy, Elizabeth?" Kit asked, catching her hand.

She knelt to his level. "I was just wondering where your father is."

"He will return," Kit said confidently. "My papa will take care of us."

Elizabeth tried not to show her disbelief. "I am sure he will. I hear a stream in that direction. Shall we find it?"

They had some trouble breaking through the underbrush but they made it to the stream. It was a wild, rushing body of water, cascading angrily over rocks, tearing at the rocky shore.

"It's cold," Kit said, stepping back. "Do you think there are any fish in it?"

"Salmon, most likely," said Miles from behind Elizabeth, and she jumped. Miles put his arm about her shoulders. "I didn't mean to frighten you."

She stepped away from him. "What about your men?"

He gave a look to Kit who was throwing forest debris into the water and watching it being swept away. He took her hands in his. "My men are gone. There's no sign of them. Elizabeth, you won't panic, will you?"

She looked into his eyes. She was frightened to be in a strange land with a child and this man she didn't trust. "No," she said firmly. "I don't want to frighten Kit."

"Good." He smiled, squeezing her hands. "We are on the southern boundaries of MacArran land now and if we walk due north we should reach some of the crofters' cottages by evening tomorrow."

"But if someone has spirited away your men—"

"My concern now is for you and Kit. If we stay in the forest perhaps we can escape notice. I don't mind a fight, but I don't want you or Kit harmed. Will you help me?"

She didn't pull away from his hands. "Yes," she said softly. "I'll help you."

He released one of her hands. "These mountains are cold even in the summer. Put this around you." He held up a large piece of woolen fabric woven in a deep blue and green tartan.

"Where did you get this?"

"This was all that was left of the meal my cook left. The food was gone but the cloth he spread it on, one of the plaids Bronwyn gave me, was left behind. We'll need this tonight." He kept her hand clasped tightly as she tossed the plaid over her arm and they walked toward Kit.

"Would you like to walk to Uncle Stephen's house?" Miles asked his son.

Kit gave his father a shrewd look. "Where is Sir Guy? A knight doesn't walk."

"A knight does what is necessary to protect his women."

Between the two males passed a long look. Kit might be only four years old but he'd known since birth that he was to be a knight. He'd been given a wooden sword at two and all the stories he'd heard were of chivalry and knighthood. Kit took Elizabeth's hand. "We will protect you, my lady," he said formally and kissed her hand.

Miles touched his son's shoulder in pride. "Now, Kit, run ahead and see what game you can find us. Even a rabbit or two will do."

"Yes, Papa." He grinned and scurried away along the side of the stream.

"Should you let him out of our sight?"

"He won't be. Kit has more sense than to stray too far."

"You seem little concerned about the loss of your men. Were there signs of a battle?"

"None." He seemed to dismiss the subject as he stooped, plucked a delicate yellow wildflower and slipped it behind her ear. "You look as if you belong in this wild place with your hair down, your torn dress held together with diamonds. I wouldn't mind giving you many diamonds, Elizabeth."

"I would prefer freedom."

He stepped away from her. "You are no longer my prisoner, Elizabeth Chatworth," he declared. "You may leave my presence forever."

She looked about the wild, rough forest. "You are very clever, Montgomery," she said with disgust.

"I take it that means you'll stay with me," he said, eyes twinkling, and before she could answer he lifted her, swirled her about in his arms, planting a kiss on her cheek.

"Release me," she said but there was a hint of a smile about her lips.

He nuzzled her earlobe. "I think you could have me at your feet if you so wished," he whispered.

"Bound and gagged, I'd hope," she retorted, pushing away from him. "Now, do you plan to feed us or do you carry that bow only because it looks good?"

"Papa!" Kit yelled before Miles could answer. "I saw a rabbit!"

"I'm sure it's waiting for me to come and slaughter it," Miles said under his breath as Kit came thrashing toward them.

A sound from Elizabeth that could only be described as a giggle made Miles turn an astonished face toward her.

Elizabeth refused to look at him. "Where is the rabbit, Kit? Your brave father will face the animal, and perhaps we'll get some supper, if not dinner."

After an hour of walking, with Miles seeming more concerned with toying with Elizabeth's fingers, they saw no more rabbits. It was later than she'd thought and it was growing dark—or perhaps the forest just seemed dark.

"We'll camp here for the night. Kit, gather firewood." When the child was gone, Miles turned to Elizabeth. "Don't let him out of your sight. I'll find us some game." With that he slipped away into the forest.

As soon as Miles was gone, Elizabeth began to feel the isolation of the forest. She followed Kit, loading her arms with dry branches. She hadn't noticed it before, but she felt as if eyes were watching her. In her brother's house she'd learned to develop a sixth sense about men who hid in corners, ready to pounce on her.

"Are you frightened, Elizabeth?" Kit asked, his eyes wide.

"Of course not." She forced a smile but she kept remembering all the stories she'd heard about the savagery of the Scots. They were wild people, torturers of little children.

"My papa will protect you," Kit said. "He was given his spurs when he was just a boy. My Uncle Raine says Papa is one of the greatest knights in England. He won't let anyone get you."

She pulled the boy into her arms. "Your papa is indeed a great fighter. Did you know that three men attacked me a few days ago? Your papa slew them in minutes and he wasn't even hurt." For all the child's bravado, Elizabeth could see that he was frightened. "I think your papa could fight off all the men of Scotland. There's no one anywhere who is as brave and strong as your papa."

A low chuckle made Elizabeth look around to see Miles holding two dead rabbits by their ears. "I thank you for the tribute, my lady."

"Elizabeth was scared," Kit explained.

"And you were right to comfort her. We must always protect our women. Would it be possible that you'd know how to skin rabbits, Elizabeth?"

She lowered Kit and took the rabbits with an air of confidence. "You'll find that a Chatworth is no Montgomery lady to sit about on satin cushions and wait for the servants to bring her food."

"You've described Stephen and Gavin's wives perfectly. Come, Kit, let's see if the Montgomery men can be useful."

In a very short time, Miles and Kit had a fire going and Elizabeth had the rabbits skinned and skewered. Miles used his ax to drive stakes into the ground and set up a turnspit for the rabbits. Leaning back on his elbows, Miles idly watched the fire while Kit turned the meat.

"You seem very relaxed," Elizabeth said, frowning, keeping her voice low. "We're unprotected in a strange land, yet you build a fire. We can be seen for miles."

He tugged on her skirt until she sat down, a few feet from him. "This land belongs to my brother and his wife, and if the MacArrans see us they'll recognize the Montgomery leopards on my cloak. The Scots rarely kill women and children outright. You'll be delivered to Stephen and all you'll have to do is explain who you are."

"But what has happened to your men?"

"Elizabeth, my men are gone with no trace of a fight. I would imagine they were escorted to Larenston, Bronwyn's castle. Right now my concern is for the safety of you and Kit. When we reach Larenston and my men aren't there, then I'll worry. Kit! You're allowing the meat to burn on one side."

He moved closer to her. "Elizabeth, you're as safe as you can be. I've scouted this area and seen no one. You're cold," he said when she shivered. He took the plaid from the ground behind her, pulled it around both their shoulders and drew her toward him.

"It's only for warmth," he said when she struggled against him, and refused to loosen his grip.

"I've heard that before!" she snapped. "The warmth is only the beginning. Do you enjoy forcing me?"

"I do not enjoy your hints that I'm like one of your brother's slimy friends," he snapped.

Elizabeth stopped struggling. "Perhaps life with Edmund *has* distorted my thinking a bit, but I don't like to be pawed."

"You've made that clear enough, but if we're to survive the night I think we need each other's warmth. Kit, break off a leg. It looks done to me."

The rabbits were barely cooked inside, charred outside, but the three of them were too hungry to care.

"I like it, Papa," Kit said. "I like it here in the forest."

"It's awfully cold," Elizabeth said, huddled in the

72

plaid. "If this is summer, what is winter like in Scotland?"

"Bronwyn thinks England is hot. In the winter she wraps herself in one of those plaids and sleeps on the snow."

"No!" Elizabeth breathed. "Is she truly such a barbarian?"

Smiling, Miles turned to his son, saw his eyes drooping.

"Come lay down beside me," Elizabeth said and Kit went to her.

Miles spread his cloak, motioned for Elizabeth and Kit to lie on it, covered them with the plaid. After tossing more wood on the fire, he lifted the plaid and crawled in beside Kit.

"You can't—" she began but stopped. There was nowhere else for him to sleep. Between them, Kit's sleeping body kept them warm. Elizabeth was very aware of Miles so close to her, but instead of frightening her his presence was reassuring.

With her head propped on her arm, she watched the fire. "What was Kit's mother like?" she asked softly. "Did she fall in love with you the first time she saw you in your armor?"

Miles gave a snort of laughter. "Margaret Sidney turned up her pretty little nose at me and refused to speak to me. I did everything I could to try and impress her. Once, when she came to the training field to bring water to her father, I turned to look at her, lost my stirrup and Raine hit me in the side with his lance. I still have the scar."

"But I thought—"

"You thought that I'd sold my soul to the devil and as a result I could have any woman I wanted."

"I had heard that story," she said evenly, not looking at him.

He caught her free hand from Kit's side, kissed her fingertips. "The devil hasn't made an offer for my soul, but if he did, I might think about it."

"You blaspheme!" she said, pulling her hand away. She was quiet for a moment. "But your Margaret Sidney changed her mind."

"She was sixteen and so very beautiful and so in love with Gavin at the time. She wanted nothing to do with a boy like me."

"And what changed her mind?"

He grinned broadly. "I persisted."

Elizabeth stiffened. "And when you got her, how did you celebrate?"

"By asking her to marry me," Miles shot back. "I told you I loved her."

"You give your love lightly. Why didn't Bridget marry you or this cousin who just bore your daughter?"

He was quiet for several moments. "I have loved only one woman; I have made love to many women. I have asked only Kit's mother to marry me and when I ask again, it will be because I love the woman."

"I pity her." Elizabeth sighed. "She will have to put up with your bastards being presented, two and three a year."

"You don't seem to mind this child of mine, and you held the girl at the inn when you thought she was mine."

"But I, happily, am not married to you."

Miles's voice lowered. "If you were my wife, would you mind receiving new children every few months?"

"I wouldn't blame your four children for your past transgressions, but if I should marry any man, which I will not do, and if my husband humiliated me by impregnating every servant girl in England, I believe that I would arrange his death."

"Fair enough," Miles said, an undertone of amusement in his voice. He turned on his side, put his arm over Kit, around Elizabeth's shoulders, and drew both of them to him. "Goodnight, my angel," he whispered and was asleep.

Chapter 6

MILES WAS AWAKENED BY KIT'S FOOT IN HIS RIBS AS THE boy painfully climbed over his father. "Be very quiet, Papa," Kit whispered loudly and juicily in the vicinity of Miles's ear. "Don't wake Elizabeth." With that he was over his father and running into the dim forest.

Miles watched his son and rubbed his bruised ribcage.

"Will you live?" Elizabeth asked laughingly from beside him.

He turned and their eyes met. Elizabeth's hair was spread about her and her face was sleep softened. He'd not realized how stern a control she kept on herself. Cautiously, smiling slightly, he moved his hand from her shoulder to her cheek, gently caressed the outline of her jaw.

His breath held when she didn't pull away. It was as

if she were a wild animal he was trying to tame and he must move very slowly so as not to frighten her away.

Elizabeth watched Miles, felt his hand on her face with a sense of wonder. His eyes were liquid, his lips full and soft. She'd never allowed a man to touch her before and never wondered what it would be like to feel a man's caress. But now she lay stretched out, facing Miles Montgomery, only inches separating their bodies, and she wondered what it would feel like to touch him. There was a dark growth of beard on his cheeks, emphasizing the sharp cut of them. A curl of dark hair touched his ear.

As if reading her thoughts, Miles lifted Elizabeth's hand, placed it on his cheek. She let it rest there for a moment, her heart pounding. It was as if she were doing something forbidden. After a very long moment, she moved her hand to touch his hair. It was soft and clean and she wondered how it smelled.

Her eyes went back to Miles's and she sensed that he was going to kiss her. Pull away, she thought, but she didn't move.

Slowly, his eyes telling her she could refuse him, he drew near her and when his lips touched hers, she kept her eyes open. What a pleasant feeling, she thought.

He just touched her lips with his and held them there, not forcing her mouth open, not grabbing her and throwing his weight onto her as other men had done, but just the light, highly pleasant kiss.

He was the first to pull away and there was a light of such warmth in his eyes that she began to stiffen. Now would come the pouncing.

"Hush," he soothed, his hand on her cheek. "No one is going to hurt you ever again, my Elizabeth."

"Papa!" Kit yelled and the spell was broken.

"No doubt he's spotted a unicorn this time," Miles said under his breath as he reluctantly rose. His jest was rewarded by the hint of a smile from Elizabeth.

Rising, Elizabeth winced at an ache in her shoulder. She wasn't used to sleeping on the ground.

Acting as if it were the most natural thing in the world, Miles began to knead Elizabeth's shoulders. "What have you found now, Kit?" he called above her head.

"A path," Kit yelled back. "Can I follow it?"

"Not until we get there. Better?" he asked Elizabeth, and when she nodded he kissed her neck and quickly began to gather their few belongings.

"Are you always so free with women?" she asked and there was curiosity in her voice. "When you visit someone's house do you freely kiss all the women?"

Miles didn't pause in burying the dead coals of last night's fire. "I can be civilized, I assure you, and usually I limit my kissing to hands—at least in public." He looked back at her, smiling, eyes sparkling. "But with you, my lovely Elizabeth, from our first . . . ah, meeting, nothing has been done in the usual manner. I can't help but feel that you were a gift to me, a very precious gift, but, nonetheless, something that is mine to keep."

Before she could answer—and, in truth, she was too stunned to answer—he caught her hand and began pulling her to where Kit glared at them impatiently. "Let's go and see where this path takes us."

Miles held her hand as Kit led them down the narrow, long-disused path. "What do you think of my son?"

78

Elizabeth smiled at the boy who was poking at a mushroom on the ground. As she watched, he straightened and began running ahead of them. "He's very independent, intelligent and quite adult for his age. You must be very proud of him."

Miles's chest swelled visibly. "I have two more at home. Philip Stephen is as exotic-looking as his mother, with a temper that sets his nurse trembling, and he's only a year old."

"And your other boy? Bridget's son?"

"James Raine is exactly opposite of Philip and the two of them are together constantly. I have a feeling it may always be that way. James gives Philip his toys when Philip demands them." He chuckled. "The only thing James will share with no one is his nurse. He screams even if I touch her."

"He must do a great deal of screaming," Elizabeth said sarcastically.

"James is silent practically always," Miles said, laughing. He leaned closer to her. "But then he does go to bed quite early."

She pushed him away playfully.

"Papa," Kit yelled, running to them. "Come and look. It's part of a house but it burned down."

Around the bend was what was left of a burned crofter's cottage, most of the roof collapsed, only one corner standing.

"No, Kit," Miles said when his son started to enter the ruin. Heavy, charred beams slanted from the one standing wall to the ground. "Let me test it first."

Elizabeth and Kit stood together while Miles grabbed one beam after another and swung his weight on it. A few bits of dirt came falling down but the beams held.

"It seems safe enough," Miles said as Kit ran inside the structure and began looking into crevices.

Miles took Elizabeth's arm. "Let's walk up the hill because, if I'm not mistaken, I think those are apple trees."

There was a small orchard on top of the hill and most of the trees were dead, but there were about a dozen scrawny, nearly ripe apples hanging from some of the branches. As Elizabeth reached for one of them, Miles's arm slid about her waist and lifted her. She caught the apple and he slowly lowered her, the front of her body sliding down his. His lips had just reached hers when Kit called out.

"Look what I found, Papa."

Elizabeth turned away to smile at Kit. "What is it?"

With a dramatic sigh, Miles set Elizabeth down.

"It's a swing!" Kit yelled.

"So it is," Miles said, holding Elizabeth's hand. He grabbed the ropes of the swing and gave them a couple of sharp jerks. "Let me see how high you can go," he said to his son.

Elizabeth and Miles stood back as Kit took over the swing, using it in an aggressive way to propel himself upward until his feet touched a tree branch.

"He'll hurt himself," Elizabeth said, but Miles caught her arm.

"Now show Elizabeth what you can do."

She gasped as Kit, still swinging very high, pulled his legs up and stood in the swing.

"Now!" Miles commanded, his arms open wide.

To Elizabeth's disbelief, Kit sent his small body flying

through the air and into Miles's arms. As Kit screamed with delight, Elizabeth felt her knees weaken.

Miles put his son down and caught her arm. "Elizabeth, what's wrong? It was only a child's game. When I was Kit's age, I used to jump into my father's arms in just the same way."

"But if you stepped away . . ." she began.

"Stepped away!" He was aghast. "And let Kit fall?" He pulled her into his arms, soothing her. "Did no one play with you as a child?" he asked quietly.

"My parents died soon after I was born. Edmund was my guardian."

That simple statement said a great deal to Miles. He pulled her away to look at her. "Now we shall make up for your lack of a childhood. Get in the swing and I'll push you."

She was glad to put away her memories of Edmund and she went readily to the swing.

"I will, Papa," Kit said, pushing the wooden bottom of the swing and not making much progress. "She's too heavy," Kit whispered loudly.

"Not for me." Miles laughed, kissed Elizabeth's ear and took the ropes. "Wipe it away, Elizabeth," he said as he pulled her far back off the ground.

"I can't now, but I will," she tossed over her shoulder.

Miles released her and she went flying. Every time she returned, he gave her a push on her bottom instead of the swing's and all Elizabeth did was laugh. Her skirt went up to her knees, she kicked off her shoes and stretched her legs out.

"Jump, Elizabeth!" Kit commanded.

"I'm too heavy, remember?" she teased, laughing.

Miles stood to the side of her. The more time he spent with her, the more beautiful she grew. Her head was back and she was laughing as he'd never seen her laugh before.

"Papa can catch you," Kit persisted.

"Yes, Papa is more than willing to catch the Lady Elizabeth." Miles grinned, standing before her. He saw a look of doubt cross her face. "Trust me, Elizabeth." He was smiling but was deadly earnest at the same time. "I won't step aside; I'll catch you no matter how hard you fall."

Elizabeth didn't play Kit's trick of standing in the swing, but she did release the ropes and go flying headlong into Miles's arms. When she hit him, the breath was almost knocked from her.

Miles clasped her tightly, then with a look of horror he said, "You *are* too heavy, Elizabeth."

His fall was the most ostentatious fake she'd ever encountered, and as he went down with great loud groans she giggled, clinging to him. With a loud, heartfelt, "Uh oh," from Miles, they began rolling down the steep hill. It was a terribly insincere roll. When Miles was on the bottom, he clutched at Elizabeth, his hands running down the length of her and when she was on the bottom, his arms and knees kept her off the ground so that not even a rock jabbed at her.

Elizabeth's giggle turned into a laugh which made her very weak and her hands were quite ineffectual at pushing him away. He'd pause with her on top just long enough for her to push at his arms, then he'd turn and she'd hang on for dear life.

At the bottom of the hill, he stopped, flung his arms outward, closed his eyes. "I'm crushed, Elizabeth," he said in a wounded tone.

Kit, wanting to join the fun, came tearing down the hill and jumped into the middle of his father's stomach, catching him unaware.

The groan Miles gave this time was genuine, and Elizabeth broke into new gales of laughter.

With great show, Miles set his son off his stomach and turned to Elizabeth. "Like to see me in pain, do you?" His voice was serious but his eyes were alive with teasing. "Come on, Kit, let's show Lady Elizabeth she can't laugh at two knights of the realm."

Eyes wide, Elizabeth stood and backed away, but Miles and Kit were too fast for her. Miles caught her shoulders while Kit threw his body weight onto her legs. Elizabeth tripped over her skirt, Miles tripped over his son and Kit just kept pushing. The three of them went down in a laughing heap as Miles began to tickle Elizabeth's ribs and Kit joined his father.

"Enough?" Miles asked, close to Elizabeth's face which was streaming with tears. "Are you willing to admit to our being the best of knights?"

"I . . . never said you weren't," she gasped.

Miles's tickling became more severe. "Tell us what we are."

"The bravest, handsomest knights in all of England —in all the world."

His hands stilled, slipping about her waist, his thumbs just under her breasts. "And what is my name?" he whispered, completely sober.

"Miles," she whispered back, her eyes on his. "Miles

Montgomery." Her arms were on his shoulders and now they slipped about his neck, lightly.

Miles bent and kissed her, softly, but there was for the first time a tiny spark between them.

Kit jumped on his father's back and Miles's face slid from Elizabeth's, and he just missed slamming into the dirt.

"Let's swing again, Papa."

"To think that I used to love my son," Miles whispered in Elizabeth's ear before he rose, his son attached to his back.

None of them had noticed that the sky had darkened in the last few minutes, and they each gasped when the first cold drops hit them. The sky opened up and nearly drowned them.

"To the cottage," Miles said, pulling Elizabeth up, his arm about her shoulders, and together they ran for shelter.

"Did you get wet?" he asked as he lowered Kit from his back.

"No, not much." She smiled up at him for just a moment before turning toward Kit.

Miles casually put his hand on Elizabeth's shoulder. "Why don't the two of you build a fire while I find us something to eat?"

Kit agreed enthusiastically while Elizabeth gave a dubious look to the torrential rain outside. "Perhaps you should wait until it slackens."

Miles gave her a smile of delight. "I'll be safe enough. Now, the two of you stay in here and I'll not be far away." With that, he slipped between the charred beams and was gone.

Elizabeth went to the edge of the shelter and looked after him. She was certain Miles Montgomery had no idea how unusual today had been to her. She'd spent an entire morning with a man and not once had any violence occurred. And the laughter! She'd always loved to laugh but her brothers were so solemn—anyone living in the same house with Edmund Chatworth soon grew to be solemn. But today she'd laughed with a man and he'd not tried to tear her clothes off. Always before, if she even smiled at a man, he'd grabbed her, hurt her.

It wasn't that Elizabeth was so beautiful that she drove men to uncontrollable passion. She knew she was pretty, yes, but if she'd heard correctly she was no match for the Revedoune heiress. What had always made Elizabeth the victim of men's aggressions was her brother Edmund. His distorted sense of humor ran to wagering with his guests as to who could get Elizabeth in bed with him. Edmund hated that Elizabeth wasn't terrified of him. When she was a child he used to bring her home from the convent where she lived most of the time and he'd often hit her, knock her down stairs. But somehow Elizabeth had escaped uninjured.

When she was twelve, she began to stand up for herself. She'd successfully held off Edmund with a lighted torch. After that Edmund's game grew more serious, and Elizabeth grew more wary, more skillful at fending off her attackers. She'd learned how to hurt men who were trying to use her. She'd persuaded Roger to show her how to use an ax, a sword, a dagger. She knew how to defend herself with a razor-sharp tongue.

After weeks with Edmund and the men he surrounded himself with, Elizabeth would escape back to her convent, usually with Roger's help, and she'd be able to rest for a few weeks—until Edmund came for her again.

"I have the fire going, Lady Elizabeth," Kit said from behind her.

She turned a warm smile on him. Children had always been her love. Children were what they seemed, never trying to take from her, always giving freely. "You've done all the work and I've just been standing here." She went to him. "Perhaps you'd like me to tell you a story while we wait for your father."

She sat down, leaning against the wall, her feet toward the fire, her arm around Kit. Tossing Miles's cloak over them, she began to tell Kit about Moses and his people of Israel. Before she was to the Red Sea opening, Kit was asleep, curled up against her.

The rain beat down on the bit of roof over their heads, leaking in three places. While she watched the fire, Miles came in out of the mist, gave her a smile and fed the fire. He was silent as he skinned and dressed a young pig, cut the meat into chunks and set them to roast on sticks.

As she watched, she couldn't help but think what an odd man he was. Or were most men like him? Roger'd always said that Elizabeth only saw the dregs of mankind, and from the way some of the young women at the convent rhapsodized over their lovers, Elizabeth'd often thought that perhaps some men weren't like the ones she fought off.

Miles knelt by the fire, his hands quickly working

with the meat. Within reach was his bow, his arrows over his back, his sword never leaving his side. Even as they'd been tumbling down the hill, Miles's sword had been attached to his hip. What sort of man could laugh with a woman and at the same time be prepared for danger?

"What are you thinking?" Miles asked quietly, his eyes intense.

She recovered herself. "That you're so wet you're about to drown the fire."

He stood, stretched. "This is a cold country, isn't it?" With that he slowly began to remove his wet clothes, spreading each piece by the fire.

Elizabeth watched him with detached interest. Nude men weren't unfamiliar to her, and often her brother's men had trained wearing the small loincloths. But she doubted if she'd ever really *looked* at any of the men.

Miles was lean but muscular and when he turned toward her, wearing only the loincloth, she saw he had a great amount of dark hair on his chest, a thick, V-shaped, curling abundance of it. His thighs were large, heavy from training in armor, and his calves were well developed.

"Elizabeth," Miles whispered. "You will have me blushing."

It was Elizabeth who blushed and could not meet his eyes when she heard him chuckle.

"Papa," Kit said, rousing. "I'm hungry."

Reluctantly, Elizabeth released the child. As much as she loved children, there had been few of them in her life. There was nothing quite like a child in her arms, needing her, trusting her, touching her.

"There's pork and a few apples," Miles told his son.

"Are you cold, Papa?" Kit asked.

Miles didn't look at Elizabeth. "I have the warm glances of a lady to keep me warm. Come eat with us, Lady Elizabeth."

Still pink-cheeked, Elizabeth joined them and it wasn't long before she got over her embarrassment. At Kit's insistence, Miles told stories of when he and his brothers were growing up. In every story, he was the hero, saving his brothers, teaching them. Kit's eyes shone like stars.

"And when you took your vows," Elizabeth said innocently, "didn't you foreswear lying?"

Miles's eyes twinkled. "I don't think they extended to impressing one's son or one's . . ." He seemed to search for a word.

"Captive?" she supplied.

"Ah, Elizabeth," he said languidly. "What would a lady think of a man whose older brothers constantly tried to make his life miserable?"

"Did they?"

She was so earnest in her question that he knew she took him literally. "No, not really," he reassured her. "We were left alone at an early age and I guess some of our pranks were a bit hazardous, but we all lived."

"Happily ever after," she said heavily.

"And what was it like living with Edmund Chatworth?" he asked casually.

Elizabeth shifted her legs under her. "He also liked . . . pranks," was all she'd say.

"Did you have enough, Kit?" Miles asked, and as he reached for another piece of pork, she saw the long gash on the inside of his wrist. It had opened again and was bleeding.

Miles never seemed to miss even a glance of hers. "The bow string hit it. You may doctor it if you wish," he said so eagerly, with so much hope, that she laughed at him.

She raised her skirt, tore off a long piece of petticoat and wet it in the rain. Miles sat cross-legged before her, his arm extended as she began to wash away the blood.

"I can't tell you how good it is to see you smile," he said. "Kit! Don't climb on those beams. Take the cloth from inside the quiver and clean my sword. And watch that you don't damage the edge." He looked back at Elizabeth. "I take it as an honor that you smile at me. I'm not sure, but I feel that you don't smile at many men."

"Very few," was all she'd answer.

He lifted her hand from his wrist and kissed her palm. "I'm beginning to think you're as angelic as you look. Kit adores you."

"I have a feeling Kit has never met a stranger, that he adores everyone."

"I don't." He kissed her hand again.

"Stop it!" She pulled away from him. "You are entirely too free with your kisses."

"I am doing very well at limiting myself to kisses. What I'd like to do is make love to you. Kit!" he yelled at his son who was waving the sword above his head. "I'll have your hide if you even consider thrusting that at anything."

In spite of herself, Elizabeth had to laugh as she thrust Miles's cleanly bandaged arm back to him. "I think you should leave your son at home when you try courting."

"Oh no." He smiled. "Kit has accomplished more than I could have in months."

With that cryptic remark, he moved to take his cherished sword from his son's reckless hands.

Chapter 7

THAT NIGHT THE THREE OF THEM SLEPT TOGETHER AGAIN, Kit firmly wedged between them. Elizabeth lay awake for a long time listening to the breathing of Miles and Kit. The past two days had been so unusual, so unlike anything she'd ever experienced before. It was like a bit of sunshine after years of rain.

When she woke she was alone on the cloak, the plaid tucked about her. Sleepily she smiled, snuggled deeper under the covers, and for a second she wished she could always stay in this place, that each day could be filled with laughter.

Turning to her back, stretching, she looked about the little shelter, saw that it was empty. Her senses had dulled over the last few days. Usually, she slept with one ear open, but somehow, Miles and Kit had managed to leave without disturbing her. She listened now for any sounds of them, smiling when she heard slow, quiet footsteps not too far away.

Stealthily, soundlessly, she left the shelter and faded into the surrounding forest. Once inside, hidden, she heard the unmistakable sounds of Kit and Miles to her left. Then who was skulking about in the undergrowth ahead of her?

Using all her years of experience at escaping her brother's friends, she slipped through the forest effortlessly. It was some minutes before she saw who was trying so hard to sneak up on them.

Lying on his stomach, his long, long body held immovable, was Sir Guy, only his head turning from side to side as he scanned the horizon where Kit and Miles scampered.

With no more sound than a breath of air, Elizabeth crept behind Sir Guy. Stooping, she picked up a small, elongated rock and clutched it in her fist. Roger had taught her that even her small, weak fist could carry some power if she held a hard object. With the rock in one hand, she bent and grabbed Sir Guy's small dagger from its sheath at his side.

The giant stood in one fluid, quick movement. "Lady Elizabeth!" he gasped.

Elizabeth stood back, at arm's length from the man. "Why are you following us? Did you betray your master and now you come to kill him?"

The scar across Sir Guy's face whitened but he didn't answer her. Instead, he turned his head in the direction of Miles and gave a high, piercing whistle.

Elizabeth knew Miles would come at the call, that it was a signal between them. If Sir Guy felt free to call his master, then Miles must know something of the reason for the giant's hidden presence.

In a remarkably short time, Miles appeared, sword drawn, alone.

"The lady asks if I mean to kill you," Sir Guy said solemnly.

Miles looked from one to the other. "How did she find you?"

Sir Guy's eyes never left Elizabeth's face. He seemed to be embarrassed and admiring all at once. "I didn't hear her."

Miles's eyes twinkled. "Give him back the dagger, Elizabeth. There needn't be any concern for Guy's loyalty."

Elizabeth didn't move. Her hand clutched the rock, hidden in the folds of her skirt, and at the same time she made note of the flat rock Sir Guy's softly clad foot was resting upon. Feet were vulnerable in even the strongest men.

"Where are your men?" she asked Miles, her eyes on Sir Guy.

"Well . . . Elizabeth," he began. "I thought perhaps . . ."

From the slight changes in Sir Guy's face, Elizabeth knew that whatever had been done had been Miles Montgomery's idea.

"Speak up!" she commanded.

"We're on MacArran land and I knew we'd be safe so I decided to walk with you and Kit. There's never been any danger."

She whirled to face him but kept Sir Guy in her view. "This was all a trick," she said evenly. "You lied about your men disappearing. You lied about being in danger. You did this all in an attempt to get me alone."

"Elizabeth," he soothed. "We were surrounded by people. I thought perhaps that if we could be alone for a time you might come to know me. And Kit—"

"Don't profane that child's name! He was not in this ugly plot of yours."

"It wasn't a plot," he pleaded, his eyes soft.

"But what of danger? You risked my life and that of your son. These woods are full of savage men!"

Miles smiled patronizingly. "True, but these savages are related to me by marriage. I'm sure we're surrounded by MacArrans even now."

"I've heard no one except this great thrashing boar."

Sir Guy stiffened beside her.

"There was no harm done." Miles smiled at her. "Give me the dagger, Elizabeth."

"No harm except lies given to a woman," she spat at him.

After that, everything seemed to happen in a single flash. She lunged at Miles with the dagger. Sir Guy's hand knocked it from her grasp, and as the little knife went flying, Elizabeth's heel came down on the two smallest toes of Sir Guy's left foot. Miles, as he turned astonished eyes to Sir Guy's cry of pain, didn't see Elizabeth's fist, wrapped about the rock, as it plowed into his stomach. With a great whoosh of pain, Miles bent over.

Elizabeth stepped back, watching as Sir Guy sat on the ground and tried to remove his boot, his face showing his pain. Miles looked as if he might lose his dinner.

"Well done," came a voice from behind her. She

whirled about to look into the face of a strikingly beautiful woman, with black hair and blue eyes, as tall as Elizabeth, which was rare. A big dog stood beside her.

"That should teach you, Miles," she continued, "that all women don't appreciate being used as a man sees fit."

Elizabeth's eyes widened as from the trees men began to drop and, coming from the direction of the cottage, an older man was leading Kit by the hand.

"Lady Elizabeth Chatworth," the woman said, "I am Bronwyn MacArran, laird of Clan MacArran and sister-in-law to this scheming young man."

Miles was recovering himself. "Bronwyn, it's good to see you again."

"Tam," Bronwyn said to the older man. "See to Sir Guy's foot. Did you break it?"

"Probably," Elizabeth answered. "When I've done it before I've found it usually breaks the man's smallest toe."

Bronwyn gave her an acknowledging look of appreciation. "These are my men. Douglas." As she called each man's name, he stepped forward, nodded at Lady Elizabeth. "Alex, Jarl and Francis."

Elizabeth gave each man a hard, appraising look. She didn't like being surrounded by men and she moved so Sir Guy was no longer behind her. The many men near her made her feel as if she were locked in a small stone cell.

Miles, rubbing his stomach, noticed the move and came to stand nearer to Elizabeth, and when Tam took a step closer, Miles touched the man's arm, his eyes giving warning. With a quick frown of puzzlement, Tam released Kit and stepped away from Elizabeth, noticing that her eyes were wary, watching.

"And where is my worthless brother?" Miles asked Bronwyn, who was quietly watching the scene before her.

"He is patroling the northern borders but I expect him to meet us before we reach Larenston."

Miles took Elizabeth's arm, tightened his grip when she tried to move away from him. "Bronwyn has a baby," he said aloud. Under his breath, he whispered, "You're safe. Stay close to me."

Elizabeth gave him a withering look that said she didn't feel he was safer than any other man, but she didn't move from his side. The men who stood close to Bronwyn were wildly dressed, their knees bare, their hair down to their shoulders, great long wide swords at their belts.

Bronwyn felt there was more wrong than just Miles's childish trick played on Elizabeth, but she had no idea what it was. Perhaps when they returned to Larenston she could find out what this tension in the air meant. "Shall we ride?"

Elizabeth stood still, not moving until Bronwyn's men were in front of her. There was a long walk to where the horses were hidden and the men were a silent group. Sir Guy hobbled along slowly, leaning on a thick staff.

"I want to ride behind the men," Elizabeth said to Miles, her jaw set.

He started to protest but stopped, murmured something to Bronwyn and at her nod, the Scotsmen and Sir Guy rode ahead, Kit settled with Tam.

"Elizabeth," Miles began from atop the horse beside

her. "Bronwyn's men mean you no harm. There's no reason to fear them."

She glared at him. "Am I to take your word for their trustworthiness? You who have lied to me? You who are of a family that is at war with my family?"

Miles glanced heavenward for a moment. "Perhaps I was wrong to play the trick on you, but if I'd asked you to spend a few days frolicking in the forest with Kit and me, what would have been your answer?"

She looked away from him.

"Elizabeth, you must admit you enjoyed yourself. There, for a few hours, you weren't afraid of men."

"I am *never* afraid of men," she snapped. "I have merely learned to be cautious."

"Your caution overtakes your entire life," he said sternly. "Look at us now, eating the dust of Bronwyn's men because you fear that one of them will attack you if you don't have him in your sight."

"I have learned—" she began.

"You have learned only the bad part of life! Most men are not like Edmund Chatworth or Pagnell. While we're here in Scotland you're going to learn that some men can be trusted. No!" he said, his eyes locking with hers. "You are going to learn that *I* can be trusted." With that he spurred his horse forward to ride beside Sir Guy, leaving Elizabeth alone.

Bronwyn glanced back at Elizabeth, then turned her horse to ride beside the blonde woman. They were a striking pair: Elizabeth with her delicate fair features; Bronwyn's strong, sculptured features.

"A lovers' quarrel?" Bronwyn asked, her eyes searching Elizabeth's face.

"We are not lovers," Elizabeth said coolly.

Bronwyn raised her eyebrows at that, thinking that it must be a first for Miles to spend any time with a woman and not possess her. "And how does a Chatworth come to ride with a Montgomery?" she asked in the same tone as Elizabeth had used with her.

Elizabeth gave Bronwyn a scathing look. "If you plan to pour out venom about my brother Roger, you should think twice."

Bronwyn and Elizabeth faced each other across the horses and after a moment—in which many signals passed between them—Bronwyn gave a curt nod. "Ask your brother about his Scots relatives," she said frigidly before reining her horse away, leaving Elizabeth to herself.

"And have you angered Bronwyn?" Miles asked when he once again rode beside her.

"Am I to listen to all manner of evilness against my own brother? That woman swore to marry Roger but went back on her word. And as a result—"

"As a result Roger Chatworth attacked my brother's back," Miles interrupted. He paused, leaned across her horse to take her hand in his. "Give us a chance, Elizabeth," he said softly, his eyes meltingly imploring. "All I ask is that you give all of us time to show you that we can be trusted."

Before Elizabeth could answer, the sound of thundering hooves came to them. With a glance up, she saw that every man had his claymore drawn, and before she could protest, Bronwyn's Scots had encircled the two women. Miles moved his horse closer to Elizabeth.

"It's that idiot husband of mine," Bronwyn said, and her pleased tone was completely at odds with her words.

Five men came to a halt before them, the leader a tall man with dark blond hair that came to his shoulders, a good-looking man who was obviously enjoying the sparks his wife was shooting at him.

"You're getting old, Tam," the blond man said lazily, leaning on the front of his saddle.

Tam merely gave a grunt and resheathed his claymore.

"Damn you, Stephen," Bronwyn hissed. "Why were you riding along the cliff like that? And why didn't you give any warning of your approach?"

Slowly, he dismounted his horse, tossed the reins to one of the men behind him and walked toward his wife. Casually, he put his hand on her ankle and started traveling upward.

Bronwyn kicked out at him. "Let me go!" she demanded. "I have more important duties than to play games with you."

With lightning quickness, Stephen caught her waist and hauled her out of the saddle. "Did you worry about me riding along the cliff?" he murmured, pulling her to him.

"Tam!" Bronwyn gasped, pushing at Stephen.

"The lad needs no help from me," Tam answered.

"But I would be willing to help," Miles said quietly.

Stephen released his wife abruptly. "Miles," he gasped, and hugged his brother when Miles was dismounted. "When did you arrive? Why are you in Scotland? I thought you were with Uncle Simon—and what's this I hear about Uncle Simon wanting your head on a platter?"

Miles gave a bit of a smile and a shrug to his brother.

Stephen grimaced as he knew he wasn't likely to get

anything from his younger brother. Miles was so close-mouthed it was infuriating.

"Miles brought Elizabeth Chatworth," Bronwyn said flatly.

Stephen turned to look through the men and upwards to see Elizabeth. For all her soft features, she looked rigid, unbending, as she sat stiffly in the saddle. Stephen started toward her but Miles caught his arm.

"Do not touch her," Miles said conversationally as he moved toward Elizabeth.

After a second's astonishment, Stephen grinned. He well understood jealousy; he'd just never seen it in his brother before.

As Miles put his arms up to Elizabeth and she hesitated, he said, "Stephen will not harm you and he'll be expecting the same courtesy." There was a twinkle in Miles's eyes.

Elizabeth couldn't help a slight smile as she glanced at Sir Guy, who had shot a couple of glances toward her that said she was part monster, part witch. They had to wait to be introduced to Stephen because Kit, who'd fallen asleep against Tam, had wakened and launched himself onto his beloved uncle. Stephen had Kit settled on one arm as he extended his hand to Elizabeth.

Elizabeth stood rigid and did not take his hand.

Miles sent his brother a look of warning and Stephen, with a knowing smile, dropped his hand.

"You are welcome to our home," Stephen said.

"I am a Chatworth."

"And I am a Montgomery *and*"—he glanced at Bronwyn—"a MacArran. You *are* welcome. Shall we walk along the cliff? It's steep and can sometimes be frightening."

"I can ride a horse," Elizabeth said flatly.

Miles took her arm, raised her fingers to his lips. "Of course you can. My clumsy brother is only trying to make an excuse to talk to you."

"Uncle Stephen!" Kit said. He'd been trying so hard to wait until the adults were finished speaking. "Lady Elizabeth hit Papa and made Sir Guy limp and we slept in the forest without a tent or anything." He smiled at Elizabeth who winked back at him.

"Made Sir Guy limp?" Stephen laughed. "Somehow I doubt that."

"Lady Elizabeth Chatworth broke Sir Guy's toes," Bronwyn said coolly.

Stephen narrowed his eyes at his wife. "I'm not sure I like your tone."

Miles spoke quickly to get his brother's attention. "How are the MacGregors?"

What followed was half-description, half-argument as Bronwyn and Stephen talked of the clan that had been the enemy of Clan MacArran for centuries—until a few months ago when a truce had been made. Bronwyn's brother Davy had married the daughter of the MacGregor.

As they talked, they walked along the treacherous cliff road, one side high rock, the other a sheer drop. Elizabeth, caught close to Miles, beside Stephen, Bronwyn ahead of them, listened with no little fascination to the exchange between the married couple. They argued heatedly but with absolutely no animosity. The men behind them talked among themselves, so this bantering was obviously not new to them. Bronwyn taunted Stephen, called him several names and Stephen merely smiled at her and told her her ideas were ridiculous. Of all the marriages Elizabeth had seen, the husband would have blackened the wife's eye if she'd said half what Bronwyn was saying.

Elizabeth glanced at Miles, saw he was smiling benignly at Bronwyn and his brother. Kit began to enter the argument, taking Bronwyn's side, running ahead to grab her hand.

"He's your son." Stephen laughed, looking at his brother.

Because Stephen looked toward Miles, toward the rock wall, he saw the rocks tumbling from above—aiming for Elizabeth. With a knight's instincts, he acted as quickly as he thought, making a leaping grab for Elizabeth. The two of them slammed into the rock wall, Stephen's big body pinning Elizabeth, crushing her as the rock fell behind him.

Elizabeth also reacted without thinking. For a few moments, her guard had been down, but with men behind her, beside her, she'd remained nervous. Her senses did not register the reason for Stephen's abrupt attack but only knew that once again a man was threatening her.

She panicked. Not just a small uproar, but Elizabeth let out a scream that startled the already nervous horses. And she didn't stop with one scream, but she began clawing and kicking like a caged wild animal.

Stephen, stunned by her reaction, tried to catch her shoulders. "Elizabeth," he shouted into her terrified face.

Miles had been struck on the shoulder and back by falling stones, knocking him to his knees. The moment he heard Elizabeth's screams he went to her.

"Goddamn you!" he bellowed at his brother. "I told you not to touch her." With a hard push he shoved Stephen away, tried to catch Elizabeth.

"Quiet!" he commanded.

Elizabeth was still in a frenzy, scratching Miles, trying to tear away from him.

He caught her shoulders, gave her a sharp shake. "Elizabeth," he said patiently, loudly. "You are safe. Do you hear me? Safe." It took another shake before she turned eyes to his—eyes such as Miles had never seen before, frightened, terrified, helpless eyes. For a moment they looked at each other and Miles used all his strength of character to will her into peacefulness. "You are safe now, my love. You'll always be safe with me."

Her body began trembling and he pulled her into his arms, held her close to him, stroked her hair. When he glanced at Stephen standing near them, he said, "Leave a horse. We'll follow later."

Elizabeth was hardly aware of the funeral-quiet procession passing them. Her fear had made her weak and all she could do was lean against Miles for support, while he stroked her cheek, her neck, her arm. After many minutes, she pulled away from him.

"I have made an ass of myself," she said with such despair that Miles smiled at her.

"Stephen didn't understand when I told him not to touch you. I'm sure he thought it was mere jealousy."

"You are not jealous?" she asked, pulling away, trying to change the subject.

"Perhaps. But your fears are more important than my jealousy."

"My fears, as you call them, are none of your concern." She succeeded in pulling completely away from him.

"Elizabeth." His voice was pleading, very low. "Don't keep all this inside you. I've told you I'm a good listener. Talk to me. Tell me what has made you so afraid."

She caught the rock wall with her hands behind her. The solid mass felt good, gave her a feeling of reality. "Why have you sent the others away?"

A flicker of anger crossed his eyes. "So I'd have no witnesses when I ravished you. Why else?" When he saw that she wasn't sure he was being sarcastic, he threw up his hands in despair. "Come on, let's go to Larenston." He grabbed her arm much too hard. "You know what you need, Elizabeth? You need someone to make love to you, to show you that your fear is much worse than the reality."

"I've had many volunteers for the task," she hissed at him.

"From what I've seen, you've known only rapists—not lovers."

With that, he practically tossed her into the saddle and mounted behind her.

Chapter 8

ELIZABETH PUT HER HAND TO HER FOREHEAD AND OPENED her eyes slowly. The big room where she lay upon the bed was empty, dark. It had been many hours since she and Miles had ridden into the fortress of Clan Mac-Arran. It was an ancient place, set on the edge of a cliff like some giant eagle using its talons to hold on. Some woman who looked as old as the castle handed Elizabeth a hot drink laced with herbs, and when the woman's back was turned, Elizabeth dumped the drink into the rushes behind a bench. Elizabeth had a knowledge of herbs and she had a good guess as to what the drink contained.

The gnarled little woman, whom Bronwyn called Morag, watched Elizabeth with sharp eyes and after a few moments Elizabeth feigned sleepiness and lay upon the bed.

"She needs the rest," Bronwyn said over her. "I've never seen anyone go insane quite as she did when Stephen pulled her from under the falling rocks. It was as if demons had suddenly entered her body."

Morag gave a little snort. "Ye fought Stephen long and hard when ye first met him."

"It wasn't the same," Bronwyn insisted. "Miles calmed her but only after a long time of shaking her. Did you know she broke Sir Guy's toes?"

"And I heard the two of ye quarreled," Morag snapped.

Bronwyn straightened defensively. "She dares to defend Roger Chatworth to me. After what he has done—"

"He's her brother!" Morag spat. "Ye would expect her to be loyal yet ye seem to think she should see your way at once. Bronwyn, there is more than one way of things in the world." She bent and spread a large blue and green plaid over Elizabeth's quiet form. "Let's leave her in peace. A messenger has come from Stephen's eldest brother."

"Why didn't you tell me?" Bronwyn said, angry at being treated as a child and more angry because she deserved the treatment.

Elizabeth lay perfectly still after the door had closed, listening for anyone's breathing. Sometimes men had pretended they'd left a room but in truth they were actually only hiding in dark corners. When she was sure she was alone, she turned over and cautiously opened her eyes. She was indeed alone.

She sprang from the bed and went to the window. It was just growing dark outside, the moonlight beginning to silver the steep walls of the gray stone castle. Now was the time to escape, now before a routine was set, before all the MacArrans were informed she was a prisoner.

As she watched, on the ground below, four men walked past, their bodies sheathed in plaids. With a smile, Elizabeth began to form a plan. A quick, silent search of the room revealed a chest of men's clothes. She pulled up the silk skirt of her gown, tied it about her waist, then pulled on a voluminous men's shirt and slipped into heavy wool socks. For just a second, she looked down at her knees, blinked at the idea of appearing in public so very bare—nude almost. There were no shoes so she had to make do with her own soft shoes, her toes tightly jammed with the added bulk of the socks. Rolling the plaid about her so it formed a short skirt and could be tossed across a shoulder took several attempts, and she was sure she still didn't have it right when she tied a belt about her waist. It was much too long to buckle.

With her breath held, she cautiously opened the door, praying that as yet no guard had been posted outside her door. Her luck held and she slipped through a narrow opening and out into the dim hall. She'd memorized the way out of the castle when Miles had led her to the room and now, as she paused to get her bearings, she listened for sounds.

Far away, to her left and below, she could hear voices. Slowly, melting into the wall, she glided down the stairs toward the main exit. Just as she was moving past the room where people were gathered, she heard the name Chatworth. She glanced toward the door to the outside but at the same time she wanted information. With no more noise than a shadow, she moved to where she could hear.

Stephen was speaking. "Damn *both* of you, Miles!" Anger permeated his voice. "Gavin has no more sense than you do. The two of you are helping Chatworth accomplish what he wants. He's coming close to destroying our family."

Miles remained silent.

Bronwyn put her hand on Miles's arm. "Please release her. Lady Elizabeth can return to England with an armed guard and when Gavin hears she's released, he'll let Roger Chatworth go."

Still Miles did not speak.

"Goddamn you!" Stephen bellowed. "Answer us!"

Miles's eyes ignited. "I will not release Elizabeth. What Gavin does with Roger Chatworth is my brother's business. Elizabeth is mine."

"If you weren't my brother—" Stephen began.

"If I weren't your brother, what I did would have no effect on you." Miles was quite calm, only his eyes showing his anger.

Stephen threw up his hands in despair. "You talk to him," he said to Bronwyn. "None of my brothers has any sense at all."

Bronwyn planted herself before her husband. "Once you fought Roger Chatworth for what you believed to be yours. Now Miles is doing exactly the same thing and yet you rage at him."

"It was different then," Stephen said sullenly. "You were given to me by the king."

"And Elizabeth was given to me!" Miles interjected

with great passion. "Bronwyn, am I welcome here? If not I and my men will leave—with Lady Elizabeth."

"You know you are welcome," Bronwyn said softly. "Unless Chatworth is prepared for war, he'll not attack the MacArrans." She turned to Stephen. "And as for Gavin holding Chatworth prisoner, I'm glad for it. Do you forget what Chatworth did to your sister Mary or that he held me prisoner for a month?"

Elizabeth slipped away after hearing those words. They were going to find that she wasn't the docile captive they assumed she would be.

Outside, a fog was rolling in from the sea and she smiled in secret thanks for the Lord's help. Her first necessity was to get a horse because she could not walk out of Scotland. Standing still, she listened, stiffly intent, trying to ascertain where the stables were.

Elizabeth was quite good at stealing horses; she'd had a great deal of practice in her short lifetime. Horses were like children. They needed to be talked to quietly, simply, with no quick movements. There were two men at one end of the stables, laughing, talking in low tones about the latest women they'd bedded.

With great stealth, Elizabeth eased a bridled horse from the far end of the long stable. She pulled a saddle from the stall wall and waited until she was outside before saddling the animal. She thanked heaven for the relative noisiness of so many people living together on a few acres of land. A creaky cart went by; a man leading four horses tied the animals not far from the stables and two of the horses started nipping each other. As a consequence, three men began shouting and cracking whips. None of the people milling about even glanced at the slight figure in the shadows, a plaid covering the person's head.

When Elizabeth mounted, she lazily followed the cart out the open gates of Larenston and, like the cart driver, raised her hand in silent greeting to the guards above her. The guards were there to keep people from entering; people leaving were of little interest to them.

The only way to reach the MacArran fortress was across a frighteningly narrow bit of land. Elizabeth's already racing heart threatened to break her ribs. The cart in front of her was unusually narrow and, even so, its wheels rode just on the edges of the road—inches in either direction and the man, cart and horse would be over the side.

When she reached the end of the road, she breathed a sigh of relief for several reasons—the end of the treacherous path and, so far, no alarm had been sounded.

The cart driver looked over his shoulder and grinned at her. "Always glad when I come off that path. Are ye goin' this way?"

Straight ahead was the easy way, through the crofters' farms where people would see her and could give a search party directions. To the right was the cliff road, the one she and Miles had ridden on. To ride along the cliff at night . . .

"Nay!" she said in her huskiest voice to the cart driver. Obviously the man would want to talk if she rode with him. She pointed a plaid-covered arm toward the cliff.

"You young'uns!" The man chuckled. "Well, good luck to ye, lad. There's plenty of moonlight, but watch yer step." With that he clucked to his horse and drove away.

Elizabeth lost no time in contemplating her fear but urged her mare toward the black emptiness before her. At night the road looked worse than she remembered. Her horse fidgeted and after only a second's hesitation, she dismounted and began to lead her.

"Damn Miles Montgomery!" she muttered. Why did he have to come to a savage place like this? If he were going to hold someone captive, he should have done it in civilized surroundings.

The howl of a wolf directly overhead made her stop muttering. Silhouetted atop the cliff were three wolves, heads low, watching her. The horse danced about and Elizabeth wrapped the reins around her wrist. As she moved, the wolves moved with her. Another one joined the pack.

It seemed to Elizabeth that she had traveled for miles but she couldn't even see the end of the cliff road. For a moment, she leaned against the rock wall, tried to calm her racing heart.

The wolves, seeming to believe their victim was admitting defeat, growled collectively. The horse reared, tore the reins from Elizabeth's hands. She made a leap for the horse, lost her footing and fell half over the edge of the cliff. The freed horse went tearing down the path.

She lay still for a moment, trying to regain her composure and to figure out how to free herself. Precariously, she clung to the edge of the cliff, one leg dangling with no support, her other foot straining to hold on. Her arms were hugging rock, her chin pressing downward. She moved her left arm, and as she did, rock crumbled from under her. With a gasp of terror she began to move her right leg to search for a foothold—but found none. Another bit of rock crumbled and she knew she had to do something.

Using every bit of strength in her arms, she tried to push herself up, inching her hips to the left. When her left knee caught on the solid rock road, she had to blink away tears of relief. Inch by slow inch, she moved her aching, bruised body back onto the road.

On hands and knees she crawled to the safety of the rock wall and sat there, tears rolling down her cheeks, her chest heaving. Blood trickled down her arms and her raw knees burned.

Above her came a great cry of animals fighting. Pushing herself away from the wall, she saw an animal attacking the wolves. "That great dog of Bronwyn's," she gasped and closed her eyes in silent prayer for a moment.

She didn't sit there long. Soon her disappearance would be discovered and she needed to be well ahead of her Montgomery enemies.

When she stood, she realized she was hurt worse than she thought. Her left leg was stiff, her ankle painful. When she wiped away the tears from her cheeks, her hand showed bloody in the moonlight. With raw palms, she began to feel her way along the road, not trusting her sight to guide her but needing the solid rock for direction.

The moon had set by the time she reached the end of the road, but instead of being frightening, the black open space was welcome to her. She pulled the plaid closer about her, ignored her weak legs and began walking.

When two pinpoints of light shone at her, chest height, she gasped, stopped, looked about for some weapon. For several moments she locked eyes with the animal, whatever it was, before it moved. The animal was almost touching her before she realized it was Bronwyn's dog.

The dog cocked its head at her quizzically and Elizabeth wanted to cry with relief.

"You killed the wolves, didn't you?" she said. "Good boy. Are you friendly?" Tentatively, she put out her hand, palm up, and was rewarded with a lick of the dog's tongue. As she began stroking the animal's big head, it nudged her hand, pushing her back toward the cliff road.

"No, boy," she whispered. Her standing still was making her feel her cuts and bruises more. And it seemed like days since she'd slept. "I want to go this way, not back to Bronwyn."

The dog gave a sharp yip at his mistress's name.

"No!" she said firmly.

The dog watched her for a moment as if considering her words, then turned toward the forest ahead of them.

"Good boy." She smiled. "Maybe you can lead me out of this place. Lead me to another clan that will return me to my brother for the reward he'll pay."

She walked behind the dog, but as she began to stumble, it stopped, nudging under her arm until she began to lean on it. "What's your name, boy?" she whispered tiredly. "Is it George or Oliver or is it some Scots name I've never heard?"

The dog slowed its step even more for her.

"How about Charlie?" she said. "I rather like the name Charlie."

With that she collapsed in a heap beside the dog, asleep, or perhaps in a faint.

The dog nudged her, sniffed her, licked her bloody face, and when nothing made her rise he settled beside her and slept.

The sun was high overhead when Elizabeth woke and looked up at the massive, shaggy head of the dog. The animal's eyes were questioning, as concerned about her as a human. There was an ugly cut covered with dried blood under one of the dog's eyes.

"Get that from fighting the wolves?" She smiled up at the dog, scratching its ears. As she started to rise, her legs gave way under her and she clutched the dog. "It's a good thing you're strong, Charlie," she said, using the dog's back to brace herself.

When she was at last on her feet, she looked down at herself and groaned. Her skirt was half tied up, half hanging down to her ankles. Her left knee was cut, scraped, still oozing blood, while her right knee was merely raw. With determination, she tossed the plaid over her arms, not wanting to see the damage done to them. When she touched her hair she felt dried bits of blood so she moved her hand away.

"Can you find some water, Charlie?" she asked the dog. "Water?"

The dog took off instantly across the rocky landscape, returning when Elizabeth could follow only at a snail's pace. The newly healed scabs had opened and there were warm trickles of blood on her body.

The dog led her to a small stream where she washed as best she could. When she met her liberators, she wanted to be as presentable as possible.

She and the dog walked for hours, staying close to the rocks and the few trees. Once they heard horses and instinctively Elizabeth hid, pulling the dog to her side. There was no way she could have held the big dog had it decided to leave her, but for the moment the animal seemed content to stay with her.

By sundown, what little strength she had left was gone, and it didn't seem to matter when the dog began barking at something she couldn't see. "No doubt it's Miles or your mistress," she said heavily and slid to the ground, closing her eyes.

When she opened them again a man she'd never seen before stood over her, legs wide, hands on hips. The dying sunlight haloed his gray hair, made shadows on his strong jaw.

"Well, Rab," he said in a deep voice, stroking the dog, "what have you brought me this time?"

"Don't touch me," Elizabeth whispered as the man bent toward her.

"If you're worried I'll harm you in any way, young woman, you needn't be. I'm the MacGregor and you're on my land. Why is Bronwyn's dog with *you?*" He eyed her English clothes.

Elizabeth was tired, weak, hungry, but she wasn't dead. The way this man said Bronwyn told her they were friends. Tears began falling down her cheeks. Now she'd never get home. No friend of the MacArrans would return her to England, and Roger's capture by a Montgomery could start a private war.

"Don't greet so, lass," the MacGregor said. "Soon you'll be in a nice safe place. Someone will tend to your cuts and we'll feed you and— What the hell!"

Elizabeth, as the man leaned closer, had pulled his dirk from its sheath and aimed for his stomach. Sheer weakness had made her miss.

Lachlan MacGregor sidestepped, took the dirk from her and flung her over his shoulder in one quick movement. "Give me no more trouble, lass," he commanded when she started to struggle. "In Scotland we don't repay kindness by stabbing someone."

He tossed Elizabeth on his horse, whistled for Rab to follow and the three of them set off at a furious pace.

Chapter 9

ELIZABETH SAT ALONE IN A BIG ROOM IN THE MACGREGOR castle, the oak door barred. The room was mostly bare except for an enormous bed, a chest and three chairs. A fireplace was along one wall, filled with logs, but no fire warmed the cold stones.

Elizabeth huddled in one of the chairs, the plaid from Bronwyn wrapped about her, her sore knees drawn in to her chest. It had been several hours since the MacGregor had tossed her in the room without so much as a backward glance. No food had been sent to her, no water for washing, and the dog, Rab, had bounded away at the first sight of the MacGregor fortress. Elizabeth was too tired to sleep, her mind in too much of a turmoil to allow her much rest.

When she first heard the familiar voice, muffled through the heavy door, her first reaction was one of relief. But she quickly recovered from that. Miles Montgomery was as much her enemy as anyone else.

When Miles opened the door and walked in boldly, she was ready for him. She sent a copper and silver goblet from the mantelpiece flying at his head.

Miles caught the object in his left hand and kept walking toward her.

She threw a small shield from the wall at him and he caught that in his right hand.

With a little smile of triumph, Elizabeth grabbed a battered helmet from the mantel and drew back her arm to throw it. He had no more hands with which to catch this object.

But before she could throw the helmet, Miles was before her, his arms drawing her close to him.

"I was very worried about you," he whispered, his face buried against her cheek. "Why did you run away like that? Scotland isn't like England. It's treacherous country."

He didn't hold her very tightly, at least not enough to cause her to want to struggle, but instead she almost wished he'd pull her closer. As it was, she had to stand very still or else his arms might drop away altogether. At his idiot words, though, she did move away. "I am attacked by wolves, nearly fall into the sea and some man throws me about like a sack of grain and *you* tell *me* this is treacherous country!"

Miles touched her temple and she did not move away from him. There was an unusual light in his eyes. "Elizabeth, you make your own problems."

"I did not ask to be delivered into my enemy's hands nor to be brought as a prisoner into this hostile country and as for that man—"

Miles interrupted her. "The MacGregor was quite angry at your taking a knife to him. A few months ago he nearly died from Bronwyn's using a knife on him."

"But they seemed to be friends."

Before she could speak another word, the chamber door opened and in walked two brawny Scotsmen carrying an oak tub. Behind them came a dozen women bearing buckets of hot water. The last woman held a tray with three decanters and two goblets.

"Knowing your propensity for not bathing, I have taken the liberty of ordering a bath." Miles smiled at her.

Elizabeth didn't answer him but put her nose into the air and turned toward the cold fireplace.

When the room was empty of people except for the two of them, Miles put his hand on her shoulder. "Come and bathe while the water is hot, Elizabeth."

She whirled on him. "Why should you think that I'd do for you what I haven't done for other men? I ran away from you at Larenston and now you seem to think I'll leap into your arms because you've shown up here. What difference does it make whether I'm held prisoner by the MacGregor or a Montgomery? If the truth be known, I prefer the MacGregor."

Miles's jaw hardened and his eyes darkened. "I think it's time some things were made clear between us. I have been more than patient with you. I have stood by silently while you hurt Sir Guy. I have shared my son with you. I have watched as you put the entire Clan MacArran in turmoil and now you've come close to injuring the MacGregor. The peace between the MacGregors and MacArrans is too new and fragile. You could have destroyed what it's taken Stephen a year to build. And look at you, Elizabeth! Have you seen yourself? There is dried blood all over you, you're obviously exhausted and you've lost much weight. I think it's time I stopped letting you have your own way."

"My . . . !" she sputtered. "I do not want to be held prisoner! Do you understand me? Can I get anything through your thick head? I want to go home to my brothers and I will do whatever I can to get there."

"Home!" Miles said through clenched teeth. "Do you have any idea what the word means? Where did you learn how to break men's toes? How to use a knife so efficiently? What made you decide all men were evil creatures? Why can't you abide any man's touch?"

Elizabeth just looked at him sullenly. "Edmund is dead," she said after a while.

"Will you always live under a cloud, Elizabeth?" he whispered, his eyes soft. "Will you always see only what you want to see?" After a long sigh, he held out his hand to her. "Come and bathe before the water cools."

"No," she said slowly. "I don't want to bathe."

She should have been used to Miles's extraordinary quickness, but as usual she was unprepared for it.

"I've had enough of this, Elizabeth," he said before tossing the damp plaid from her. "I've been patient and kind but from now on you're going to learn a little obedience—and trust. I am not going to harm you; I have *never* harmed any woman but I cannot stand by and allow you to hurt yourself."

With that, he tore the front of her dress away, exposing her breasts.

Elizabeth gasped, crossed her arms in front of her and jumped back.

Easily, Miles caught her, and in two swift tears he had her nude. He didn't seem to pay any attention to her body as he picked her up and carried her to the tub where he gently set her into the water.

Without a word, he picked up a cloth, soaped it and began to gently wash her face. "Struggle and the soap will be in your eyes," he said, making her hold still.

She refused to speak to him while he washed the upper half of her body, glad for the soap that hid her red face as his hands glided lingeringly over her high, firm breasts.

"How did you hurt yourself?" he asked conversationally as he soaped her left leg, careful of the ugly cuts and scrapes on her knee.

The water was relaxing her and there was no reason not to tell him. She lay back in the tub, closed her eyes and told him of the night she'd spent along the cliff road. Halfway through the story, a glass of wine touched her hand and she drank of it thirstily. The intoxicant immediately went to her head and, dreamily, she kept talking.

"Rab stayed with me," she concluded, drinking more wine. "The dog understood that I didn't want to go to Bronwyn, but instead he led me to Bronwyn's friend." The wine was making her so relaxed she didn't even feel angry at the dog or the MacGregor or anyone else.

"Miles," she said conversationally, unaware of the pleasure she gave him in using his Christian name. "Why *don't* you strike women? I don't believe I've met a man who doesn't use force to get his way."

He was gently washing her toes. "Perhaps I use a different kind of force."

That was all he was going to say and for a while they were silent. Elizabeth didn't realize that he kept her glass full of wine and by now she had drunk nearly an entire decanterful.

"Why didn't you speak up to your brother this morning? Or was it yesterday morning?"

Miles's momentary pause in washing her was his only sign that he understood her question. She'd never really asked something so personal before, as if she were interested in him.

"My three elder brothers are very pig-headed men. Gavin's never heard anyone's opinion except his own and Raine likes to imagine himself as a martyr for all lost causes."

"And Stephen?" she asked, drinking more wine, watching him through lowered lashes. His hands on her felt so very, very good.

"Stephen fools people into believing he's a willing compromiser, but when it comes to the point, he insists upon his own way. Only for Bronwyn was he willing to look at someone else's view, and she had to fight him—and still fights—for everything. He makes jests about what to her is life and death."

Elizabeth considered this for a moment. "And you are their little brother. No doubt they will always consider you someone to be instructed, someone who must be taken care of."

"And is that the way you are treated also?" he half whispered.

The drink, the hot water, made her loosen her

tongue. "Roger thinks I have only a quarter of a brain. Half is missing because I am a woman, half of that gone because he remembers me in swaddling clothes. When I told him some of what Edmund was doing to me, he wasn't sure whether to believe me or not. Or perhaps he didn't want to see the things his own brother did or allowed to happen.

"Damn!" she said, half rising from the tub. With a violent jerk she threw the goblet across the room, slamming it into the stone wall. "I *am* half a woman. Do you know what it feels like to watch Bronwyn and your brother, to see them laugh and love? The two of them sneak little touches when they think no one is looking. Whenever a man touches me, I—"

She broke off, her eyes wide, her head reeling from the drink. "Make love to me, Miles Montgomery," she whispered huskily. "Make me not afraid."

"I had planned to," he said throatily as he pulled her into his arms.

She still stood in the tub, and as Miles's mouth came down on hers, she kissed him back—kissed him with all the passion, all the anger she felt at having been cheated of a normal attitude toward love. While other women were learning how to flirt, Elizabeth's brother had been gambling, promising his little sister's virginity to the winner, and Elizabeth had learned to use a knife. She had preserved her precious virginity and for what? The convent? For a life where she grew harder and angrier every year until she turned to stone—an un-loved, useless old woman?

Miles pulled back from her slightly, controlling the kiss, keeping her from hurting herself as she tried to grind her lips against his teeth. His hands were playing up and down her wet back, his fingertips caressing the indentation of her spine.

His lips moved to the corner of her mouth, his tongue touching the tip of hers before he trailed to her cheek, kissing her while his hands toyed with her skin.

Elizabeth tilted her head back and to one side as Miles's teeth ran along her neck and to her shoulder. Perhaps this was the true reason why she'd never allowed a man to touch her. Maybe she'd always known that unless she fought like a demon she'd succumb like this—wantonly, unashamedly.

"Miles," she whispered. "Miles."

"Always," he murmured, nibbling her ear.

With one swift motion he lifted her from the tub and carried her to the bed. Her body was wet, her hair cold and clinging to her, but Miles wrapped a towel about her and began rubbing. The briskness of his rubbing sent new warmth through her and everywhere, every time he touched her she wanted more. She had a whole lifetime of touching to make up for.

Suddenly Miles was beside her, nude, his glorious skin warm, dark, inviting.

"I am yours, Elizabeth, as you are mine," he whispered as he placed her hand on his chest.

"So much hair." She giggled. "So very much hair." She buried her fingers in the short black curling stuff and pulled. Obediently, Miles rolled closer to her, snuggled her golden body to the length of him.

"What does it feel like?" she asked anxiously.

"You'll not know for a long while." He smiled. "When we become one, there'll be no fear in your eyes."

"Become one," she whispered as Miles again began to kiss her neck. He kissed her neck for a very long time before he moved to her arm, his tongue making little swirling motions inside her elbow. It was odd how little vibrations seemed to be traveling from her fingertips, across her breasts to her other fingertips.

She lay still, eyes closed, arms open, legs open as Miles touched her. Those big hands that could wield a sword, could protect a child from harm, could control an unruly horse, were tenderly, slowly setting her body on fire.

When his hand moved from her throat to her cheek, she turned her head and kissed the palm, put both her hands on his and began to make love to that hard delicate hand, scraping it against her teeth, tasting his skin, running her tongue around and around the hairs on the back of his hand.

She was rewarded by a primitive sound from Miles that set her heart racing.

"Elizabeth," he groaned. "Elizabeth. How I have waited."

Elizabeth decided she wasn't really in the mood for more waiting. Instinctively she tried to wiggle further under Miles, but he refused to allow that. Instead, he brought his mouth to her breast and Elizabeth nearly came off the bed.

Miles chuckled at her reaction and she felt his laughter all along the length of her. Love and laughter, she thought. That's what Miles had added to her life.

Miles's lips on her breasts soon made her stop thinking. He straddled her hips, on his knees, his hands about her waist, squeezing, caressing, and gradually he began using his fingers to guide her hips into a slow, undulating rhythm.

She caught the rhythm easily. Her breathing deepened and her hands on Miles's arms tightened, her fingers digging into his muscles. His body surrounding her, warm, hard, sculptured, was all she was aware of as her whole body began to move sensuously.

"Miles," she whispered, her hands moving to his hair. She was not gentle as she pulled his face to hers, sought his lips in a kiss such as she'd never dreamed of before. There was sweat on both of them, salty, hot sweat.

Elizabeth drew her knees up, clutched Miles's hips and when she did, he entered her.

There was no pain as she was more than ready for him, but for a moment she trembled with the force of her reaction. Miles held still, also slightly trembling, until Elizabeth started the slow rhythm he'd taught her with his hands.

Slowly, together, they made love. After only moments, Elizabeth lost herself in a sea of passion she'd never known existed before. As Miles increased his speed, she locked her legs about him and gave herself up to her senses. With one blinding flash, Elizabeth's body convulsed and her legs began to shake violently.

"Hush," Miles soothed as he lifted onto one elbow and stroked her temple. "Hush, my angel. You're safe now."

He withdrew from her, pulled her into his arms. "My promised angel," he whispered. "My angel of rain and lightning."

Elizabeth didn't understand his words completely but

she did, perhaps for the first time in her life, feel safe. She fell asleep instantly, her body so close to Miles's that she could scarcely breathe.

When Elizabeth awoke, she stretched luxuriously, feeling each and every muscle of her body, wincing when she pulled the torn skin of her knees. Her eyes opened and the first thing she saw was a long table covered with steaming food. She was sure she'd never been so hungry in her life. Grabbing Bronwyn's plaid from the floor, she tossed it about her body haphazardly and went to the table.

Her mouth was full of a bit of poached salmon when the door opened and Miles walked in. Elizabeth froze, her hand halfway to her mouth as she began to remember the previous night. There was such a disgustingly *knowing* look in Miles's dark eyes that Elizabeth began to grow angry. Before she could even sort her feelings, Miles casually began to discard the Scots clothes he wore.

What right did he—! Elizabeth thought, choking on the salmon as she tried to speak. But he did have a right. After the way she'd acted last night, he had every right to believe the very worst of her. But still she'd like to wipe that expression off his face.

Elizabeth didn't really consider what she did, but beside her were two heaping platters of warm, soft tarts, baked to a golden turn, heavy with summer fruit. With a smile, her eyes locked with Miles's, she slipped her hand under a tart and, still smiling, sent it flying toward him.

He wasn't expecting missiles sent at him and the pie

hit his collar bone, splashing his cheek, running down his chest in a warm ooze of cherries and juice.

Elizabeth knew that whatever happened now it was worth it for the look on Miles's face. He was totally, completely, shocked. With her hand over her mouth to cover a giggle, Elizabeth sent two more pies flying at him, hitting his bare hip with the first one, the chair behind him with the other one.

Miles looked at Elizabeth with an odd expression, discarded the rest of his clothes and kept walking toward her.

The plaid Elizabeth had worn fell from her body and Elizabeth, eyes wide, began to throw pies in earnest, using both hands. She wasn't sure but she thought she saw murder in those gray eyes.

Miles kept coming, only moving when a tart came flying at his face. His entire body was covered in a mixture of peaches, cherries, apples, dates, plums, all running down his muscular body in a glorious riot of colors—and flavors, Elizabeth thought irrelevantly.

When he reached the table, his piercing eyes held hers and she didn't dare move. He bolted over the table to stand beside her and Elizabeth, breath held, looked up at him. But as she looked, a cherry, plump and juicy, ran down his forehead, his nose, and hung for just a second before plopping down onto the floor. Another giggle escaped Elizabeth.

Slowly, tenderly, Miles drew her into his arms. "Ah, Elizabeth," he said, "you are such a joy."

As his lips came near hers, she closed her eyes, remembering all too well the sensations of last night. He bent her backward in his arms and Elizabeth gave herself over to the strength of him. He had power over her. All he had to do was touch her and she began to tremble.

But lips did not touch hers. Instead, she received a face full of juicy, syrupy peach pie. As peaches ran into her ears, her eyes flew open. Gasping, she looked up into Miles's devilish face.

Before she could even protest, with a wicked little smile, he lifted her and set her on the table—smack in the middle of the second platter of tarts. Fruit juice oozed over her legs, somehow did the impossible and traveled up her spine. Her hands were covered, peaches dripped off her chin, her hair was glued to her body.

With utter disgust, she lifted her hands, brushed them against each other, saw that did no good whatever, and on second thought, she ate two apple slices from the back of her wrist.

"A little too sweet," she said seriously, looking at Miles. "Perhaps we should complain to the cook."

Miles, nude before her, showed that his mind was not on the cook. Elizabeth's eyes widened in mock dismay. It was difficult, if not impossible, to retain one's composure while sitting in a puddle of fruit pies. She opened her arms to her sticky lover and he came to her.

When Elizabeth kissed Miles's neck and came away choking on a cherry pit, their laughter began. Miles noisily began eating peaches from her forehead while Elizabeth nibbled plums from Miles's shoulder.

Miles grabbed her, rolled onto his back amid a great clatter of dishes and the squish of food, and set her down on his swollen manhood. There was no more laughter as their thoughts turned serious and they made love with vigor, twice changing positions, ending with Miles on the bottom.

Elizabeth lay quite still on top of him, weak, exhausted, thinking she might die before she had energy to rouse herself.

But Miles, with a grunt, lifted both of them and removed a small earthenware bowl that had once contained a sauce of some sort from the small of his back, and flung it to the floor.

Elizabeth raised herself and absently scratched her thigh. "You are a sight, Miles Montgomery," she said, smiling, brushing a poached egg from his hair. The yellow was working its way down toward his scalp.

"You are not exactly presentable at court." With another groan of pain, he removed a serving fork from under his buttocks.

"What do you think your MacGregor is going to think of this?" Elizabeth asked, moving off Miles. She sat up, cross-legged beside him and surveyed the room. The walls, floors, furniture were covered with smashed tarts, and the table was a disaster, everything overturned, dripping, running together—except for a couple of dishes at the very end of the table. On her hands and knees, Elizabeth crawled toward the undisturbed food, squealed once when Miles gave her buttocks a sweet caress, but came back with a bowl of chicken cooked with almonds and a small loaf of wheat bread.

Miles, still stretched on his back on the table, raised himself on his hand. "Still hungry?" he teased.

"Starved." She grabbed a spoon from under Miles's ankle and dug into the stew, and when Miles turned soulful, forlorn eyes up to her, she began to feed him also. "Don't get used to this," she commanded as she shoveled more food into his mouth.

Miles merely smiled at her and occasionally kissed her fingers.

All in all, they found quite a bit of undestroyed food on the table. Elizabeth hung over the side, with Miles holding an ankle and a wrist, and retrieved a whole roast partridge which had caught on the leg stretchers. Miles refused to feed himself and Elizabeth was "forced" to feed him, even to stripping the meat from the partridge bones.

"Worthless is what you are," Elizabeth said, scratching. The food on her body was beginning to dry and it *itched!*

"What you need," Miles murmured, running nibbling kisses up her arm, "is—"

"I don't want to hear any of your suggestions, Montgomery!" she warned. "Last night you got me drunk and pounced on me in a tub and now . . . this!" There were no words to describe the fragrant mess about them. "Damn!" she cursed, using both hands to scratch her thigh. "Is there nothing normal about you?"

"Nothing," he reassured her as he lazily stepped down from the table and began to dress. "There's a lake not far from here. How about a swim?"

"I have no idea how to swim."

He caught her waist and lifted her from the table. "I'll teach you," he said so lewdly that Elizabeth laughed and pushed against him.

"Underwater?" she said, and when Miles seemed to consider this seriously, she nearly ran from him, slipping once on an ooze of cod livers but catching herself on the table edge. In record time, she'd slipped into a tartan skirt, a saffron-colored shirt and tossed a plaid about her shoulders. The skirt had been in the line of fire of a cheese tart.

"Do I look as bad as you?" she asked as he pulled food from his hair.

"Worse. But no one will see us." With that cryptic sentence, he walked toward a tapestry on the far wall, pulled it aside and revealed a staircase built inside the thick stone walls. He took Elizabeth's hand and led her into the dark, cold passage.

Chapter 10

Two hours later they were washed and Miles was drying Elizabeth with a plaid.

"Quite useful, aren't they?" she murmured, wrapping the tartan cloth about her cool body. The Scots summer was not conducive to lying about nude.

"Many things about the Scots are practical as well as pleasant—if you'd give them half a chance."

She stopped drying her hair. "What does it matter to you whether I like the Scots or not? I understand your wanting to get me into your bed but I don't understand this constant . . . interest, I guess, in my welfare."

"Elizabeth, if I'd merely wanted you in my bed I could have taken you that first day when you were delivered to me."

"And you would have lost part of yourself to my ax blade," she snapped.

After a moment's surprise, Miles began to laugh. "You and that ax! Oh Elizabeth, you were such a charming sight with your leg sticking out and surrounded by so much hair. You were—"

"You do not have to laugh *quite* so hard," she said stiffly. "It was not humorous to me. And I may yet escape you."

That sobered him. He pulled her down to the ground beside him. "I don't want to have to go through more nights like those. Rab was missing and we found dead wolves along the cliff and the mare you rode came back limping. We were really afraid you'd fallen over the cliff."

She pushed at him because he was holding her so tightly she couldn't breathe. As she looked up at him, she frowned. She'd always thought that if a man did take her virtue, she would hate him, but hate was far removed from what she felt for Miles. Between them now was a soft sense of sharing, as if they'd always been here and always would be.

"Is it always like this?" she whispered, looking up at the trees overhead.

There was a pause before Miles answered. "No," he said so softly it could have been the wind.

She knew he understood what she meant. Perhaps he was lying to her, perhaps tomorrow he'd again be her enemy, but right now he wasn't.

"There were never days like this when my brother was alive," she began, and when she started she couldn't stop. Although she'd fought Miles at every opportunity, she now knew that in truth she'd never been in any real danger—not the danger she'd experienced for most of her life. In the last few weeks she'd seen courtesy; she'd seen love between Bronwyn and Stephen, Miles and his son—and love that asked very little in return was something she'd not seen in her lifetime.

Instead of telling a horror tale of all the atrocities Edmund had committed, she talked of the way she and her two other brothers had bound themselves together. Roger had not been very old when his parents died and he'd been turned over to the rule of his treacherous brother. He'd done all he could to save his younger siblings but at the same time he wanted to live his own life. Every time that Roger slipped in his vigilance, Elizabeth was summoned from her convent and used in Edmund's nasty games. Roger, in remorse and guilt over his lapse, would strike out and renew his vows to protect Brian and Elizabeth, but always, Edmund's slimy ways would undermine Roger's good intentions.

"He's never had anyone but us," Elizabeth said. "Roger is twenty-seven but he's never been in love, never even had the time to while away a summer afternoon. He was old by the time he was twelve."

"And what of you?" Miles asked. "Didn't you consider that you deserved some time for laughter?"

"Laughter." She smiled, snuggling against him. "I don't think I remember any laughter in my life until a certain young man rolled down a hill with me."

"Kit is a delightful child," Miles said with pride.

"Kit, ha! It was someone larger who, even as he rolled, protected his fine sword."

"Noticed that, did you?" he said softly, tucking a strand of her hair behind her ear.

For a moment they were silent, with Elizabeth looking at him in puzzled silence. "You are not a kidnapper," she said at last. "I have seen you with men and with women and if you are nothing else in life, you are kind to women. So why do you not release me? Is it because, as you said, I have so many . . . problems?" She said the last stiffly.

He did not take her question lightly and it was a while before he answered. "All my life I've seemed to enjoy the company of women. I like nothing better than to lie about with a beautiful woman in my arms. My brothers seemed to think this made me less of a man but I don't guess one can change how one is. As for you, Elizabeth, I saw something I'd never seen before —a man's hatred and anger. My sister-in-law Judith could probably organize all of England, yet she needs my brother's strength and love. Bronwyn loves people and could make anyone do her bidding, but she's unsure of herself and needs Stephen's stubborn belief in himself to back her."

He paused. "But you, Elizabeth, are different. You could probably exist alone and you wouldn't even know there was more to life."

"Then why . . ." she began. "Why hold someone like me prisoner? Surely some soft, docile woman would be more to your liking."

He smiled at the insult in her tone. "Passion, Elizabeth. I think you are surely the most passionate human on earth. You hate violently and I am sure you will love just as violently."

She tried to move away but he pinned her to the ground, his face near hers. "You'll love only once in your life," he said. "You'll take your time in giving your love but once it is given, no power on earth—or hell—will break that love."

She lay still under him, gazing up into those deep gray orbs that burned into her.

"I want to be that man," he said softly. "I want more than your body, Elizabeth Chatworth. I want your love, your mind, your soul."

When he bent to kiss her, she turned her head away. "You don't ask much, do you, Montgomery? You've had more than I've given any other man—but I don't think I have more to give. My soul belongs to God, my mind to myself and my love goes to my family."

He rolled away from her and began to dress. "You asked me why I keep you prisoner and I've told you. Now we'll return to the MacGregor's and you will meet his men. The MacGregor is angered over your taking a knife to him and you will apologize."

She did not like his attitude. "He is a friend to the MacArrans who are related to my enemies, the Montgomerys"—she smiled sweetly—"therefore I had every right to try and protect myself."

"True," he agreed, handing her her clothes, "but if the MacGregor isn't appeased, it could cause problems between the clans."

She began to dress sullenly. "I don't like this," she muttered. "And I'll not enter a hall of strange men without a weapon."

"Elizabeth," Miles said patiently. "You cannot wield an ax at every gathering of men you enter. Besides, these Scots have some beautiful women of their own. Perhaps they won't be so enraptured with your charms that they're driven to insane acts of lust."

"I didn't mean that!" she snapped, turning away from him. "Must you laugh at . . . ?"

He put his hand on her shoulder. "I don't mean to

laugh at you, but you have to begin to realize what is normal and what isn't. I'll be there to protect you."

"And who will protect me from you?"

At that, his eyes lit and he ran his hand down the side of her breast. "You will be pleased to know that no one will protect you from me."

She pulled away from him and finished dressing.

What Miles had planned for Elizabeth was, to her, sheer torture. He clamped his fingers down on her elbow until pain shot up her arm, and he forced her to shake hands with over a hundred of the MacGregor men. When she finished, she collapsed in a chair against the wall and shakily drank the wine Miles handed her. When he complimented her as if she were a dog that'd performed a trick correctly, she sneered at him, which made him kiss her fingers and laugh.

"It will get easier," he said confidently.

Indeed, it did get easier, but it took weeks. Miles never let up on her for a moment. He refused to let her walk behind the men and when she turned constantly to check the men's whereabouts, he made her be still. They rode on a hunt and once Elizabeth was separated from Miles. Three MacGregors found her, were quite cordial to her, but by the time she reached Miles, there was terror in her eyes. Instantly, he pulled her onto his horse, held her and soothed her and when that wasn't enough, he made love to her under a beech tree.

There was one man at the MacGregors who Miles warned her against: Davy MacArran, Bronwyn's brother. Miles had a fierce dislike for the boy who was actually older than himself. Miles said, with great contempt, that Davy had tried to kill his own sister.

"For all the arrogance of my brothers," Miles said, "they would give their lives for me as I would for them. I have no use for men who go against their families."

"As you are asking me to do?" she retorted. "You are asking me to forsake my brothers and give myself body and soul to you."

There was a flicker of anger in Miles's eyes before he left her alone in the room they shared.

Elizabeth went to the window to look down at the men in the courtyard below. It was an odd feeling to know that if she wanted she could walk in that courtyard and not be molested. She need have no fear that she would have to fight for her life. There was no urge on her part to test her knowledge but it was pleasant to consider.

The MacGregor walked by and the powerful strut of the big man almost made her smile. His vanity had taken a beating at Bronwyn's hands and again at Elizabeth's, and when Miles had practically pushed Elizabeth before him, the MacGregor'd hardly looked at her. This had *never* happened to her before and before she knew what she was doing, she found herself practically coaxing him to talk to her. It had taken only minutes before she felt him twining about her fingers. He liked pretty women and he was old enough that he was beginning to wonder whether pretty women liked him. Elizabeth soon dispelled that idea.

Later Miles looked at her in disgust. "You changed quickly from the frightened rabbit to the temptress."

"Do you think I make a good temptress?" she taunted. "Lachlan MacGregor is a widower. Perhaps—"

She didn't finish because Miles kissed her so hard he

nearly bruised her lips. With her fingertips on her lower lip, she watched his broad back as he moved away from her—and smiled. She was beginning to realize that she had some power over Miles, but as yet she didn't know the extent of her power.

Now, as she watched the courtyard, men, wearing the MacArran cockade, rode into the area. The MacGregors falsely acted with nonchalance, but Elizabeth saw that all the men's hands were very close to their sword belts. Miles came from inside the MacGregor's stone house and talked to the MacArrans.

Elizabeth watched for only a moment before turning back to the room with a sigh, and she began to gather Miles's belongings. She knew without a doubt that they would be leaving.

Miles opened the door, paused for a moment, saw what she was doing and began to help her. "My brother Gavin has come to Larenston."

"With Roger?" She paused with her hand on a velvet cape.

"No, your brother has escaped."

She whirled to face him. "Unharmed? With all his body parts?"

Miles's eyes widened for a moment. "As far as I know, everything is attached." He caught her hands. "Elizabeth . . ."

She pulled away. "Perhaps you should have one of the MacGregor's beautiful lasses to pack your fine belongings." With that she fled to the stairs behind the tapestry.

In spite of everything she could do, tears began to

fall. She tripped in the black darkness, barely caught herself from falling and ended up sitting down hard on a stone stair as several rats squealed in protest at her disturbance.

Sitting there, crying as if her life were over, she knew she had no reason to cry. Her brother was no longer a prisoner as she was; he was unharmed. And now Gavin Montgomery had come, no doubt to force his younger brother to release her. By this time tomorrow she'd probably be on her way home. No more would she have to shake hands with strange men. No more would she be a captive, but she'd be free to go home to her own family.

A sound on the stairs above her made her turn and although she couldn't see him, she knew Miles was there. Instinctively, she held her arms out to him.

Miles grabbed her so hard she knew her ribs would crack, and all she did was cling to him all the more tightly. They were like two children hiding from their parents, frightened of tomorrow, making the most of now.

To them there was no dust or filth, no angry little eyes watching them as they fumbled with each other's clothes, their lips joined, never parting. The violence with which they came together was new to Elizabeth, as Miles had always been gentle with her, but when her nails dug into his back, he reacted. The stairs bit into the back of her as Miles lifted her hips and took her with a blinding, fierce passion, but with no more fierceness than Elizabeth sought him. She braced her feet against the stairs and pushed upward with all the force of her strong young body.

The flash of light that tore through them left them both weak, trembling, holding onto each other as if to let go meant they'd die.

Miles was the first to recover. "We must go," he whispered tiredly. "They wait below for us."

"Yes," she said. "Big brother calls." Even in the darkness, she could feel Miles's eyes on her.

"Don't be afraid of Gavin, Elizabeth."

"The day a Chatworth is afraid of a Montgomery—" she began but Miles kissed her to silence.

"That's what I like! Now if you can keep your hands off me long enough, we'll ride to Larenston."

"You!" She started to strike him but he bolted up the stairs before she could, and when Elizabeth tried to move, she winced at a hundred bruised places. She emerged from behind the tapestry bent over, her hand to her back. Miles's conceited chuckle made her straighten painfully. "If women didn't always have to be on the bottom—" she snapped, then stopped when she saw the MacGregor leaning against a chest.

"I was going to say I hoped you enjoyed your visit, Lady Elizabeth." The big man's eyes twinkled so merrily that Elizabeth busied herself in packing, pointedly ignoring him, so pointedly that she didn't hear him move behind her. When his hands touched her shoulder, she gasped, but Miles caught her arm, warned her with his eyes.

"We've enjoyed ye, Elizabeth," the MacGregor said as he removed the crude pin she wore at her shoulder and replaced it with a large round silver one, bearing the MacGregor standard.

"Thank you," she said quietly, and to the amazement of all three of them, she quickly kissed the MacGregor's cheek.

Miles's hand on her arm tightened and he looked at her with such pleasure that his whole body fairly glowed.

"Sweet lass, come and see me again."

"I will," she said and smiled genuinely because she meant her words.

Together the three of them walked down to the courtyard and the waiting horses. Elizabeth looked at all the MacGregor men with curiosity because she knew she was going to miss them. With a sense of wonder at what she was doing, she voluntarily shook hands with some of the men. Miles stayed close to her and she was well aware of his presence, and grateful for it, but her fear at touching the men and being touched by them was only just that—fear, not terror.

She was glad when she came to the end of the line and could mount her horse. Behind her were Bronwyn's men, strangers to her, and she could have cried out at the injustice of having to leave a place she was just beginning to trust.

Miles leaned across and squeezed her hand. "Remember that I am here," he said.

She nodded once, kicked her horse forward and they were off.

For how long will you be here? she wanted to ask. She knew much about Gavin Montgomery. He was a greedy, treacherous man whose jilting of Alice Chatworth had nearly driven her insane. And Gavin was the head of the Montgomery family. For all Miles's bravado, he was only twenty years old and Gavin had the guardianship of his young brother. Would Gavin take her away, use her in his own games against the Chatworth family? Miles believed Roger'd killed Mary Montgomery. Would this Gavin use Elizabeth to repay the Chatworths?

"Elizabeth," Miles said. "What are you planning?"

She didn't bother to answer him, but kept her head high as they entered Larenston.

Miles helped her from her horse. "No doubt my eldest brother is inside, waiting to get his hands on me," Miles said, eyes twinkling.

"How can you laugh about this?"

"The only way to deal with my brother is to laugh," he said seriously. "I'll come to you later."

"No!" she gasped. "I'll meet your brother with you."

Miles cocked his head, studied her. "I do believe you mean to protect me from my brother."

"You are a gentle man and—"

At that Miles laughed so loud, he startled the horses. He kissed her cheek heartily. "You are a dear, sweet child. Come along then and protect me if you want, but I'll keep an eye on Gavin's toes."

Gavin, Stephen and Sir Guy waited for them in the upstairs solar. Gavin was as tall as Miles but his face was more sculptured, hawklike, and his expression was of pure unadulterated rage.

"Is this Elizabeth Chatworth?" Gavin said through clenched teeth. He didn't wait for an answer. "Send her away. Guy, see to her."

"She stays," Miles said in a cool voice, not bothering to look at either of his brothers. "Sit, Elizabeth."

She obeyed him, sinking into a chair that dwarfed her.

After one angry glance at Elizabeth, Gavin turned to Miles who was pouring himself a glass of wine. "Goddamn you to hell and back, Miles!" Gavin bellowed. "You walk in here as if you hadn't nearly caused a private war between our families and you bring this . . . this . . ."

"Lady," Miles said, his eyes growing dark.

"If she were a lady, I'd swear she isn't now after having spent weeks with you."

Miles's eyes turned black. His hand went to his sword but Sir Guy's hand made him pause.

"Gavin," Stephen warned, "you have no right to make insults. Say what you have to."

Gavin moved closer to Miles. "Do you know what your little escapade is costing our family? Raine can't even show his face but must hide in a forest, and I have spent the last month in the company of that bastard Chatworth—all in an attempt to save your worthless japing hide."

Elizabeth waited for Miles to retort that Raine's outlawing was not Miles's fault, but Miles remained silent, his eyes still dark, locked on his eldest brother.

A muscle in Gavin's jaw worked frantically. "You will release her to me and I will return her to her brother. I'd hoped that by now you'd come to your senses and let her go. I'm sure you've taken her virginity and that will no doubt cost me much, but . . ."

"Will it cost you or Judith?" Miles asked calmly, turning his back on his brother.

A silence fell on the room and even Elizabeth held her breath.

"Stop it, both of you," Stephen interceded. "And for God's sake, Gavin, calm down! You know how Miles is when you insult his woman-of-the-moment. And you, Miles, you're pushing Gavin too far. Miles, Gavin has held Chatworth in order to give you some time to release Lady Elizabeth, and you can imagine that he was, ah, disappointed when Chatworth escaped and still you held Elizabeth. All you have to do is send her back with Gavin and all will be well."

Elizabeth again held her breath as she watched Miles's back and after a moment she felt Gavin watching her. It was then she decided she didn't like the man. She returned his arrogant look with one of her own. She looked away to see Miles watching them.

"I will not release her," Miles said softly.

"No!" Gavin bellowed. "Does the family mean nothing to you? Would you rather risk our name, the name of generations of Montgomerys, merely for the spread of a woman's thighs?"

Gavin wasn't expecting the fist that plowed into his face, but it didn't take him but seconds to recover and leap at Miles.

Chapter 11

STEPHEN AND SIR GUY USED ALL THEIR STRENGTH TO restrain the two men.

It was Gavin who calmed first. He shook Stephen's arms away, walked toward the window and when he looked back, he had control over himself. "Send Lady Elizabeth away," he said quietly.

Sir Guy released Miles and Miles nodded to Elizabeth. She started to protest but knew that now was not the time. Miles was not going to turn her over to his brother, of that she was sure.

When the men were alone, Gavin sank into a chair. "Brother against brother," he said heavily. "Chatworth would love to know what he's doing to us. Stephen, pour me some wine."

When he held the cup, he continued. "King Henry has ordered this feud between the Montgomerys and

Chatworths to cease. I have pleaded that our family is innocent in everything. Raine attacked Chatworth because of what had been done to Mary and I know you are innocent in the kidnapping of this Elizabeth."

Gavin drank deeply. He was used to these one-sided conversations with his young brother. Getting words from Miles was much worse than teeth pulling. "Has your Elizabeth told you of the young singer who was with her when Pagnell rolled her in a carpet? You should ask her because that singer has recently married Raine."

Miles's eyes widened slightly.

"Ah! At last I get some response from my brother."

"Gavin," Stephen warned. "How is Raine's wife involved in all this?"

Gavin waved his hand. "Pagnell was after her for some reason, tossed her in a dungeon and Elizabeth Chatworth tried to save her. In so doing, the Chatworth woman got caught and in jest was delivered to our lecherous little brother. God's teeth, why didn't you return her to Chatworth as soon as you found out who she was?"

"As he returned my sister?" Miles asked quietly. "When did you start being such a peacemaker?"

"Since I have seen my family torn apart by this hatred. Hasn't it occurred to you that the king will have some say in all this? He's punished Raine by outlawing him and Chatworth has been heavily fined. What will he do to you when he hears that you hold the Chatworth woman?"

"Miles," Stephen said. "Gavin's concern is for you. I know you've grown to care for the girl but there's more here than you think."

"Elizabeth deserves more than to be sent back to that hellhole of Chatworth's," Miles said.

At that, Gavin groaned, closed his eyes for a moment. "You've been around Raine too long. Whatever you think of Chatworth, no matter what he's done, he's done it with the belief that he was in the right. I've spent weeks with him and—"

"You are well known to side with the Chatworths," Miles said evenly, referring to Gavin's long affair with Alice Chatworth. "I'll not release her and no words from anyone will make me do so. The woman is mine. Now, if you will excuse me, I'd like to see Bronwyn."

In spite of her surety that she would be allowed to stay with Miles, Elizabeth still paced the floor. She cursed herself because she knew that she wanted to stay in Scotland, wanted to stay in a place where she could learn to be unafraid. Roger, she thought, dear, protective, angry Roger was in England somewhere, looking for her, frantic to find her, yet she hoped with all her heart that he'd not succeed.

"Just a little more time," she whispered. "If I can but have one more month I'll leave readily. And I shall have memories to last me a lifetime."

She was so absorbed in her own thoughts that she didn't hear the door open behind her, and when she heard the light footsteps, she whirled about, ready to do battle.

"Did . . . did you enjoy the MacGregors?" Kit stammered, unsure of what the fury on her face meant.

Instantly, Elizabeth's face changed. She knelt, opened her arms to the child and held him very, very close.

"I missed you so much, Kit," she whispered. When her eyes cleared, she held him away from her. "I stayed in a big room with a secret staircase behind a tapestry and your papa and I had a pie fight and we went swimming in a very cold lake."

"Bronwyn gave me a pony," Kit answered, "and Uncle Stephen took me riding and what kind of pies?" He leaned forward and whispered loudly, "Did you make Papa angry?"

"No." She smiled. "Not even when I hit him square in the face with a cherry tart. Come and sit down by me and I'll tell you about how Bronwyn's dog saved me from wolves."

It was some time later that Miles found them together, asleep, both looking perfectly content. For a long time Miles stood over them, quietly watching. When he heard the muffled sounds of horses in the courtyard below and knew it was Gavin leaving, he bent and kissed Elizabeth's forehead. "I'll give you more children, Elizabeth," he murmured, touching Kit's cheek. "See if I don't."

"I most certainly will not!" Elizabeth said to Miles, her face set grimly. "I have nearly killed myself doing what you want but I will not remain here alone while you chase about the countryside having a good time."

"Elizabeth," Miles said patiently, "I am going hunting and you will not be here alone. All the MacArrans—"

"MacArrans!" she shot at him. "All those men near me for three days! No, I will not stay here. I'll go on the hunt with you."

"You know I'd love to have you but I think you need

to stay here. There will be times when I can't be with you and you need to learn . . ." He stopped when she turned away.

"I don't need you or any other man, Montgomery," she said, shoulders stiff.

Miles touched her but she moved away. "Elizabeth, we've been through too much together to let this come between us. I think you should stay here with Kit and the men and try to conquer some of your fear. If you don't think you can do that, tell me and of course you can go with me. I'll be downstairs."

Elizabeth didn't look at him before he left the room. Nearly two months had passed since that day Gavin had first arrived, and during that time Elizabeth had found out what happiness was. She and Miles and Kit had spent lovely, long days together, playing in the newly fallen snow, laughing together. And Christmas had been such as she'd never experienced before—a family together.

Bronwyn had taught her a great deal, not by lectures but by example. Elizabeth rode with Bronwyn a few times and visited some of the crofters. There were a few instances of panic and once when Elizabeth drew a knife on a man who was following her too closely, Bronwyn had interceded and calmed Elizabeth. After that there was no more of the initial hostility between the women. Bronwyn seemed to adopt Elizabeth as a young sister rather than look on her as a potential rival. When Bronwyn started ordering Elizabeth about just as she did everyone else, Miles and Stephen relaxed. Three times Elizabeth told Bronwyn she could drop herself off the cliff road and Bronwyn had laughed heartily.

Rab also seemed to have adopted Elizabeth and quite often he'd refuse to obey either woman, skulking off into the shadows instead. When Stephen called the dog a coward, both women turned on him.

And daily, Miles and Elizabeth drew closer. Sometimes, while she watched Miles training, the upper part of his body bare, glistening with sweat, she felt her knees go weak. *Always,* Miles sensed her presence during those times and the hot looks he turned on her would make her tremble. Once, Stephen's lance had just missed Miles's head because Miles was concentrating on Elizabeth's lustful looks. Stephen had been so angry he'd started choking Miles.

"Another inch and I could have killed you," Stephen screeched in rage.

Both Bronwyn and Elizabeth, as well as Rab and Sir Guy, entered into that fracas. Stephen, his entire body red with fury, had demanded that Miles take Elizabeth away from the training ground. Miles, completely unruffled by his brother's anger, had agreed readily. And what a memorable afternoon that had been! In spite of Miles's outward calm, Stephen's unusual anger had upset him and he alternately attacked Elizabeth and clung to her. They made love in the bed, across a chair, the arm nearly breaking her back, and against a wall. Unfortunately, Miles slammed Elizabeth against a tapestry and she grabbed it. The heavy, dusty rug fell on them, knocked them to the floor—but they kept on until they started coughing. Locked together, they crawled from under the tapestry and continued on the cold stone floor. When they appeared for supper that night, flushed and exhausted, the entire Clan Mac-Arran set up a howl of laughter. Stephen was still angry and all he'd say was to issue an order for Elizabeth to stay away from the training ground.

Two whole months and one week together, almost five months since her "capture," she thought.

But now she knew that time was running out.

Gavin sent a messenger to Miles. Roger Chatworth and Pagnell had gone to the king together and Roger'd told King Henry that Raine Montgomery was trying to raise an army against the king, and that Miles was holding Elizabeth in bondage. The king declared that if Miles did not release Elizabeth, he'd be declared a traitor and all his lands confiscated. As for Raine, the king threatened to burn the forest.

Gavin had pleaded with Miles to release Elizabeth. Miles spent days hardly speaking, but sometimes looking at her with great longing, and Elizabeth began to realize that their days together were numbered. Miles began to push her to spend time with the MacArrans, almost as if he were trying to prepare her for the future—a future without him.

Elizabeth was torn both ways. She did want to learn how to cope with her terror of men, but at the same time she wanted to spend every moment with Kit and Miles.

"Damn!" she muttered, alone in the room. How had she come so far from independence to utter dependence?

Gavin had come to Scotland again, this time in a rage that made his first one seem mild, and for the first time Elizabeth felt some guilt at wanting to stay in the peaceful MacArran household. When Miles came to their room, she asked him to allow her to leave with Gavin. She'd planned to say she wanted to save both his family as well as hers but Miles never gave her a chance. Both Stephen and Gavin's rages together were nothing compared to Miles's. He cursed in three languages, he threw things, tore a chair apart with his bare hands, took an ax to a table. It took both Tam and Sir Guy to hold him.

Gavin and Stephen had obviously seen their little brother like this before. Even Gavin gave up and went home after Miles's display. And Elizabeth was left weakened, looking down at the drugged Miles with tears in her eyes. Roger and Miles, she thought over and over, Roger and Miles. She had a home with two brothers, one of whom was tearing the Isles upside down to find her, yet she sat and cried over her enemy, a man who'd also protected her, who'd shown her patience and kindness and taught her that life could be good.

Drowsily, Miles opened his eyes. "Did I frighten you?" he asked huskily.

She could only nod.

"I frighten myself. They don't happen too often." He caught her hand, held it to his cheek like a child's toy. "Don't leave me again, Elizabeth. You were given to me; you are mine." With that often repeated refrain, he slipped away into sleep.

That had been four days ago, a mere short four days ago, but now he was planning to leave her alone for three days while he and Stephen went boar hunting. Perhaps Miles didn't sense her feeling of dread. Perhaps he was just sure enough of himself that he thought he could always keep her at his side. But Roger was on his way to Scotland and when he arrived with his army, what would she do? Could she stand by and see the

MacArrans fight her brother? Could she watch a personal fight between Roger and Miles? Would she hold Kit in her arms and watch Miles die or would she hold Miles at night and taste the blood of her brother?

"Elizabeth?" Bronwyn asked from the doorway. "Miles said you're not going on the hunt."

"No," she said with some bitterness. "I'm to stay here and surround myself with men. Men behind me, men beside me, men watching my every move."

Bronwyn was silent for a moment, watching the blond woman. "Are you worried about Miles or your brother?"

"Both," Elizabeth replied honestly. "And were you ever worried about bringing an English husband into the midst of your Scotsmen? Did you wonder if you could trust him?"

Bronwyn's eyes danced with mirth. "The thought crossed my mind. All Stephen wanted was for me to admit that I loved him. But I was sure there was more to love than just some undefinable feeling."

"And is there?"

"Yes," Bronwyn said. "For some women I think they love a man in spite of what he is, but for me I had to know Stephen was what my clan needed as well as what I wanted."

"What if you'd loved him, loved him deeply, but your clan hated him? What if your staying with Stephen meant you would have alienated your clan?"

"I would have chosen my clan," Bronwyn answered, watching Elizabeth intently. "I would give up many things, even my own life, to keep from starting a war within my family."

"And that's what you think I should do!" she spat.

"You think I should return to my brother. Now, while Miles is gone, is a perfect time. If I could have a few of your men I could . . ." She stopped as she locked eyes with Bronwyn.

At last Bronwyn spoke. "I honor my husband's brother. I will not help you to escape."

Elizabeth put her arms around Bronwyn. "What am I to do? You saw how Miles acted when I said I should return to Roger. Should I try to escape again? Oh Lord!" She pushed away. "You are my enemy as well."

"No." Bronwyn smiled. "I'm not your enemy, nor are any of the Montgomerys. We've all grown to love you. Kit would follow you to the ends of the earth. But the time will come when you'll have to choose. Until that moment arrives, no one can help you. Now come downstairs and kiss Miles goodbye before he starts wrecking more of my furniture. We have little enough as it is. And, by the way, how did that tapestry get on the floor?"

Elizabeth's red face made Bronwyn laugh loudly as they descended the stairs.

"Elizabeth." Miles laughed, pulling her into a darkened corner where she kissed him enthusiastically. "I'll only be gone for three days. Will you miss me so much?"

"You are the lesser of evils. If you come back and half-a-dozen men have their toes broken, it will be your fault."

He caressed her cheek. "After Sir Guy's experience, I don't think they would mind."

"What do you mean?"

"Bronwyn put that ugly giant in the care of some

little flirt and now the two are inseparable. She has him fetching water for her and no doubt if he could hold a needle, he'd embroider her shirt collars."

Elizabeth almost kicked Miles at that because the shirt he wore under the Scots plaid was one she'd embroidered for him.

"Here, my little captive, behave yourself or I'll send you home."

Her eyes hardened at that, but Miles only laughed and nuzzled her neck. "What you feel is in your eyes. Now kiss me again and I'll be back very soon."

Minutes later she stood with empty arms and a heavy heart. Something was going to happen and she knew it. Her first impulse was to hide in her room, to remain there for three days, but she knew Miles was right. Now was a good time to try and overcome some of her fears.

By early afternoon she'd arranged an expedition of her own. She and Kit would ride out with ten Mac-Arran men, Tam included, to a ruin Bronwyn had told her about. Kit could go exploring and she could work on swallowing her fear.

By the time they reached the ruin, Elizabeth's heart was pounding but she was able to smile at Tam as he helped her from her horse. When she heard a man behind her, she didn't turn quickly but tried to act in a normal manner. As she turned to face Jarl, she was rewarded with a smile of great pride from the young man, and Elizabeth let out a small laugh.

"Does everyone know about me?" she asked Tam.

"My clan has a great respect for you because you can slip about the woods as well as any Scotswoman, and we like people who are fighters."

"Fighters! But I have submitted to my enemies."

"Nay, lass." Tam laughed. "Ye've only come to your senses and seen what fine people we Scots are—and to a lesser degree, the Montgomerys."

Elizabeth joined in the laughter with him, as did the men around them.

Later, as Elizabeth sat on a stone of the ancient fallen-down castle, she watched the men below her, realized that she wasn't really afraid of them and thought how good that felt. She owed much to Miles Montgomery.

Because she was so intent upon the sight before her and perhaps because her wariness had dulled in the last few months, she didn't at first hear the whistle coming from the trees behind her. When it did penetrate her peace-drugged brain, every cell of her body came alert. First she looked to see if any of the MacArrans had heard the sound. Kit was playing with young Alex and making a great deal of noise while the others looked on fondly.

Slowly, as if she were going nowhere really, Elizabeth left the boulders and disappeared into the trees with all the noise of a puff of smoke. Once inside, she stood still and waited and her mind was taken back to the days of her childhood.

Brian had always been the one to be protected. Older than Elizabeth but seeming younger, he'd never been able to develop the protective techniques that Elizabeth had. If a man attacked Elizabeth, she had no qualms about drawing a knife on him, but Brian couldn't. Time after time Elizabeth had rescued Brian from some gaggle of men Edmund had brought to their home. While Edmund roared with laughter, shouting

158

insults at his weakling of a brother, Roger and Elizabeth had soothed the young, crippled Brian.

There had been so many days that Brian had spent in hiding, without food or drink, that they'd devised a way of signaling. Roger and Elizabeth were the only ones who knew the high-pitched whistle and they'd always come when Brian called.

Now, Elizabeth stood still, waiting for Brian to appear. Was he alone or with Roger?

The young man who stepped into the clearing was a stranger to Elizabeth and for a moment she could only gape at him. He'd always been handsome in a delicate way, but now he looked wraithlike and his face was that of some terrible specter.

"Brian?" she whispered.

He gave her a curt nod. "You look healthy. Does captivity agree with you?"

Elizabeth was nearly knocked speechless by this. She'd never heard her young brother say such a thing to anyone, much less to her. "Is . . . is Roger with you?"

Brian's sunken features darkened even more. "Do not say that vile name in my presence."

"What?" she gasped, moving toward him. "What are you talking about?"

For a moment, his eyes softened and he lifted a hand to caress Elizabeth's temple, but fell away before he touched her. "Many things have happened since we last saw each other."

"Tell me," she whispered.

Brian moved away from her. "Roger kidnapped Mary Montgomery."

"I had heard that but I can't imagine Roger . . ."

Brian turned on her with eyes like hot coals. "Do you

think he's related to Edmund with no taint of blood? Do you think any of us escaped the evil that controlled our eldest brother?"

"But Roger . . ." she began.

"Do not even speak the name to me. I loved the woman Mary, loved her such as I could never love again. She was good and kind without a single wish to harm, but he—your brother—raped her and she cast herself from a window in horror."

"No," Elizabeth said calmly. "I cannot believe it. Roger is good. He doesn't harm people. He never wanted this war between the Montgomerys and Chatworths. He took in Alice when her own family wouldn't have her. And he—"

"He attacked Stephen Montgomery's back. He lied to Bronwyn MacArran and held her prisoner for a while. When Mary died, I released Bronwyn and took Mary back to Gavin. Did they tell you of the rage of Miles Montgomery when he saw his sister? It lasted for days."

"No," Elizabeth whispered, vividly imagining Miles's fury. "They have said little about any of the war." After the first few days, it seemed to be a silent mutual agreement that she and Miles would not speak of their families' problems.

"Brian," she said softly. "You look tired and worn. Come back to Larenston with me and rest. Bronwyn will—"

"I'll not rest as long as my brother is alive."

Elizabeth gaped at him. "Brian, you cannot mean what you say. We'll contact Roger, then we'll sit down and talk about this."

"You don't understand, do you? I mean to kill Roger Chatworth."

"Brian! You can't forget a lifetime of good in one day. Remember how Roger always protected us? Remember how he risked his life to save you the day Edmund ran you down and crushed your leg?"

Brian's face didn't lose any of its hardness. "I loved Mary and Roger killed her. Someday you'll understand what that means."

"I may love a hundred people but that will not make me stop loving Roger, who has done so much for me. Even now he searches for me."

Brian looked at her in question. "You slipped away easily enough from your guard. If you're held so loosely, why don't you escape and go to Roger?"

Elizabeth moved away from him but Brian caught her arm. "Do the Montgomery men hold such attraction for you? Which is it? The married one or the boy?"

"Miles is far from being a boy!" she snorted. "Sometimes age is deceptive." She ceased when she saw Brian's expression.

"Do you forget that I was there at the Montgomery estate? So it's Miles you've come to love. A good choice. He's a man with enough fire to match your own."

"What I feel for any Montgomery doesn't change what I feel for Roger."

"And that is? What keeps you from going to him? These Scots can't be too difficult to escape. You deceived Edmund for years."

She was silent for a moment. "It isn't just Miles. There's a peacefulness here that I've never known before. No one puts knives to my throat. There are no distant screams at Larenston. I can walk down a corridor and not have to slide from shadow to shadow."

"I saw a glimpse of that once," Brian whispered, "but Roger killed it and now I mean to kill him."

"Brian! You must rest and think what you're saying."

He ignored her. "Do you know where Raine Montgomery is?"

"No," she said, startled. "He's in a forest somewhere. I met a singer who'd been with him."

"Do you know where I can find her?"

"Why do you care where this Raine is? Has he done something to you?"

"I plan to beg him to teach me how to fight."

"Not to fight Roger?" she gasped, then smiled. "Brian, Roger will never fight you, and look at you. You aren't half the size of Roger and you look as if you've lost weight. Stay here and rest a few days and we'll—"

"Don't patronize me, Elizabeth. I know what I'm doing. Raine Montgomery is strong and knows how to train. He'll teach me what I need to know."

"Do you really expect me to help you?" she asked angrily. "Do you honestly think I'd tell you where this Montgomery was even if I knew? I'll not aid you in your madness."

"Elizabeth," he said softly. "I came to say goodbye. I have waited in these woods for weeks, waiting for a time to see you, but you're always heavily guarded. Now that I have seen you I can leave. I will fight Roger and one of us will die."

"Brian, please, you have to reconsider."

As if he were an old man, he kissed her forehead.

"Live in peace, my little sister, and remember me kindly."

Elizabeth was too stunned to reply, but as Brian turned away, Scotsmen began to drop from the trees. Stephen Montgomery, sword drawn, planted himself before Brian Chatworth.

Chapter 12

"DO NOT HURT HIM," ELIZABETH SAID HEAVILY, WITHOUT the least fear that Stephen would harm her young brother.

Stephen caught her tone and resheathed his sword. "Go with my men and they'll feed you," he said to Brian.

With one last look at Elizabeth, Brian left the clearing, surrounded by MacArrans.

Elizabeth stood glaring at Stephen for a moment and in that time she understood a great deal.

Stephen had the courtesy to look somewhat embarrassed. With a sheepish grin, he leaned against a tree, took the dirk from the sheath on his calf and began to whittle on a stick. "Miles knows nothing about this," he began.

"You used me as bait to capture my brother, didn't you?" she blurted.

"I guess you could say that. He's been in the woods for days, skulking about, living on bare sustenance, and we were curious as to who he was and what he wanted. Twice while you were with Miles he came near but my men frightened him away. We decided to let you go to him. You were never alone; my men and I were directly overhead, swords and arrows drawn."

Elizabeth sat down on a large rock. "I don't much like being used like this."

"Would you rather we killed him on sight? A few years ago a lone Englishman couldn't have ridden onto MacArran land and lived to tell of it. But the boy seemed so . . . frantic that we wanted to find out about him."

She considered this a moment. She didn't like what he'd done but she knew he was right. "And now that you have him, what do you plan to do with him?" Her head came up. "Does Bronwyn know of this cat-and-mouse game of yours?"

She wasn't sure, but she believed Stephen's mouth whitened a bit. "As I love life, I am thankful she does not," he said with great feeling. "Bronwyn does not do things in secret—at least not too many anyway. She would have hauled the boy into Larenston and Miles . . ." He broke off.

"Miles's hatred of the Chatworths runs deep," she finished.

"Only of the men." He smiled. "Roger Chatworth caused our sister's death and Miles isn't likely to forgive that. You've only seen the side of him he shows to women. When confronted with a man who's hurt a woman, he is unreasonable."

"You were sure Brian was a Chatworth then?"

"He has that look about him."

Elizabeth was quiet for a moment. Brian *had* had some of Roger's look just now, a look of defiance and anger, covered by an expression of I-don't-care. "You heard what Brian said. Can we hold him here and keep him away from Roger?"

"I think he might go mad. He doesn't look too far from that now."

"No," she said heavily. "He doesn't." She looked up at Stephen expectantly.

"I believe I'll do just what Brian asks: I'll take him to my brother Raine."

"No!" Elizabeth said, standing up. "Raine Montgomery will kill him. Didn't he attack Roger?"

"Elizabeth," Stephen soothed. "Raine will take to the boy because Brian helped Mary. If Raine is nothing else, he's fair. And besides that," Stephen said with a little smile, "my brother will work Brian so hard the young man won't have time to hate. Within three days Brian will be so tired, all he'll think of is sleeping."

She studied him a moment. "Why should you help a Chatworth? Mary was your sister also."

"I thought you believed we Montgomerys lied about your brother's involvement in her death."

"If Miles killed a stranger's sister, would you hate your brother without so much as asking Miles why? Perhaps Roger was involved, but perhaps there were reasons for his actions. I do not and will not hate either of my brothers without just cause."

"Well said." Stephen nodded. "I do not bear any

love for your brother Roger for what he's done, but my quarrel is with him, not with his family. My brothers don't feel the same way, which is why Gavin was so rude to you. To him family is everything."

"And is Raine the same way? Will he hate Brian on sight?"

"Perhaps, which is why I'm going with Brian. I'll be able to talk to Raine, and if I know my brother, he'll end by adopting your young Brian." He tossed the stick away and resheathed his knife. "And now I must be off. It will take us days to find my brother."

"Now?" she asked. "You'll leave before Bronwyn and Miles return from the hunt?"

"Oh yes." He grimaced. "I don't relish being around when my lovely wife finds out I tricked her into leaving Larenston so I could tend to this English trespasser alone."

"Or Miles," she said, eyes sparkling. "I don't believe he'll take this calmly."

Stephen groaned, making her laugh. "You, Montgomery, are a coward," she pointed out.

"Of the worst sort," he agreed readily, then turned serious. "Will you pray for me while I'm gone? Perhaps if Raine and Brian get along, we can make some progress in ending this war."

"I would like that," she answered. "Brian is a sweet, gentle man and Roger loves him very much. Stephen," she said in a low voice, "if I ask you a question, will you answer me honestly?"

"I owe you that much."

"Has anyone seen Roger?"

"No," Stephen answered. "He's disappeared. The MacGregors are looking for him and my men are always alert. We nearly lost you once and it won't happen again. But no, so far there is no sign of Roger Chatworth."

For a moment they stood quietly, looking at each other. A few months ago this man was her enemy, as were all men. With one step forward, she came close to him, reached up and put her hand to his cheek.

Stephen seemed to understand the full impact of the honor she was bestowing upon him. He caught her hand, kissed the palm. "We Montgomerys are heart-breakers," he said with dancing eyes. "We'll end this feud with love words instead of swords."

She pulled away from him as if she were insulted, but her laughter escaped. "I will indeed pray for you. Now go before my Miles finds you and gives you a good thrashing."

He lifted one eyebrow at that. "Poor little brother, when some woman decides she owns him." With that he left her alone in the clearing.

Elizabeth sat alone for quite some time and now that she was listening carefully to the sounds around her, she could hear the MacArrans. There were still two men in the trees above her. Far off she could hear Kit's laughter and Tam's deep rumbling answer.

In the last months her senses had dulled greatly. Before her swam the angry face of Brian and she knew that once she, too, had felt such hatred. She hoped with all her being that Stephen would be able to take some of Brian's hate away, or perhaps this Raine Montgomery could do it.

With a heavy heart, she returned to the ruins and the laughter of Kit. In a few days, she'd have Miles's anger to deal with and that would take her mind off her problems.

Bronwyn returned to Larenston the next day and went first to her five-month-old son, Alexander. The child had a wet nurse as Bronwyn was too often away to feed him, but she made sure the boy knew who his mother was. As she was contentedly cuddling her son, Rab at her feet, Elizabeth told her about Brian and how Stephen had taken him to Raine.

For a moment, Bronwyn's eyes flashed. "Damn him!" she muttered but calmed when Alex let out a yowl. "Hush, love," she cooed. When Alexander was quiet, she looked back at Elizabeth. "I don't like that he used you. He should have brought your brother here. Stephen forgets that Brian Chatworth released me from your brother's clutches. I wouldn't have harmed the boy."

"I think Stephen was more concerned about Miles— that *he* might harm Brian." Elizabeth leaned forward and caressed Alex's silky head.

Bronwyn's keen eyes missed nothing. "And when is your child due?" she asked evenly.

Elizabeth met Bronwyn's eyes.

Bronwyn stood, carried her son to his cradle. "Morag told me you've had no flow since you've been here. You've not been ill?"

"Not at all. I wasn't sure what was wrong with me at first, but it didn't take long to understand. Who have you told?"

"No one. Not even Stephen. Especially not Stephen. No doubt he'd want to celebrate. Are you planning to marry Miles?"

Elizabeth tucked the soft plaid around Alex's feet. "He hasn't asked me, but even if he did, there is more between us than marrying and having babies. Roger won't give up merely because I become a Montgomery. He'd have to know I go of my own free will and that I wasn't forced."

"And would Miles have to force you?" Bronwyn asked quietly.

Elizabeth smiled. "You know as well as I that he's forced me in nothing. But I don't think Miles would like marriage to me. I'd demand fidelity from my husband and Miles Montgomery doesn't know the meaning of the word."

"I wouldn't underestimate any of the Montgomery men," Bronwyn answered. "They may seem to be an arrogant, inflexible lot but there's more to them than pretty faces and virile bodies."

"They are indeed that." Elizabeth laughed as they left the room.

The next day Bronwyn returned to the hunt and it was while Elizabeth was being a helpless maiden in distress and Kit was saving her from a three-headed, fire-breathing dragon that Elizabeth suddenly stopped.

"Elizabeth!" Kit said impatiently, wooden sword brandished over his head.

She couldn't explain what was wrong with her but chills were covering her body. "Miles," she whispered. "Here!" she said to the woman holding Alex. "Take care of Kit."

With that she tore toward the stairs, down and out into the courtyard. When she reached the stables, she had her hand on a saddle before Douglas was beside her.

"I can't let you leave," Douglas said, regret in his voice.

"Out of my way, you fool," she spat at him. "Miles is in trouble and I'm going to him."

Douglas didn't waste time asking her how she knew this since no messenger had come from the hunting party, but he stepped out of the stables, gave three low whistles and in seconds two of his brothers were there.

Elizabeth wasn't used to saddling her own horse and it was a slow process, but the men didn't help her. Douglas checked the tightness of her cinch before catching her foot and practically tossing her into the saddle. Elizabeth didn't even flinch when he touched her.

As they started off, Elizabeth gave no thought as to where she was going but cleared her mind, visualized Miles and set off at a frightening pace, Douglas, Jarl and Francis behind her. The four horses thundered down the narrow, steep-sided road out of Larenston, turned right and headed along the cliff.

Elizabeth had no fear of the road nor did she worry about the men behind her. Once she was again on flat land, she paused only seconds. To the left was the MacGregors, and to the right was unknown territory. She kicked her horse to the right, somehow knowing this was the way.

One of the men yelled at her in warning once and she flattened herself against the horse's sweaty neck as she barely missed being hit by a tree branch. Other than that, the men were silent as they rode hard to keep up with her.

After a long time of riding, Rab came bounding from the underbrush, barking hard. He seemed to expect

Elizabeth and had come to guide her the last part of the way.

Elizabeth was forced to slow her horse to a brisk walk as the four of them and Rab made their way through thick undergrowth into a clump of trees so dense the sunlight was hidden.

Rab began to bark again before the people came into view. Bronwyn and her men were standing in a group, looking down at something on the ground. Sir Guy was kneeling.

Bronwyn turned at her dog's bark and lifted surprised eyes to Elizabeth.

Her horse was still moving as Elizabeth slid to the ground and ran forward, pushing through the people.

Miles lay on the ground, eyes closed, his entire body covered in blood. His clothes were torn and she could see great gashes in his flesh, in his left thigh, in his right side.

She pushed Sir Guy away, knelt, pulled Miles's head into her lap and began to wipe the blood from his face with the hem of her skirt.

"Wake up, Montgomery," she said firmly with no sympathy or pity in her voice. "Wake up and look at me."

It seemed an eternity before Miles's lashes fluttered. When he did look at her he gave a little smile, let his eyes shut again. "Angel," he whispered and was silent.

"Water," Elizabeth said to the stunned faces over her. "I'll need water to wash his wounds, and is there a crofter's house near here?" Bronwyn only had time to nod before Elizabeth continued. "Go and clear the place out. Take the crofters to Larenston but leave me alone with him. Send Morag and her herbs and I'll need sharp steel needles and thread. Guy! Fetch a big plaid and we'll carry him to the hut. Well!" she snapped. "Get busy, all of you."

Instantly, men went off in all directions.

Bronwyn flashed Elizabeth a quick grin. "Are you sure you aren't a Scot?" With that she was off toward Larenston.

Elizabeth, alone for a few moments, held Miles. "You'll be all right, Montgomery," she whispered. "I'll see to it."

She wasted no more time on sentimentality but took the dagger that lay on the ground beside him and began cutting away his clothes in order to examine his wounds. There seemed to be more blood on him than a man's body could hold.

Rab came up to her as she was slicing away Miles's shirt. "Where's the blood from, Rab?" she asked. "Go and find what did this to Miles."

With two great barks, the dog left them alone.

To Elizabeth's relief there was only the one gash on Miles's upper body, and that wasn't deep but would have to be sewn. There were several long bloody cuts on his left arm but nothing serious. His legs were another matter. The wound on his thigh was deep and ugly and there were more cuts on one ankle.

She shifted him once to try to see his underside to look for wounds.

With a groan of pain, Miles opened his eyes, looked at her. "You'll have to get on top, Elizabeth, or else I'll bleed all over you," he said with a glance down at his bare body.

"Quiet!" she commanded. "Save your strength to get well."

As she spoke, Rab began pulling the carcass of an enormous, long-tusked boar into the clearing. The dead animal's face was covered in blood and there were several knife wounds in its side.

"So you won a fight with a boar," she said in disgust, tenderly wrapping him in the plaid she wore about her shoulders. "I don't guess it occurred to you not to ride out alone."

Before she could say another word, Rab dragged another boar carcass to lie beside the first one, this one also slashed.

Elizabeth began to wipe Miles's dirty face. "We're going to take you not far from here where it's warm and where it'll be quiet. Now I want you to rest."

Sir Guy with a man and woman came thrashing through the undergrowth, their arms slung with great heavy plaids.

"There's a strong barley broth on the fire," the woman said, "and oatcakes on the hearth. Bronwyn'll send more plaids if ye need them."

Sir Guy, kneeling, pulled the plaid off Miles's body and studied the wounds, looking up in surprise when Rab pulled a third boar carcass into the clearing.

"How many of them are there?" Elizabeth asked.

"Five," Sir Guy said. "His horse must have thrown him into a family of them. He had only his sword and the little dagger but he killed all five of them and managed to drag himself here. Rab led us to the boars but ran off before we found Lord Miles."

"He came to get me," Elizabeth said. "Can you carry Miles?"

Without much show of effort, Sir Guy carefully picked up his young master as if he were a child.

Instantly, his wounds began to renew their vigor in bleeding.

"Careful!" Elizabeth half screeched, and the look Guy gave her made her quiet.

Sir Guy led the way as he carried Miles through the trees toward the crofters' cottage, and laid him gently on a cot against one wall. It was a tiny, dark, one-room hut, the open hearth the only source of light. There was a crude table and two chairs and no other furniture besides the cot. A pot of water simmered over the fire. Immediately, Elizabeth dipped clean cloths that had been left for her in the water and started washing Miles. Sir Guy lifted him, helped her remove the shreds of his clothes from under him. To Elizabeth's relief, there were no more wounds on the back of him other than minor cuts and bruises.

She had him almost washed when Morag and Bronwyn arrived together, Morag carrying a big basket of medicines.

"I can't see as well as I used to," Morag said, looking down at Miles, nude, the two wounds gaping redly. "One of ye will have to tend to him."

"I will," Elizabeth said quickly. "Tell me what to do and I can do it."

Sewing a man's flesh was far different from sewing on cloth, Elizabeth soon discovered. The muscles of her body tightened each time she slid the needle inside Miles's skin.

Miles lay still, not moving, barely breathing, his body pale from the loss of blood as Elizabeth stitched. Bronwyn threaded the needles, cut and helped to knot.

When Elizabeth finished at last, she was trembling.

"Drink this," Bronwyn ordered.

"What is it?" Elizabeth asked.

"Lord only knows. I learned long ago not to ask what Morag puts into her concoctions. Whatever it is, it'll taste vile but it will make you feel better."

Elizabeth drank the brew, leaning against the wall, her eyes on Miles. When Morag started to hold a cup to Miles's pale lips, she thrust her mug at Bronwyn and went to him.

"Drink this," she whispered, holding his head. "You must get your strength back."

His eyes moved, his lashes barely parted as he looked up at her. "Worth it," he whispered as he drank Morag's brew.

Morag gave a derisive snort. "He'll stay on his back for a year if ye pamper him."

"Well, let him!" Elizabeth snapped back.

Bronwyn laughed. "Come sit down, Elizabeth, and rest. I want to know how you knew Miles had been wounded. We'd only just found him when you rode up."

Elizabeth sat on the floor by Miles's head, leaned back and shrugged. She had no idea how she'd known he was injured—but she had.

Her moments of rest were short-lived. Seemingly seconds later, Morag had something else for Elizabeth to feed Miles.

Night came and Bronwyn went back to Larenston. Elizabeth sat beside Miles, watching him, knowing that he didn't sleep, while Morag nodded in a chair.

"What . . ." Miles whispered. "What is Raine's wife like?"

Elizabeth thought he was delirious since she'd never met Raine or his wife.

"Singer," Miles said. "Pagnell."

Those words were enough of a key to make her understand. She was surprised that one of the Montgomery lords would marry a lowly little singer. Elizabeth told Miles the story of meeting Alyxandria Blackett, of hearing her extraordinary voice and later her attempt to rescue the singer from Pagnell's clutches —which led to Elizabeth's own capture.

Miles smiled at that and searched for her hand. Still touching her, he fell asleep just as the sun began to rise.

Morag woke and began to mix another batch of herbs, dried mushrooms and several things Elizabeth didn't recognize.

Together they changed the bloody bandages on Miles's wounds and Morag applied warm, wet, herb-filled poultices over the sewn cuts.

Miles slept again in the afternoon and Elizabeth left the little cottage for the first time. Sir Guy sat outside under a tree and only looked up in question when he saw her.

"He's resting," she said.

Sir Guy nodded and stared off into space. "Not many boys could fall into a pack of five boars and come out alive," he said with pride.

There were tears in Elizabeth's eyes as she placed a trembling hand on the giant's shoulder. "I will do all in my power to see that he gets well."

Sir Guy nodded, not looking at her. "You have no reason to help him. We've treated you badly."

"No," she answered. "I have been given more than courtesy; I have been given love." With that she turned away toward the stream that ran through the MacArran land. She washed, tidied her hair, sat down for a moment's rest, wrapped in her plaid, and when she woke it was night. Sir Guy sat not far away from her.

Sleep-dazed, she hurried back to the cottage.

Miles was awake and the frown he wore disappeared when he saw her.

"There she is," Morag scolded. "Now maybe you'll drink some of this."

"Elizabeth," Miles said.

She went to him, held his head while he drank nearly a cup of the brew and continued to hold him until he fell asleep.

Chapter 13

"You will not walk," Elizabeth said to Miles with steely firmness. "I have lost too many nights' sleep in trying to heal your wounds without watching you break them open."

He looked up at her with meltingly soft eyes. "Please, Elizabeth."

For a moment she almost relented, but stopped herself with a laugh. "You are a treacherous man. Now be still or I'll tie you to the bed."

"Oh?" he said, eyebrows raised.

Elizabeth blushed at what he was obviously thinking. "Behave yourself! I want you to eat more. You'll never get well if you don't eat."

He caught her hand and, with surprising strength, pulled her down beside him. Or perhaps it was that Elizabeth had no will to resist him. He was half sitting up, propped on pillows against the corner of the room, his legs on the cot before him. Carefully, she stretched beside him. It had been four days since Miles had been gored but his youth and natural resistance had made him recover quickly. He was still weak, still in pain, but he was starting to heal.

"Why have you stayed with me?" he asked. "One of Bronwyn's women could have tended me."

"And have her jump in bed with you and tear your stitches?" she asked indignantly.

"I'll tear my stitches if you make me laugh. How could I have touched another woman when you're so close?"

"When I'm gone, I'm sure you'll manage to gather your courage."

His hand tangled in her hair, pulled her head back and his mouth took hers possessively. "Haven't you learned yet that you're mine?" he half growled. "When are you going to admit that?"

He didn't give her a chance to answer as he kissed her again, and much of the worry Elizabeth'd felt in the last days went into that kiss to make it one of desperation.

The touch of cold steel against Miles's throat made them break apart. Instinctively, he reached for his own sword but met only bare flesh under the plaid he wore.

Over them stood Roger Chatworth, his eyes full of hate, his sword pressing against the vein in Miles's neck.

"Do not," Elizabeth said, moving away from Miles. "Do not harm him."

"I would like to kill all the Montgomerys," Roger Chatworth said.

Miles, in one quick motion, moved sideways, caught Chatworth's wrist.

"No!" Elizabeth screamed and clung to her brother's arm.

Miles's bandages began to redden.

"He's hurt," Elizabeth said. "Would you kill a man who can't fight back?"

Roger turned his full attention to her. "Have you become one of them? Have the Montgomerys poisoned you against your own blood relations?"

"No, Roger, of course not." She tried to remain calm. There was such a wild look in Roger's eyes that she feared to anger him. Miles lay against the wall, panting, but she knew that at any moment he'd leap again and tear his wounds further. "Have you come for me?"

There was a sudden hush in the little room as both men watched her. She had to leave with Roger. If she did not, he'd kill Miles. She knew that very well. Roger was tired, angry, beyond all rational thinking.

"It will be good to go home," she said, forcing a smile.

"Elizabeth!" Miles warned.

She ignored him. "Come, Roger, what are you waiting for?" Her heart was pounding so hard she could barely hear her own voice.

"Elizabeth!" Miles shouted at her, his hand clutching at the hole in his chest.

For a moment Roger looked from one to the other, hesitating.

"I'm growing impatient, Roger! Haven't I been away long enough?" She turned on her heel to leave, paused at the door. Her eyes stayed on Roger's, not daring to look at Miles. She couldn't risk even one look at him or she'd lose her resolve.

Slowly, puzzled, Roger began to follow her. A horse waited obediently not far from the cottage. Elizabeth kept her eyes on the animal, not daring to look around because she knew she'd see the body of Sir Guy. Only his death would have kept the giant from protecting his master.

Another shout, stone-shaking, came from the cottage. "ELIZABETH!!"

Swallowing the lump in her throat, Elizabeth allowed Roger to help her on his horse.

"We must have food," Roger said and turned away from her.

"Roger!" she yelled after him. "If you harm him I—" she began and saw that he was ignoring her. She dismounted in a flash and was after him—but not in time.

Roger Chatworth ran his sword through Miles's arm and as Miles lay there bleeding, Roger said, "Raine's wife spared my life and it's to her that you owe your filthy life now." He turned to Elizabeth in the doorway. "Get on the horse or I'll finish the job, if he doesn't bleed to death as it is."

Trembling, feeling very ill, Elizabeth left the cottage and mounted the horse. Within seconds, Roger was behind her and they set off at a grueling pace.

Elizabeth sat before her embroidery frame, working on an altar cover of St. George slaying the dragon. In one corner was a boy who looked remarkably like Kit and St. George . . . the saint had some of the look of

Miles Montgomery. Elizabeth stopped for a moment as the child in her womb kicked her.

Alice Chatworth sat across from her, a mirror held to reflect the unscarred half of her face. "I was so beautiful then," Alice was saying. "Absolutely no man could resist me. All of them were ready to lay down their lives for me. All I had to do was hint at something I wanted and it was given to me."

She switched the mirror to the misshapen side of her face. "Until the Montgomerys did this!" she hissed. "Judith Revedoune was jealous of my beauty. She is such an ugly, freckled, red-haired thing that she was worried over my dear Gavin's love. And well she should have been."

Elizabeth gave an exaggerated yawn, ignored Alice's look of hate and turned to Roger, who was standing by the fireplace, mug of wine in hand, his face brooding. "Roger, would you like to go for a walk with me in the gardens?"

As usual, Roger looked at her stomach before he looked back at her face.

"No, I have to talk to my steward," he half mumbled, his eyes searching her face.

She could feel what he wanted to say, what he'd said many, many times: You've changed.

She'd been back with her brother and her "family" for two weeks and it brought home to her how much she *had* changed in her five months with the Montgomerys. The time had not been enough to make any changes in the Chatworth household, but it was enough for Elizabeth to have started the makings of a new person.

For all her insistence that Roger was different from Edmund, she saw that Roger had actually not enforced his own beliefs within his household. In many ways, the Chatworth house was the same as when Edmund was alive. The reason Roger could easily have Alice live with him was that he was oblivious to her. Roger lived with such inner turmoil, with all his love and care given to Elizabeth and Brian, that he was truly unaware of a great deal that went on around him.

Elizabeth had no more than dismounted her horse, tired after days of travel, when two of Roger's men, who had once been with Edmund, began to make snide comments to her. They hinted that they could hardly wait to catch her alone.

Elizabeth's first reaction had been fear. It had been as if she'd never left the Chatworth estates. Her mind raced over her repertoire of debilitating tricks to use on the men. But her thoughts went back to Sir Guy and how she'd broken his toes, how he'd hobbled for weeks—and later she'd sat with him, saw tears of worry gathering in his eyes over a man they both loved.

She would not return to her skulking, fearful ways. She'd come a long way in conquering her fear of men and she wasn't going to throw all she'd learned away.

She'd turned to Roger and demanded that he send the men away immediately.

Roger'd been very surprised and had quickly hustled her out of the stables. He'd tried to patronize her but Elizabeth wouldn't listen to him. The idea that his dear little sister would talk back to him shocked as well as hurt him. To his mind, he'd just rescued her from a hellhole and she was ungratefully complaining.

For the first time in her life, Elizabeth told her brother the whole truth about Edmund. Roger's face had drained of blood, he'd staggered backward into a chair and looked as if someone had beaten him. All these years he'd thought he'd protected his dear little sister but, in truth, she'd lived in hell. He had no idea Edmund had summoned her from her convent whenever Roger left the estates. He didn't know that she'd had to defend herself from his men.

By the time Elizabeth finished, Roger was ready to kill the men in the stables.

Roger Chatworth's fury was something to be reckoned with. Within three days, he'd put fear in the hearts of his household. Many men were dismissed and if a man so much as looked at Elizabeth with slanted eyes, she went to Roger. No more was she going to stand for such insolence. Before, she'd not known how a lady should be treated, as her only experience was with Edmund, but now she'd had five months in a place where she didn't have to be afraid of walking in a garden alone.

Roger had been taken aback by her demands and she realized how she and Brian had always protected him. Roger could be so kind and at the same time so cruel. She tried only once to talk to him about the Montgomerys, but Roger'd exploded with such hatred, she feared for his life.

Since it had been months since he'd seen her, he quickly noticed the changes in her body, remarked that she'd put on weight. Elizabeth had put her chin in the air and, with no regret, stated that she carried Miles Montgomery's child.

She had expected rage—she was prepared for rage but the deep, deep hurt in Roger's eyes threw her off balance.

"Go. Leave me," he'd whispered and she obeyed.

Alone in her room, Elizabeth'd cried herself to sleep as she had every night since leaving Miles. Would Miles realize she'd gone with Roger to save her lover? Or would Miles hate her? What would they tell Kit about where Elizabeth had gone? She lay on her bed and thought of all the people she'd come to care about in Scotland.

She longed to send a message to someone in Scotland but there was no one she could trust to deliver it. But yesterday, as she took her afternoon walk, an old woman she'd never seen before offered her a basket of bread. She started to refuse it until the woman lifted the cloth and showed a MacArran cockade. Elizabeth grabbed the basket quickly and the old woman was gone before Elizabeth could thank her. Greedily, she tore into the basket.

There was a message from Bronwyn saying she well understood why Elizabeth'd returned with Roger—but Miles didn't. Sir Guy had been hit with three arrows but they thought he'd live. While Miles was untended, he'd gone into a rage, torn all his stitches apart. When Morag found him he was in a fever and for three days they didn't believe he'd live. Stephen had returned from Raine's outlaw camp as soon as he heard Miles had been injured. He bore the news that Raine was taking young Brian under his wing and Stephen had every hope of there soon being peace between the two families. Bronwyn added that Miles was recovering slowly and he refused to mention Elizabeth's name.

Today, as Elizabeth thought of that last sentence, her skin grew cold, making her shiver.

"You should have a cloak," Roger said from behind her.

"No," she murmured, "my plaid is enough."

"Why do you flaunt that thing in front of me?" Roger exploded. "Isn't it enough that you carry a Montgomery within you? Do you have to slap me in the face every time I see you?"

"Roger, I want this hatred to end. I want—"

"You want to be my enemy's whore!" he snarled.

With one quick angry look she turned away from him.

He caught her arm, his eyes soft as he looked at her. "Can you see this from my side? I spent months in hell looking for you. I went to Raine Montgomery to ask where you were, yet he drew a sword on me. If his new wife hadn't stepped between us I'd be dead now. I went to the king on my knees and do you think that was easy? I bear no love for the man since he's fined me so heavily for what happened to Mary Montgomery, but for you I'd have gone on my knees before the devil."

He paused, put his hands on both her arms. "And getting in and out of Scotland was no easy task either, yet when I found you you were cuddled beside Montgomery as if you wanted to become a part of him. And the playacting you did! I felt as if I were the enemy because I was rescuing my own sister from a man who'd held her captive and taken her virtue. Explain all this to me, Elizabeth," he whispered.

She leaned her head forward to touch his chest. "How can I? How can I tell you what has happened to me in the last few months? I've seen love and—"

"Love!" he said. "Do you think that if a man takes you to his bed, he loves you? Has Montgomery sworn undying love to you? Has he asked to make a Chatworth his wife?"

"No, but—" she began.

"Elizabeth, you know so little of men. You were a pawn in this feud. Don't you know that the Montgomerys are laughing because a Chatworth bears a Montgomery child? They'll think they've won."

"Won!" she spat at him, pulling away. "I hate this all being thought of as a game. What should I tell my child, that he was a chess piece, used by two families in their silly war?"

"Silly? How can you say that when Brian is out there somewhere, possibly hating me because of the Montgomerys?"

She hadn't told him of seeing Brian in Scotland. "Did it ever occur to you, Roger, that perhaps *you* caused Brian to leave? I would like to hear your side of what happened to Mary Montgomery."

He turned away from her. "I was drunk. It was a hideous . . . accident." He turned back, his eyes pleading. "I can't bring the woman back and the king has punished me more than enough with his fines. Brian has left me and you return from my enemy bloated with his child, and instead of the love you once gave me, now all you do is question me, doubt me. What more punishment do you intend for me?"

"I'm sorry, Roger," she said softly. "Perhaps I have changed. I don't know if Miles loves me. I don't know if he'd want to marry me to give our child a name, but I do know that I love him and if he asked me, I'm sure I'd follow him wherever he led."

Only Roger's eyes showed the pain he felt at her words. "How could you turn against me so completely? Is this man so good in bed that your screams of pleasure make you forget the love I bear you and have always had for you? Does five months with him wipe out eighteen years with me?"

"No, Roger. I love you. I will always love you, but I want you both."

He smiled at that. "How very young you are, Elizabeth. You want a man who, I hear, is also wanted by half the women of England. You want a man who takes you to his bed, gets you with child and never speaks of marriage. And what kind of marriage would it be? Will you care for all his bastards as you have for his eldest son?"

"What do you know of Kit?"

"I know a great deal about my enemies. Miles Montgomery likes women. You are one of many to him and I respect the man for at least not lying to you and saying you were going to be his one and only love."

He touched her arm. "Elizabeth, if you want a husband, I can find someone for you. I know several men who'd take you bearing another man's child, and they'd be good to you. With this youngest Montgomery you'd be miserable inside a year."

"Perhaps," she said, trying to think rationally. Maybe Miles's hands on her had made her lose reason. He'd always been kind to her, but then he'd been kind to serving girls. If she did desert her brother for a Montgomery, Roger would hate her, and what would she feel for Miles years from now? What if, as a practical joke, someone else "gave" him a pretty young girl? Would he decide she belonged to him also? Would he bring her home to Elizabeth, smiling, expecting her to care for the girl as she did for his bastard children?

"Let me find someone for you. I'll bring many men for your approval and you can choose who you want. At least look at them. If you want to remain unmarried, you can."

She looked at him with love. He'd be laughed at for allowing his sister to bear a child out of wedlock. Some would say she should be killed if she refused to wed. Roger had suffered much disgrace over the last few years, yet he was willing to risk more for her sake.

At her smile, he grinned, and for the first time he looked as if he had a reason for living.

"Yes, I'll look at your men," she said from her heart. She would try with all her might to fall in love with one of them. She'd have a kind, loving husband, children to love and her brothers, because somehow she'd reunite Brian and Roger.

Elizabeth learned a great deal about love in the next few days. Never, before she met Miles, had she had any idea what love was. She'd never even considered loving a man, but then Miles came along and changed that. Within five months of his patience and humor he'd made her love him. She knew she'd always have a soft spot for Miles but there were many men who were good and kind in the world. All she had to do was fall in love with one of them and it would solve everything.

But Elizabeth underestimated herself.

Roger began parading men before her like so many studs ready to service her. There were tall men, short men, thin men, fat men, ugly men, men so handsome you merely gaped at them, swaggering men, bold men,

men who made her laugh, one who sang beautifully. On and on they came.

At first Elizabeth was flattered by their attentions, but after just a few days, her old fears began to return. A man touched her shoulder and she jumped high, put her hand on her eating dagger at her side. After a week, she was finding excuses to remain in her room, or else she was always in Roger's company.

Then suddenly, Roger left the estates. He said nothing to her but rode out with eight men at a furious pace. A servant said Roger'd received a message from a dirty, black-toothed man and within seconds Roger'd left. The message was tossed into the fire.

Elizabeth was close to tears knowing that there were eleven male guests below and she was their hostess. She couldn't talk to one man with any coherence because she was always concerned with where the other men were. All Miles's months of patient training were disappearing. Once she brought a brass vase down on the head of a man who'd dared to walk up behind her.

With her skirts flying about her, she fled to her room and refused to return to the hall.

She lay on her bed a long time and all she could remember was Miles. Every time she met a man, she compared him to Miles. Some utterly splendid man would be introduced to her and all she'd think was, he moves his hands too quickly or some other such nonsense. And one night, she'd allowed a man to kiss her in the garden. She'd caught herself just before she brought her heel down on his little toes, but she couldn't keep herself from wiping her mouth with the back of her hand. The poor man'd been terribly insulted.

Elizabeth tried very hard, but not a single man even interested her. As the days passed, she wished she could see Bronwyn and ask advice. She was considering writing a letter when the bottom dropped out of her world.

A haggard, wasted Roger returned bearing the mutilated body of Brian.

Elizabeth greeted him but Roger merely looked through her as he tenderly carried Brian's body upstairs and locked himself in a room. For two days he stayed locked inside with Brian's body and when he emerged, his eyes were sunken and black.

"Your Montgomerys did that," he said hoarsely as he strode past Elizabeth and Alice.

They buried Brian that afternoon but Roger didn't reappear. Elizabeth planted roses on the grave and shed tears for both her brothers.

Alice hounded Elizabeth mercilessly, screeching that the Montgomerys should die for all they'd done. She was fascinated by lamps full of hot oil and waved them around maniacally. She said Elizabeth's child would be born with the mark of Satan and would be cursed for all eternity.

One by one, the male guests left the bereaved and somewhat insane household and Elizabeth was left alone with her sister-in-law.

In early March a messenger wearing full regalia came from the king.

It was a day before the men Elizabeth sent out could find Roger where he'd been—alone in a shepherd's stone hut. He looked to be a skeleton of himself, his cheeks gaunt under a beard, his hair long and dirty, his eyes wild and frightening.

He silently read the message in Elizabeth's presence, then tossed it into the fireplace.

"Tell the king no," he said calmly before leaving the room.

Elizabeth could only gasp, and wonder what message the king had sent. With as much calmness as she could muster, she dismissed the king's men and sat down to wait. Whatever Roger had refused to do would no doubt soon be known to them when the king heard of the refusal. She put her hand on her growing belly and wondered if her child would live to worry about being called a bastard.

Chapter 14

Six days after the king's messenger had come and gone, Elizabeth was alone in the garden. She had not seen or heard from Roger in days and Brian's death was making Alice lose what sanity she had. It wasn't that the woman cared for Brian but it was the fact that a Montgomery had killed him. Elizabeth thought of this Raine with hatred.

A shadow moved across her path and involuntarily she gasped before looking up—into the dark, intense eyes of Miles Montgomery. His eyes contemptuously swept her up and down, made note of the ivory satin of her gown, the double rows of pearls, the blood-red ruby at her breast.

Elizabeth felt she wanted to drink in all of him, that she couldn't get enough of him. There were dark, faintly yellow shadows under his eyes and he was thinner. Obviously he wasn't fully recovered from his fever.

"Come," he said hoarsely.

Elizabeth didn't hesitate as she followed him through the garden and into the forest park of the Chatworth estates. Supposedly these boundaries were guarded, but somehow Miles had entered undetected.

He didn't speak to her, didn't look at her and it wasn't until they reached the two waiting horses that she realized what was wrong: He hated her. His rigid body, his cold eyes all screamed it.

She became rigid herself when they reached the horses. "Where are you taking me?"

He turned toward her. "The king has ordered us to marry. Your brother has refused the order. If we disobey, both your brother and I will be declared traitors and our lands confiscated." His eyes touched on the ruby. "You need have no fear. After the marriage I will return you to your precious brother, but even you would not like to have all the things that mean so much to you taken away."

He turned away from her. Elizabeth tried to mount her horse but her long skirt and trembling body made that impossible. Miles came up behind her and, touching her as little as possible, flung her into the saddle.

Elizabeth was too stunned, too much in a state of shock, to even think as they set off quickly to the north. Her eyes were so dry they burned and all she thought of was the way the horse's mane whipped in the wind.

They halted less than an hour later on the outskirts of a small village, before a pleasant little house beside a church. Miles dismounted, didn't look at her as she struggled to get down from her horse.

A priest opened the door to them. "So this is the lovely bride, Miles," he said. "Come along, I know how impatient you are."

As Miles strode ahead, ignoring Elizabeth, she ran after him, caught his arm. The look he gave her as he glanced from her hand to her face made her breath catch. She dropped her hand. "After this is over, could we talk?" she whispered.

"If it doesn't take too long," he said coolly. "My brother is waiting for me."

"No," she said, trying to regain her dignity. "I'll not keep you long." With that, she gathered her skirts and walked ahead of him.

The marriage was over in minutes. There were no witnesses from either family, only a few strangers who the priest knew. For all the feeling either participant put into the words, they could have been negotiating a grain contract.

When they were pronounced man and wife, Miles turned toward her and Elizabeth held her breath. "I believe we can talk in the vestry," was all he said. Chin up, Elizabeth led the way.

When they were alone in the room, he lazily leaned against the wall. "Now you have your chance to say what you want."

Her first impulse was to tell him where he could spend the rest of his life but she calmed herself. "I didn't know of the king's order that we marry. If I had I would not have refused. I would do a great deal to settle this feud."

"Even to sleeping with your enemy?" he taunted.

She gritted her teeth. "Roger has been very upset at Brian's death." For a moment her eyes flashed fire.

Miles's nostrils flared. "Perhaps you hadn't heard that Raine survived your brother's poison."

"Poison!" she gasped. "Now what do you accuse Roger of?"

"Not Roger," Miles said. "Your brother Brian poisoned Raine."

"Well, Brian certainly paid for the attempt! I hear Raine is a large man. Did he enjoy tearing my slight brother apart? Did he enjoy hearing Brian's frail bones snap?"

Miles eyes hardened. "I see that once again you have heard only one side. Did Roger say Raine killed Brian?"

"Not in so many words, but . . ."

Miles came away from the wall. "Ask him then. Have your perfect brother tell you the truth about who killed Brian Chatworth. Now, if you have nothing else to accuse me of, I must go."

"Wait!" she called. "Please, tell me the news. How is Sir Guy?"

Miles eyes turned black. "What the hell do you care? Since when have you cared about anyone except your treacherous brother? Guy nearly died from your brother's arrows. Perhaps he should practice his marksmanship. Another inch and he'd have reached Guy's heart."

"And Kit?" she whispered.

"Kit!" Miles said through clenched teeth. "Kit cried for three days after you left but now he won't even allow Philip's nurse in the same room. The nurse's name is Elizabeth."

"I never meant . . ." she began. "I love Kit."

"No, Elizabeth, you don't. We were nothing to you.

You repaid us all for holding you against your will. You are, after all, a Chatworth."

Her anger exploded in her. "I'll not stand for more of your insinuations! What was I supposed to do when my brother held a sword at your throat? Should I have stayed with you? He would have killed you! Can't you understand that I left with him in order to save your ungrateful life?"

"Am I supposed to believe that?" he said, low. "You stand before me dripping pearls, wearing a ruby that costs more than all I own and tell me you followed your brother in order to save me? What has made you think I'm stupid?"

"Tell me then," she shot back, "what should I have done?"

His eyes narrowed. "You claim your brother loves you so much, you should have told him you wanted to stay with me."

She threw up her hands at that. "Oh yes, that would have worked so well. Roger no doubt would have resheathed his sword and gone home docilely. Roger's temper is second only to yours. And, Montgomery, how was I to know you *wanted* me to remain with you?"

He was silent for a moment. "My wants have always been clear. I hear you have been sleeping with many men lately. I'm sure your marital status won't interfere with your activities, although my child will curb you for a while at least."

Very calmly, very slowly, Elizabeth stepped close to him and slapped him across the face.

Miles's head snapped to one side and when he looked back at her, his eyes were ablaze. With one quick, violent gesture he caught both her hands in one of his, pushed her back against the stone wall. His lips came down on hers hard, plundering.

Elizabeth reacted with all her pent-up desires and pushed her body into his hungrily.

His lips made a hot trail down her neck. "You love me, don't you, Elizabeth?"

"Yes," she murmured.

"How much?" he whispered, touching her earlobe with the tip of his tongue.

"Miles," she murmured, "please." Her hands were held against the wall, above her head, and she desperately wanted to put her arms around him. "Please," she repeated.

Abruptly, he pulled away from her, dropped her hands. "How does it feel to be turned down?" he said coldly, but a vein in his neck pounded. "How does it feel to love someone and be rejected? I pleaded with you to stay with me but you chose your brother. Now see if he can give you what you need. Goodbye, Elizabeth . . . Montgomery." With that he left the room, closing the door behind him.

For a long while Elizabeth was too weak to move, but she finally managed to make her way to a chair and sit on it. She was there, in a daze, when the priest entered, obviously agitated.

"Lord Miles had to leave but an escort awaits you outside. And this was left for you." When Elizabeth didn't react, the priest took her hand and closed it around something cold and heavy. "Take your time, dear, the men will wait."

It was several minutes before Elizabeth gathered her strength enough to stand. The object in her hand fell and clanged against the stone floor. Kneeling, she picked it up. It was a heavy gold ring, sized small enough to fit her hand, set with a large emerald that was incised with three Montgomery leopards.

Her first impulse was to toss the ring across the room, but with a grimace of resignation, she slipped it on her left hand and left the room to go to the guard waiting for her.

Roger met her a half-mile from the estate with an armed guard, swords drawn. She kicked her horse ahead to meet him.

"Death to all Montgomerys!" he cried.

Elizabeth grabbed his horse's bridle, succeeding in nearly pulling her arm from its socket and making Roger's horse rear. Both of them fought their horses for a moment.

"Why do you come riding with Montgomerys?" Roger bellowed.

"Because *I* am a Montgomery," she shouted back.

That statement successfully made Roger pause.

"How dare you not tell me of the king's order that I marry Miles!" she yelled at him. "What else have you lied to me about? Who killed my brother Brian?"

Roger's anger made his face turn red. "A Montgomery—" he began.

"No! I want the truth!"

Roger looked at the guard of men behind her as if he were planning their deaths.

"You tell me the truth here and now or I ride with them back to Scotland. I have just been married to a Montgomery and my child has every right to be raised as one."

Roger was breathing so hard, his chest was swelling

to barrel size. *"I* killed Brian," he shouted, then quietened. "I killed my own brother. Is that what you wanted to hear?"

Elizabeth had expected any answer but that one and she felt deflated. "Come back to the house, Roger, and we'll talk."

When they were alone in the solar, Elizabeth demanded that Roger tell her everything about the wars between the Chatworths and the Montgomerys. It wasn't an easy story to listen to and it was even harder to get Roger to tell the unbiased truth. Roger's view of the events was colored by his emotions.

In Scotland he'd seen a chance to marry Bronwyn MacArran, which would have been an excellent match for him. He did tell the woman a few falsehoods in order to make him appear more favorable to her—but what were a few lies in courtship? He'd even maneuvered Stephen Montgomery into fighting for her, but when Stephen won so easily Roger'd been enraged and attacked Stephen's back. Roger's humiliation at that had been too much to bear. He'd kidnapped Bronwyn and Mary merely to show the Montgomerys he was a power to be reckoned with. He never meant the women any harm.

"But you did harm Mary," Elizabeth said angrily.

"Brian wanted to marry her!" Roger defended himself. "After all I'd suffered at the hands of the Montgomerys and then Brian wanted to marry their old, plain, spiritless daughter. No one else in England would have her. Can you imagine how the Chatworths would have been laughed at?"

"Your pride sickens me. Brian lies dead rather than married. Did you get what you wanted?"

"No," he whispered.

"Neither have I." She sat down. "Roger, I want you to listen to me and listen well. The anger between the Montgomerys and Chatworths is over. My name is now Montgomery and my child will be a Montgomery. There will be no more fighting."

"If he tries again to take you—" Roger began.

"Take me!" She stood so fast the chair fell over. "This morning I begged Miles Montgomery to take me with him, but he refused. And I don't blame him! His family has lost someone they loved because of you, yet they have not killed you as probably they should have."

"Brian—"

"*You* killed Brian!" she shouted. "You have caused all of this and so help me God, if you so much as look at a Montgomery wrong, I'll take a sword to you myself." With that she left the room, nearly tripping over Alice who, as usual, was eavesdropping.

It was three days before Elizabeth could control her anger enough to even think. When she did think, she decided to look at what she had and do something with it. She was not going to have her child growing up as she had. She would probably never live with Miles so the closest thing to a father her child would have was going to be Roger.

She found Roger brooding before the fireplace and if she'd been a man, she would have pulled him out of his chair and given his backside a good swift kick.

"Roger," she said in a voice filled with honey, "I never noticed before, but you're getting a roll about your middle."

He put his hand to his flat stomach in surprise.

Elizabeth had to repress her smile. Roger was a very good-looking man and he was used to women noticing him. "Perhaps at your age," she continued, "a man should grow stout and his muscles weak."

"I'm not so old," he said, standing, sucking in his stomach.

"That was one thing I liked about Scotland. The men were so trim and fit."

He cocked his head at her. "What are you trying to do, Elizabeth?"

"I'm trying to keep you from living in a world of self-pity. Brian is dead and even if you fall in bed drunk every night for the rest of your life, you won't be able to bring him back. Now go get those lazy knights of yours and put them to work."

There was just a hint of a smile in his eyes. "Perhaps I do need some exercise," he said before leaving the room.

Six weeks later, Elizabeth was delivered of a very large, healthy baby boy whom she named Nicholas Roger. The child showed right away that he had inherited Gavin Montgomery's high cheekbones. Roger took to the child as if he were his own.

When she was up from her childbed, she began to work on making a home for little Nicholas. The first thing she did was order a guard near the baby at all times because Alice seemed to think the child was Judith and Gavin's and Elizabeth didn't trust the crazy woman's actions.

Nicholas was barely a month old when the first letter arrived from Judith Montgomery. It was a reserved letter inquiring after the child, saying Judith regretted not meeting Elizabeth but Bronwyn sang her praises. There was no mention of Miles.

Instantly, Elizabeth wrote back, raving about little Nick, saying he looked like Gavin and did Judith have any advice for a new mother?

Judith responded with a trunkful of exquisite baby clothes that her son, now ten months old, had outgrown.

Elizabeth, with a bit of defiance, showed the clothes to Roger and told him she'd started a correspondence with Judith Montgomery. Roger, sweat-drenched from the training field, said nothing—but Alice had a great deal to say, all of which was ignored by everyone.

It wasn't until Judith's fifth letter that she mentioned Miles and then seemingly only in passing. She said Miles was living with Raine, both men were without their wives and both men were miserable. That news made Elizabeth's whole week seem wonderful. She laughed at Nick and told him all about his father and his stepbrother Kit.

In September, Elizabeth sent Judith bulbs for her garden, and tucked away inside was a doublet, very adult-looking, that Elizabeth had made for Kit. Judith wrote back that Kit loved the doublet but both he and Miles were under the impression Judith had made it, which made Gavin laugh because Judith was always too busy to have the patience to sew.

Just after Christmas, Judith sent a long, serious letter. Raine and his wife had reunited and Miles had come to visit them before returning to his own estates. Judith was appalled at the change in Miles. He'd always been a loner but now he rarely spoke at all. And worst of all, his love of women seemed to have disappeared. The women were still drawn to him but he looked at them suspiciously and without the least concern. Judith had tried to talk to him but all he'd said was, "I'm a married man, remember? Husbands and wives should remain faithful to each other." With that, he laughed and walked away. Judith pleaded with Elizabeth to forgive Miles and she also warned Elizabeth that all the Montgomery men were insanely jealous.

Elizabeth replied with a long, long letter of anger. Miles was the only man who'd ever touched her; she'd begged him to take her with him when they were married but he refused. She told how she'd gone with Roger only to save Miles's life. She ranted for pages about what a fool she'd been to believe in her brother so blindly, but it was Miles who was keeping them apart, not her.

As soon as Elizabeth sent the letter off with the messenger, she wanted it back. In truth, she'd never met Judith Montgomery. If just a small portion of what Alice thought was wrong with the woman was right, Judith was a monster. She could hurt Elizabeth's chances with Miles.

The month before an answer came nearly drove Elizabeth mad. Roger kept asking her what was wrong. Alice did more than that—she sneaked into Elizabeth's room, found Judith's letters and read them, giving a detailed account to Roger afterward. When Roger merely turned away, Alice threw herself into a fit of rage which lasted nearly a whole day.

Judith's answer to Elizabeth was short: Miles would

be camping twenty miles from the Chatworth estate on
16 February, just outside the village of Westermore. Sir
Guy was willing to help Elizabeth in any way he could.

This letter Elizabeth slept with, carried about with
her and finally hid behind a stone in the fireplace. She
walked about on a cloud for a few days, then came
down. Why should she think Miles would want her
again? What could she do to make him want her?

"You are mine, Elizabeth," he'd said. "You were
given to me."

A plan began to form in her mind. No, she couldn't,
she thought. A giggle escaped her. She just really
wouldn't have the nerve. What if she "gave" herself to
Miles again?

As Elizabeth was in the solar conjuring delightful,
naughty visions, Alice was in Elizabeth's room, slipping
about and searching. When she found Judith's latest
letter, she took it to Roger, but this time he didn't turn
away. For the next few days there were three people in
the Chatworth house who were making plans—all in
direct opposition to each other's.

Chapter 15

"I MOST CERTAINLY WILL NOT!" SIR GUY SAID AS HE looked down at Elizabeth. His voice was low but it seemed louder than a shout.

"But Judith said you were willing to help me."

Sir Guy drew himself up to every inch of his extraordinary height. The scar across his face was a brilliant purplish red. "*Lady* Judith"—he emphasized the word —"had no idea you'd ask something so preposterous of me. How can you think of such a thing?" he said in a shaming voice.

Elizabeth turned away from him, gave a swift kick to the carpet on the ground. It had seemed such a good idea at the time: She'd get Sir Guy to deliver her to Miles, nude, rolled in a carpet. Perhaps the repeat of the scene would make him laugh and he'd forgive her. But Sir Guy refused to cooperate.

"Then what am I going to do?" she asked heavily. "I know he won't see me if I ask him straightforward."

"Lady Alyx sent her daughter to Lord Raine and the child acted as an emissary."

"Oh no! I'll not let Miles get his hands on Nick. Miles would hire another nurse and add the boy to his collection. I'd never see Miles *or* Nick again." She leaned against a tree and tried to think. If she did arrange a meeting with Miles she doubted if he'd listen to her. Her only real chance was to make his eyes darken with passion and then he wouldn't be able to help himself. Perhaps she could talk to him, after they'd made love.

As she was thinking, she toyed with her long black cloak, a lovely thing of velvet lined with black mink. It covered her from neck to feet. A new light came into her eyes as she looked back up at Sir Guy. "Can you arrange to give me some time alone with Miles? Not in his tent but in the woods? And I mean really alone! No doubt he'll call for his guard, but I want no one to come."

"I don't like that idea," Sir Guy said stubbornly. "What if there were some real danger?"

"True," she said sarcastically, "I might wrestle him to the ground and take a knife to his throat."

Sir Guy lifted one eyebrow and ostentatiously shifted off the foot Elizabeth'd injured.

Elizabeth gave him a small smile. "Please, Guy, I haven't hurt a man in a long time. Miles is my husband and I love him and I want to try to make him love me again."

"I believe Lord Miles more than loves you—he's

obsessed with you, but you've hurt his pride. No woman anywhere has ever given him any trouble."

"I'll not apologize for leaving Scotland with Roger. At that time it's what I had to do. Now, will you give me time alone with my husband?"

Sir Guy took his time before he nodded once. "I will no doubt come to regret this."

Elizabeth shot him a dazzling smile, her whole face lighting up. "I will make you godfather to our next child."

Sir Guy snorted. "In one hour Lord Miles will be standing here. I will give you an hour with him."

"Then you'll find us in an embarrassing situation," she said frankly. "I mean to seduce my husband. Give us at least three hours alone."

"You are no lady, Elizabeth Montgomery," he said, but there was a twinkle in his eye.

"Nor do I have any pride," she agreed. "Now go while I ready myself."

When she was alone, Elizabeth lost some of her bravado. This was perhaps her only chance to win her husband back and she prayed that everything would go well. With trembling hands, she began to unbutton her gown. She hoped she knew Miles well enough to know that he might be able to resist her logically, but could he resist her physically?

She hid her clothes under leaves and, nude, she wrapped the concealing cloak about her body. To the world she'd appear to be a lady of decorum. When she was ready, she sat down on a stump and began to wait.

When she first heard someone walking toward her, she stiffened, recognizing Miles's step, quick, light, purposeful. She rose to meet him.

At his first sight of her there was a look of welcome, of eagerness, but then his vision clouded and he looked at her coldly. "And have you misplaced your brother?" he asked.

"Miles, I have arranged this meeting in order to ask if we might live together as man and wife."

"All three of us?"

"Yes." She smiled. "The two of us with our son Nicholas."

"I see. And what, pray tell, will your brother do without the sister he has so often killed for?"

She stepped closer to him. "A great deal of time has passed since we last saw each other, and I'd hoped that by now you'd conquered some of your jealousy."

"I am not jealous!" he snapped. "You had a decision to make and you made it. Now I will have someone escort you back to your brother. Guards!"

A look of puzzlement crossed Miles's face when no men appeared at his call, but before he could say a word, Elizabeth opened her cloak, revealing her nude body. Miles, gaping, could only gasp.

Elizabeth let the cloak fall closed but held it open to reveal the length of her from her waist to her toes, rather like when she'd first met him and was draped in the fur pelts. Stealthily, like a huntress, she walked toward him, put her hand to the back of his neck.

Involuntarily, his hand went to touch the satin skin of her hip.

"Do I have to beg, Miles?" she whispered, her eyes on his lips. "I have been wrong in so many things. I have no more pride. I love you and I want to live with you. I want more children."

Slowly, Miles's lips moved closer to hers. He appeared to be using all his willpower to resist her. "Elizabeth," he murmured, his lips touching hers lightly.

Long-repressed and banked fires ignited between them. Miles's arms slid under the cloak, pulled her off the ground as he clutched her to him, his kiss deepening. His mouth moved over her face as if he meant to devour her. "I've missed you. Oh God, there were times when I thought I'd go insane."

"I'm sure I did," she answered, half laughing, half crying. "Why couldn't you realize I loved only you? I could allow no other man to touch me."

He kissed away her tears. "I hear John Bascum had four stitches taken in his head from where you struck him."

She kissed his mouth and stopped him from talking. Without either of their realizing it, they were starting toward the ground. Elizabeth's fingers were buried in the fastenings of Miles's clothes, while his hands roamed eagerly over her body.

"Unhand her!" came a deadly voice from above them.

It took both Elizabeth and Miles a moment to understand who was speaking.

Roger Chatworth held his sword on Miles.

Miles gave Elizabeth a hard look and began to stand. "She is yours," he said to Roger, his chest heaving.

"Damn you to hell, Roger!" Elizabeth shouted up at her brother, grabbing a handful of stones and throwing them at his head. "Just once, can't you stay out of my life? Put that sword away before someone gets hurt!"

"I will hurt a Montgomery if he—"

"You may try," Miles sneered, drawing his sword.

"No!" Elizabeth screamed, jumping up to stand between the two men, facing her brother. "Roger, let me make this clear. Miles is my husband and I am going to return to his home with him, that is if he'll have me after the fools you've made of both of us."

"Some husband he is," Roger sneered. "He doesn't come near you for months, hasn't even seen his own son. Is this what you want, Elizabeth? You'd give up the home I've provided for a man who cares nothing for you? How many women have you impregnated since Elizabeth, Montgomery?"

"More than you could in a lifetime," Miles replied calmly.

Elizabeth stepped closer to Miles as Roger lunged. "If I had any sense I'd tell both of you to go to the devil."

"Let me rid you of him," Roger said, but when his sword tip touched Elizabeth's cloak, he halted. "Have you no shame? Have you greeted this man like . . . like this?"

"Roger, you are a pigheaded fool who understands only what is pounded into your head." With a swirl of velvet and mink she turned, stood on tiptoe and planted her mouth on Miles's. Miles was beginning to understand that this time Elizabeth was choosing him over her brother. He caught her to him in a rib-crushing embrace and kissed her with promises of tomorrow.

Roger, fuming, so angry he was trembling, was unaware of the man sneaking up behind him. Nor did he hear the swoosh of air as the club came down on the side of his head. Silently, he crumpled to the ground.

Miles and Elizabeth would have been oblivious to the crashing of a tree but something made Elizabeth's eyes flicker open. A club was coming down on Miles's head. She pushed him to the left just enough so that the club struck her and not him.

Miles did not at first realize what had made Elizabeth go so completely limp. With one hand supporting her, he turned, but too late to avoid the blow that felled him.

The three men, dirty, burly men, stood over the two men and a woman on the ground.

"Which one is Montgomery?" one man asked.

"How would I know!"

"So which do we take?"

"Both!" said the third one.

"And the doxy?" a man asked, using his club to part Elizabeth's cloak.

"Throw her in with them. The Chatworth woman said there might be a woman and to get rid of her, too. I'm plannin' to make her pay for each body. Now, get that man's clothes off while I tend to this one."

The third man cut a long strand of Elizabeth's blonde hair and tucked it into his pocket. "Come on, hurry up. The wagon won't wait all day."

When Elizabeth woke, the pounding, galloping pain in her head was so bad she wasn't sure she ever wanted to wake up. Even the ground under her seemed to be moving. As she started to sit up, she fell backward, banging her head not on the ground but on wood.

"Quiet, sweetheart," came Miles's voice from behind her.

She turned to meet Miles's intense stare. He wore nothing but his loincloth, his arms behind him at an unnatural angle, his ankles tied. Beside him, snoring, was Roger, also bound.

As Elizabeth's head cleared, she realized her own wrists and ankles were also bound. "Where are we?" she whispered, trying not to let her fear show.

Miles's voice was deep, strong, comforting. "We're in the hold of a ship and I would imagine we're bound for France."

"But who? Why?" she stammered.

"Maybe your brother will know," Miles said flatly. "Right now we must free ourselves. I'll roll over to you and use my teeth to untie your hands, then you can free me."

Elizabeth nodded, willing herself to calmness. If Roger'd had anything to do with their capture, he wouldn't also be here, she told herself. When her hands were free, she gave a great sigh of relief, turned to Miles and instead of freeing his hands, she opened her cloak, pressed her bare body against his and kissed him. "Have you thought about me?" she whispered against his lips.

"Every moment." Eagerly he leaned forward to kiss her again.

Laughing, she pushed him away. "Shouldn't I untie you?"

"The parts of me that need freedom have it," he said as he moved his hips closer to hers.

Elizabeth buried her fingers in his shoulders and invaded his mouth with her own.

Only the loud, wakening groans of Roger made her pull away.

"If I didn't hate your brother before, I would now," Miles said with feeling as Elizabeth sat up, leaned over him, and began to untie the ropes on his wrists.

"What is this?" Roger demanded. He sat up, fell down again and finally managed to sit. "What have you done now, Montgomery?"

Miles did not answer the challenge but rubbed his wrists as Elizabeth worked on the ropes on her own ankles. As Miles began to untie his ankles, Roger exploded again.

"Do the two of you plan to free yourselves and leave me here? Elizabeth, how can you forget . . ."

"Do be quiet, Roger," Elizabeth said. "You've done more than enough harm already. Do you have any idea where this ship is taking us?"

"Ask your lover. I'm sure he's the one who planned this."

Miles didn't bother to answer Roger as he turned to Elizabeth. "I want to know whether I have your loyalty for the moment. If someone opens the hatch I'll jump him while you use the ropes to tie him. Can I depend on you?"

"Whether you believe it or not, you have always had my loyalty," Elizabeth said in a cold voice.

"Have you tried demanding our release?" Roger asked. "Offer them money."

"And will you empty your pockets for them?" Miles asked, glancing at the small strip of cloth that Roger wore.

No one said any more as the hatch began to open and a foot appeared on the ladder.

"Down!" Miles commanded and both Roger and Elizabeth feigned sleep as they sprawled on the wooden floor. Miles silently slipped to the far side of the ladder.

The sailor stuck his head down, seemed satisfied with the two prisoners' silence and took another step. At the same moment he realized one prisoner was missing, Miles grabbed both the man's feet and sent him sprawling. There was no sound except a heavy thud, lost in the creaking and groaning of the ship.

Roger lost no time in springing into action as he lifted the sailor's head by his hair. "He'll be out for a while."

Miles was unbuttoning the man's clothes.

"And do you expect me to remain here while you take his clothes and escape?" Roger demanded. "I'll not leave myself at the mercy of a Montgomery."

"You will!" Elizabeth hissed. "Roger, I am sick of your distrust. *You* are the one who has caused most of the problems between the Montgomerys and Chatworths, and now if we're to get out of this, you must learn to cooperate. What can we do, Miles?"

Miles was watching her as he struggled into the too-small clothes. Sailors were often chosen because of their diminutive size since small men could maneuver more easily inside the confines of a ship. "I will return as soon as I've found out anything." With that he was up the ladder and out.

Elizabeth and Roger tied and gagged the unconscious sailor and left him in a corner.

"Will you always side with him?" Roger asked sulkily.

Elizabeth leaned back against the wall of the ship. Her head hurt and her empty stomach was growing queasy from the motion. "I have a great deal to make up to my husband. Perhaps Miles was right and there was something I could have done the day you came to us in the crofter's hut. You've never been one to listen to reason, but perhaps I could have at least tried."

"You insult me! I have always been good to you."

"No! You've always taken advantage of what good you've done for me. Now listen to me. However we got into this mess, we must get out. You must cooperate."

"With a Montgomery?"

"With *two* Montgomerys!" she snapped.

For a few moments Roger was quiet. "Alice," he muttered. "She brought me the letter from Gavin Montgomery's wife. She knew where you were meeting your . . ."

"Husband," Elizabeth supplied. "Oh Roger!" she gasped. "Nicholas. He's with Alice, alone. We must get back to my son."

Roger put his hand on her arm. "The child has a guard and they have orders not to let Alice near the boy. They won't disobey me."

"But what will happen to him if we don't return?"

"No doubt the Montgomerys will take over his care."

Their eyes met and it was a moment before Roger realized what he'd said. He was very close to admitting that, just perhaps, he'd been wrong in his accusations of the Montgomerys. Maybe all Elizabeth's thousands of words had begun to sink in.

They turned, breath held, as the hatch door opened, and expelled it when Miles entered.

Elizabeth flew to him, clasped his neck, nearly knocking the bundles from his hands. "We think it was Alice who arranged everything. Oh my Miles, you weren't hurt?"

Miles looked at her suspiciously. "You blow quickly from hot to cold and back again. No, I had no trouble. I brought food and clothes." He tossed Roger a loaf of hard bread and handed a bundle of clothing to Elizabeth. After one glance at the bound and gagged sailor, silent, eyes wide open in fear, Miles sat down with Roger and Elizabeth.

Besides the bread, there was dried meat and a vile-tasting grog which Elizabeth gagged over.

"What did you see?" Roger asked.

Miles realized that Roger was swallowing a great deal of pride to ask such a question. "It's an old ship, falling apart, and it's run by a crew that's mostly drunk or dying. If they know we're prisoners, they're not interested."

"They sound like the type of men Alice would know," Elizabeth said in disgust. "Are we headed toward France like you thought?"

"Yes. I recognize the coastline. When it's dark we'll slip out, take one of the rowboats and row ashore. I don't want to risk a welcoming party when the ship docks." He looked to Roger and Roger gave a nod of his head.

"And how do we get back to England?" Elizabeth asked, chewing.

"I have relatives about four days' ride from where we'll land. If we can get to them we should be safe enough."

"Of course we have no horses or food to last us the journey," Roger said, drinking deeply of the awful brew.

"Perhaps we can manage," Miles said quietly, taking the jug. There was a slight emphasis on the word "we."

"Yes, maybe we can," Roger answered just as quietly.

They ate in silence and when they'd finished, Roger and Elizabeth dressed in the sailors' clothes. The striped cotton shirt stretched taut across Elizabeth's breasts and she was pleased to see a flicker of interest in Miles's eyes. She'd already proved that though he might still be angry with her, he still desired her—and hadn't he said he'd thought of her "every moment"?

When it grew even darker in the smelly little room, Miles again slipped up the ladder and this time he was gone a frighteningly long time. He returned empty-handed.

"I stocked the rowboat with all the food I could find." He looked at Roger. "I must trust you to protect my back. Elizabeth will be between us."

Roger, like Miles, was too tall to stand in the hold. Miles could pass as a sailor in his ill-fitting clothes, a day's growth of black beard on his cheeks, his eyes wild and fierce, but Roger couldn't. Roger's heavier form had split the seams of the shirt and his aristocratic blondness could not be mistaken for that of a dirty seaman. And Elizabeth in the form-fitting clothes was hopeless. Her features were too delicate to ever look like a man's.

Under the watchful eyes of the bound sailor who was trying to disappear into the woodwork, they made their way up the ladder. Miles stayed several paces ahead, a small knife in his hand. It was the only weapon he'd returned with and he'd offered no explanation as to how he'd obtained it.

The cool night air made Elizabeth realize how hideous the hold had been and her head began to clear as a breeze rushed over her. Miles caught her arm, giving a slight impatient jerk, and she gave her attention back to the moment.

There were three men on deck—one at the helm, two sauntering about on opposite sides of the ship.

Miles ducked, to disappear in a tangle of enormous ropes, and instantly Roger and Elizabeth followed his example. Crouching until her legs ached, they inched along the ship wall, slowly, carefully so as to make no sound.

When Miles stopped, he waved an arm and Roger seemed to understand. He slipped over the side of the ship, and Elizabeth held her breath, expecting to hear a splash as Roger fell, but none came. The next moment Miles motioned her over, too. Without another thought, she threw a leg over the side of the ship and the rest of her followed. Roger caught her and silently lowered her to a seat in the rowboat.

Her heart was pounding as she watched Roger, Miles helping from above, begin to lower the little boat down the side of the ship. Muscles in Roger's arms strained as he took the weight, not letting it drop and hit the water loudly. Elizabeth made a move to help but Roger impatiently motioned her away. As she moved back to her seat, her foot caught on something. It was all she could do to stifle a scream as she saw a hand near her foot—the hand of a dead sailor.

Suddenly, the rowboat lurched and she heard Roger's intake of breath as he fought to control their plunge. For some reason Miles had abruptly released the ropes overhead. Roger managed to set the boat into the water with only a whisper. Pulling back, he looked up toward the ship.

Miles was nowhere to be seen and for a moment Elizabeth felt panic. How deep did Roger's hatred run? Could she fight Roger if he decided to leave Miles behind?

But Roger merely stood in the boat, looking up expectantly, his legs wide apart and braced against the rolling boat.

When Elizabeth was near tears of worry, Miles looked over the side, saw where Roger was and the next minute he tossed a body into Roger's arms. Roger seemed to be waiting for just this and he didn't fall when the body hit him. The next moment Miles was traveling down the rope with lightning speed and he was only half-in when Roger pushed off and began to row. Miles kicked the second dead sailor's body beside the other one, grabbed the second oars and started rowing.

Elizabeth couldn't say a word as she watched the two of them working together, the boat gliding away into the night.

Chapter 16

"LET'S GET RID OF THEM," WERE THE FIRST WORDS SPOKEN after an hour of silence.

Miles nodded in agreement and kept rowing as Roger slipped the two bodies into the water.

Roger resumed rowing. "We'll have to have other clothes. Something plain that won't arouse suspicion."

"Suspicion of what?" Elizabeth asked. "Do you think the sailors will try to find us?"

Roger and Miles exchanged looks that made Elizabeth feel like an outsider.

"If we let it be known that we're of the Montgomerys or Chatworths," Roger began patiently, "we'd be held for ransom within minutes. Since we travel without a guard we must travel incognito."

"As musicians perhaps," Elizabeth added. "We should have Alyx with us."

The mention of Miles's new sister-in-law made Roger reminisce about the time Alyx saved his life. The telling took until dawn, when the men finally reached shore.

"Keep your cloak about you and stay close to me," Miles ordered under his breath. "They'll be setting up a market soon and we'll see if we can find some clothes."

Even though light was just breaking, the town square was alive with people bringing in goods to sell. Roger, in his clothes with burst seams, his arrogant stance, caused many looks, as did Elizabeth, her hair dirty and tangled but her body covered in an expensive cape. But it was Miles who received the most looks—all from females.

A pretty young woman, surrounded by young men, looked up from her wares and met Miles's dark eyes.

Elizabeth stepped forward, hands made into claws. With a chuckle, Miles caught her arm. "How'd you like to have the lady's dress?"

"I'd like to have her hide nailed to my door."

Miles gave Elizabeth such a hot look that she felt her heart begin to beat faster. "Behave yourself and obey me," he said, walking toward the woman who was giving him such heated looks.

"And what can I do for you?" the woman fairly purred, her language a gutter French.

"Could I persuade you out of your clothes?" Miles half whispered, his fingers caressing a large cabbage as he spoke a perfect, classical French.

Elizabeth could have been part of the roadway for all the attention the woman paid her.

"Aye, you could," she whispered, her hand closing over Miles's. "And what would you like to offer in return?"

Miles drew back, his eyes alight, that half-smile of his that Elizabeth knew so well on his lips. "We'll barter a cloak, fur lined, for three suits of clothes and provisions."

The woman looked Elizabeth up and down. *"Her cloak?"* she spat.

By now two of the men had walked toward the group and from the look of them, they were the woman's brothers. Elizabeth, angry at Miles's flirting, even if it were for a good cause, looked up through her lashes at the men. "We have had a most unfortunate accident," she said in French, not quite as good as Miles's, but adequate. "We were hoping to trade this unworthy cloak for a few garments, although perhaps your sister's would be a bit small." At that she casually let the cloak fall to her hips, revealing a skin-tight shirt and pants even tighter. Miles angrily pulled the cloak back to her shoulders but not before the young men gasped in appreciation.

"Will there be a trade?" Miles said through clenched teeth, not looking at Elizabeth.

The brothers agreed readily, the sister having been pushed into the background.

A few minutes later, Elizabeth stepped into a doorway and changed clothes under the cover of her cloak. The dress she wore was plain homespun, loose, comfortable, concealing.

When Miles and Roger were also dressed plainly but with tight hose displaying their muscular thighs, they filled packs with food and set off toward the south.

They were well out of town before Miles spoke to Elizabeth. "And did you learn that trick while at your

224

brother's house? You seem to have recovered quickly from your fear of men."

"And what was I supposed to do? Stand by and let that slut maul you? No doubt you would have taken her against the wall if she'd asked that price."

"Perhaps," was all Miles said and lapsed into one of his infuriating silences.

"Why is it that you accuse me of all manner of bad doings? I have never done anything to deserve your mistrust. I stayed with you in Scotland and—"

"You ran away and nearly killed the MacGregor. You left with your brother," Miles said flatly.

"But I had to!" Elizabeth insisted.

Roger had been walking on the other side of Elizabeth, silent until now. "I would have killed you, Montgomery, if she hadn't gone with me. And I wouldn't have believed whatever she said about wanting to stay with you."

"Why are you telling me this?" Miles asked Roger after a pause.

"Because Elizabeth's ranted at me for a long time about how . . . wrong I've been. Perhaps there's some truth in her words."

They walked in silence for some time, no one speaking his or her thoughts.

As the sun rose higher, they stopped and ate, drinking water from a roadside stream. Elizabeth caught Miles watching her several times and she wondered what he was thinking.

They passed many travelers on the road, rich merchants with donkeys laden with gold, many wandering peasants, musicians, blacksmiths and once a nobleman escorted by twenty armed knights. For an hour afterward Roger and Miles made derogatory remarks about the knights, ranging from their colors to their old-fashioned armor.

As the sun started its descent, the men looked about for a place to spend the night. Although they risked being arrested as poachers, Roger and Miles chose to stay in the king's forest, away from the campers along the roadside.

As they ate, Miles and Roger talked about training, mentioned a few people they both knew and generally acted as if they were old friends. Elizabeth walked away into the shadows and neither man even noticed. Several minutes later she was near tears as she leaned against a tree and listened to the night sounds.

When Miles's hand touched her shoulder, she jumped away.

"Is something wrong?" he asked.

"Wrong!" she hissed at him, her eyes filling with tears. "How could anything be wrong! You held me prisoner for months, made me fall in love with you, yet when I sacrificed everything to save your worthless life, you hated me. I have borne your child, I have conspired with your relatives and your own man to win you back, yet all I get from you is coolness. I've kissed you and you've responded but you've offered me nothing on your own. What must I do to make you understand that I didn't betray you? That I didn't choose my brother over you? You heard Roger say he would have killed you if I hadn't gone with him." She couldn't continue as the tears were choking her.

Miles leaned against a tree, several feet away from her. The moonlight silvered his hair and eyes. "I thought only my brothers were subject to the old demon of pride. I thought Raine was a fool when he refused to forgive his wife for going to the king to beg for a pardon. I could have forgiven you a king but you chose one man over me, someone else's home over mine. And when I heard the stories of all the men you'd bedded I knew I could have killed you."

When she started to protest, he put up his hand. "Perhaps it's because I've dealt with so many unfaithful wives, women who've risen from my bed and put on their wedding clothes. Maybe that distorted my view of all women. And finally, you were my prisoner but you came to me so easily."

"I fought you!" she said hotly, insulted.

Miles merely smiled at her. "Raine said I was jealous, and the irony of it was that I was jealous of the same man as he was. Raine believed his wife Alyx had a great affection for Roger Chatworth."

"Roger, I'm sure, knew nothing of this."

"So I gathered when he told the story of Alyx saving his life. Alyx did it to save Raine because my brother is a hotheaded, stubborn man who never listens to reason."

"Raine!" Elizabeth sputtered. "Did he rage so that he tore his stitches? Did he have to be drugged to make him sleep?"

Miles gave her a quick smile, teeth flashing. "Raine wears out lances when he's angry. I have my own way."

He was silent for a long moment. "How is our son?" he asked quietly.

"He has high cheekbones like your brother Gavin. There is no doubt of the family resemblance."

"I never doubted it, not truly. Elizabeth . . . ?"

227

"Yes," she whispered.

"Why did you leave me? Why didn't you return to me within a week or so? I waited every day; I prayed for your return. Kit cried himself to sleep. So many mothers have left him."

Tears were rolling down Elizabeth's cheeks. "I was afraid of Roger. He wasn't sane. Brian had vowed to kill Roger and I was afraid that if I weren't there to stop him, Roger'd declare war on all the Montgomerys. I hoped to make him see the truth; I hoped to learn the truth about the hatred of the two families."

"And the men?" Miles said. "Pagnell told everyone of how you were delivered to me and every man who courted you made sure I heard all the details."

Elizabeth put her hand up. "You were not only the first man to make love to me, you were the first man to speak to me without a leer on his face, the first man to make me laugh, the first man to show me kindness. Even you have said I know nothing about men."

"So you found out," Miles said bitterly.

"In a way, I did. I thought about it dispassionately and I knew that it would be better if I loved any man but a Montgomery. If I were married to someone else perhaps Roger would forget that I carried a Montgomery's child and maybe some of his hatred would leave him. So I decided to meet some men and see if maybe I loved you merely because you were the first."

Miles was silent, his eyes burning into her.

"Some of the men made me laugh, some were kind, some made me feel beautiful, but none of them did all things. As the weeks went by, instead of fading, everything about you became clearer. I remembered your every gesture and I began comparing the men to you."

"Even to the size of—"

"Damn you!" Elizabeth cut him off. "I did not bed any of the men and I have a feeling you know that, yet you want to hear me say it."

"Why didn't you take them to your bed? Some of the men you met are very successful with women."

"As you are?" she spat at him. "Here you stand demanding celibacy from me, yet what about you? When I tell you there have been no other men will you allow me to come to your pure bed? This morning I had to drag you from a woman. How do you think I've felt while holding your son and knowing that at that moment you could be in bed with one or two—or more—women?"

"More?" he mocked, then lowered his voice seductively. "There have been no women since you."

Elizabeth didn't believe she'd heard correctly. "No—" she began, eyes wide.

"My brother Raine and I moved into one of his keeps and in a rage we dismissed every woman, even the laundresses. We trained all day, drank all night and cursed women constantly. Raine came to his senses first when his wife sent their daughter to him. Little Catherine made me miss my own children so I went back to Gavin's for Christmas and Judith—" He ran his hand through his hair.

"I used to think Gavin was hard on his sweet little wife but I'd never been on the sharp side of her tongue. The woman never left me alone. She was merciless. She talked constantly about our son, sighed over the

VELVET ANGEL

fact that her son would never know his cousin and she even hired a man to paint a picture of an angel with long blond hair holding a little boy inside my shield. Inside my shield, mind you! I told Gavin I was going to wring his wife's neck if he didn't do something but Gavin laughed so hard I never mentioned it again. When she received your letter about how you were willing to forgive me, Judith launched into me with renewed force."

Miles closed his eyes a moment in memory. "She enlisted Alyx's help and Alyx came up with a dozen songs about two lovers who were held apart by a stupid, vain man who just happened to look exactly like me. One evening at dinner Alyx led twenty-two musicians in a song that made everyone laugh so hard two men fell off their stools and broke ribs. Alyx was at her best."

Elizabeth was so astonished at his story she could barely speak. "And what did you do?"

He winced in memory. "I very calmly bounded over the table and took Alyx's throat in my hands."

"No!" she gasped. "Alyx is so tiny, so—"

"Both Raine and Gavin drew swords on me and as I stood there, about to kill this pretty little songbird, my brothers' swords at my neck, I realized I wasn't myself. The next day Judith arranged the meeting between us." His eyes twinkled. "The meeting where you wanted Sir Guy to deliver you to me in a carpet."

Elizabeth wouldn't look at him. She thought Sir Guy had been on her side, yet all along he'd been reporting —and laughing—to Miles. How the two of them must have slapped each other's backs at her wanting to seduce her own husband. What had happened to that prideful woman who'd once stood on a cliff edge and vowed never to submit to any man?

"Excuse me," she whispered as she swept past Miles on her way back to Roger.

Miles caught her in his arms, pulling her close to him. When Elizabeth saw that he was smiling at her with such a *knowing* little grin, she brought her elbow down hard into his ribs and was rewarded with his whoosh of pain. "I hate you, Montgomery!" she yelled into his face. "You've made me beg and cry and taken all my pride." She tried to hit him again but he pinned her arms to her side and she couldn't move.

"No, Montgomery," he said, moving his lips near hers. "You love me. You love me so much you're willing to beggar yourself for me. I've made you cry in passion and I've made you cry tears of love."

"You've humiliated me."

"As you've done to me." He held her as she struggled against him. "Every woman has come to me easily but only you have made me work. Only with you have I been angry, jealous, possessive. You were given to me and you are mine, Elizabeth, and never again will you be allowed to forget it."

"I never did—" she began but he cut her off by kissing her. Once his lips touched hers, she was lost. She could no more argue with him than she could have run away.

His arms loosened their grip on her just long enough for her to slide her arms about his neck and pull him even closer.

"Never, *never* forget it again, Montgomery," he whispered by her ear. "You will belong to me always— in this century and in the next. Forever!"

Elizabeth barely heard him as she stood on tiptoe and raised her mouth to his.

She had no idea how much she had missed him physically. He was the only man on earth she could be with so trustingly, the only man she wasn't wary of. All the years of holding herself in reserve were showing themselves in her eagerness, her ferocity. She put her hands in his hair, feeling it curl about her fingers, and pulled his head closer.

A low, throaty laugh came from Miles. "A tree you said? Take the woman against a tree?" he said.

Miles knew what she wanted—not a sweet, gentle lovemaking but one of all the fury she felt. His hands began tearing at her clothes, one hand on the ties of her linen underwear, the other on his own trunk hose. Elizabeth kept kissing him, her mouth wrapped around his, tongues entangled.

When her back slammed into a tree, she merely blinked and applied her teeth to Miles's neck, tearing at his skin as if she meant to flay him.

Miles lifted her, put her legs about his waist, her skirt bunched between them. Neither of them cared for the niceties of removing their clothes. His hands on her bottom, he lifted her, set her down on his shaft with the force of a falling anchor.

Elizabeth gasped, buried her face in Miles's neck and held on for dear life as his strong arms lifted her up and down. Her head went back as she felt a scream building inside her. Sweat began to drip off Miles and he rubbed the salty stuff on her, plastering her hair to the both of them.

With one last, fierce thrust that sent Elizabeth into

an ecstasy, Miles pulled her to him, shuddering, his hot body erupting again and again.

Elizabeth, her body tight, convulsing in waves of pleasure, felt quick tears in her eyes. Slowly she came back to earth, her legs feeling weak, aching from clasping Miles with every ounce of her strength.

He leaned away to look at her, caressed her wet hair, kissed her temple. "I love you," he said tenderly, then smiled roguishly. "And besides that you're the best . . ."

"I understand." She laughed. "Now are you going to let me down or are you going to kill me against this tree?"

With one more kiss, Miles set her feet on the ground and gave an ungentlemanly, prideful laugh when Elizabeth's legs collapsed under her and he had to hold her to keep her from falling.

"Braggart!" she hissed, clutching him, but she gave him a smile and kissed the hand holding her arm. "Am I really the best?" she asked as if it meant nothing to her. "You still find me attractive even after I've borne a child?"

"Tolerably so," Miles said seriously.

Elizabeth laughed, smoothed her skirts and tried to regain her composure as they walked back to where Roger waited.

Chapter 17

THE THREE OF THEM WALKED TOGETHER FOR TWO DAYS
and they were blissful ones for Elizabeth. There were
nights of lovemaking and days of love. Miles gave her
his complete attention. They held hands and talked
softly or laughed uproariously at the silliest things.
They made love beside a stream and later bathed in its
icy water.

Roger watched them with an air of aloofness, and
sometimes Elizabeth felt a pang of guilt for the pain she
knew she was causing him. A few times he made
remarks about Miles's unknightly behavior but Miles
said that until he reached his relatives, he was a
carefree peasant.

Their progress was slow and the four-day journey on
horseback was stretching into several more days on
foot.

On the fourth day, the trio left the roadside just before noon to rest and refresh themselves. Roger, after directing an unnoticed look of contempt toward his sister and Miles, walked away from them, deeper into the forest. When he'd first heard his sister had been taken prisoner, his pain had been great—but now he could see that he'd lost her much more completely than if she were a prisoner.

Reminiscing over his problems, he walked past the earth-torn edge of the little gully without paying the least attention. He was several feet past the obvious signs of a struggle before he recognized them. Turning back, he examined the earth.

He'd been walking along the edge of a steep-sided bank that fell away to a stream of rushing water and, clearly, on the edge were the signs of someone falling. Often, after a battle, Roger'd had to search for his men who were wounded and lost, and now his knight's instincts rose like the hairs on his neck. Immediately, he started down the side, skidding in his haste.

What he saw at the bottom was not what he expected. Sitting on a rotten piece of log, her feet hidden under a jumble of large rocks, was a pretty young woman, richly dressed in burgundy velvet trimmed about the neckline with large golden amethysts. Her dark eyes, almost too big for her face, looked up at Roger with pleasure.

"I knew you'd come," she said in English that was pleasantly and softly accented.

Roger blinked once in confusion but ignored her remark. "Did you fall? Are you hurt?"

She smiled at him, making her eyes turn liquid. She looked to be quite young, a child really, wearing a dress much too old for her. Dark hair peeped from under a pearl-embroidered hood. More pearls draped down the front of her dress.

"My foot is caught and I cannot move it."

Women! Roger thought, moving to examine the rocks that pinned her feet. "You must have heard me above. Why didn't you call out to me?"

"Because I knew you'd come for me."

Insane, Roger thought. The poor girl was possessed by spirits. "When I lift this rock I want you to move your foot. Do you understand me?" he said as if talking to an idiot.

She merely smiled in answer and when the rock was moved, she pulled her foot from under it.

Her right foot was pinned differently and Roger saw that if he moved one stone, another would fall and perhaps break her ankle. She was a little thing and he doubted her fragile bones could stand much.

"Do not be afraid to tell me," she whispered. "I'm not a stranger to pain."

Roger turned to look at her, at her big eyes looking at him with so much trust, and that trust both frightened him and made him feel powerful.

"What is your name?" he asked, studying and considering the rocks around her little foot.

"Christiana, my lord."

Roger's head came up sharply. His dirty peasant's clothes had not fooled her, so perhaps she wasn't stupid after all. "Chris then." He smiled. "May I borrow your eating dagger? I'll put together something to hold those rocks while I move these." He pointed.

She handed him the knife quickly and he bit his lips

to keep from cautioning her about handing knives to strangers. The jewels on her dress were worth a fortune and the pearl necklace she wore was without equal.

He moved but a few feet from her to cut several tree branches. Removing his doublet, he pulled out his shirt and cut strips of cloth from the tail to use in building a platform to fit under the rocks.

"Why is no one searching for you?" he asked as he worked.

"Perhaps they are; I don't know. I dreamed of you last night."

He gave her a sharp look but said nothing. Girls everywhere seemed to be full of romantic ideas of being rescued. It was hard for a man to live up to.

"I dreamed," she continued, "of this forest and this place. I saw you in my dream and I knew you'd come."

"Perhaps the man in your dream was merely fair-skinned and resembled me," Roger said patronizingly.

"I saw many things. The scar by your eye—you received it from your brother when you were only a boy."

Involuntarily, Roger's hand went to the curved scar by his left eye. He'd come close to losing his eye that day and very few people who knew how he got the scar were still alive. He doubted if even Elizabeth knew.

Christiana merely smiled at his look of surprise. "I have waited all my life for you."

Roger shook his head to clear it. "That was a lucky guess," he said. "About the scar I mean. Now hold very still while I prop these rocks up." There was no need to tell her to be still as she'd hardly moved since he'd arrived.

The rocks were not small and Roger had to sweat some before he could move the largest one. And even as it rolled away, more came crashing down onto the weak, makeshift platform he'd created. With lightning speed he jumped onto Christiana, knocking her backward and rolling her away from the crushing boulders. Even as he moved her, he heard her intake of breath as the rocks scraped away some of her skin.

The sound of the rocks filled the air and Roger covered Christiana's body with his own, protecting her from dust and fragments. When it was safe, he started to pull away from her but she put her hands on the sides of his head and pulled his lips to hers.

For a long time Roger'd been concerned only with bringing his brother and sister back to him and he'd had no time for women. He'd had no idea his desires were so pent-up inside him. Once, years ago, he'd been almost carefree, laughing with pretty young girls, tumbling about with them in clandestine meetings, but his anger at the Montgomerys had changed all that.

At the first touch of the girl's lips, Roger's first thought was: serious. She may look to be little more than a child, but she was a woman and her purpose was one of seriousness. She kissed him with such intensity that he drew back from her.

"Who are you?" he whispered.

"I love you and I have waited always to meet you."

Roger, lying on top of her, looked deeply into her dark eyes, eyes that seemed to be trying to pull his soul out of his body, and he was frightened. He moved off her. "We'd better get you back to your parents."

"I have no parents," she said, sitting up.

Roger looked away from her eyes that seemed to be accusing him of deserting her. Part of him wanted to run away from this strange woman and another part wanted to fight to the death to keep her near him.

"Let me see your ankle," he said at last.

Obediently, she turned and held out her foot to him. He frowned when he saw it, cut and bruised, blood running freely. "Why didn't you show this to me?" he snapped. "Here"—he handed her back her knife—"cut off some of your underskirt. I can't afford to lose more of my shirt. It's the only one I have at the moment."

She smiled at that and began slicing away at a fine lawn petticoat. "Why are you here in France and dressed like that? Where are your men?"

"You tell me," he said nastily, taking the strips from her. "Perhaps tonight you'll dream the rest of my life."

As soon as he turned away toward the stream, he regretted his words, but damn! the woman gave him chills. He could still feel her kiss—an odd combination of a woman who wanted to jump into his bed and a witch who wanted his soul.

At that thought he smiled. He was getting fanciful. She was a young girl who needed his help, nothing more or less. The best thing he could do would be to dress her ankle and return her to her guardians.

When he returned to her with dampened cloths, he could see tears glistening on her lashes, and he was immediately contrite. "I'm sorry, Chris," he said as if he'd known her always. "Damn! Give me your ankle."

A small smile came through her tears and he couldn't help returning it, and she smiled broadly as she put her foot in his hand.

"Let me have your knife again and I'll cut away your hose," he said, after he'd gently removed her embroidered slipper.

Without a word, Christiana slowly raised her dress on one side to the top of her thigh and unfastened her hose. Her eyes on Roger, and his on her slim curvy leg, she inched the hose downward toward her bloody ankle. When she reached her calf she held up her leg. "You may remove the rest."

Roger suddenly felt sweat breaking out on his body and a flame of desire so hot shot through him that his veins seemed to be on fire. With shaking hands, he removed her stocking, one hand on fabric, the other on the back of her bare knee.

The sight of blood on her ankle soothed him somewhat and he began to calm. "You are toying with things you don't understand," he said tightly, wetting her ankle to get the torn stocking off.

"I do not play children's games," she said softly.

Roger tried to concentrate on the task before him as he carefully cleaned her ankle, then bound it. "Now we must return you," he said as if he were her father, but his left hand was still on her ankle and began to caress her leg as his hand moved upward. He replaced her dagger in the sheath at her side.

Her eyes locked with his. She didn't move away but seemed to welcome him.

Roger came to his senses abruptly. No matter how appealing this urchin was, she wasn't worth his life. Someone would be looking for her soon and if he, looking to be a peasant, were found making love to her, obviously a noblewoman, no one would ask questions before they put a sword through his heart. And besides, he wasn't sure he liked the idea of being intimate with this strange young woman. What if she were a witch and she did mean to take his soul?

"Why did you stop, my lord?" she whispered in a throaty voice.

Primly, he pulled her skirt down. "Because you're a child and I'm— Do you always offer yourself to strangers?"

She didn't respond to the question but the answer was in her eyes. "I have loved you always and will love you always. I am yours to command."

Roger felt himself getting angry. "Now see here, young woman! I don't know who you think I am nor who you are, but I think it's best that you get back to your people and I to mine. And I hope you pray to God—if you believe in Him—for forgiveness for your actions."

With that he bent, tossed her small body over his shoulder and began to climb the steep bank.

By the time he reached the top of the bank, both his anger and his passion had calmed. He was too old and too sensible to allow a romantic bit of a girl to bother him.

He stood her before him, holding her shoulders to steady her, and smiled. "Now where may I take you? Do you remember which way you came from?"

She looked confused for a moment. "Of course I remember the way. Why are you sending me away? Would you kiss me again? Would you kiss me as if you loved me in return?"

Roger held her at arms' length. "You are too forward

and no, I will not kiss you again. You must tell me where you belong."

"I belong with you but—" She stopped as a blast from a stag's horn sounded. Her eyes changed to wild, frightened. "I must go. My husband calls. He must not find you. Here!"

Before he could speak, she'd taken her little dagger from her side and crudely cut the largest amethyst from the front of her dress. An ugly, irreparable hole was left in the expensive velvet.

"Take this," she offered urgently.

Roger's back stiffened. "I do not take tribute from women."

The horn sounded again and Christiana's fright increased. "I must go!" She stood on tiptoe, quickly kissed his tightened lips. "I have a beautiful body," she said, "and lovely soft hair. I will show you sometime."

When the horn sounded a third time, she gathered her skirts and began to run awkwardly, her ankle bending every few steps. She'd not gone far when she turned and tossed the amethyst toward him. He made no move to catch it. "Give it to the woman who travels with you. Is she your sister or your mother?"

The last words were called over her shoulder as she disappeared from his sight.

Roger stood still, rooted into place for a very long time, his eyes staring sightlessly toward the place where she'd disappeared. His head felt strange, light, as if he'd just been through some experience that wasn't real. Had the girl really existed or had he fallen asleep and dreamed her?

"Roger!" came Elizabeth's voice from behind him. "We've been looking for you for an hour. Are you ready to travel? There are a few hours before night-fall."

Slowly, he turned toward her.

"Roger, are you all right?"

Miles had left his wife's side and was looking about the area. Sometimes men who'd been wounded had Roger's look—just before they fell down. Miles saw the amethyst on the ground, but before he could touch it, Roger swept it into his hand, fingers closing tightly around it.

"Yes, I'm ready to go," he said tersely. Before he left he gave one last look about the forest, his thumb rubbing the jewel in his hand. "Her husband!" he muttered angrily. "So much for love." He thought about throwing the amethyst away, but he couldn't do it.

It was Miles who was truly aware of Roger's distant moodiness that night. Miles had snared a rabbit—illegally—and it was turning over a spit as the three of them sat around the fire. He didn't want to worry Elizabeth, telling her there was no danger—and indeed the life of the French peasant seemed carefree compared to life at her brother's house—but Miles was always on guard, always aware of potential danger. At night he slept lightly and he gained respect for Roger as he saw that the knight was also wary.

Elizabeth lay sleeping, her head in her husband's lap. Roger sat apart, turning something over and over in his hand. Miles was not a person to directly ask after something that wasn't his concern, but Roger felt the younger man's interest.

"Women!" Roger finally said with great disgust and

pocketed the amethyst. But as he stretched out on the cold forest floor, his hand sought the jewel and held it all night.

The morning dawned bright and clear and Elizabeth, as usual, was extraordinarily happy. Another day and they'd reach the French Montgomerys. Then they could go back to England and their son and, like a fairy tale, live happily ever after.

"You seem especially happy." Miles smiled down at her. "I think you like this peasant life."

"For a while," she said smugly, "but don't get the idea I'll always wear rags. I'm an expensive woman." She rolled her eyes at him flirtatiously.

"You will have to earn your keep," he said arrogantly, looking her up and down.

"I do that well enough. I—"

She stopped as the clatter of many horses and many men forced them to the side of the road. It was obviously a rich group of men, their horses draped in silks, their armor painted and well tended. There were about a hundred men and baggage wagons, and in the middle was a young girl, her hands tied behind her back, her face bruised, but she held her head high.

Elizabeth shivered as she remembered all too well how it felt to be a captive, but this girl looked as if she'd been beaten.

"Chris," Roger whispered from beside her and it was a heartfelt sound.

Miles was watching Roger intently and when Roger made a move forward, Miles caught his arm. "Not now," Miles said quietly.

Elizabeth turned back toward the passing procession. So many men for such a small girl, she thought sadly.

Her head turned with a snap. "No!" she gasped up at Miles. "You can't possibly be considering rescuing the girl."

Miles looked back at the knights and didn't answer Elizabeth. When she spoke again he turned such hot eyes on her that she became silent.

The trio stood for some time after the knights went past. Elizabeth's mind kept screaming no, no, no! Miles couldn't risk his life for a woman he didn't know.

As they started walking again, Elizabeth began her plea as calmly and rationally as she could. "We'll be at your relatives' soon and they'll know who the girl is, who holds her prisoner—and why. Perhaps she killed a hundred people. Perhaps she deserves her punishment."

Both Miles and Roger looked straight ahead.

Elizabeth clutched Miles's arm. "I was held prisoner once and it hasn't worked out badly. Perhaps—"

"Be quiet, Elizabeth!" Miles commanded. "I can't think."

Elizabeth felt herself begin to shiver. How could he, weaponless, rescue a girl guarded by a hundred armored knights?

Miles turned to Roger. "Should we volunteer our services as wood gatherers? At least we'll gain entrance to their camp."

Roger gave Miles a calculating look. "This isn't your fight, Montgomery. The girl was beaten because of me and I'll get her out alone."

Miles kept looking at Roger, his eyes blazing, and after a moment, Roger gave in.

After one curt nod, Roger looked away. "I don't know who she is except that her name is Christiana. She gave me a jewel, cut it from her dress, and no doubt that's why she's been beaten. She has a husband and she is terrified of him."

"A husband!" Elizabeth gasped. "Roger, please, both of you, listen to reason. You can't risk your lives for a married woman. How long have you known her? What does she mean to you?"

"I never saw her before yesterday," Roger half whispered. "And she means nothing to me—or perhaps she does. But I cannot let her be beaten because of me."

Elizabeth began to realize there was no sense in arguing further. She'd never seen Roger do something so foolhardy but she was sure Miles would risk his life for a scullery maid. She took a deep breath. "Once, on the road, a peasant offered me a bouquet of flowers and she was allowed past the guard to give them to me."

"You will remain behind," Miles said in dismissal.

Elizabeth didn't answer but set her jaw. The odds were better if three people attacked a hundred than if there were just two.

Chapter 18

THEY FOLLOWED THE GUARD UNTIL NEARLY SUNSET, when the men made camp, and quite easily Miles and Roger, forsaking their usual shoulders-back stance, slipped among the knights, their arms loaded with wood. In the shadows of the trees, Elizabeth watched. Her early offer of help seemed to be hollow, the words of a braggart. Now, watching all those men, it was as if she'd never left her brother's house. Even as she stood hidden, she glanced behind her to make sure none of the men was there, ready and waiting to touch her.

Both Miles and Roger had given her strict orders that under no circumstances was she to leave her hiding place. They'd made it clear that they had enough to do without worrying about her also. Roger'd given her the girl's amethyst and Miles'd told her how to get to his relatives—in case anything happened to either of them.

247

Elizabeth'd felt a hint of panic at the pronouncement but she'd kept her fears to herself. The men wanted her to wait far away but she'd stubbornly insisted on a place where she could watch. They'd refused to tell her their plan and Elizabeth began to suspect they had no real plan at all. No doubt Miles intended to hold the men at swordpoint while Roger fled with the girl.

Watching, she saw a scuffling, awkward old man, who she couldn't quite believe was her proud brother, move slowly toward where the girl was tied. She sat, leaning against a tree, hands and feet bound, head lowered.

When Roger awkwardly dropped the entire load of wood on the girl's feet, Elizabeth held her breath. She didn't know how much contact Roger'd had with the girl and she looked too young to have much sense. Would she give Roger away?

There was a brief flicker across the girl's face—but that could have been from pain—and then her face calmed. Elizabeth almost smiled. The girl was certainly not stupid. There wasn't another movement or expression from her as Roger began to clear the fallen wood away. A knight, cursing Roger, kicked him in the leg, and as Roger rolled, kicked him again in the ribs. And even as Roger took the blows, Elizabeth saw the flash of a knife as he cut the bindings from the girl's feet under the cover of the wood.

But Elizabeth saw something Roger couldn't: Behind him an older man, richly dressed, hung with jewels, his garments interwoven with gold wire, had never taken his sunken little eyes off the bound girl. The dying sunlight caught just a bit of a flash of Roger's knife.

On the far side of the camp, Miles kicked a burning

log out of the fire, setting some grasses on fire. He slipped away before he could receive punishment for his actions and several knights began to fight the fire.

But the diversion wasn't enough. The men guarding the girl didn't glance at the fire—and the old man continued to glare at her with hatred.

The dark seemed to be coming quickly but there was enough light for Elizabeth to see a shadowy Miles slip a sword from a scabbard.

He did plan to fight! she thought. He planned to create some commotion so Roger could get the girl away. If fire had failed, perhaps a little clashing steel would work.

Elizabeth rose from her safe ditch, made a quick prayer for forgiveness for sinning and began unbuttoning her coarse woolen gown all the way to her waist. Perhaps she could get the men's attention—and especially the attention of the old man.

Her entrance was quick and dramatic. She ran into the clearing, leaped the last few feet, so close to one of the fires that she almost straddled it. Hands on her thighs, legs spread, she bent forward, the open bodice gaping, and practically touched the old man's head with her breasts. Slowly, seductively, she began to sway her shoulders, back and forth, from side to side, one raised, the next one higher, always working back until she was leaning backwards over the fire. With one hand she pulled the cotton cap from her head and let her hair cascade down to her knees. It hung over the fire, turning almost red in the light and looking as if it were part of the flames.

When she straightened, her hands insolently on her hips, she gave a laugh—a loud, arrogant, challenging laugh—and she had everyone's attention. The old man looked at her with interest and at last his eyes weren't on the girl not two feet from Elizabeth.

Elizabeth had never danced before but she'd seen enough lascivious entertainments at her brother's house to know what could be done. One of the knights began to play a lute and another a drum. Elizabeth began to undulate slowly—not just her hips, but her entire body moving every inch from fingertips to toes. And she used her magnificent hair to advantage, swirling it about, slapping men across the face with it. When one knight came too close, Elizabeth swept downward, grabbed a rock and plowed her fist into the man's stomach.

Everyone laughed uproariously at the knight's pain and from then on it was more a chase than a dance. For Elizabeth it was a nightmare come true. She was back in her brother's house and his men were pursuing her. She forgot about the last months of freedom but regressed to a time when she had to survive.

On her toes, she whirled about a knight and lifted his sword from his belt. With garments flying, hair tangling about her body, she dodged at the men trying to catch her. She didn't hurt any of them but she managed to draw blood now and again. Forcing herself to laugh and keep up the charade of dancing, she jumped atop a table set with food, kicking plates and goblets everywhere. When a knight's hand touched her ankle, she moved away, her heel "accidentally" coming down on his fingers. He went away with a cry of pain.

Elizabeth's nerves were at the breaking point as the men began to clap in rhythm. Bending, she turned her hair around and around in time to their applause.

Hoping that by now Roger and Miles had had time to release their captive, she threw her skirts high, the men cheering at the sight of her legs, and leaped to the ground directly in front of the old man.

She landed in a low bow before him, head low, hair a curtain about her. Panting, sides heaving, she waited.

With great ceremony, the man rose and put one bony hand under Elizabeth's chin, lifting her face to meet his.

Out of the corner of her eye, Elizabeth could see that the girl was gone and now it would be only moments before someone noticed.

Elizabeth rose and, praying for more time, hoping to distract the men, shrugged her shoulders and let the top of her dress fall away to her waist.

There was a great hush among the people, almost all of whom were behind her. The old man's eyes greedily roamed over her exquisite, high, firm breasts. Then, with a smile showing blackened teeth, he removed his own heavy cloak and put it about Elizabeth's shoulders.

Holding onto the ties in a degrading manner, he began to pull Elizabeth into the darkness of the forest.

Concealed in her hand was a knife she'd taken from one of the knights. As the old man turned, he saw that the bound girl was gone, but before he could call out, Elizabeth moved forward, caught his earlobe between her teeth, pressed the knife to his ribs and growled, "Walk!"

They were enveloped in the darkness before the cry was given that the prisoner had escaped.

"Run!" Elizabeth commanded the old man, pushing on the knife.

Quickly, he turned and backhanded Elizabeth across the face.

But before he could move, Roger leaped from the trees, his big hands around the old man's throat. Perhaps it was the surprise or the excitement of Elizabeth's dance, but Roger barely touched him and the ugly old man fell dead at their feet.

Roger lost no time but caught Elizabeth's waist and shoved her up into a tree.

Knights swarmed across the ground under them, their drawn swords glinting in the moonlight. Roger put his arms around Elizabeth and held her close, her head buried in his shoulder. She was trembling over her entire body and even now, in the safety of her brother's arms, she could still feel the men's hands clutching at her.

"Miles," she whispered to Roger.

"Safe," was all Roger'd say as he pressed her even closer.

They waited for some time, through all the hue and cry of finding the old man dead. Finally, two knights carried the body back to the camp and the search for the girl seemed to be ended as the men saddled horses and began to ride out.

Roger held Elizabeth a while after the forest was quiet.

"Come," he commanded. "Montgomery waits for us."

Roger climbed down first, then caught Elizabeth, who still wore the old man's cloak. The velvet swirling about her, she ran after Roger through the cold, damp forest.

Elizabeth hadn't realized how worried she'd been

about Miles's safety until she saw him again. He emerged from a stagnant pond, holding the hand of the girl. Both of them were wet, slimy, and the girl's teeth were chattering.

After one grateful look at Miles for his safety, Elizabeth removed the old man's cloak and put it around the girl's shoulders.

"It is his!" Christiana said, stepping away from the cloak as if it were evil.

Roger caught the cloak, tossed it back to Elizabeth and removed his own doublet, wrapping the girl in it. She melted into Roger's arms as if she were part of his skin.

"We must go," Miles said, taking Elizabeth's hand. "They'll be back for her soon."

They traveled all night. Elizabeth knew she was past exhaustion but she kept going, sometimes stealing looks at the girl who'd caused this flight. Wearing Roger's doublet, which dwarfed her, she looked even younger and more fragile than she first appeared. She was never more than an inch or two from Roger's side even though sometimes branches hit her face. As for Roger, he didn't seem to want her any farther away.

Elizabeth hardly looked at Miles because his eyes blazed with anger and a few times he threatened to crush her hand in his. Once, she tried to talk to him and explain why she'd had to disobey his orders and enter the rescue, but Miles looked at her with eyes blackened with rage, and Elizabeth practically crawled back inside the concealing cloak.

Toward morning, Miles said, "We'll join the travelers on the road and we must get her some clothes."

Christiana still wore her bejeweled dress, the pearls

about her neck. It somehow emphasized her fallen status—she still wore her riches but now her fine dress was torn, her hair matted, her cheek bruised and the slime from the pond was dried and still clinging to her.

When at last they stopped beside the road, near a large group of travelers just waking, Elizabeth nearly fell in an exhausted heap. Miles caught her to him, pulled her across his lap. "If you ever do anything like that again, wife—" he began but stopped when he kissed her so hard her mouth was bruised.

Tears came to her eyes, tears of joy that he was safe. There'd been a time, when she saw Miles draw a sword, that she was sure she'd never see him alive again. "I would risk all for you," she whispered and fell asleep in his arms.

It seemed like only moments before Elizabeth was wakened again and they began walking just a short distance behind the other travelers. The girl, Christiana, now wore a coarse woolen dress with a large concealing hood.

At midday they stopped and the men left the women alone while they went to the travelers to negotiate for bread and cheese, using the hated cloak.

Elizabeth leaned against a tree, her body trying to relax, but Christiana's nearness prevented rest. She couldn't help resenting the girl who'd nearly caused their deaths.

"Will you hate me for long, Elizabeth?" Christiana asked softly.

Elizabeth gave her one startled look before turning away. "I do not . . . hate you."

"You are not accustomed to lying," the girl said.

Elizabeth turned on her. "My husband could have been killed rescuing you!" she said fiercely. "As well as my brother! What hold do you have on Roger? Have you bewitched him?"

Christiana did not smile nor did she frown. Her big eyes blazed with intensity. "I have always dreamed of a man like Roger. I have always known he'd come for me. Last year my uncle gave me in marriage to a cruel man but still I knew Roger would come. Three nights ago I dreamed and I saw his face. He was traveling in coarse clothes and with a woman related to him. I knew that he'd finally come."

Elizabeth looked at the girl as if she were a witch.

Chris continued, "You curse me for putting the man you love in danger, but what would you risk to be with your man? Perhaps if I were braver I could have gone to the torture and death my husband planned for me, but instead I sat in camp tied to the tree and prayed with all my might for my Roger to come."

She looked away, down the road to where Miles and Roger were approaching, and an inner light appeared in her eyes. "God has given me Roger to repay me for what has happened to me before. Tonight I will lie with Roger and after that I am ready to forsake all life, if need be. I have risked his life, yours and your kind husband's for this one night with my beloved."

She put her hand over Elizabeth's and her eyes were pleading. "Forgive me if I have asked too much of all of you."

Elizabeth's anger evaporated. Her hand took Christiana's. "Don't talk of death. Roger needs love perhaps more than you do. Stay beside him."

For the first time, Chris gave a bit of a smile and a single dimple showed in her left cheek. "Only force will take me away from him."

Elizabeth glanced upward, saw Roger standing over them, his face showing puzzlement. He's bewildered by all this, Elizabeth thought. Chris confuses him as much as she does us.

They rested only minutes, ate hurriedly and were again on their way.

That night, as Elizabeth snuggled in Miles's arms, she had her first chance to talk to him. "What do you think of this young woman you risked your life for?" she asked.

"I know she's dangerous," he answered. "She was married to the Duke of Lorillard. As a child I used to hear of his cruelty. He's been through seven or eight rich, highborn young women. They all seem to die within a few years of marriage."

"Is Chris highborn?"

Miles gave a snort. "She's descended from generations of kings."

"How do you know all this?"

"From my French relatives. They've had a few dealings with the Lorillard family. Elizabeth," he said solemnly, "I want you to keep these." He closed her hand over the long strand of pearls Christiana'd worn yesterday. "Tomorrow, late, we should reach the home of my relatives but in case we don't . . . No!" He put a finger to her lips to quiet her. "I want to tell you the truth so you can be prepared. The Lorillard family is powerful and we've taken the life of one member and now harbor another. They'll tear the countryside apart looking for us. If anything happens, take the pearls and go back to England to my brothers. They will take care of you."

"But what about your French relatives? Couldn't I go to them?"

"I'll tell you the story someday, but for now let's just say that the Lorillards know me. If I'm captured, the way to my people here will be blocked. Go home to my brothers. Will you swear that? No more attempts to rescue me, but get home to safety."

She refused to answer him.

"Elizabeth!"

"I swear I will go home to your brothers." She sighed.

"And what about the rest?"

"I will make no more promises!" she hissed at him, turning her face up to his to be kissed.

They made love slowly and deliberately, as if tomorrow would never come. Miles's words of warning made Elizabeth feel desperate, as if they had only a few hours together. Twice, tears came to her eyes, tears of frustration that they'd been so close to safety and one woman's lust had put them in danger.

Miles kissed away her tears and whispered that she was to live for the moment and she could save her anger and hatred until later when they had the leisure.

She fell asleep holding Miles as tightly as she could and during the night she moved on top of him. He woke, smiled, kissed the top of her head, pulled a wad of her hair out of his mouth, hugged her and went back to sleep.

Roger woke them before daybreak and after one look, Elizabeth was sure he'd never been asleep. Christiana appeared from the trees, her eyes alive, her lips full and reddened, whisker burn on her neck and the side of her face. As they began to walk, Elizabeth saw Roger constantly cast looks toward Chris—looks of awe and pleasure. By noon, he had his arm around the girl, pulling her close to him. And once, to Elizabeth's surprise, he caught Chris in his arms and kissed her passionately. Roger'd always been decorous, aware of his place in life, his knightly vows, and he never made public displays of affection.

Miles caught Elizabeth, pulled her away from the spot where she stood gaping at her brother.

It was an hour before sunset when men burst from the trees, swords drawn and pointed at the throats of the four travelers.

A man, old, ugly, stepped from behind the knights. "Well, Montgomery, we meet again. Take them!" he commanded.

Chapter 19

ELIZABETH SAT STILL ON THE HORSE FOR JUST A MOMENT as she saw, through tears, the ancient Montgomery fortress. So many things had changed in the last few weeks that she wasn't sure either England or the massive stronghold would still be there.

One of the horses of the three big men behind her stamped impatiently, bringing Elizabeth to her senses. With a great cry, she used the ends of her reins as a whip and spurred the horse forward. For all that she'd never visited the Montgomery estates, she knew the plan of it well. In Scotland, Miles had told her about the place, even drawn a sketch in the dirt.

She headed for the heavily guarded back gate, the family entrance. As she came to the walls that surrounded the narrow entrance, she barely slowed her horse.

259

Immediately, guards, arrows aimed, challenged her.

"The wife of Miles Montgomery," one of the men behind Elizabeth bellowed upward.

Six arrows landed in the ground before Elizabeth's horse, and the tired animal reared, one hoof breaking two shafts. Elizabeth used all her strength to control the frightened animal.

Three armed knights now stood between her and the closed entrance.

"I am Elizabeth Montgomery and these men are with me," she said impatiently but with some respect. Not many places were guarded like this any more.

As if they were statues, the knights held their ground as more men dropped from the walls and aimed swordpoints at the men behind Elizabeth.

When twenty Montgomery knights were assembled, one guard spoke to her. "You alone may enter. Your men stay here."

"Yes, of course. Take me to Gavin. He can identify me."

The reins of Elizabeth's horse were taken from her and she was led into a clean, spacious courtyard before a large house. More buildings were tucked inside the high surrounding walls.

One of the guards entered the house and moments later a pretty woman appeared, her face smudged with flour, sesame seeds dotting her hair.

"Take me to your master," Elizabeth ordered the woman. "I have news that concerns him."

"Are you Elizabeth?" the small woman asked. "Do you have news of Miles? We were told you'd both been killed. Henry! Help her from her horse and bring the men with her inside and feed them."

At that moment Bronwyn appeared in the doorway and behind her the little singer Elizabeth'd met years before, Alyx.

"Elizabeth!" Bronwyn cried, running forward.

Elizabeth nearly fell into her sister-in-law's arms. "I am so glad to see you! It's been such a long journey. Where's Stephen? We have to return and get Miles and Roger. They've been taken by a French duke and we have to ransom them or rescue them or—"

"Slow down," Bronwyn said. "Come inside and have something to eat and we'll make plans."

"Henry!" the woman behind Elizabeth commanded. "Fetch my stepfather and Sir Guy. Send them to me and prepare seven horses for a journey. Send a rider ahead immediately and have a ship prepared for travel to France. I want *no* delay. Is that understood?"

Elizabeth had stopped, gaping at the woman she'd first thought was a servant.

"May I present Lady Judith?" Bronwyn said with some amusement.

Judith brushed her hand at a stray strand of hair and a flurry of golden sesame seeds fell away. "Do you know where Miles is held?"

"Yes, I've just come from there."

"And ridden hard by the look of you," Bronwyn said.

"Hello, Alyx," Elizabeth said, extending her hand to the quiet woman who had moved to stand beside Bronwyn.

Alyx nodded in greeting and smiled shyly. She'd never felt so insignificant before as she did now, surrounded by her magnificent sisters-in-law.

At that moment Sir Guy came running. The giant

looked as if he'd lost weight. Behind him came Tam, his sturdy form fairly making the ground shake.

"You have word of my Lord Miles?" Sir Guy called, his eyes roaming over Elizabeth. "We were told you were dead."

"And who told you this?" Elizabeth asked, voice rising. "Did no one search for us?"

"Come inside," Judith said, her hand on Elizabeth's arm. "Tell us what has happened."

Minutes later Elizabeth sat at a big table, eating energetically of the vast quantity of food set before her, while telling her story. Around her were her three sisters-in-law, a man she didn't know—John Bassett, Judith's mother's husband—Sir Guy and Tam.

With her mouth full, she told hurriedly of how the three of them were tossed into the hold of a ship, how they'd escaped and traveled south until Roger decided to risk their lives for a bit of a girl who was someone else's wife.

Bronwyn interrupted with a barrage of hatred directed toward Roger Chatworth but Tam ordered her to be quiet. Surprisingly, Bronwyn obeyed the older man.

Elizabeth briefly told of their rescue of the young Christiana.

Judith asked many questions, both about Elizabeth's participation in the rescue and about Christiana. "I know of her," Judith said. "And I know of her husband and his family. The younger brother, not the duke, hates Miles."

"Why?" Elizabeth blurted.

"There was a young woman who—"

Elizabeth put up her hand. "Tell me no more. I think

it's the younger man who holds Miles and Roger. The duke died in Roger's hands."

"He enjoys killing!" Bronwyn said.

Elizabeth didn't waste time defending her brother but continued with her story, telling of the old duke's sudden death. She stopped eating when she told of their capture by the dead duke's brother. Miles had been wounded when he pulled a knight from his horse, tossed Elizabeth into the saddle and slapped the horse's rump. She'd gone tearing down the weed-infested, rutted road, working hard at trying to get the dangling reins. When she did have control of the horse, she glanced backward to see half-a-dozen men chasing her. She whipped her horse forward and spent the next hours trying to escape them.

Elizabeth skipped over the next ten days of her story hurriedly. She used the pearls of Christiana's necklace to purchase her way back to England. Praying she wasn't hastening her own death, she hired three men off the road, men who'd once been soldiers, but their master had died and the successor wanted younger men.

The four of them traveled night and day, changing horses often, sleeping for only a couple of hours at a time.

When they reached the coast, Elizabeth had paid ten pearls for a ship and crew to take them back to England and she'd slept for the whole three days of sailing. They arrived in the south of England, purchased horses and a few supplies and took off again, never pausing until they reached the Montgomery estates.

"So," Elizabeth concluded, "I have come to get Miles's brothers. We must set out at once for France."

A knight entered, whispered something to Judith and left. "Lady Elizabeth," Judith said, "there are things you don't know. Soon after you, Miles and your brother were cast into the ship, Alice Chatworth"—Judith nearly choked on the name—"couldn't resist bragging about what she'd done. She sent a messenger and a letter telling us everything."

Alyx spoke for the first time, her voice soft but easily heard. "Raine, Stephen and Gavin left for France immediately while we"—she nodded toward Judith and Bronwyn—"came here to wait for news."

"Then the men are already in France?" Elizabeth asked, rising. "I must leave now. If I may have some men I'll find Miles's brothers and lead them to the place where Miles is held."

"Do you know the Duke of Lorillard's castle? Do you know where his brother lives?" Judith asked, leaning forward.

"No, but surely—" Elizabeth began.

"We can't risk it. The duke was a 'friend' of my father." Judith sneered at this. "I know where all four of the Lorillard estates are and I doubt if any other Montgomery does. Raine might, since he's fought in tournaments in France, but if the men have separated . . . no, it's decided." She stood.

"Like hell it is!" roared the man at her side, John Bassett, as he rose to tower over her.

Judith merely blinked at his voice but remained calm. "The horses are ready and we will ride soon. Bronwyn, do you have enough of those tartan skirts of yours? They'll be comfortable on the long journey."

John grabbed her arm harshly. "You'll not go risking

your life again," he said. "You nearly killed us all when you went after Gavin. This time, young lady, you'll remain here and let the men handle this."

Judith's eyes turned as hot as molten gold. "And where will you look for my husband?" she seethed. "Have you ever been to France? And if you by chance found him, where would you tell him to look for Miles? Use what sense you have, John! Leave the other women here but Elizabeth and I must go with you."

Alyx looked at Bronwyn and then let out a yell of "NO!" that made dust trickle down from the ceiling.

Alyx's face turned a becoming shade of pink and she looked down at her hands. "I mean that Bronwyn and I would rather go with you. Perhaps we can help," she whispered.

"Bronwyn," Tam began while Sir Guy was looking down his nose in an intimidating way at Elizabeth. Instantly, the room erupted into argument. Alyx, having no man to tower over her, slipped away unnoticed, ran up the stairs to Bronwyn and Stephen's room and pulled several plaids from a trunk. Even upstairs she could hear the loud voices downstairs.

On impulse, she grabbed a bagpipe from the wall. Multicolored tartans over her shoulders, she set the pipes to wailing as she started downstairs. By the time she reached the Great Hall, where everyone stood looking up at her, they were silent.

She dropped the pipe from her mouth. "If you men ride without us," she said into the silence, "we will leave, alone, an hour later. Do you ride with us or before us?"

The men were quiet, jaws working, lips in tight lines.

"While we are wasting time," Alyx continued, "Miles is being held prisoner, or perhaps being tortured at this very moment. I suggest we ride—NOW!"

Judith walked forward, took Alyx's face in her hands, kissed both of her sister-in-law's cheeks. "We ride!" Judith declared, taking the plaids from Alyx's shoulders and tossing one to Elizabeth. "John, see to the supplies. Guy, go to my steward. We'll need gold for this journey. Tam, make sure we have arrows aplenty and check the strings on the bows. Bronwyn, make sure we have horses that can travel. Alyx, bring something to make music with. We may need it."

Elizabeth began smiling at the first order. "And me?" she asked as everyone started off in different directions to obey Judith.

"Come with me," Judith said, starting up the stairs.

Halfway up the stairs, Judith paused, her eyes boring into Elizabeth's. "Alice Chatworth contracted small-pox and although she lived, the unscarred side of her face was badly pocked." Judith paused. "She took her own life by casting herself from the battlements of one of her estates." She looked away, then under her breath said, "The same wall old Ela fell from."

Elizabeth didn't understand the last statement but as she followed Judith up the stairs, she was glad Alice was dead. At least now she could be sure of her son's safety.

Elizabeth had heard talk of what a worker Judith Montgomery was but she soon decided Judith was a demon. She allowed no one any weakness—nor any rest.

They made the trip to the south of England in just two days, changing horses often. No one spoke but merely rode as hard and fast as possible. In many places the roads were so bad they were nonexistent, and they tore through newly plowed fields while farmers raised fists in anger. Twice Tam and Guy jumped from their horses, used battle axes to chop down fences. Behind them sheep grazed.

"The owner will take Judith to court," Elizabeth said, for the huge sheep pens were obviously owned by someone rich.

"This land belongs to Judith," Bronwyn called over her shoulder as she kicked her horse forward.

Alyx and Elizabeth exchanged looks of awe before they, too, set their horses at the usual spine-jarring pace.

When they reached the southern tip of England at dawn the third morning, a ferry waited to take them to the island where more of the Montgomerys lived.

"My clan is small compared to this family," Bronwyn said tiredly before she sat down in the wet bottom of the ferry, pulled her plaid over her head and fell asleep.

An hour later they were awakened and, as sleepwalkers, they mounted fresh horses and rode to the Montgomery estates. Even as tired as she was, Elizabeth felt the age and serenity of the fortress, the stones laid over two hundred years before by the knight known as the Black Lion.

Inside the gates, Judith touched Elizabeth's arm and nodded toward a child peeping out from a doorway. She was about a year and a half old, with dirty hair, torn clothes and the wary look of a hungry dog.

267

"One of Miles's children," Judith said, watching Elizabeth's face.

A surge of anger shot through Elizabeth. "She shall be mine when I return." With one last look, Elizabeth swept past the others and into the house.

They stayed at the old castle only long enough to eat, then were off on the ship that waited for them. All seven of them immediately curled up on deck and went to sleep.

Many hours later, when they were refreshed, the women began to discuss their plans.

"We will have to gain access to the castle," Judith said. "Alyx's music will open any door to us. Can either of you play or sing?"

Bronwyn swore she had a voice of lead; Judith admitted to being tone deaf. Elizabeth whispered, her throat dry, "I can dance."

"Good!" Judith declared. "Once we're inside—"

"You will do nothing," John Bassett said from behind her. "You will point out the new duke's estate to us and we will find your husbands and bring them to it. They will rescue Lord Miles." With that he turned on his heel and left them.

Judith gave her sisters-in-law a little smile. "Years ago I had a little trouble when I attempted to rescue Gavin. John has never forgiven me, and since he married my mother he feels responsible for me." She leaned forward. "We'll have to be more discreet in our planning."

Elizabeth leaned against the side of the ship and suppressed a laugh. There Judith sat, so very pretty, so tiny, her hands in her lap, looking for all the world like a demure, helpless young lady. It was hard to believe her fierce spirit. Bronwyn stood by the rail, the sun flashing off the water and highlighting her strong-featured beauty. Elizabeth knew Bronwyn for the passionate, brave, loyal woman she was. And Alyx, so quiet and shy, looking as if she were afraid of all of them, yet Elizabeth had seen glimpses of her spirit through Alyx's magnificent voice.

And Elizabeth? Did she fit with these women? She wondered if she could stand up under Judith's scrutiny.

They purchased horses as soon as they stepped ashore in France and Judith led them southwest. For the last day Judith had been agreeing with everything the men told her. Once Bronwyn punched Elizabeth so that she looked up at John Bassett when he swelled out his chest as he lectured Judith. Tam also gave Bronwyn curt orders. Sir Guy spoke only once to Elizabeth.

Glancing up at him through her lashes, looking demure and angelic, she asked him how his toes were. The giant's scar whitened and he walked away. Bronwyn held her ribs as she nearly split her sides laughing. Judith, when told the story of Sir Guy's toes, gave Elizabeth a look of admiration and speculation.

Alyx merely tuned her lute and that act seemed to show whom she thought was going to win the power battle.

John Bassett rented rooms in an inn not far from the duke's estates, the one the locals said he was residing in at present. The three men had to leave the women alone as they went to search for the husbands. John looked as if he were going to cry when he met with stubborn silence as he begged Judith to swear to God that she would wait for the return of the men.

"Must I put a guard on you?" John asked, exasperated.

Judith merely looked at him.

"I've a good mind to take you with me, but we'll have to split up and it takes more than one mere man to control a hellion like you. There should be a special saint to guard husbands like Gavin."

"You're wasting time, John," Judith said patiently.

"She's right," Guy said, not looking at any of the women.

John caught Judith to him, kissed her forehead. "May the Lord protect you." With that, the three men left.

Judith leaned against the door and let out a deep sigh. "He means well. Now, shall we get to work?"

Elizabeth soon came to realize what a magnificent planner Judith was—and she knew how to use her gold. She hired a total of twenty-five people to spread word of the world's greatest singer and the universe's most exotic dancer. She planned for the excitement of expectation to be feverish by the time Alyx and Elizabeth appeared, for she wanted all eyes on them while she and Bronwyn slipped away.

In the early afternoon, Judith dressed in rags, blackened one front tooth with a nasty mixture of gum and soot and delivered fresh-baked bread to the duke's castle. She came back with wonderful news.

"Miles is alive," she said, scratching and discarding the filthy clothes. "The duke always seems to have prisoners and he always keeps them in the top of the tower. This tastes awful!" she said, scrubbing at her teeth. "It seems the whole Lorillard family are masters of torture and right now they're working on the girl.

"I'm sorry, Elizabeth," Judith added quickly. "From the gossip, I don't know if she's still alive or not, but the two men are."

"What about Miles's wound?" Elizabeth asked.

Judith put out her hands, palms up. "I couldn't ask directly and all I could find out was that the prisoners are always kept in the top of the tower."

"That should be easy," Bronwyn said. "We merely attach wings to our horses and fly to the top."

"There's a staircase," Judith said.

"Unguarded?" Bronwyn asked.

"The door to the rooms where the prisoners are kept is guarded but another stair branches up to the roof." Judith slipped a clean shift over her head. "There are windows in the rooms and if we could go down from the roof . . ."

Only Bronwyn was aware of the tight white lines forming at the corners of Judith's mouth. At times Judith seemed fearless, but she had an absolute terror of high places. Bronwyn touched Judith's arm. "You stay and dance to Alyx's music. Elizabeth and I will lower ourselves and . . ."

Judith put up her hand. "I could as likely dance as I could make the horses fly. Alyx would be singing, I'd never be able to keep the rhythm and I'd start looking at the tables and thinking of how many storage bins were needed for that much food. I'd probably forget to dance and start ordering the servants about."

All three women unsuccessfully tried to suppress giggles, both at Judith's accuracy and her forlorn expression.

Judith rolled her eyes at them. "I'm strong and I'm small and I can most easily go down a rope and slip inside a window."

No amount of talking could persuade Judith of any other course and soon they sat down to rest, each with her own thoughts of the dangers to come. Elizabeth never spoke of her fear of the men touching her and Judith's terror of high places wasn't mentioned again.

As dusk approached, Judith sank to her knees and began to pray and soon the other three women joined her.

Chapter 20

Alyx was the one who surprised the women the most. For the last few days she'd had the least to say, had followed her outspoken, beautiful sisters-in-law without a suggestion or complaint. But as soon as Alyx had a musical instrument in her hands and was told to perform, she far outstripped her sisters in flamboyance.

Judith and Bronwyn, dressed in filthy, concealing rags, blended into the procession that followed Alyx and Elizabeth. Elizabeth, strutting, already drawing attention to her well-endowed body, wore cheap cloth of garish, outlandish colors that would have attracted attention on their own.

As soon as Alyx entered the Great Hall of the old castle, she let out a note that made everyone pause. Bronwyn and Judith had never heard the full volume of

Alyx's voice and they halted for a moment, listening with some awe.

"I'll give you a rhythm," Alyx whispered to Elizabeth. "Follow it with your body."

Every eye was on Alyx and the beautiful woman beside her. Abruptly Alyx let her voice drop and once again the audience began to breathe, and with a mixture of laughter and applause, they began to move about. "Now!" Judith hissed at Bronwyn and the two women disappeared into a darkened hole in the wall.

With their very heavy skirts flung over their arms, they tore up the old stone stairs, up two flights, three flights, and as they neared the top, a noise made them flatten themselves against the wall. Listening with every pore, they waited for the guard to pass the opening.

Judith pointed to a crack of blackness on the left, away from the vigilant guard. They slipped into the opening with a whisper of sound. Rats squealed in protest and Bronwyn kicked one of the nasty things back down the stairs.

At the top of the stairs was an overhead door—a locked door.

"Damn!" Judith whispered. "We need a key."

But before she even spoke, Bronwyn went to the narrow trapdoor and began to run her hands along the edges. As she reached the far edge, she turned and gave Judith a triumphant smile, her teeth and eyes showing white in the darkness. Bronwyn threw an iron bolt and the door swung up easily. One loud squeak made them stop but they heard no sound of footsteps on the stairs. They squeezed through the opening and were on the roof.

For a moment they paused and breathed deeply of the clean night air. As Bronwyn turned to Judith, she saw the little woman was looking at the battlements with fear in her eyes.

"Let *me* go," Bronwyn said.

"No." Judith shook her head. "If something happened and I had to pull you up, I couldn't do it. But you can lift me."

Bronwyn nodded as she saw the sense in Judith's words. With no more sound, they removed their outer, coarse woolen skirts and began uncoiling heavy rope from the underside. Judith had paid four women to spend the afternoon sewing these skirts. Now the moonlight shone on their skirts of plaid, blue and green for Bronwyn, golds and browns for Judith.

As soon as Bronwyn's rope lay in a coiled heap, she went around the roof of the round tower to peer down from the crenelated battlements. "There are four windows," she informed Judith. "Which one holds Miles?"

"Let me think," Judith said, rope on her forearm. "That window is over the stairs, the opposite one facing the stairs, so the cell must be one of those two." She pointed to her right and left.

Neither of them had to mention that if Judith appeared in the wrong window it could mean her death.

"Come on, let's go," Judith said as if she were on her way to her own execution.

Bronwyn had used ropes all her life and, easily, she knotted a sort of seat for Judith. The full tartan skirt was pulled between her legs and fastened into the wide leather belt. Her heart already racing, Judith stepped into the rope sling, part around her waist, some between her legs.

As she stood on the battlement, Bronwyn smiled at her. "Concentrate on your job and don't think about where you are."

Judith only nodded since fear had already closed her throat.

Bronwyn wrapped one end of the rope around a stone crenelation and used that to lower Judith slowly.

Judith repeated psalms to herself, swearing her trust in God, as she looked for toe holds. Three times pieces of wall crumbled away under her feet and each time her heart jumped to her throat as she paused, expecting any moment to have a guard above her cut the rope that held her life.

After long, slow moments, she reached the window and as her foot caught the stone sill, a hand grabbed her ankle.

"Quiet!" a voice commanded as Judith gave a sharp gasp of terror.

Strong hands caught her calves, then her hips, and pulled her inside the window. Judith, so very glad to once again be on firm ground, clutched the inside of the sill so hard she threatened to break her fingers.

"Aren't you the one that's terrified of high places?"

Judith turned to look into Roger Chatworth's calm face. His shirt hung in rags on his strong body. "Where's Miles?" she said in a half-gasp, half-croak.

A sound from outside the cell made Roger grab her protectively.

"Talkin' to yourself, Chatworth?" the guard called out but didn't bother to walk toward the cell.

"No one better," Roger called back, holding Judith's trembling body.

"Who is above?" Roger said into her ear.

"Bronwyn."

Judith's answer was rewarded by an under-breath curse from Roger. She wanted to pull away from him but at the moment any comfort felt good. Roger drew her, still attached to the rope, to a far corner of the little room. "Miles is in the opposite cell," he whispered. "He's been wounded and I'm not sure he has the strength to climb your rope. The guard will sleep soon and we'll get out. I'll go first and then pull you up. But you cannot stay in this room alone. You must sit on the sill and if the guard looks in, you must jump off. Do you understand? As soon as I reach the top I'll pull you up," he repeated.

Judith let his words sink in. This was her family's enemy, had been the cause of Mary Montgomery's death. Perhaps he meant to kill Bronwyn and cut the rope holding her. "No . . ." she began.

"You have to trust me, Montgomery! Bronwyn can't pull you up and you couldn't possibly climb the rope. Damn women! Why didn't you send some men?"

That did it. Her eyes blazed. "You ungrateful—"

He put his hand over her mouth. "Good girl! Whatever I don't like about the Montgomerys, I like their women. Now let's waste no more time." With that, he led, half pulled, Judith to the window, picked her up and set her on the sill. "Put your hands here"—he indicated the ledge of the sill—"and hold on. When I start to pull you up, use your hands and feet to keep from hitting the wall." He gave her a little shake since Judith was staring glassily at the ground far, far below her. "Think about your husband's anger when he finds out you rescued a Chatworth before his brother."

Judith almost smiled at that—almost. She did lift her

head and visualized Gavin and imagined being in his safe arms. She swore she'd never again do anything so stupid as try to rescue a man again. Unless of course Gavin needed her. Or his brothers. Or one of her sisters-in-law. Or perhaps, too, her mother. And her children by all means. And—

The tug on the rope as Roger grabbed it above her head nearly sent her flying. "Mind on your work, woman!" he commanded.

She ducked his feet as he swung above her and, her senses once again alert, she tilted her head back and watched him climb the rope, hand over hand.

Bronwyn greeted Roger at the top with a knife aimed at his throat and held him there, suspended over the wall, hands supporting his body weight.

"What have you done with Judith?" Bronwyn growled.

"She waits below for me to pull her up and every minute you delay comes closer to costing her her life."

At that moment, several things happened. One, Judith, either in fear or necessity, swung away from the windowsill and the momentum almost made Roger lose his grip.

"Guards!" came a shout from below.

"The door!" Roger said, fighting to stay on the wall. "Lock the door!"

Bronwyn reacted at once, but by the time she reached the door, a guard was already through it. She didn't hesitate as she slipped her knife between his ribs. He fell atop the door and Bronwyn had to push him aside to shove the bolt home.

She ran back to where Roger was pulling on Judith's

rope, and leaned between the crenelations to help. "What happened?" Bronwyn asked before Judith was even over the roof.

"Alyx and Elizabeth were tossed in the cell with Miles. I stayed and listened as long as I could but when the guard looked for Chatworth, he called out. What happened to him?"

Bronwyn assisted Judith onto the roof. "There," she nodded toward the dead man not far away.

"Who heard him call?" Roger demanded.

"I'm not sure anyone did," Judith said. "Hurry! We must get them out of this place."

"There isn't time. Where are your husbands?" Roger asked.

"Here in France but—" Judith began but stopped as Roger took the second rope from the roof floor and tied it to a battlement. "They're on the other side."

Roger ignored her. "There isn't time. The old man will be up here in minutes. We've got to get down and get some help."

"You coward," Bronwyn hissed. *"You* escape. Judith and I will rescue our family."

Roger grabbed her arm harshly. "Shut up, you idiot! Do you forget that Elizabeth is my sister? I haven't time to argue but if we're all caught there'll be no one to lead a rescue. Now, can you get down that rope yourself?"

"Yes but—" Bronwyn began.

"Then do it!" He half tossed her over the wall, all the while securely holding her hands. "Go, Bronwyn!" he ordered, then gave her a quick smile. "Show us some of your Scots blood."

As soon as Bronwyn disappeared over the side, Roger grabbed Judith by the armpits and lifted her. "Good! You weigh no more than my armor." He half squatted. "Hang onto my back with all your strength."

Judith only nodded and obeyed, buried her face in Roger's shoulder and closed her eyes. She didn't look when he lowered himself over the side. Sweat broke out on his neck and she was aware of how he was straining.

"Are you going to let an Englishman beat you?" Roger spat across the void to Bronwyn.

Judith opened one eye and looked with admiration at her sister-in-law. Bronwyn had the rope wrapped around one ankle, the opposite foot on top, her hands easing herself down. At Roger's words, she speeded up her travel.

Judith didn't even consider leaving Roger's safe, broad back merely because they stepped onto land. As if it were something he did every day, he peeled her hands then her legs away from his body.

Trembling, Judith watched as he ran to the bottom of Bronwyn's rope. She was still several feet from the ground. "Jump, Scot!" he ordered up at her.

There was a slight hesitation but Bronwyn obeyed, let go of the rope and landed heavily into Roger Chatworth's waiting arms. "You must weigh the same as my horse," he murmured while setting her down. "Is it too much to hope that you women have horses nearby?"

"Come, enemy," Bronwyn said, motioning with her arm.

Roger grabbed Judith's arm since she was standing still, looking straight up with horror to where she'd been. "Run!" he said and gave her a sharp slap on her rump. "Let's get my sister and Chris out of this!"

Miles was standing in the middle of the room as if waiting for them, when the door was thrown open and Elizabeth and Alyx were pushed inside.

"To keep you company, Montgomery." The guard laughed. "Enjoy tonight because it'll probably be your last one alive."

Miles caught Elizabeth before she fell, then reached for Alyx.

Without a word, expertly, he sat down on the floor, arms about both women's shoulders, as Elizabeth began kissing his face enthusiastically.

"They were told you were dead," Elizabeth said between kisses. "Oh Miles, I didn't know if I'd ever see you again."

Miles, smiling slightly, his eyes alight, kissed each woman's forehead. "I can die peacefully now."

"How can you joke—?" Elizabeth began, but Miles kissed her lips and calmed her.

The three of them came alert as the single guard called out as he ran up the stairs toward the roof. A heavy thud followed the guard's disappearance.

In the silence, eyes looking upward, Miles said, "Bronwyn?"

Both women nodded.

Miles took a deep breath, sighed. "Tell me what you've done."

Alyx was quiet as Elizabeth told of their rescue plan, how Judith was going down the wall and into Miles's cell. Alyx was watching Miles, leaning against his strong shoulder, happy for his comfort, and she saw his eyes darken. Raine would wring my neck if I told him of such a plan, Alyx thought and hot tears came to her eyes.

"Alyx?" Miles said, interrupting Elizabeth's story. "We'll get out of here. Right now my brothers . . ."

She wiped her eyes with the back of her hand. "I know. I was just thinking that Raine will have my hide for doing this."

Miles's eyes twinkled. "Yes, he will."

"You're hurt!" Elizabeth suddenly announced, her hand running over a dirty bandage about his ribs. There wasn't much of his shirt left but what there was, Elizabeth had been exploring under.

She leaned away from him. Only moonlight came into the little room but even in that light, as she parted his shirt, she could see all the scars. Running her fingertips along one, she spoke, "You had no scars when I first met you and you've received all of them through me."

He kissed her palm. "I'll put a few scars on you—scars you get from bearing twenty of my children. Now I want both of you to rest because I imagine morning will bring . . . new events."

Elizabeth's main concern in life had been seeing Miles safe again and now that she leaned against him, knew he was strong and well, she was content. She closed her tired eyes and slept instantly.

Not so Alyx. She had not been traveling as long as Elizabeth and wasn't as tired. She closed her eyes and was still but her mind raced.

After an hour, when the cell was barely growing light, Miles gently moved the women off him and went to stand before the window. With half-shuttered eyes, Alyx watched him, saw his awkward movements.

"Come join me, Alyx," he whispered, surprising her that he knew she was awake.

Alyx stepped over a sleeping Elizabeth and as she drew near Miles, he pulled her to him, his front to her back. "You've risked much to save me, Alyx, and I thank you."

She smiled, put her cheek against his wrist. "I'm the one who got us caught. The duke had seen me play in England somewhere, remembered me and also remembered that he'd heard I'd become a Montgomery. What do you think Bronwyn said when she saw Roger on the roof instead of you?" She turned in his arms. "You do think they got away, don't you? No guards were waiting for them at the bottom of the ropes, were they? Raine will come?"

With a smile he turned her back toward the window. "I *know* they got through. Look there, far to the west."

"I see nothing."

"In the haze, see the little sparkles?"

"Yes," she said excitedly. "What are they?"

"I could be wrong but I believe they're men in armor. And there, more to the north."

"More sparkles! Oh Miles." She turned, hugged his ribs tightly then suddenly let him go. "You're hurt worse than you told Elizabeth," she said accusingly.

He tried to smile but there was pain in his eyes. "Will you tell her and give her more to worry about? She was brave dancing for all those strange men, wasn't she?" he said proudly.

"Yes," Alyx said, turning back around. Together

they stood there as the day began to dawn, watching the little pinpoints of light as they grew nearer and nearer.

"Who are they?" Alyx asked. "I know there are Montgomerys in France but there must be hundreds of knights approaching. Who are the others?"

"I doubt if there are any others," he answered. "There are Montgomerys all over France, and in Spain and Italy. When I was a boy and first earned my spurs it bothered me that I could go nowhere that I didn't have an uncle or a few cousins breathing down my neck, but now I believe every one of my relatives to be beautiful."

"I have to agree with that."

"There!" he said, pointing straight ahead. "Did you see it?"

"No, I saw nothing."

He grinned happily. "It's what I've been waiting to see. There it is again!"

Briefly, for less than a second, Alyx saw a different flash.

"It's my Uncle Etienne's banner. We've always joked about the Montgomery banner he carries. It's nearly as big as a house, but Etienne says just the sight of those three gold leopards will send most people running—and he wants to give them time to leave."

"I saw it!" Alyx gasped. On the horizon had appeared three flashes of gold, one above the other. "The leopards," she breathed. "Who do you think—?" she began.

"Raine will be leading Uncle Etienne. Stephen is coming with the men from the north and Gavin will arrive from the south."

"How can you know that?"

"I know my brothers." He smiled. "Gavin will wait a few miles away for his brothers and all three armies will attack at once."

"Attack?" she said through her teeth.

"Don't worry." He ran his hand along her temple. "I don't believe even the Duke of Lorillard will try to stand against the combined forces of the Montgomerys. He'll be given a chance to surrender to us peacefully. And besides, his fight is about Christiana, not with the Montgomerys."

"Christiana. The girl Roger Chatworth rescued? What has happened to her?"

"I don't know but I'll find out," Miles said with such feeling that Alyx was silenced. She knew better than to try to argue with one of the Montgomery men about something he planned to do. Together they watched the approaching armies of knights and when Elizabeth awoke, Miles held her also.

Trying to cheer them, he made a bawdy jest about Elizabeth's garish clothes.

"If Judith and Bronwyn liberated Roger Chatworth and the three of them went for help, which brother do you think they reached first?" Alyx asked.

Neither Miles nor Elizabeth had an answer for her.

"I pray it wasn't Raine," Alyx whispered. "I think Raine would strike first and listen second."

In silence, they watched their rescuers approach.

Chapter 21

RIDING NEXT TO RAINE AND ETIENNE MONTGOMERY WAS
Roger Chatworth, his mouth set in a grim line, his right
arm—his sword arm—bound tightly but still bleeding,
and next to him was Bronwyn sporting what promised
to be an extraordinary example of a black eye. Roger's
arm was the result of Raine's first sighting of his enemy
and Bronwyn's eye came about when she placed herself
between Raine and Roger. Judith would have joined
the fracas but John Bassett leaped from his horse,
knocked her to the ground and pinned her there.

It took four men to hold Raine and keep him from
tearing Chatworth apart but he did finally calm somewhat and allowed Judith and Bronwyn, who was nursing her swollen eye, to tell him what had happened. All
the Montgomerys were remounted halfway through the

story. When Judith told of Alyx being thrown in the cell with Miles, Raine once again leaped for Roger. Roger held him off with a sword held in his left hand while Raine's relatives calmed them both.

They were all quiet now as they approached the old Lorillard castle.

Gavin Montgomery sat in steely silence atop his horse, three hundred armed men behind him, and watched the approaching Montgomerys. Beside him sat Sir Guy, the giant's scarred face immobile. Guy didn't like to remember Gavin's explosion when he found out Judith had come to France with the men.

"She has no sense in these matters!" Gavin'd roared. "She thinks waging war is like cleaning a fish pond. Oh Lord," he prayed fervently, "if she is still alive when I find her, I will kill her. Let's ride!"

Stephen ordered his men to the eastern side of the castle while he and Tam rode toward where Gavin waited on the south.

"Women?" he bellowed long before he reached Gavin.

"None!" Gavin answered so loudly his horse lifted both forefeet off the ground.

In a cloud of dirt, Stephen and Tam turned west and headed for Raine. When Stephen saw Bronwyn, he nearly cried with relief, then frowned at her swollen eye. "What happened?" he shouted over the sound of the horses, not touching her but eating her with his eyes.

"Raine—" was all Bronwyn got out before Stephen let go with a bellow of laughter. He looked fondly at Raine's big form held rigidly in the saddle.

Bronwyn didn't bother to look at her husband again but moved to the far side of Tam.

"Stephen," Judith called. "Is Gavin with them?" She pointed south.

Stephen nodded once and Judith, John behind her, was off like a shot of lightning toward the southern group of Montgomerys.

There was no fighting.

The new Duke of Lorillard, obviously just roused from his bed, his eyes red, his skin gray green from a night of excess, had not lived to his great age of fifty-eight by trying to fight the nearly one thousand angry men who now surrounded his house. Showing his faith in the honor of the name Montgomery, he walked into the armed knights and told Gavin that if he were given his freedom, the Montgomerys could have whatever, or whomever, they wanted from his castle without the loss of a single life.

Raine didn't want to accept the man's terms because the duke was surrendering not only his land but two of his sons as well. Raine believed that a man who'd do that should die.

Both Bronwyn and Judith pleaded for the easiest way to rescue the people from the tower.

In the end, it was Gavin, as the oldest, who made the decision. The duke and five of his guard were allowed to ride away after all the gates had been ordered opened.

Amid protests, the women were ordered to stay

behind while the three brothers, Roger and a dozen cousins rode into the duke's crumbling fortress.

Either the occupants didn't know—or didn't care—that they were under attack, or perhaps, as Stephen suggested, it was a common occurrence. They did not rouse themselves from their drunken stupors. Men and women sprawled about the floors and across benches.

Cautiously, swords drawn, the men stepped between the bodies and searched for the stairs Bronwyn and Judith had told them of.

At the top of the stairs the three brothers put their shoulders to a locked door that opened to the room containing the cells.

"Here!" Roger said, grabbing a key from the wall and unlocking the heavy wooden door.

They were greeted by Miles, looking calm and pleased with himself, an arm around each woman.

Alyx ran, leaped into Raine's arms where he held her very close, his eyes moist as he buried his face in her neck. "Every time you get near your sisters-in-law," he began, "you do something like this. From now on—"

With a laugh, Alyx kissed him to silence.

Elizabeth left Miles's arms and went to Roger, caressed his cheek, touched his bloody arm. "Thank you," she whispered. She turned to Gavin, their eyes meeting, and she nodded curtly to him. She couldn't forget the insults he'd paid her.

Gavin, with a grin that softened his sharp features, opened his arms to her. "Could you and I start again, Elizabeth?" he asked quietly.

Elizabeth went to him, hugged him and when Bronwyn and Judith arrived, more hugs and kisses were exchanged.

Miles's words broke the spell of happy reunion. With eyes locked with Roger's, he said, "Shall we go?"

At Roger's curt nod, Miles took a sword from the hand of a young cousin.

"Now's not the time for a fight," Stephen began but quieted at Miles's look.

"Chatworth has helped me. Now I go with him."

Miles didn't answer but left the room behind Roger.

"With him?" Raine exploded. "Have you forgotten that he killed Mary?"

Miles didn't answer but left the room behind Roger.

"Raine," Alyx said in her softest voice. "Miles is wounded and so is Roger and I'm sure they're going after this woman Roger wants."

"Christiana!" Elizabeth said, coming out of her stunned state. She'd had no idea where her brother and husband were going. "Judith, Bronwyn." She turned.

Without hesitation, all four women started for the door.

Without a word, in unison, the men caught their wives about their waists, Raine catching both Alyx and Elizabeth, and carried them to the cell where they promptly locked them inside. For just a moment the men blinked at both the variety and the virility of the curses coming from the women. Judith intoned from the Bible, Bronwyn in Gaelic, Elizabeth used a soldier's language. And Alyx! Alyx used her magnificent voice to shake the stones.

The men grinned triumphantly at each other, motioned to their young cousins to follow and left the room.

"I never thought I'd see the day I'd help a Chatworth," Raine muttered, but stopped when he heard the clash of steel.

Six guards, awake, alert, were guarding the room that held Christiana, and they attacked Roger and Miles on sight.

Miles's side wound opened instantly as he ran a sword through one guard, stepped over the fallen body and went for two more men. Roger's sword was knocked from his left hand, he tripped over the body of the man Miles'd killed, fell, grabbed the sword in his right hand, came up and killed the man looming over him. His arm wound tore open.

As another man came at Roger, he raised his wounded arm helplessly. But as the guard's sword neared Roger's belly, the guard fell forward, dead. Roger rolled away in time to see Raine pull his sword out of the dead man's back.

The three brothers welded together to protect Roger and Miles and quickly dispatched the remaining guards. They wiped their swords on the nearby bed-hangings.

It was Raine who offered his hand to Roger and for a moment Chatworth only looked at it as he would an offer of friendliness from a deadly serpent. With eyes wide in speculation, Roger accepted the offer and allowed Raine to help him stand amidst the fallen bodies. Their eyes locked for just seconds before Roger went to the bed and pulled back the hangings.

In the center was Christiana, curled into a ball, wearing only a thin bit of wool, her body black and blue. Her eyes were swollen shut, her lips cracked.

Slowly, Roger knelt by the bed and touched her temple.

"Roger?" she whispered and tried to smile, which caused her lower lip to start bleeding.

With a look of fury on his face, Roger bent and lifted her.

Raine's hand came to rest on his shoulder. "We'll take her south to our family."

Roger only nodded and carried Chris out of the room.

Gavin assisted Miles in standing.

"Where are the women?" Miles asked.

His brothers were oddly silent and seemed to grow a little fearful.

"We, ah . . ." Stephen began.

Gavin's head came up. "I think I'll ride ahead. Here." He tossed a key to Miles. "Maybe you better look after the women."

"Yes," Stephen and Raine added hastily, all three stumbling over each other to get out of the room.

Miles looked at the key in his hand, realizing it was the key to the cell where he'd been locked. "You didn't!" he said but his brothers were gone.

For a moment he stood there and, at last, he began to laugh, laugh as he'd never laughed before. A few years ago he and his brothers had been living alone in their safe little world of mere battles and wars. Then, one by one, they'd married four beautiful, charming women— and really learned what war was.

Just now he and his brothers had taken a castle and killed several men and they'd taken no notice of the danger, but when faced with four furious women locked in a cell, they turned cowards and ran.

Miles started for the door. Thank God he'd not been involved in locking the women up! He pitied his brothers when at last they saw their wives again.

Like hell he did! He thought of every time they'd treated him as their "little brother." Now they were going to pay for every trick they'd ever played on him.

He tossed the key up, caught it and, grinning, started toward the cell full of beautiful women. He just might lock himself *inside* for a few days.

What Happened to Everybody

CHRISTIANA RECOVERED COMPLETELY, MARRIED ROGER Chatworth and ten years later, after they'd almost given up hope, they had a daughter, who, to Roger's chagrin, married one of the Montgomerys from the south of England. The Chatworth name died out except, now and then, a child would be named Chatworth Montgomery.

Miles and Elizabeth either created or adopted a total of twenty-three children and one of their sons, Philip, was a great favorite of Henry VIII. Later, two of Miles's grandsons went to the new country of America and remained there.

Raine was hired by Henry VIII to train his young knights and Alyx became lady-in-waiting to Queen Catherine. The court was a happy place and the king listened to and put into action some of the reforms Raine wanted. Raine and Alyx had three daughters, the middle one inheriting Alyx's musical talent. There's a legend that some of our great singers of today are descended from Alyxandria Montgomery.

Bronwyn and Stephen had six children, five boys and a girl. Bronwyn's name became a legend in her clan and even today Clan MacArran children sing her praises. Bronwyn's daughter married Kirsty MacGregor's son. He took the name of MacArran and eventually became laird.

Lachlan MacGregor married one of Tam's daughters, became so enraptured with her that he turned clan business over to his men. Davy MacArran fought for power, won and became a MacGregor. But Lachlan's daughter, Davy's wife, wasn't the docile little thing everyone believed and in the end it was she who was actually the MacGregor.

Judith and Gavin held onto the Montgomery estates. They prospered and left the estate in such good shape financially that today it's one of the largest, richest private homes in the world. One of Judith's descendants runs the whole place. She's a small, pretty young woman with odd-colored eyes, unmarried because she's never met a man who's accomplished in his life half what she's done in hers. Next week she has an appointment to meet a thirty-year-old American, self-made millionaire, who says he's a descendant of a knight named Miles Montgomery.

I have great hopes for them.

Jude Deveraux
Santa Fe, New Mexico
June, 1982

Two great books— one great price!

Each book features two classics by your favorite authors together in one collectible volume!

Coast Road • ***Three Wishes***
Barbara Delinsky

The Taming • ***The Conquest***
Jude Deveraux

Twin of Ice • ***Twin of Fire***
Jude Deveraux

Velvet Song • ***Velvet Angel***
Jude Deveraux

Angel Creek • ***A Lady of the West***
Linda Howard

Shades of Twilight • ***Son of the Morning***
Linda Howard

Guardian Angel • ***The Gift***
Julie Garwood

Castles • ***The Lion's Lady***
Julie Garwood

Honey Moon • ***Hot Shot***
Susan Elizabeth Phillips

Scandalous • ***Irresistible***
Karen Robards

Homeplace • ***Far Harbor***
JoAnn Ross

The Callahan Brothers Trilogy
JoAnn Ross